Praise for Sharan

"Sharan Newman will change the way you think about the Middle Ages. Her Catherine LeVendeur series brings the twelfth century to life with compassion, intelligence, and wit, in tales rich with detail and unforgettable characters. This series is not to be missed!"
—Jan Burke

"A truly fascinating perspective on medieval life, this gem is a 'do not miss' for historical mystery fans." —*Booklist*

"Reading a Sharan Newman novel is like journeying back to medieval times. The sights and sounds of Paris are so vividly described that they mesmerize readers as they enjoy a fine tale of mystery."
—*RT Book Reviews* (4 ½ stars) on *To Wear the White Cloak*

"Seasoned with wit and humor, this is a recommended read for mystery lovers and historical devotees alike."
—*Publishers Weekly* on *To Wear the White Cloak*

"Newman, author of the much acclaimed Catherine LeVendeur medieval mysteries, always does her research for her brilliant historicals." —*Library Journal* on *The Shanghai Tunnel*

"Newman deftly illustrates the complex family and religious intrigues of the time and shows the real action—and the humor—behind convent, tavern, and cathedral doors."
—*Mystery Scene* on *Heresy*

Also by Sharan Newman from Tom Doherty Associates

The Shanghai Tunnel

CATHERINE LEVENDEUR MYSTERIES
Death Comes as Epiphany
The Devil's Door
The Wandering Arm
Strong as Death
Cursed in the Blood
The Difficult Saint
To Wear the White Cloak
Heresy
The Outcast Dove

GUINEVERE
Guinevere
The Chessboard Queen
Guinevere Evermore

The Witch in the Well

SHARAN NEWMAN

A TOM DOHERTY ASSOCIATES BOOK
NEW YORK

This is a work of fiction. All of the characters, organizations, and events portrayed in this novel are either products of the author's imagination or are used fictitiously.

THE WITCH IN THE WELL

Illustration on page 319 by Lisa Newman

A Forge Book
Published by Tom Doherty Associates, LLC
175 Fifth Avenue
New York, NY 10010

www.tor-forge.com

Forge® is a registered trademark of Tom Doherty Associates, LLC.

The Library of Congress has catalogued the hardcover edition as follows:

Newman, Sharan.
    The witch in the well / Sharan Newman.—1st ed.
        p. cm.
    "A Tom Doherty Associates book."
    ISBN 978-0-7653-0881-8
    1.LeVendeur, Catherine (Fictitious character)—Fiction. 2. France—History—
Medieval period, 987–1515—Fiction. 3. Women detectives—France—Fiction.
4. Witches—Fiction. 5. Wells—Fiction. I. Title.

    PS3564.E926W57   2004
    813'.54—dc22

                                                                2004050622

ISBN 978-0-7653-1124-5

First Hardcover Edition: December 2004
First Trade Paperback Edition: March 2010

Printed in the United States of America

P1

For Edgar,
without whom Catherine would not have survived

The Witch in the Well

One

The keep at Vielleteneuse, near Saint-Denis. Tuesday 3 ides
August (August 9) 1149. Feast of Saint Alexander, burnt at
the stake in 295, patron saint of charcoal burners.
28th Av 4909.

> *D'un lay vos dirai l'aventere:*
> *Nel tenez pas a troveure,*
> *Veritez est ce que je dirai. . . .*

I'm going to tell you a tale of an adventure:
Don't believe it's only a story,
It is the complete truth. . . .

—The *lai* of *Guingamor,*
II. 1–3

*I*t was the hottest summer in living memory. Blind Garna
said so and no one doubted her. She had been the midwife for
every soul now alive in the village. She swore that it was worse
even than the year the crops had all shriveled to dust before the
vigil of the Feast of Saint James when the forest had sponta-
neously burst into flame.

The heat sucked moisture from men, animals, plants, the earth itself. The summer spared no one, from village hut to castle.

Marie, lady of Vielleteneuse, yawned over her embroidery. After a week of working on it, the blue and yellow flowers on the green linen seemed insipid. The material crumpled under her perspiring hands and the needle kept slipping from her fingers. She looked over at her husband's sister, Catherine, hoping for sympathy. But Catherine was poring over some musty parchment, apparently unaware of the heavy air.

Suddenly, Marie sat bolt upright. From below their tower the afternoon lethargy was cut by shouts and cries of anger. They were being attacked! She heard the shouts of the guards as they tried to stop the invaders. The clanking of metal against wood echoed harshly up the spiral staircase.

Startled from her reading, Catherine looked up. The noise was coming closer. She realized that the troop had managed to get past the guards and was even now climbing the narrow steps to the solar.

"Marie!" Catherine called a warning to her sister-in-law. "They're coming!"

"I have ears," Marie answered. She put her embroidery safely back in its box. "Are you ready?"

Catherine shook her head as she hid the parchment under a cushion. "There are too many for me!"

She ran to the window to call for help but it was too late. The hordes were upon them.

Marie stood proudly, her hands on her hips, defying them to attack.

"Not one of you touch me until you've washed!" she ordered the intruders as they burst into the room. "Hubert, put down that stick before you fall on it! Beron, stop poking your brother! Mabile, just what have you been eating? Evaine, give the baby to your aunt. Why did you run away from your nursemaids?"

Gingerly, Catherine reached out her arms and took her youngest child, Peter, from her niece. He was as filthy as the others, his tunic stained with grass, mud, and, she sniffed, probably horse dung, although it might be his own. At only a bit past the age of one, Peter wasn't about to look for a chamber pot.

Her other two children, James and Edana, were somewhere amidst the cluster of cousins. Catherine didn't even try to identify them under the muck. She held Peter out at arm's length. The child let out a hungry wail. Catherine sighed and set him down long enough to strip off his short tunic before she nestled his naked body against the slit in her clothing. Peter relaxed at once and sucked eagerly at her breast.

"He's still getting mud all over you," Marie observed. "That's what comes of not getting a wet nurse."

Catherine shrugged. She'd heard the argument before, but all the authors she had consulted said that a child could ingest weakness and unwholesome traits if fed by a hired woman. Nursing him herself was sometimes inconvenient, but necessary to the moral development of her son. And, although she knew Marie would laugh, Catherine loved being able to hold Peter, to snuggle his solid, healthy body against her. It was worth a bit of grime.

"We'll have to change, anyway," she reminded Marie, "if my brother is bringing back his hunting party to be fed tonight."

"They'll get cold chicken and trout pies unless they've brought down a deer," Marie answered. "Yes, I know. I suppose I should see what else the cooks have come up with. There are berries enough and greens, I suppose. Although who would want to eat in this heat, I can't imagine. Now," she returned to the children, "Evaine, get these wild animals back to their nurses to be washed and dressed. Beron and James, don't forget you are to help serve tonight."

The two six-year-olds were hopping with excitement. After much pleading, they had convinced their parents that they were old enough to carry the hand towels and small trays of sweetmeats at dinner. They had been practicing all week and spent their idle hours speculating on how much they could snitch from the platters.

Catherine finished feeding the baby, who had fallen asleep. She held him until the nurse finally appeared to clean and dress him again. As he lay in her lap, she let her fingers play in his soft curls, golden as summer wheat. He seemed so sturdy, but Catherine knew how fragile children were. She had lost one at birth and another to a winter ague. No sacrifice was too great to ensure their safety.

With a sigh, Catherine gave her youngest into the nursemaid's care and resigned herself to an evening in tight sleeves, hot slippers, and an elaborate headdress. It was the price she paid for spending the summer out of the miasma of the Paris air. Vielleteneuse was a small town well north of the city. Even though it was on an important roadway, hence the need for a fortified castle, it was cooler and quieter than Paris, with healthy breezes to sweep away foul humors that could cause sickness. At least it had been until this suffocating heat had settled in.

Still, she thought, as she stood impatiently later that afternoon waiting to be fitted into her sleeves, it would be nice if the price for the children's safety didn't include heavy, elegant robes.

Elegance was Catherine's main objection to life at Vielleteneuse. She wouldn't mind living in the castle if her brother, Guillaume, didn't take his position so seriously. Although their father had been only a merchant, Guillaume had been raised at the castle of their maternal grandfather, Gargenaud. The lords of Boisvert were very minor nobility in terms of property, but they had the pride that comes with knowing that not only had their ancestors fought with Charlemagne, but that they were able to name the links of that lineage all the way down to the present, almost four hundred years later.

Guillaume intended that he and his children live up to that heritage. His oldest son, Gerard, was now a page in the household of the count of Vermandois, regent of France. The boy was home for a visit until Saint Matthew's Eve and Guillaume took every possible opportunity to show him off to friends, neighbors, and important visitors.

Although much less concerned with position than Guillaume, Catherine's husband, Edgar, had encouraged her to pass the worst of the summer at the castle.

"It's time our children learned how to behave properly," he had told her. "And speak. They sound like the urchins in the streets of Paris. Half the time I can't understand what they're saying, their speech is so slurred and full of *parleroie de vilain*."

Catherine had agreed. Whatever the children did in their lives, they would receive no advancement unless they were well spoken and knew how to behave among the nobility.

Of course, now that Catherine's children were in the country, they had begun to sound like the peasants who lived near the keep. Added to that, James was learning vulgarities from the men-at-arms that Catherine could only guess the meaning of, despite her classical education.

Still, she reminded herself, Canon Hugh of Saint Victor had written that no knowledge is useless. Perhaps Edgar would explain the words to her when he returned from Lombardy.

Catherine smiled at the thought of the conversation, trying to ignore the twist of worry in her stomach at the thought of her husband so far away. Edgar's party had been well protected, she reminded herself. The mountain passes were clear in the summer and he wore enough charms and herbal bags to keep him safe even from the sweating sickness. He would return soon. It wasn't as if he had gone off with King Louis on that disastrous expedition to the Holy Land. There were many women who had already learned that they were now widows and many others who would never know the fate of the men they loved.

"Ow!" Catherine was brought out of her thoughts by a piercing pain in her arm.

"Stop fidgeting and you won't get stuck," her maid, Samonie, told her. "If you don't stay still, I might easily sew your inner sleeve to your robe. A fine fool you'd look then!"

Catherine settled obediently. As a trickle of sweat slid down her back, she wondered again if there might not be some less tortuous way to educate the children.

She was barely sewn together and hadn't yet started winding the long scarf around her looped-up braids, when she heard a clatter of horses' hooves on the hard earth of the bailey below. Samonie went to look.

"It's Lord Guillaume," she told Catherine. "Whatever is he doing here? He shouldn't be back for hours. Nothing is ready!"

"Is anyone hurt?" Catherine asked.

"Don't think so," the maid answered. "Everyone seems to be upright in the saddle, even young Gerard. Wait! One of the men has something . . . someone slung in front of him. If they've brought down some poacher for sport, we'll have mobs hurling rotten turnips and waving torches by nightfall. Idiots!"

Alarmed, Catherine gave up on style and draped the scarf loosely over her head. Together, she and Samonie hurried down the stairs and out into the bailey, where a crowd had gathered.

"Guillaume!" she called. "Why are you back so soon? What happened?"

Her brother looked down at her and waved angrily at the body slung across the horse.

"Fetch Marie!" he shouted. "Tell her to make up a bed. Some old woman. I don't know where she came from. One minute the path was clear and the next, she was right there. I couldn't avoid her!"

Catherine tried to push through the throng. At least the woman hadn't been hit by an arrow. But if Guillaume's horse had knocked her down, there wasn't much hope that she still lived. Ernul was bred for fighting, short and solid with powerful legs. A blow from one of his hooves could cripple a grown man.

As the body was carried past her, Catherine was surprised to see movement from inside the blanket. She grabbed the nearest servant.

"Go! Run for the priest!"

The man nodded and left at once. At least there might be time for the last rites.

Marie was at the top of the stairs to the keep. She took one glance at the slight body in the knight's arms and moved aside, pointing to the corner where a bed was hurriedly being set up. Before following him in she waved down to Samonie.

"I'll need your help!" she called.

"Go," Catherine told the maid. "I'll be up soon. Call if you need me."

"Just keep all those louts from stomping around," Samonie answered. "Good thing we were going to eat in the courtyard tonight."

Catherine wasn't sure that would be possible. At the moment, the place was full of horses, hunters, dogs, and various onlookers all getting in the way.

"Watch out!"

A load of nets and snares landed on the ground right next to her. Catherine jumped back and collided with a squire trying to lead three horses to the stables.

"Sorry, sorry, my lady," he said. But his tone asked what she was doing there instead of being up in the solar at her sewing.

Guillaume was in the center of it all, still mounted, shouting orders. Catherine tried to find a path to him through the commotion, but there didn't seem to be one. Finally, she grabbed at the first man moving toward the keep and followed in his wake.

"Hamelin!" She touched the man's shoulder. "What's going on? Who is that old woman?"

The young sergeant stopped abruptly, causing Catherine to bump against his back. He turned around. His usually cheerful expression was somber.

"I don't know who she is," he said. "Not from any of the vil-
lages around here, I can swear to that. It was a bad day all round.
No game but a few rabbits. Heat that stuck us all to our saddles.
Even the forest seemed bent on tripping us up. And then, out of
nowhere, this crone leaps onto the path, right in front of Lord
Guillaume. It was a miracle she wasn't killed outright."

They both crossed themselves. Hamelin shook his head and
shoulders, as if trying to cast off the memory of the woman
falling under Ernul's hooves. He leaned closer to Catherine.

"Osbert says that he saw her come out of a tree trunk," he
whispered. "As Lord Guillaume approached, it just opened up
and tossed her out."

He stared at her, daring her to laugh.

But Catherine didn't. There was something about this day,
the long afternoon shadows, the muggy air, the way that even the
loudest voices around her seemed muted. She felt the heaviness
pressing upon her, like a harbinger of evil.

She took a deep breath to clear her head.

"Osbert may have been mistaken," she told Hamelin. "That
sort of thing doesn't usually happen outside of Brittany."

Catherine gave him a doubtful smile. After a moment,
Hamelin chuckled, albeit nervously.

"You're right," he agreed. "No one else saw it, or will admit
they did, at least."

His laughter helped to dissipate the vague fear that had
gripped Catherine's stomach. She was glad she had asked Hamelin for information. For a young man, he had an air of *gravitas*
about him that usually came with years of experience. One reason, she supposed, that her brother trusted him so much. He
didn't come from a great family. He had simply been the man
chosen by the rest of his village to fulfill the duty of providing a
soldier for the lord's guard. But his natural talent had brought him
to Guillaume's notice and Hamelin had been rewarded enough to

decide to stay at the keep, earning more responsible positions each year.

Catherine put a hand on his arm. "Thank you," she said. "Now can you make a pathway for me to get back into the keep without ruining my clothes any further?"

A low cot stood in an alcove off the Great Hall. Marie had called for candles, but for now the only light was what filtered dimly in through a small window of thick green glass. As Catherine approached, her sight clouded after the bright day outside, she thought that instead of a withered crone, a young woman lay on the bed, her face the color of the moss that grows on stones by a stream. Then her eyes adjusted to the gloom, and the woman became aged again, her thin white hair tangled with bits of twigs. She gave a heart-wrenching moan.

"Water!" Marie shouted.

Samonie rushed past Catherine, carrying a pitcher and basin, drying towels, and bandages draped over her arm. She knelt next to the bed and began wetting the cloths.

"Will you need more, my lady?" she asked Marie.

"I don't think so," Marie answered. "She doesn't seem to have any cuts or broken bones."

She looked at Samonie in amazement, not believing her own words.

"How can this be?"

"Perhaps Lord Guillaume was able to avoid her, after all," Samonie suggested. "And she fainted from terror."

Marie shook her head. "No, that's impossible. I saw the hoof marks on her cloak when she was carried in. They tore through the fabric."

She felt again all over the body of the unconscious woman. "Nothing. Not even swelling. There must at least be some terrible bruises." She raised her voice. "Where is the girl with the candles?"

"I'm coming, Mother!"

Evaine entered the hall, carefully balancing a pair of candle-holders.

"There was no fire inside so we had to go to the storeroom for the candles and then to the kitchens to light them. I'm sorry it took so long."

"Thank you, *ma douz*," Marie said. "Give one to Samonie and the other to Catherine. Now, you two, hold them up so that I can see her better."

Catherine hurried over to do her part. The candles tilted as she took the holder, causing the hot wax to drip onto her fingers.

"Ouch," she said absently, trying to look over Marie's shoulder. Samonie had the better view from the other side of the bed.

After a moment, she noticed that Evaine was still there. Catherine smiled down at her niece.

"It was good of you to bring the candles," she told the child. "Don't worry, your mother doesn't think the woman is that badly hurt after all."

Evaine smiled. "Oh, I'm so glad. I was praying for her all the way up the staircase. Who is she?"

"We don't know," Catherine answered. "She'll have to tell us when she wakes up."

Marie overheard this. "Evaine dear," she said quietly. "Perhaps you should go find your father and ask if he can come here a moment."

Even in the dim light, Catherine could see Evaine's blush. "He went down to the pond with other men to wash, Mama. You told me not to . . ."

"Yes, I did," Marie answered hastily. "Then could you go to the doorway and watch for Father Anselm? He should be here soon."

"Yes, Mama." Evaine gave a sigh and went to sit on the top step until the priest came.

Marie waited until she had gone before uncovering the old

woman's body. Catherine bent closer, careful not to tip the candles again. "Oh, dear Virgin!" she gasped.

In the middle of the woman's stomach was the deep black print of a horse's hoof. The bruise radiated out from it, an ugly purple. The stain was still spreading across her skin.

"She must have landed directly beneath the horse." Samonie shook her head. "I don't see how her back didn't break."

"Will she survive?" Catherine asked.

"I doubt it," Marie said. "We can try leeches, if any can be found in this weather, to draw out the excess blood, but that's the only treatment I know of for such things."

"I think the damage is too great," Samonie added. "The blow must have crushed her stomach and bowels. I hope Father Anselm hurries."

"Do you think she'll wake?" Catherine stared in horror at the enormous angry discoloration that now covered the woman's stomach from her withered breasts to her sparse white private hair. She wished Marie would cover the poor thing.

"I hope not," Marie answered. "Her pain would be horrible. I should have a numbing draught ready, though, in case she does." At last she pulled a sheet over the woman's nakedness. "Catherine, will you sit here with her while Samonie mixes the draught? I must go see what preparations are being made to feed the household."

Reluctantly, Catherine agreed.

Except for an occasional person passing through, the Great Hall behind her was deserted. From outside Catherine could hear the servants calling to one another as they set up tables and benches in the bailey for dinner that evening. She knew the moment when the men came back from the pool by the increase in masculine laughter. It seemed that the hunting party had recovered from the shock of the accident. It was only when she heard the deep, distinctive bark of James's dog, Dragon, that she realized that her son must have gone bathing with them. That

would undoubtedly mean a number of new phrases for her to try
to explain.

The noise was muffled by the thick stone walls that made the
scorching heat bearable. The candles flickered by the bed, their
light blending with the green from the window, causing it to appear as if the woman were lying under a willow tree, thin
branches passing over her face in the wind. She didn't seem to be
suffering. Catherine murmured a prayer for her comfort and that
of her soul. She dipped the end of one of the cloths in the basin
and started to moisten the woman's face.

Suddenly her wrist was caught and held in an iron grip that
pulled her down, almost against the woman's face. She grabbed at
the arm with her free hand, dropping the cloth.

The woman's eyes snapped open.

Catherine inhaled to scream, but only a squeak emerged. Instead of the rheumy, pale eyes of age, what glared at her were a
pair of glittering bright orbs, black as polished onyx.

"Wha . . . wha . . . wha?" Catherine forced out.

She tried again to pull free, but now those eyes held her more
powerfully than the hand about her wrist.

The old woman forced Catherine's face closer to hers. She
opened her mouth.

"The water," she croaked.

"Water, yes. I have water here." Catherine twisted to reach
the pitcher.

The hand jerked her back.

"Water," the woman said again. "They have dammed the spring.
Monsters! The evil is coming for all Andonenn's children. You
must save her! Save her before the well is empty!"

"What? Who?" Catherine wasn't warm now, but freezing.
This wasn't a human being lying on the bed, but some incubus, a
servant of the devil. "*Domine!*" she prayed. "*Misereatur mei, dimis-
sis pecatis meis, perducat me ad vitam eternam.*"

"Stop babbling and listen!" The woman's voice was fainter

now but the intensity remained. "You must release her or she will die and all her children with her."

"But who?" Catherine cried. "I don't understand! Who will die?"

The hard fingers relaxed their hold on her. The woman's terrifying eyes lost their focus and began to close.

"Please!" Catherine begged. "Tell me, who must I save?"

The voice was no more than a leaf on the breeze now, a long, long exhalation that took the spirit of the woman with it.

A moment later, Catherine straightened. The woman was still in death. Catherine couldn't believe she had made out those last words.

"Your mother, Catherine," the old woman had gasped. "You must save your mother."

Two

The keep at Vielleteneuse: Later that day.

. . . si vit une peucele
Vestue d'une purpre bise
E d'une mut bele chemise . . .
A une fontenine veneit
Ke suz un grant arbre surdeit.

. . . he saw a maiden
Clothed in a purple coth
And a most beautiful gown . . .
She went to a fountain
That gushed from under a huge tree.

—*Lai de Désiré*, ll. 134–136, 141–142

I don't understand why you don't believe me!" Catherine said for the hundredth time. "Why should I lie about such a thing?"

"Catherine," Marie's voice was edged with the effort to re-main patient. "I'm only saying that it's unlikely that the woman could have roused before she died, much less been able to speak, with her stomach crushed like that. Perhaps you were dozing. Dreams so close to the surface of waking can often seem real."

"Marie, I was not dreaming!" Catherine circled the small tower room, her feet crushing the brittle straw and dried herbs strewn over the floor. The scented dust tickled her nose.

Marie coughed and motioned for Catherine to sit down again.

"Very well," she said. "Then what else could it have been? A vision? A visitation? Why? From what you've said, this woman told you that you have to save your mother before the well goes dry. Are you sure that's what you heard? It makes no sense to me."

Catherine rubbed her forehead. "Something of that sort. She talked about a spring, I think. Perhaps not a well. I was so startled that I didn't hear it completely."

"Exactly!" Marie leapt on this. "So even if she did wake for a moment before she died, she might have been babbling. You are trying to create sense where there is none."

Catherine remained unconvinced. Marie got up and went to the window, hoping it would be cooler there. The evening sun was still hot enough to cause dry hay to smolder. The walls in the keep below were sweating as heavily as the people. This heat even pulled water from stone. Finding no relief, Marie turned to face Catherine.

"I can't believe you're giving any credence to this," she said. "You're the one who always tells me to think logically. On top of the fact that the poor thing was a hair from death when they brought her in, and could hardly have said anything coherent, there are many reasons why none of what you thought you heard makes sense. First of all," she held up her thumb. "What danger could your mother be in? She is quite safe in the convent. She's being well cared for. We received a message not six months ago saying that she's much better. She's become tranquil there, even content. She now believes that you and your brothers and sister are still small. She talks to you all the time."

Catherine bit her lip. Marie continued.

"Second," she held up her first finger. "A dream about a well that fails is natural at this time of year. Everything is drying up. We pray constantly for rain. The weather is making everyone light-headed. Why can't you admit that this is what happened to you?"

Catherine shook her head. "You don't understand. It wasn't like a dream or a *fantasia*. It was terribly real. And Marie, if the woman was delirious, then how did she know my name?"

"Catherine!" Marie threw up her arms in exasperation. "*If* she actually woke and *if* she said anything clearly, then why wouldn't she use your name? She may not have really been un-conscious when we were fussing over her. Then she would have heard me tell you to stay with her. Now, isn't that a better expla-nation than yours?"

Reluctantly, Catherine agreed. Marie knew that common sense could shake Catherine, no matter what she thought she had seen. It was one of her more endearing faults. Catherine sighed as she got up and dusted off the back of her skirts.

"I suppose it's just as well I've said nothing to Guillaume about it," she said. "My brother has less tolerance than you for such things."

"Well, I'm only sorry that you told Father Anselm," Marie answered. "Now he's all a dither about whether this woman can be buried in the churchyard. The villagers don't want the people who died with their sins forgiven to resent having a sorceress buried among them. They fear that the dead will try to throw her out of her grave."

That made Catherine laugh. "I'll speak to him," she prom-ised. "I'm sure we can arrange something."

"Do it now," Marie added when Catherine didn't move. "Even in the cellars, her corpse is ripening by the minute."

Catherine went down the winding stairs to the chapel, hoping that Father Anselm was taking his afternoon nap on the cool stone floor, as was his custom in the summer. But the little room was empty. She was turning to leave when she heard a scuffling noise coming from the direction of the altar.

"Father?" she said.

The noise stopped.

Curious, Catherine came a few steps closer. There was something sticking out from behind the stone table. Something pale against the dark wall.

"Hello?" she said.

All at once she realized what she was looking at. Two pairs of feet, one mirroring the other.

"Oh!" She backed toward the door. "I beg your pardon."

Catherine hurried on down to the hall, trying not to laugh. A few years ago she would have been shocked and embarrassed. Ten years of marriage had changed that. Now she only felt a touch of envy coupled with the wish that Edgar would return home soon. She was glad she hadn't seen who it was, however. She had no interest in overseeing other people's morals. That was what the priest was for, after all.

The thought crossed her mind that one of the pair might have been Father Anselm, himself. That was an unpleasant image! So when she reached the bottom of the stairs and found the priest at the middle of a group of angry people, her expression was more cheerful than the situation called for.

"Catherine!" The priest greeted her with relief. "You've read the Fathers of the Church. Tell them that it's wrong to bury the poor woman in unconsecrated ground unless we are certain that she died in mortal sin."

"Well," Catherine hedged. "I haven't read all the Fathers. I know that Tertullian said that we should always assure the poor a decent burial."

"But not the damned!" a woman from the town broke in. "I don't want a wicked old woman sharing the same land with my father and my children."

"But what if she wasn't wicked?" The priest was clearly teetering on a theological precipice.

Catherine felt she had to throw him a rope.

"Shall I ask my brother if she can be put in our private cemetery?" she asked. "My own first child, baptized as she was born and died, lies there."

Anselm gave her a look of intense thankfulness. "Oh, yes, please do!" he said. "And, if it turns out that she was excommunicant, we can always dig her up and move her."

All eyes turned to Catherine for confirmation.

"Certainly," she told them. "They do that all the time, even to popes."

"Excellent." Anselm waved the townspeople away. "Should I plan a Mass for her? Prayers at the graveside?"

"Guillaume will have to decide that." Catherine backed away. "Or Marie. I'll tell them. Perhaps we could all recite Psalm Forty-two at evening prayers tonight?"

"Quite appropriate," Anselm beamed. "Thank you, Lady Catherine. When should we bury her?"

Catherine inhaled. The air was rank enough with the smell of the living.

"As soon as a grave can be dug," she announced. "Guillaume will agree with me, I'm sure. I'll go tell him now."

Her brother gave a grimace when Catherine told him what arrangements she had made, but he didn't protest.

"I'll set some men to digging when the sun is lower," he said. "Marie is rummaging through the stores for the last of the smoked meat to feed all these people tonight. I asked her what we were expected to eat this winter. Do you know what she told me?"

"That you'd better start bringing down deer and wild boar?" Catherine guessed.

"Humph," Guillaume snorted. "If we don't get rain soon,

there'll be no bread to go with the meat, supposing we shoot any."

Catherine suddenly realized how worn her brother looked. He hadn't changed from his hunting leathers yet. His body was streaked with sweat and grime. His face was as tanned as his tunic and there were fine lines around his eyes. There were streaks of gray in his dark brown beard, although he was only thirty-four, five years older than Catherine. She often felt the burden of caring for her husband and children. Guillaume had a whole town to protect and the abbot of Saint-Denis to answer to if he failed.

The dinner that evening was sparse, but adequate. It was too hot for most people to have any appetite. Catherine spotted James and his cousin finishing off a tray of honey cakes. She signaled to Marie's oldest daughter, the long-suffering Evaine, to take the tray away from them, but from the smears on their hands and faces, Catherine predicted there would be two little boys with stomachaches hanging over the chamber pots before morning. It might be wise to prepare an emetic now.

The morning came all too soon, the sun striking leaves already curled and brown with thirst. The tolling of the chapel bell reminded everyone that there would be a funeral Mass before anyone could break their fast. For once Catherine was glad that Father Anselm tended to omit large parts of the text.

They had just raced past the elevation of the Host when there was a shriek of terror from just below the window.

"I told you!" The sound was shrill, yet Catherine thought the speaker was a man. "Didn't I say she wasn't human? Didn't I?"

Guillaume signaled the priest to continue. Then he jerked his head toward two of his knights to go down and find out what was wrong.

They returned swiftly. Marie turned her head as they went over to Guillaume and spoke in low urgent voices.

"Attend, my lady!" Father Anselm said in panic as she knocked against the chalice. "You might have spilled the Sacred Blood."

Marie went white with horror and took a timid sip of the proffered cup. She blessed herself quickly and returned to her place.

"What is happening?" she whispered to Catherine.

Catherine shook her head. "I can't hear them. Something about the woman's body."

"Oh, I hope it hasn't exploded," Marie murmured.

Catherine gave her a look of consternation.

"It happened once when I was a child," Marie spoke close to her ear. "In a summer like this. You can't imagine what the smell was like."

Catherine could, but tried not to.

The Mass ended rapidly and Father Anselm paused to catch his breath.

Guillaume approached the altar and turned to face the household.

"It seems that the burial will have to be delayed." He spoke through teeth clenched in anger. "The woman's body is no longer in the cellar."

The small chapel emptied in an instant as everyone rushed to see.

Catherine had stopped to check on her son and his cousin, who were, as predicted, suffering from a surfeit of honey cakes. By the time she reached the bailey, the usual confusion had become chaos.

"I tell you, Father, no one has been down there!" Hamelin was shouting at the priest over the din. "Bernat, you were on guard, tell him."

Bernat, a burly, good-natured man, nodded agreement. "I swear it, Father. I've been at the door all night. Not a soul went up or down into the cellar the whole time. But, when I went down this morning, the body had vanished!"

"Really?" Anselm was shorter and slighter than the knights but, in an argument, he had the advantage of knowing all their sins. "Then would you like to tell me just where the body of that unfortunate woman is?"

Hamelin moved past Father Anselm, heading for the steps.

"It must be down there," he insisted. "Perhaps you weren't looking in the right place."

Anselm was at his heels. "Unless Bernat stowed her in a beer vat, I just searched every possible spot."

Hamelin grabbed the lantern from the priest, and started down into the cellar. The crowd started to follow, but a sharp word from Guillaume halted them in midstride.

A few moments later Hamelin returned, holding the lantern with one hand and making the sign to ward off evil with the other.

Anselm gave a cry of triumph.

"What did I tell you?" he said.

"Well, I tell you that it's impossible!" Bernat snatched the lantern from Hamelin. "We carried her down and she didn't come back up. Maybe she melted."

"Are you sure she was dead?" Catherine stood on tiptoe as if this would help her be heard. "It seemed so to me, but I only knew she'd stopped breathing."

Bernat gave her a look of exasperation. "It doesn't matter!" he shouted. "*No one* came up those stairs. There was a guard there all night. Someone is playing tricks and I'm going to find out who!"

"You'll have to go to Hell to do it!" a man from the crowd cried out.

There was a chorus of agreement from the people in the bailey.

"She was a demon," one of the nursemaids said flatly. "Didn't Osbert say she came from inside a tree? We're all cursed!"

Catherine felt a shiver start at the nape of her neck and run down her spine. Logic was rapidly evaporating. The eerie vision of the woman, both young and old, now seemed less a dream. But if what she had said was true then . . .

"It's not a curse!" Catherine said abruptly, thinking aloud. "It's a warning."

The silence was as sudden as a thunderclap. Everyone turned to look at her.

"Catherine," Guillaume said, his voice blade sharp. "What are you running on about?"

Marie rushed to her side. "It was just a dream she had. It means nothing!"

Catherine stopped her next words. "Yes," she said with an effort. "Just a dream."

Her brother glared at her and then nodded toward the keep. Catherine knew she would soon be interrogated thoroughly. For now, she remembered that Guillaume was the lord here and to be obeyed. Marie tugged at her sleeve and the two women returned inside, leaving the lord to restore order.

It was midafternoon before the villagers were convinced to return to their homes and the servants to their work. They went muttering and grumbling, but they went. Guillaume gave a sigh of relief. At least for now his authority held.

He mounted the steps to the keep slowly, trying not to show how weary he was. He wasn't looking forward to talking with his little sister. Catherine had always been a puzzle to him, too bookish and, in his mind, not gifted with much useful learning. His rare conversations with her always left him wondering how they could have been born of the same parents. His other sister,

Agnes, was much more sensible. It was a shame she'd married so far away in Germany. He doubted that he'd ever see her again.

He sensed the man climbing the stairs behind him and his hand automatically went to his knife.

"My lord!"

Guillaume relaxed slightly.

"Hamelin." He spoke without turning around. "Have you found what happened to the woman's body?"

"No, my lord." There was a pause. "I swear that no one passed me during my watch in the night. Is there no other way from the keep? Some passage known only to a few?"

Guillaume's back stiffened. "Are you suggesting that someone close to me is in the habit of stealing corpses?"

"No! I mean, of course not." Hamelin tried to find words that would not earn him dismissal. "But there must be a sensible explanation. You don't think she simply vanished, do you?"

Now Guillaume did face his knight. He smiled without mirth.

"Or that she turned herself into a serpent and slithered through a crack in the stones?" he asked. "No, I don't. I think that someone went in and got her, either living or not. I want to know who and why. And, if Bernat is being honest when he says nothing passed him, I want to know how."

Hamelin's face went red.

"My lord, I will find the answer," he said. "Even if it earns me expulsion from your service."

Guillaume's expression softened. "If you made no plans to deceive, nor were bribed to look the other way, then you needn't fear my anger. This woman may have some power over the minds of others. If so, we must discover her reason for using it on us. I can think of nothing in the keep or the village that anyone would desire enough to contrive such an elaborate illusion."

Hamelin's shoulders relaxed. He could face anything but being cast out of Guillaume's service. Even demons.

They had reached the entry to the keep. Marie was waiting for her husband. She didn't need to ask if the body had been found.

"Come in," she said gently. "There's a basin of water and cloth to wipe the grime from your face and hands. I've put a platter of new cheese and strawberries on the table by the hearth downstairs. Take what you like, Hamelin."

The knight didn't need to be asked twice. It was the most refined dismissal he had ever received.

Guillaume followed Marie up to their private room.

"You know that things like this only happen when Catherine is staying with us," he grumbled.

Marie handed him a damp towel.

"I didn't realize we'd ever lost a body before," she commented. "You can't blame your sister. She is as puzzled as the rest of us."

"Hummph," Guillaume said from behind the facecloth. "Well, then, she shouldn't be. All that learning she's supposed to have, she could give us the profit of it."

Marie took the cloth and handed him a cup of flat beer and cucumber juice. Her husband sniffed it and then drained the cup.

"Foul stuff," he said. "But it cools the throat. Now, have you managed to learn what my clever sister meant by 'a warning'?"

Marie pursed her lips, trying to find the right words.

"She had a strange experience while watching the woman." Marie paused while she thought of a way to describe it without alarming Guillaume. "I'm sure Catherine had fallen asleep and dreamed the whole thing, but she told me that the woman came to life and told her that the well was drying and she had to save her mother. Total nonsense, of course."

"What?"

She couldn't believe the croaked word had come from Guillaume. She'd never heard her husband sound so frightened. Marie moved closer to where Guillaume had just sat heavily on their bed.

She sat down next to him and put her hand on his cheek, turning his face to hers.

"This means something to you?" she asked. "Is your mother in danger? I thought she was safe in the convent."

Guillaume's face was pale and his skin cold to her touch. His eyes were a hand's breadth from hers, but Marie felt he wasn't seeing her.

"What's wrong?" She tapped his cheek to bring him back.

Guillaume gave her a look as bleak as damnation.

"The prophecy," he whispered. "It can't be. Why now? Who could want such retribution? What could we have done?"

"My dear." Marie swallowed and started again. "Husband, you are making my blood freeze even in this heat."

"It can't be!" Guillaume stood up so abruptly that Marie was thrown to the floor. "I won't believe it. It's only a legend, a tale for children. Catherine made it all up just to scare me. Does she think we're back in the nursery? I'll get the truth of this from her now."

He strode from the room.

The sun was taking a long time to set that day. Long arrows of light pierced the woods around the village and keep. They glistened on the ripples of the Seine, turning the water gold. The rising wind picked up dust from the arid fields and roads and splashed it onto the sere plants. The color of the world was shades of brown.

The two horsemen approaching the castle keep did nothing to alter the monotony of the landscape. They wore dull beige cloaks of light wool and dark brown felt hats to fend off the sun. The watcher at the edge of the forest had the impression that they were in a hurry, but the heat was forcing them to little more than a walk.

"Any water left in the skin?" the rider in front slowed to ask.

"Enough," the other answered, tossing a flopping leather bag to him. "But it tastes of the mule."

Solomon took a long drink anyway. The bag deflated. He wiped his mouth and then pushed back his hat and sprinkled the last drops onto his thick black hair.

"Sorry," he told his partner. "We're almost there, though, and you at least can be sure of the offer of a beer and a bath from your lout of a brother-in-law."

"So can you. After the reaming Catherine gave him the last time you were there," Edgar chuckled. "Guillaume will make no more comments about a Jew polluting his pond."

Solomon's expression was sour. "There are times when it would give me immense satisfaction to tell him that he and I are first cousins."

Edgar's pale skin blanched even more at the idea. He knew, well, he was fairly sure, that Solomon would never do such a thing. The knowledge would tear Catherine's family apart. She and her sister, Agnes, knew that their father was a convert. Agnes had been horrified, but agreed to say nothing. However, their brother had no suspicion, and Edgar prayed he never would. Guillaume barely tolerated his father's many connections with Jewish traders and that only because it gave him the extra funds to live like the lord he wanted to be. There was no telling what he would do if he found out that many of those merchants were his relatives.

Solomon laughed at his friend's face.

"Don't worry," he said. "I'm not eager to claim him as kin, either. And I don't want him to throw me out until we find out what that message means."

"It may be just as much a mystery to him as to us," Edgar commented.

At that moment they rounded a bend in the road and saw the village and keep of Vielleteneuse only a league away. Edgar tried to push his flagging mount to a trot. The horse simply walked more slowly.

"It looks peaceful enough there," Solomon said. "There's washing flapping from the crennels."

"The messenger said that this was his next stop." Edgar looked worried. "You'd think there'd be more activity."

"Not if Guillaume knew it was all nonsense." Solomon pushed back his cloak. The heat was worse than the dust. His faded green tunic was dark with sweat.

Edgar took off his hat and fanned his face with it. His pale blond hair stuck damply to his forehead.

"Old Gargenaud may have gone mad," he conceded. "He's got to be almost as old as Adam by now. But then why would anyone be willing to humor his delusions enough to send messengers out in this weather?"

Solomon yawned, shaking his head. They were in the village now. Most of the houses were set in a long row, with the fields stretching out behind up to the forest. Edgar noticed first that there seemed to be more people about than usual. They were clustered in groups where the fences joined or around a beer barrel in the common green. Although he had known most of them for years, the women barely nodded at him as they passed. The men just stared.

"Saint Mungo's sacred salmon!" Edgar shouted at the group by the beer. "What's happened here? Why are you all standing about like this?"

One of the men disengaged himself from the spigot and came over as Edgar dismounted. The man's eyes carefully avoided the strap around the stump at the end of Edgar's left arm.

"Ask at the keep, my lord," he told Edgar. "There's curses and sorcery about and it'll bring famine this winter, mark me. If we aren't all blighted with boils before."

The bleak despair in his voice filled Edgar with dread. He spun about and put his foot in the stirrup, catching the strap around his wrist on the pommel to steady himself, and swung up again. Before his rear touched the saddle he heard a shrill voice.

"Papa! Papa!"

James came racing down the narrow path from the keep. He

was pulling Edana by the hand. Right behind them strode Catherine, barefoot, with Peter on her hip.

Edgar's relief rolled him back out of the saddle and onto the ground where he was pounced upon by his entire family.

Solomon watched them a moment with a wistful air. Then he, too, dismounted. Catherine reached up an arm for him to pull her to her feet.

"You're sooner than expected," she said as she hugged him. "Not that I'd ever complain. You won't believe the strange thing that happened yesterday."

"Uncle Guillaume caught a witch when he was hunting," James was telling his father. "She magicked herself dead and then ran away."

Edgar looked up at Catherine.

"A bit terse, but those are the main points," she admitted.

He managed to get up, children still clinging to him. Peter was trying to pull on the loop still hanging from his father's left arm. Solomon plucked him up and swung the child to his shoulders.

"Piss on me, young man," he warned. "And you'll find yourself back with your nurse before you finish dripping."

Peter laughed without understanding. He gripped Solomon's thick hair with both hands and bounced.

"Solomon, that may be the bravest thing you've ever done," Edgar said.

"Not at all." Solomon grinned. "I can't see Guillaume aiming a crossbow at me if I'm carrying his nephew. I'll take these barbarians up with me."

His progress up the path would be slow, since James and Edana were doing their best to trip him as they grabbed at his sleeves in the hope of finding presents. It gave Catherine and Edgar a moment to speak privately.

Catherine filled in James's account of the mysterious woman, including the conversation that Marie still insisted could not have taken place.

"I know it's strange," she ended. "But I'm sure it really happened."

Edgar put his arm around her.

"I missed you," he said.

Catherine gave a deep sigh and pressed against him, despite the amused stares of the villagers.

"Perhaps the heat and my lack of marital comfort caused me to see things," she said thoughtfully. "Do you think we could sneak out to the field beyond the pear orchard tonight? It would be so much cooler."

"What makes you think we could find a spot?" Edgar kissed the top of her head. "Half the people we know will be there."

"Maybe not," she smiled. "They might stay in for fear of the witch."

Edgar stopped and looked at her sharply. "*Carissima*, I know you are an ardent wife but I can't imagine you inventing a chat with a dying woman just so that we could secure a place to lie alone."

"No." Catherine became serious again. "I wish I had."

Edgar sighed. "I wish you had, too. This makes it harder to discount the message from your grandfather."

"Message? What message? When?"

Edgar started back up the path, more quickly now.

"You should have had it by now," he told her. "The rider left early this morning, well ahead of us. Lord Gargenaud has ordered all his family to come at once to Boisvert. 'Every descendant,' the man told me. He said to tell you that if the spring dries, then all who are of the blood of Andonenn will die."

Three

Vielleteneuse, that evening.

La fontaine estoit bele et clere et delitouse;
Al fons avoit gravele qui n'ert pas anuiouse,
Onques Tagus n'en ot nule tant presciouse . . .
La gravele estoit d'or sel quierent gens wisose.

The fountain was beautiful, clear and charming;
The gravel at the bottom was not gritty,
There has not been any so precious since the Tagus . . .
Where the gravel was of gold, or so say idle folk.

—*Elioxe*, II. 134–138

I can't believe you never heard the story," Guillaume told
Catherine. "You'd think our mother would have told you, or Uncle Roger."

The children had been put in bed, and Solomon not very
tactfully requested to find somewhere else to be, to Catherine's
fury. However, he seemed more amused than angry and set off to
the village to find the beer keg.

Marie, Guillaume, Catherine, and Edgar were sitting in the solar, waiting for the night breeze to make it cool enough to sleep.

Catherine winced at the mention of her mother and uncle. She felt responsible both for her mother's unbalanced mind and Roger's death ten years before. Edgar leaned forward, ready to defend her, but Marie anticipated him.

"You never told me, either," she reminded her husband. "Perhaps Madeline and Roger didn't think it a proper tale for a young girl."

Catherine wiped away the sweat dripping from her hair into her eyes.

"Whatever the reason, it's time we all learned of this," she said sharply. It hurt her deeply that this had been kept from her. Why hadn't anyone told her the story when she was a child? Wasn't she part of the family, too?

"I haven't been to Boisvert since I was ten," she said. "But you could have said something about this legend when you came back from there. Now, tell me why Grandfather should summon us there so abruptly and why we should obey?"

Guillaume scratched at a flea in his beard that had survived the last dunking in the pond. He shifted on his cushion, shuffling his feet in the straw until Catherine wanted to upend him onto the floor. At last he made up his mind to speak.

"You all know that our family goes back at least to the time of Charlemagne. Our ancestor Richard," he began. They nodded. "Well, the line really begins with Richard's grandmother, Andonenn, the lady of the spring."

"The what?" Catherine tensed. She sensed a myth coming.

"Sneer if you like," Guillaume said. "But that's the tale. Richard's grandfather, Jurvale, was a knight of the court of Charles the Hammer. He was strong and brave and of the line of Brutus. He had lost his property when the Saracens invaded France and didn't regain them even when the infidel had been turned back at Poitiers. And yet, he wasn't bitter.

"Richard hoped that by serving his lord faithfully, he would be given land of his own to re-create his family fortune, but many years went by and none was offered to him."

Guillaume's speech became more rhythmic, as if reciting a lesson.

"It chanced that one day, while hunting in the forest with other friends of the court, Jurvale spotted a twelve-point buck. Everyone gave chase, but soon the others fell behind until only Jurvale was left following the deer deeper into the woods."

"Guillaume!" Catherine interrupted. "Everyone knows this story. The deer turns into a woman who offers to grant him a wish if he spares her life and . . ."

"No, that's not what comes next," Guillaume snapped. "Anyway, just because something of the sort happened to others, doesn't mean it didn't happen to him, too."

"Catherine, let your brother tell the tale," Edgar said.

It took a moment for Guillaume to remember the thread. He wasn't a man inclined to storytelling.

"As a matter of fact, the deer got away." He looked pointedly at Catherine. "But it was past sundown and Jurvale was in a country that was unknown to him. He tethered his horse to a great oak tree and made camp for the night, hoping that daylight would show him a way home.

"When he woke the next morning, he found that someone had covered him with a soft blanket, as light as feathers. Although it was a kind gesture, Jurvale was afraid, even when he saw that his sword still hung in its belt from the branch above his head. Soon, he became aware of the sound of falling water. Drawing the sword, he advanced toward it."

"I thought this was the ancestress of the counts of Flanders," Catherine interrupted again. "She was bathing naked in a pond, surrounded by swans."

"Swans?" Guillaume was baffled. "Why swans? They're filthy birds with not a bit of tender meat to them."

"Catherine," Edgar warned. "If you keep diverting him we'll be here all night."

Catherine remembered where she really wanted to be at that moment, before all of the private spots in the field were taken.

"I'm sorry," she said. "Please finish."

"It seems you know it all already." Guillaume crossed his arms and stared at the ceiling.

Catherine sighed. "It was wrong of me to interrupt," she told him. "Perhaps you're right. The legends may be similar because they come from the same truth. I do want to learn what happened to Jurvale."

"Legend? I don't know about its being a legend." Guillaume wasn't prepared to give in. "When I was a boy I saw a book where it was all written down. An *old* book."

He knew this would impress her. Catherine finally showed some interest.

"Now," Guillaume went on. "He did come upon a maiden at a spring but she was properly dressed and sitting next to it, not splashing about naked! The water gushed out of a crevice in a rocky hillside and formed a pool in a hollow among the trees.

"The woman greeted him and told him her name was Andonenn and that she was the heiress of all the land fed by the spring. Our ancestor saw that she was beautiful and well bred and wished to make her his wife, but he knew that he was only a poor knight with nothing that he could give her for a dower. He admitted this to her, adding that he served a great lord who could find her a husband her family would approve of."

Guillaume stopped at this point, reached out and took his wife's hand. He gave her a tender smile. Catherine looked away, blinking. Sometimes her brother surprised her.

"The woman laughed at this and told Jurvale that she was now the lady of the land and could choose her own husband. At this, Jurvale sat down next to her and they talked all that day, stopping only when Andonenn sent for food and wine to be brought to them. By evening they had agreed to wed.

"The next morning, Andonenn and her servants and men-at-arms led Jurvale back to the court of Lord Charles. Everyone there was astonished by her beauty and the fineness of her clothing and jewelry. Even her horses were arrayed in the finest Spanish leather, studded with gold and precious stones . . ."

"Guillaume." This time Edgar stopped the tale. "This is not a night for the complete version. I will take it as understood that she was very rich. Now, what about the well and the curse?"

"Very well." Guillaume tried to think how to condense the story. "So, after being married by the bishop and many days of feasting and tournaments, Jurvale and his wife returned to her country. He then swore an oath to Lord Charles that he would always be his true vassal."

He broke off again. "I can't tell this shortly!" he complained. "It's a long history. The *jongleur* took six nights to finish it. Let's see . . . Jurvale and Andonenn built a fortress on the hill and dug a well that tapped into the spring where they had first met. Then the rocks grew to cover the source and now, no one knows where it is, only that the water still flows and the well is always full. Our ancestor had sons who grew up and went out to make their fortunes and then they had sons, but Jurvale and Andonenn still remained young and strong. In the time of Charlemagne, Richard was the eldest descendant and should have inherited, but Jurvale seemed to be immortal. There was gossip that Andonenn was a sorceress who kept them young through black arts. But that wasn't true!"

He glared at them, embarrassed, then looked down. The next part he seemed to be telling to his beard. They all had to lean closer to make it out. "She was one of the river people, a sort of fairy, I suppose. But a good Christian, not like that bitch who whelped the counts of Anjou. She was the guardian of the spring and would live as long as the water flowed."

"This was our great-great-whatever-grandmother?" Catherine asked. "Solomon will love this!"

"Catherine! How can you even think of telling that man?" Guillaume sprang up. "This is our family's story. It's not for outsiders. Especially the next part. Not even the *jongleurs* know this. Swear you will tell no one not of our blood, Catherine, or I'll say no more."

Catherine nodded. "I swear," she said earnestly.

Once again she was glad that her brother had never learned just what their father's blood was and that Solomon shared it, too.

"But if Andonenn is immortal, where is she now?" Marie asked.

"That's what worries me." Guillaume sat down again. "It is said that she finally retreated back into her country under the hillside and after she left, Jurvale at last grew old and died. His great-grandson became lord and swore allegiance to Charlemagne's son, Louis. But things become muddled here. Grandfather told me that Andonenn still watches out for her children, at least those who remain at Boisvert. The lords have always had unusually long lives. There has never been a time when a child was the sole heir. And the keep has never fallen, not to the Northmen nor the Angevins nor the counts of Champagne, although we became their vassals."

Guillaume leaned back, as if satisfied. He poured a mug of beer and emptied it.

The others waited. Guillaume filled the mug again.

"That's wonderful, a fine legacy," Edgar said at last. "But what about the curse?"

Guillaume shrugged, uncomfortable again. "It's something to do with a treasure,"

"Isn't it always?" Catherine commented. "No, wait. I said nothing. Make an end to the story before I go mad with curiosity and the heat."

"They say," her brother started again with reluctance. "They

say that our ancestor, Richard, brought something from Charlemagne's court at Aix-la-Chapelle, soon after the emperor died. It
was something of great value and power. Charlemagne's heir,
Louis, wanted to destroy it. Andonenn agreed with her grandson
that it must be kept safe and so she took it with her when she retreated into the hill. There's some that say it was the reason she
left.

"Louis's wife, the evil Judith, learned that the treasure had
been taken far from her reach. Andonenn's power was stronger
than hers and Judith could not penetrate into the realm guarded
by the spring. In her fury, she cursed all the descendants of Jurvale and Andonenn. She prophesied that the moment the spring
ceased to flow and Andonenn's magic failed, all of them, all of us,
would be struck down dead, wherever in the world we might try
to hide.

"And now the time has come," he finished.

As one, Edgar, Catherine, and Marie reached for the beer
pitcher.

"You can't believe this," Catherine said, after a moment of
shocked reflection.

But her voice shook as she thought of the tangle of cousins
sleeping now in the room below them. Even if this fantastic story
were true, she told herself, a three-hundred year-old curse
couldn't hurt them now. Of course not. It was all nonsense. But
who was the woman in the woods? Could Andonenn have sent a
messenger of her own to warn her children? And what had happened to the man her grandfather had sent? Why wasn't he here
to tell the tale?

Guillaume leaned back in his chair, wiped his brow and
looked around for his cup. Marie handed it to him.

"When I lived at Boisvert," he said, "I never thought to doubt
the story. No one ever died within the castle. Not while I was
there. No fatal accidents or illness. Grandfather said that the water made us invincible. It made me feel special, stronger. All of us

boys, it made us train harder, maybe take more chances. We thought we couldn't die."

"But many of your family have died," Edgar objected. "Your uncle and your young brother to start with. And our little Heloisa."

"Andonenn's power only reaches as far as the spring flows," Guillaume reminded him. "Once we go beyond the water, she can't protect us."

"If that were true, then why would any of you leave?" Edgar asked.

Guillaume shrugged. "A man can't hide behind his mother's skirts all his life."

Edgar opened his mouth to reply. Then he nodded slowly.

"So are we going to go?" Marie asked. She knew who would have to make all the arrangements if they did.

Guillaume threw up his hands, forgetting the full cup.

"I want to speak to this messenger," he said. "Why hasn't he arrived? I don't see how all the surviving descendants of Andonenn can be found. There must be hundreds by now. And what good would it do us to go back if the well is empty? If the curse is true it seems a lot of bother to go all the way to Blois when we could die just as easily here."

Catherine started to laugh and then realized that he wasn't joking.

"Edgar, did the man tell you why Grandfather sent for us all?" she asked.

He shook his head.

"I had the feeling that he would rather have spoken to you," he said. "Now that I think of it, he might well have been one of your cousins. He gave the impression that only family should hear what he had to say. It worries me that he didn't reach you. He said the matter was grave."

"If the message is really from Boisvert then there is no ques-

tion of ignoring it. We must save our mother." Guillaume sighed.
"And not let the treasure be destroyed."

After that there was nothing more to say.

Edgar and Catherine didn't go to the field that night. Without discussion, they retired to a bed in an alcove off the staircase
within hearing range of the children's room. Perhaps this story
was no more than moonbeams but they both felt it was better to
keep close to their own treasures.

"You don't seem too upset by the idea that I'm descended
from a water fairy," Catherine commented as Edgar helped her
out of her tight sleeves along with the rest of her clothing.

"The way you get sick at the sight of a boat, I find the idea
difficult to believe," he answered. "And it does seem that all the
best families have similar stories. My uncle Aethelraed always insisted that our great-grandmother was a selchie."

"What's that?"

"A bit like a mermaid, only with seals." Edgar lost his con-
centration as he carefully unrolled her stockings.

"You mean a woman with flippers?"

"No," he laughed. "Seal in the water, human on land."

"Well, that makes more sense than a water sprite hiding in a
rocky hill with some mysterious treasure. At least you'd get out
more." She closed her eyes. "Mmm . . . what are you doing?"

"You know quite well," he said.

There was no more speculation that night.

Edgar and Catherine slept through the bells for Mass the next
morning but they couldn't ignore the children bouncing on them
shortly after.

"Mama!" Edana pulled at the coverlet. "Papa! Why are you
sleeping in your bodies?"

"Uh, it was very hot last night." Edgar was too pale to hide
the blush as his daughter stared at him.

"Have you washed your faces?" Catherine knew better than to bother with explanations that would only lead to more questions.

She threw a loose *chainse* over her head as Edgar pulled the sheet farther up.

"Come with me," she told Edana and James. "I imagine your brother wants his breakfast."

Edgar dressed quickly after they had left and went down to the village to find Solomon.

"What's the gossip on this vanishing dead woman?" he asked when he found Solomon at the tavern poking gingerly at something that might be fish pie.

"Good morning to you," Solomon answered. "I'll tell you, if you tell me what Lord Lance-up-his-ass is so upset about."

In a low voice, Edgar did. By the end of the story, Solomon realized that he had eaten the entire pie without tasting it, for which he was profoundly grateful.

"And you say Guillaume seems to believe this?" he asked. "It sounds like a thousand other tales told from the corner by the fire on a winter night."

"I know," Edgar said. "And yet, there is something at the root of it, I think. It can't be by chance that this strange old woman should show up now. What do the villagers say about her?"

"The usual," Solomon shrugged. "That it's a sign, probably of something bad. But no one knows why. Oddly enough, your brother-in-law is fairly popular among his people. Even with the bad crops these past few years, they trust him. He doesn't overtax them and he keeps his men mostly in check. No one has accused him of bringing evil upon them. If anything, they're sure this woman was some demon jealous of their loyalty to him."

"So no one has suggested that her body was stolen by someone at the castle?" Edgar asked. "They leap right to the idea that she wasn't human?"

"Well, the story of her emerging from a tree trunk to throw

herself under Guillaume's horse seems to have inclined them in that direction," Solomon explained.

"Makes sense," Edgar admitted. "Perhaps you and I should ride out that way and see if we can find any trace of sorcery."

Solomon got up. "Or a big hollow tree right next to the path?"

"Exactly." Edgar smiled grimly. "I don't want to fight Catherine over taking all of us to Boisvert. I can see that she's half-afraid this tale might be true. I've got to prove to her that she has no reason to fear for our children."

"And if we can't?" Solomon asked.

Edgar sighed. "Then I suppose I'll finally get to meet the immortal lord of Boisvert."

Only a few days ride from Villeteneuse and even closer to the castle of Boisvert, in the comital town of Blois, someone else was listening to the legend of the undying spring.

"Does it work miracles?" she asked.

"It's supposed to keep people young forever," the man answered. "Or at least alive. The current lord, Gargenaud, is reputed to be over a hundred now."

The woman tapped her gnarled hands impatiently on the table.

"That's not immortal," she snapped. "Especially if he's deaf and blind, with his fingers curled in on themselves, his back twisted like a willow leaf, and only three teeth left."

The man stared at the wall above the woman's head.

"I hear he recently married again," he said.

The woman snorted. "A Shulamite to warm his bed? That means nothing. Go find the truth of this."

"And if the well does bring youth?" the servant asked.

"Fill me a flask of it," she laughed. "Whether they let you or no."

He knelt in obedience.

"What if the other rumors are also true, that the water is receding?"

The woman gave a long, tired sigh.

"Then," she told him, "Lord Gargenaud is going to need my help. At last."

The woman sat hunched over the table for a few moments after the man had gone. Then, slowly, she raised her head, letting her shoulders drop and the bent back straighten. She rubbed her clawlike fingers, pulling at the swollen knuckles until the hands, too, were straight.

When she stood, she no longer looked elderly, but like a woman still in her prime. As she muttered to herself, however, her voice creaked like that of one who had spent a long life shouting into the wind.

"So, all this time, all this time," she said in wonder. "Who'd have thought you'd pick a place so close by for your hidey-hole? Well, to give you your due, it worked. But no longer, my sister. It's time to root you out and take you into the sunshine for your sins to be shown to all."

She didn't cackle gleefully, but there was a space in the air that indicated satisfaction with the way things were starting to go.

Marie went to the window of the keep as a crash told her another of the large clay water jugs had fallen onto the stones. She sighed and returned to where the bailiff awaited the last of her instructions.

"I don't see why they can't come here, where we still have water, by God's grace. We can't bring enough with us to do any good."

The bailiff, Conon, had served her many years.

"I understand that it's a family matter," he said, hinting that someone should have told him all about it.

Marie nodded absently, her head full of lists.

"Lord Guillaume's grandfather," she said. "I've never met

him. Now, we should be back before winter, but you are to see that our share of the harvest, such as it is, is collected. Half to go into the grain sheds and half to be sent to Boisvert. There's enough smoked meat and salted fish to be distributed to the villagers on the appropriate feast and fast days. Should we, by some horrible chance, be delayed until after the Nativity, Hamelin has marked the wine casks you can open. Abbot Suger's bailiff will be by around Michaelmas for what we owe the abbey."

Conon already knew all this but waited in respectful silence for her to finish.

"I suppose that should take care of most problems," Marie concluded doubtfully. "You can always send a messenger if necessary. Lord Guillaume can be back in two days."

Conon nodded but didn't take his leave.

"What is it?" Marie asked. "You act as if you have mice in your *brais*."

"Yes, my lady," he said. "I mean no, of course I don't. It's that my wife wanted you to speak to Lord Guillaume about the drought."

"He has done everything he can," she answered sharply. "We pray for an end to it every day. He has asked Abbot Suger to authorize digging a trench from the river to the fields but the abbot hasn't responded."

"I know, my lady," Conon replied. "We don't hold you at fault. But the women, that is all of us, that is . . ."

Marie was starting to understand.

"They want to do the old rite, don't they?" she asked.

"Nothing else has helped," Conon pleaded. "Beyond the drought, too many odd things have happened lately. Many among us think that it's time to call upon the sylphids of the forest and streams."

Marie thought about it. "Perhaps it might help. I can't see how any harm could come of it. It's not as if they were demonic spirits. Anything that brings us relief can only be on the side of good. Yes, I'll let my husband know and see to it that all his men are accounted for on the night."

"No fear there," Conon said. "Any man found within the square won't be walking straight for a month."

"Very well," Marie told him. "Let them know we won't interfere. Just be sure that no one mentions this to Father Anselm or my sister-in-law. Catherine gets very upset at anything she can't find in the Fathers of the Church."

Edgar and Solomon rode slowly through the forest.

"This must be the spot." Solomon pulled his horse up. "There are fresh tears in the underbrush and deep clefts in the dirt where the men tried to keep their horses from running into the one ahead."

"But the trees here are thin," Edgar objected. "How could the woman have hid behind them?"

Solomon gave him a perplexed look.

"I don't know," he said. "I suppose this means you're going to Blois?"

Glumly, Edgar nodded.

Marie had a quiet word with her husband, who agreed about keeping the ritual a secret from Catherine. Guillaume had been castellan of Vielleteneuse for nearly twenty years, and he knew that there were things done for the good of the crops and the village that the pope might not approve of. Following the old ways didn't make anyone a bad Christian, he felt. In times like these it was best not to neglect the ones who had been caring for the land longer than Christians had lived on it. He just didn't think his sister would see the sense of this.

Catherine knew Edgar thought they shouldn't make the journey to Boisvert. He had agreed in the face of Guillaume's insistence, but she knew he wasn't happy about it.

"If you really are opposed, we can send word that it's impossible to make the journey," she suggested. "I'm not eager to see my mother's family again. There are many who blame me for her madness and, even more, for my uncle Roger's death."

"I am just as much to blame as you," Edgar reminded her. "It was to save me that you wove the tales that made your mother think you were blessed. And Roger might well have killed us both, if his own madness hadn't overcome him."

"Reason enough for us both to stay home," Catherine said. "If only I were absolutely sure that there was nothing in this curse."

They were standing at the edge of the field watching James and his cousins pretend to hunt down monsters. Catherine tried not to wince as the boys happily whacked at each other with wooden swords.

"Good blow, son!" Edgar shouted as James dispatched a withered sapling.

"Edgar." Catherine tried to bring him back to the subject. "I can feel you simmering. Shall I tell Guillaume we aren't going?"

Edgar kept his eyes on the field for another moment. Then he turned to his wife.

"I don't want us to go," he admitted. "I think it may be a ploy on your grandfather's part to extract money from the rest of us. That was why he let your father into the family in the first place."

Catherine agreed that it was not impossible. Edgar raised his hand to stop her.

"But when my father ordered me home to Scotland, you came with me." He smiled at her tenderly. "I didn't want to go then, either. Or course, I was right."

He raised his left arm and looked at her. Even after five years, he couldn't stand to see the empty space where his hand had been.

Catherine took his wrist. The stump never bothered her as much as how close she had come to losing him.

"My grandfather is strange, but not cruel." She didn't add,

"As your father was." But the memory floated between them of the sword shining in the candlelight and the blood and Edgar's hand on the floor of the chapel, fingers outstretched.

Catherine took Edgar's right hand in her own.

"I don't know if there is anything to this curse," she said. "It sounds like one of a hundred tales that every old family has. For all I know, Grandfather finally feels death approaching and wants to see his progeny before he goes. That isn't such a great thing to do for an old man. It shouldn't be as dangerous as other journeys we've been on."

"Like going to Scotland to avenge the death of my brothers?" Edgar said it at last. "Or all the way to Trier to save your sister from a murder charge?"

"Or even just to Reims to keep a friend from being burnt as a heretic," Catherine added. "Next to all of that, a few days' journey to Blois seems . . ." She happened to glance at the field where the boys were playing. She caught her breath in horror.

"James!" she screamed. "Stop that! Stop it at once! Edgar! Do something!"

Edgar was already running across the field to where his son had knocked one of the other boys down and was now hitting him mercilessly with sword and fist.

"Enough!"

Catherine didn't know where her brother had come from. Guillaume reached the children before Edgar and lifted James off his victim.

The boy struggled a bit and then dropped the wooden sword. He looked around as if puzzled to find himself hanging from his uncle's arm.

Edgar arrived and bent over the child on the ground.

"Bertie, are you all right?" he asked.

Guillaume's second son managed to stand on wobbly legs.

"I'd have got you if I hadn't dropped my shield!" He glared up at James.

"Next time, don't be so clumsy," Guillaume told him. "Now go have your mother bandage those cuts."

He handed James over to Edgar.

"You've got a fine warrior here," he said. "Another couple of years, send him to me for training."

Edgar took his son without comment. A part of him was proud of James's fierce attack. A much greater part was terrified that the child was already becoming as brutal as his own father and brothers in Scotland.

James knew he was in trouble.

"I'm sorry, Papa," he said, still confused. "I didn't mean to hurt Bertie. I forgot."

"Forgot what?" Edgar asked.

"That he wasn't really a monster."

Edgar tightened his grip. He was more confused than James.

He didn't know what to tell his son. However, Catherine was almost upon them and it was clear that she had plenty to say.

After the failure to discover a simple explanation for the appearance of the old woman, Solomon had offered to go back to Paris to make arrangements for the journey to Blois. He returned to Vielleteneuse just at twilight. The village was quiet and the castle windows showed only a few candles. He had brought sausage and bread with him as well as a skin of wine made by his old friend, Abraham. Rather than enjoy them under the scornful gaze of Christians, he decided to wander down to the river for a peaceful solitary meal.

The sound of the running water and the flow of wine made him sleepy and it was full dark when he awoke.

That was when he heard the chanting.

Normally, Solomon found the melody of women's voices very appealing. However, there was something in the rhythmic sound, coming ever closer, that told him this was no place for a man. Slowly, he rose to a crouch and made his way up the riverbank and back toward the town.

He hadn't gone ten paces when two shapes appeared from the field and blocked his path.

"*Heu, peterin!*" one of them said.

It was a woman's voice, harsh with anger.

"You know the price, *om sordois*." The other stepped close to him.

Solomon felt the prick of a knifepoint.

"Price for what?" he cried. "I fell asleep by the river. Now I'm going back to the keep. That's all."

"And tell them all what you saw?" the woman with the knife snorted. "Not likely."

"I saw nothing!" Solomon insisted. "And could you move that knife a little higher? To my heart, perhaps, or my throat."

There was a low chuckle from the other woman.

"There's always a few who think they can have a peek and get away with it," she said. "You're lucky the Holy Virgin doesn't strike you blind."

"Maybe she didn't because she knows I didn't see anything." Solomon tried to back away, but felt others coming up behind him. "I tell you, I woke up, heard voices, and decided to leave before I interrupted anything. That's all."

There was laughter at this. Other women had gathered to enjoy his plight.

"Cut 'em off quick, Rose," one woman called. "We have no time to play."

Solomon had been in danger of death many times before, but nothing had made him as terrified as he was at this moment.

Suddenly a lantern was held up to his face.

"Here, now," the first woman said. "You're that one with Lady Catherine, aren't you? What would she say about this?"

"That I'd made a perfect fool of myself," Solomon sighed. "But she'd also tell you that I'm not a man who needs to creep about in fields to get an eyeful."

"I'd let you in the barn when my man was out," called a voice from the rear.

The knife didn't budge, but the atmosphere seemed to lighten.

Very carefully, Solomon reached down and turned the blade away.

"You're doing an invocation to the river, aren't you?" he asked. "No one thought to tell me or I wouldn't have been a league from this place. My aunt knows about it. She said it worked when she was a girl in Troyes. A child pulls an herb up by the roots and then the other maidens sprinkle her with water. That's all I know of it."

"That's right, young man." The woman with the knife wasn't convinced of his innocence. "The job is done by the virgins of the village and we mean to see that they remain so."

"And fine guardians you are." He backed a step, still trying to find a way out of the circle. "I wouldn't want to disturb the rite for anything, truly. The drought has been bad for all of us. Look," he said. "I swear on the soul of my mother that I came to this place all unknowing. My partner, Lord Edgar, and his wife, Lady Catherine, will be my gauge in this."

"By the way," he added. "Who is protecting your daughters while you're busy with me?"

There was a moment of silent consternation then the group dissolved into individual worried mothers and aunts.

"Let him go, Rose," one said. "We don't want trouble with the castle."

Reluctantly, Rose moved away a pace. Solomon dared take a deep breath.

It was too soon. Before he could react she slashed at his groin with the knife. He felt the point of it slide along his thigh before she turned and ran.

He waited until he reached the slopes of the bailey before he checked the wound.

His linen tunic had been cut through, but his riding pants had been too tough for the metal. Apart from the thin scratch on his leg, he was unharmed.

"Thank you, Lord." He knelt in the dust. "Blessed be Your holy Name, I am eternally grateful that You made me a common trader, who always covers his privates with leather *brais*."

He got up carefully, checking to be sure no one had seen his lapse into faith. Then he woke up the guard at the keep and went in to bed.

He fervently hoped that the morning would bring rain.

Four

Vielleteneuse, Thursday, 3 ides August, August 11, 1149.

Les aventures trespassees
Qui diversement ai contees,
Nes ai pas dites sans garants.
Les estores on trai avant
Ki encore sont a Carlion
Ens el moustier Saint Aaron. . . .

The tales of long ago that I have often told,
I don't tell them to you without proofs.
I came across them at Carlion
In the monastery of Saint Aaron. . . .

—*Lai de l'Aubépine*, II. 2–7

*T*he next morning, to Solomon's amazement, the sky was full of clouds. The hot air had a breeze in it that smelled like rain. He actually recited the morning prayers out of grateful relief. Now no one would be tracking him down for desecrating the rite. He was just congratulating himself on another narrow escape when Edgar yanked him from the breakfast table and hustled him out into the bailey.

"They've found the body of the messenger from Boisvert," he told Solomon. "Some peasants were out fishing at dawn and pulled him up in their nets."

"Are you sure it was him? Has he been dead long?" Solomon asked. What if the women had snared another unfortunate man out to catch a glimpse of naked girls?

"At least since yesterday," Edgar said. "He hadn't been in the water so long that I didn't know his face. Even more, the pouch containing the letter with Lord Gargenaud's seal was still hanging at his belt."

"Accident?"

"He had an arrow through his chest," Edgar said. "Worse, there was no sign of theft. It wasn't a chance attack. Someone didn't want him to reach the rest of Gargenaud's relatives. They must have been laying in wait for him."

Solomon didn't need time to think.

"I say we pack up and return to Paris at once," he said. "Let Catherine's grandfather rot. It's not worth risking your lives."

"I know," Edgar snapped. "That's what I think we should do, too."

He was silent for a moment, staring at the floor as if there were a message in the broken rushes and bits of trash.

"But . . . ?" Solomon prompted.

Edgar shook his head as if to clear it. His fine blond hair flopped across unshaven cheeks.

"I *think* that we should go back home at once," he spoke from behind clenched teeth. "But I *feel* that we must go to Boisvert. I can't tell you why; I don't know myself. Perhaps there is a curse that must be lifted, as Giullaume believes. What if by hiding we condemn all the others?" He grimaced. "All right, tell me I'm howling mad."

"Oh, you are," Solomon said. "But it's beginning to appear

that this is not just some moldy legend. Spirits don't shoot arrows. There's a living person who doesn't want the message to reach the family. Maybe there's something more tangible at stake here than a curse."

"Somewhere in the story," Edgar told him, "Guillaume did mention that this magical ancestress of theirs also guarded an ancient Carolingian treasure."

"I thought so," Solomon said. "There's always something like that in these tales. What if the old man wants it discovered, perhaps divided among his descendants? And what if only those present have a chance at it?"

"That's nothing to me," Edgar protested. "We don't need a treasure. We're doing well enough on our own."

"For now," Solomon agreed. "But the wheel of life goes down often enough. And what if this is something that was once owned by Charlemagne himself? Would you want to deprive your children of a share in that?"

Edgar gave him a look of disgust.

"What side are you arguing on?" he asked.

"Neither. I want you to make the decision clearly," Solomon answered. "I'm only throwing the *merel* on the table so you can make up your mind which ones to play."

Edgar threw up his hands.

"I've already told Catherine that we're going. If this poor man's murder doesn't alter her mind, we'll leave from Paris within the week."

"Murder hasn't stopped her yet," Solomon said. "Now, it so happens that I have friends in the town of Blois that I've been meaning to visit. Perhaps I should see you safely to Boisvert on my way."

Edgar grinned. "You don't fool me. You want to us find out just what form this treasure of Charlemagne takes."

"You never know," Solomon smiled. "They say he was very tolerant toward the Jews, even sent one to Baghdad on a mission.

Maybe it's a holy treasure, like articles taken from the Temple in Jerusalem or even the tablets Moses brought down from the mountain. Imagine, the Commandments, themselves, etched by the hand of the Creator! That might be something the pious King Louis would want destroyed. Something that proved your faith isn't necessary."

Edgar glanced over Solomon's shoulder. There had been a movement farther down the hall, as if someone had stopped in the shadows and then moved on.

"Right!" he said loudly. "What nonsense! Hiding in a cave in Blois? Now who's howling? Come along, old friend. We'll go down to the storeroom and see if we can find the jewels that Dido gave Aeneas before he sailed away. I've heard that there are boxes of them hidden all over France."

Solomon understood at once. He should have known bet-ter than to say such things anywhere but in their own home. He wondered who had been listening and how much they had heard.

At that moment, Catherine was reconsidering any journey that would mean continued association with her older brother. The two of them had been arguing since the morning meal and every word made it clear to her that they would never agree.

"How can you not be upset about this?" she asked again. "It was your son that mine was pounding on. Bertie could have been badly hurt."

"Nonsense." Guillaume waved his hands, wishing he could brush her off like the flies circling his head. "Bertie is a head taller than James. If he can't hold his own against a smaller boy, then he deserves a good pounding. Anyway, they're friends. James wouldn't have harmed him seriously."

"But, Guillaume, don't you see," Catherine watched him swat at the flies and longed to suggest that he go wash the honey from his beard if he wanted to get rid of them. "James insists that he didn't mean to do it. He was so involved in the game that he really thought Bertie was a monster. Doesn't that worry you?"

"Hmph! Think that myself often enough about Bertie. Ow!" He had slapped at a fly just as it landed on his cheek. "There's nothing wrong with getting carried away in a battle, Sister. What do you think we're training them for? Are you planning to shove James into the Church? I can tell you now, he'd make a lousy monk and our family doesn't have the clout to get him a bishopric. Now," he pushed her toward the door, "why don't you get on with your packing and leave James to me and his father. Hmm?"

Catherine was still fuming when Edgar found her. At first she listened to the news about the messenger with little attention. It was only when she realized that he had been murdered that she calmed down.

"The poor man!" She crossed herself. "Do you think the old woman had anything to do with his death?"

The question surprised Edgar. "Not unless she was handy with a crossbow and could shoot it from her grave, wherever that is."

"Marie thinks that the villagers bribed the guards to steal her body so that she wouldn't be buried in consecrated ground with their relatives." Catherine was thinking aloud. "The townspeople say she went back to Hell where she came from. What if she wasn't a sorceress or a witless old woman, but someone sent by Grandfather's enemies to divert the messenger? Perhaps she fell under Guillaume's horse and died before she could finish the task."

"Then the man would have reached the castle," Edgar pointed out. "And who would send an old woman to stop a man on horseback? Catherine, the two deaths are not connected. You act as if there's some grand conspiracy at work here."

Catherine rubbed her arms. She felt as if ants were crawling across her skin.

"Don't you sense it, Edgar?" she asked. "It's as if we're living on the point of a spear. Any moment, I expect us all to crash into something."

Edgar stepped back and looked her up and down.

"*Carissima,*" he asked quietly. "Are you pregnant again?"

"No!" she answered.

"Well then, is it about that time?" Edgar spoke with the timidity of a man who had endured too many 'that times.'

"No, last week," Catherine sighed. "Maybe it's just the weather. There was a breeze this morning but it faded. It's as hot as ever but the sky is such an odd yellow. I think we'll have rain soon. Our prayers must finally have been granted."

"I hope so." Solomon had told Edgar about the rite in the meadow, and they agreed that Catherine would not approve. But it bothered him to keep anything from her.

"A good storm should bring cooler air," he said. "We could safely return to Paris. Solomon thinks there might be danger if we go to your grandfather's. You sound as though you agree with him."

"And you don't?" she asked. "This man's death seems to prove it."

Edgar sighed. He reached out to put his arms around her and felt a spark leap from her clothing. It stung his good hand.

"I think there's danger everywhere," he said. "But if someone, human or not, doesn't want us to go to Boisvert, then that may be the safest place for us to be."

Catherine took him in her arms and managed to hug him without repercussion.

"Thank you, *carissime,*" she whispered. "It's foolish, I know, but I have this incredible longing to see the home of my forebears again and to show it to our children even though logic tells me to stay away."

"I understand," Edgar said, although he didn't. He would have been happy to learn that his ancestral home in Scotland had been swallowed by the earth.

∽

Hamelin and Osbert were not happy to be given another body to guard.

"At least there's no doubt that this one's dead," Osbert said, wrinkling his nose. "Why don't we just stick him straight in the ground? The hole's already dug."

"Father Anselm is just waiting on a coffin," Hamelin told him sourly. "He asked if I could keep the corpse from running off for that long."

"In this heat, we'll need a vat," Osbert replied. He stared at the canvas around the body as if expecting it to commence oozing.

Outside the clouds thickened, turning the daylight musty. A long roll of thunder crossed the sky. The sound of it echoed in the stone cellar. Hamelin shuddered.

"Do you think the saints are angry because we let the women make offerings to the river?" he asked.

Osbert rubbed his nose. "It'd be pretty mean of them," he answered. "After the way they ignored us all summer."

"It's dry as tinder for miles around," Hamelin continued. "One spark from the sky and there'd be nothing left, not woods nor village nor keep. Only us in this pile of stone."

"Saint Hubert's yowling hound!" Osbert cried. "As if I'm not all over gooseflesh as it is! It's just a storm brewing. I don't care if it was saints or devils that sent it, if it rains enough to save my barley crop."

He crossed himself with a muttered prayer and another crash resonated from above.

"That one was almost over our heads," Hamelin said.

The world was silent for a moment. In the lantern light, Osbert was sure he saw the body shift under the shroud. He stood with a cry that was cut off by the clatter of footsteps outside. They were accompanied by shouted orders and cries of fear.

"Something's wrong!" Hamelin grabbed the lantern and headed for the steps out.

"Wait!" Osbert hurried after him, grabbing the light. "What if it's a trick, like last time? Do you want to be made a fool of again?"

Hamelin slowed. He glanced from the body to the door leading out to the bailey. The noise outside was growing.

"I'd rather be a fool than not come to the aid of my lord," he decided. "Here, take the lantern. You stay."

"Alone!" Osbert bumped against him in his haste. "Sit by myself and watch that thing rise to do God knows what to me?"

They emerged into a terror worse than that they had left. The air was full of smoke and people running about trying to save their belongings or themselves. Water fell, not from the sky, but from the cistern on the roof that had shattered when lightning hit the tower.

"Holy Mother!" Osbert exclaimed. "It was better with the corpse!"

There was no way to get water up to the keep in time. Everyone knew that if the rain didn't begin soon, there would be nothing left on the hilltop but a smoking shell of blistered stone.

Solomon pushed his way through the people fleeing through the gate. He climbed onto a *perron* to see better, twisting to keep his balance until he saw Edgar's blond head a hand's breadth above all the others. He jumped down and made his way there.

"Is everyone accounted for?" he gasped in the acrid air.

"Yes!" Edgar shouted back. "The children were all outside, thank God. The nursery is nothing but flame. Catherine helped Father Anselm save the vessels for the Mass. Marie thought to grab the jewelry boxes and got the servants to bring out the wall hangings and silver dishes. No one is inside now, I hope. The fire is burning down through the wood, floor by floor."

"Where's Catherine?" Solomon coughed on the words. The wind was whipping around the outside of the keep as the fire roared within. "There's nothing to keep this from jumping to the village and then the forest."

"She went with the others to the river," Edgar said. "Go and watch out for them. I have to stay until the animals are all brought down or until Guillaume realizes that it's too late to save them."

"Just so you aren't one of the roasts." Solomon put his hand on Edgar's shoulder. "I won't bear the burden of supporting your family, understand?"

"Coward," Edgar grinned. "Now go!"

As he made his way through the panicked village and down to the river, Solomon bumped into an elderly woman. He mumbled an apology, but as he moved on, she caught his arm, digging her nails into his flesh.

"I know you." Her eyes narrowed. "You tried to pollute the ritual. If this is your doing, I'll find you. Them at the castle can't protect you forever and my knife is razor sharp."

"Sorry, you must be thinking of someone else." Solomon pried her hand loose and ran. It was bad enough being blamed for things because he was a Jew. Now it was as much of a crime to be a man.

He found Catherine clad only in her *chainse*, with baby Peter on her hip. Edana clung to her mother, but James was not to be seen.

"Where's Edgar?" she greeted him.

"Herding pigs, I think," he answered. "He'll be down soon. Are you all right?"

"For now," she answered. "James is with his cousins. They're supposed to be wetting blankets for the men to wear to fight the fire, but I think they're just splashing each other."

She tore a piece of her dampened *bliaut* with her teeth and knotted it around Edana's head and face and then made another

one for the baby, who squirmed in her arms, refusing to be muffled. Solomon held him while she tied it over his nose and mouth.

"Another day and we would have been gone," she said.

"That's so," Solomon said.

He kept Peter in his arms and took Edana's hand.

"You're worn out, Catherine," he said. "Come, sit down.
You're safe enough here; the wind is blowing away from the river."

Catherine did as he bade. She set Edana in her lap and let
Solomon take care of the baby. The little girl was frightened into
stillness. She tried to burrow into Catherine's breast, sucking her
thumb and rubbing her cheek against the warm linen of the *chainse*.

"Home, Mama," she whispered over and over.

Catherine held her tightly, kissing her forehead and cheeks.
"It will be all right, *ma douz*," she murmured. "We'll be home
soon."

They were still sitting there when Edgar found them. With
him was their maid, Samonie, and her son, Martin.

"Your brother is still up there," Edgar told Catherine. "He
can't see that there's nothing more to be saved."

"I got what I could from the stores," Samonie added. "Dried
apples and some cheese is all but it will keep us on the road to
Paris. What we need is a safe corner to stay the night."

Catherine gave her a wan smile. "Thank you, Samonie. I'm
glad you thought of our bodily needs. After my children, I only
worried about the Gospel and patens."

"I'd have expected nothing less of you, Mistress." Samonie
smiled. They had been through too much together for the division in their rank to matter much.

Catherine smiled back, then coughed as she inhaled the
blowing ash. She looked around. The rest of the villagers were
huddled near or even in the river. The water was low and the current sluggish. A few people were passing leather buckets up from
the water to wet down the roofs of the houses, but most just
watched with dazed resignation.

Marie herded her children over next to Catherine.

"Look," she said. "The wind is pulling the flames upward, into the sky. If only the rain will begin, then the village might yet be saved. I don't understand. Is it a judgment or a blessing?"

She was shivering in the heat. Catherine looked around for a dry blanket to wrap her in. Poor Marie! Everything she owned, the home she had ruled for twenty years, destroyed before her eyes. Catherine didn't understand it, either.

Dusk was falling and the clouds still refused to open. Guillaume finally came down the hill to them. They could hear him shouting orders in a rasping voice, sending people back up to throw dirt over patches where the fire had jumped the motte.

"Everything inside is gone," he told them. "But by some miracle the stone walls and the ditches were too much for the fire to escape into the town. At least so far."

He looked around with bloodshot eyes. His face and beard were streaked with soot and sweat.

"The granary is undamaged, not that there was much in it," he muttered. "You can smell the last of the dried meat burning, if that's not the body in the cellar."

Edgar looked at Guillaume's face. He wasn't making a bad joke; he was too tired.

"I can't go to Boisvert now," Guillaume went on. "This isn't a time to leave my people unprotected."

Marie took the end of her sleeve and began to wipe his face. As she did, the first drops of rain began to fall. Within moments, it was pelting down hail that stung their raw skin.

Everyone scurried into the nearest refuge. In the melee Catherine, still holding Edana, was separated from the others. She found herself pushed into the corner of a hut that reeked of fish.

"Edgar!" she called. "Solomon!"

Her voice was canceled by the explosion of hailstones on the roof and the cries of the others crushed in with her.

She concentrated on making a space large enough for Edana to breathe. Someone in the room had begun a *Nostre Père* and soon everyone was praying together.

"This is what comes of arrogance," someone hissed in her ear.

Catherine tried to turn away but there was no place to go in the darkness. She concentrated on the prayer.

"More will come if you don't do as you were told."

"Go away!" Catherine begged. "Who are you? What do you want?"

There was a low chuckle. "You have to save your mother. You can't escape the prophecy. Sweet baby!"

Catherine felt a hand reach around her and brush Edana's cheek. The child whimpered. Catherine grabbed at the hand, but only caught empty air. She wrapped both arms tightly about her daughter.

"It's all right," she said. "I won't let her hurt you. Mama's here, *ma douz*."

Edana's body relaxed as Catherine rocked her. Catherine continued long after the child had fallen asleep on her shoulder. She only wished someone now could comfort her.

The rain eased sometime after sunset. Catherine emerged to a world that seemed to match her nightmares of Hell. The air smelt of things burning and even the untouched houses of the village were streaked with black. The crops that had managed to withstand the drought were now flattened by the hail. Puddles of mud and ash had collected everywhere. All the paths were slick and people trudging up and down were soon layered with gray-brown slime.

Catherine's overfull breasts ached. Even though Peter was partially weaned now, she worried that he was crying for his dinner. No one in the fishing hut had brought any food or drink, so she and Edana were also suffering.

Catherine started back up to the keep out of habit. She got only a few steps before she looked up and saw the ruin that the lightning had wrought. In the darkness, white smoke shone swirling amidst the shell of the castle. She stood in the middle of the common staring about, unsure of which way to move.

"My lady?" Hamelin seemed to appear before her from nowhere.

Catherine blinked, then focused on his face. The guard bowed and held out his arm for her to lean upon.

"You husband has been searching for you," Hamelin continued. "Lord Guillaume has lodged all of you in the tavern for now. It wasn't damaged although the beer is very warm. Let me take you there."

Once she saw that everyone was accounted for, Catherine's relief was overwhelmed by chagrin.

"How did all of you manage to wash?" She looked at their clean hands and faces and then down at herself. "I want soap and water before anything else, even food."

Guillaume had set up a table in an alcove of the inn, where he listened to reports of what had been lost and what little saved. Father Anselm sat next to him, laboriously writing down the totals.

"And then . . . The cows of Rabel wandered . . . uh . . . traversed . . . um . . . the garden of Auda and . . . What was the last part?"

"Father." Guillaume was losing patience. "Can't you write more quickly?"

The priest shrugged in apology. "I learned to read for the Mass," he explained. "I don't have much need to write."

"Catherine!" Guillaume stood and shouted for her. "Peter has swilled enough. He can finish up with sausage. The lad's got a couple of teeth; time for him to chew something besides you. I need you to write the list of what's been lost for Abbot Suger."

Catherine gave Peter another few gulps and then released him. He had almost finished, anyway. She folded the flap over the slit in her clothing and joined her brother at the table.

They didn't finish with the last recital of woe until the lamps had been lit and most of the village gone back to their smoky but untouched homes. Catherine had written as shortly as she could, but the wax tablet was full with squiggles running down the side.

"I should get this on parchment as soon as possible," she said. "Before I forget what all my abbreviations mean. Guillaume," she checked to be sure everyone else was busy elsewhere, "something strange happened to me this afternoon."

She told him about the voice in the hut.

"I think it was the same old woman that your horse stepped on," she finished. "And don't tell me that she's dead."

Guillaume sighed and rubbed his eyes. Every muscle in his body ached, including some he hadn't used in days. His head was full of speculations about how they were going to survive the winter, or even autumn. Under this worry was the fear that the fire had been a warning. Catherine's story only deepened his fear.

"How can I leave my wardship?" he asked her. "Without the keep to protect them, these people will be prey to any brigands who may come by. The abbot will certainly want rebuilding to start at once."

"I know." Catherine put her hand over his. "I don't know what to do, either. It all seems like something from a winter night story. Yet, the messenger was killed on his way to you. Not struck down from the sky or appearing from a gnarly oak. A harmless man was murdered to keep you from going to Boisvert. What would the abbot think about that?"

Guillaume sighed and withdrew his hand.

"You know as well as I do that he would consider it a personal insult," he said. "Abbot Suger has strong opinions of those who challenge his authority or who threaten his people."

"That's right." Catherine stood up, stretching her tired back and hands. "Why don't you go and explain it to him, yourself. Edgar and Solomon want us to return to Paris for a few days before we set off. If the abbot agrees, you can meet us there."

"I suppose." Guillaume was reluctant. "I'm surprised he hasn't sent someone down here already. The smoke must be visible from Saint-Denis."

Then he looked at her sharply. "What do you mean, 'Solomon'? What has he to do with any decisions? That Jew doesn't intend to come with you, does he?"

Catherine wished that just once she could tell Guillaume that Solomon was family, too. But this wasn't the time.

"He has the right to help us decide anything that might affect the trade he and Edgar do," she explained. "He has offered to come with us on his way to visit the Jewish community in Blois. I don't think he has any interest in staying at Boisvert."

Guillaume was pacified, but not pleased. He spent the rest of the evening in the corner in deep conversation with his bailiff.

Catherine had only a few words with Marie before they left the next morning. Considering how her sister-in-law had reacted to the first story about the old woman, she didn't think the most recent encounter would be appreciated. And Marie had enough to cope with at the moment. Catherine was amazed that she seemed so calm, with most of her possessions now fluttering in the wind across the countryside.

But Marie did have something on her mind.

"Catherine, I don't want to worry you," she began.

Catherine was mildly amused.

"What more could there possibly be?" she asked. "A plague?"

"No, of course not," Marie answered. "But, I've just been

wondering. Edgar says that all of the descendants of Lord Garge-naud must return to Boisvert. Have you thought about what that means?"

"Well, I don't know how many there are," Catherine admit-ted. "He's outlived three wives, at least. So there are likely cousins I've never . . ."

"Not cousins, Catherine," Marie said. "I was thinking of your mother."

"Oh, sweet Virgin!" Catherine was thunderstruck. "It never occurred to me. They can't mean to take her from the convent!"

Madeleine de Boisvert had been in the care of the Cistercian nuns of Tart for the past ten years. Her guilt over marrying a bap-tized Jew had been exacerbated by Catherine's decision not to en-ter a convent. Eventually, her mind had broken. The ritual and routine of the religious life helped her survive, but nothing had brought back her senses.

Marie shrugged. "I don't know. But, even though the nuns say she's much calmer, she apparently thinks that you and your brother and sister are still children. Or she may believe that you ascended bodily into heaven. Either way, seeing you might not be good for her."

Catherine sagged against the wall of the tavern. Edgar had al-most finished overseeing the loading of the packhorses, not that there was much left for them to carry. She really didn't need something else to worry about. Perhaps that was why she hadn't even considered that anyone would be so foolish as to wish her poor mother to leave the refuge where she was cared for in her gentle madness.

"I'm sorry, Catherine," Marie said, "but I didn't know if I'd be able to mention it before you got there. I thought you should be prepared."

"Yes, yes, of course," Catherine told her. "You're right. It's thoughtful of you to consider it amidst all this trouble."

"But you wish I hadn't." Marie gave a wry smile.

"Well, yes," Catherine said. "However, as you say, at least now I'll be able to prepare for the possibility."

As they followed the river downstream toward Paris, Catherine's mood began to lighten. Once away from the heavy layer of smoke, she could smell the remnants of rain in the forest. It was as if the dust of the world had been washed away to make it ready for guests. The shock of the fire receded. They were all safe. Guillaume would manage as he always did. She had let the oppressive heat and odd occurrences affect her mind. They would have a short, pleasant visit at Boisvert with relatives she had never met or could barely remember. She would show the children where she had played on her rare visits there. The abbess of Tart would never be so ill-considered as to disrupt her mother's life on a whim. Everything was going to return to normal soon.

When she caught a glimpse of a pale, greenish face looking down at her from the overhanging branches of an oak tree, Catherine closed her eyes and didn't open them until the road had twisted, leaving the apparition far behind.

Five

Paris, Wednesday (feria quarta) 9 kalends September (August 24) 1149. Feast of Saint Bartholomew, apostle to India. He was martyred by being flayed alive. The patron saint of tanners and leatherworkers. 11 Elul 4909.

> *E Lorois, ki les esgarda*
> *De la merveillese segna*
> *Jamais ne verra sa pareille.*

> Seeing this, Lorois crossed himself
> At this wonder, for never had he seen the like.

—*Lai de Trot*, II. 135–137

*D*o you know what I like best about the baths?" Catherine asked Edgar as they steamed together in a large, curtained tub near their home.

"I know what I like best," Edgar answered and demonstrated.

"Exactly," Catherine laughed. "We can do whatever we like and not worry about one of the children coming in."

"Yes, I feel strongly that children should learn about copulation from watching dogs and goats, just as we did," Edgar said. "And not from their parents."

"Well, that explains a lot." Catherine let herself float against him.

"Are you complaining, my lady?" he asked.

"Not at the moment." She sighed.

There was an interval of silence and near-drowning.

When they had both recovered, Catherine reluctantly pulled herself from the warm water and draped a linen sheet over her shoulders. Then, over his protests, she scooped a finger into the pot of face cream she had brought and began rubbing it into Edgar's left wrist around the part where the leather strap chafed his arm. Gently she smoothed it over the scarred skin that was still tender, even four years after the hand had been cut off.

"Stop wriggling," she told him. "You're worse than James."

He tried to pull away. He didn't like her paying so much attention to an ugly stump. She knew it and continued her ministrations.

"Now that we're home again," she said. "I'm beginning to feel a bit foolish about my insistence that we go to Grandfather's. Since Guillaume is so involved in getting at least part of the keep rebuilt before winter, he may not want to bother with it, either."

"Catherine, are you forgetting that a man died trying to deliver the summons?" Edgar asked, keeping his eyes from what she was doing.

She was silent a while, her fingers massaging the cream up his arm with hard strokes.

"No," she said finally. "But it all seems so unreal now. I think I was bewitched by the heat and that strange old woman. There probably is no emergency. It's more likely that Grandfather is senile and bored and wants to stir up some excitement to amuse himself."

She put the leather patch back on his arm, winding the straps around to secure it. "Don't you agree?" she asked him.

He lifted himself out of the tub to sit next to her. Catherine looked down.

"Anything else in need of a soothing cream?" she asked, distracted for the moment.

"They say one should always oil a sword before sheathing it," Edgar suggested. "Of course that's a very ambiguous adage."

"You don't have any obvious bruises," she said after making an examination. "Nor rust, I'm glad to say."

"I thank you for that, *carissima!*" He grabbed her in a tight embrace that almost sent them both back into the water.

"Now, about going to Blois?" Catherine asked reluctantly. "What should we do?"

Edgar sighed. He and Solomon had been debating the matter since their return to Paris. As the summer waned, more people were returning to the city. There was business to be transacted. Could they afford to spend even a few weeks away, especially when they had just completed a journey to Italy and back?

"It may be that this was just a whim on your grandfather's part," he answered. "The messenger might have been the victim of brigands who were interrupted before they could loot his body. In that case, it would make no sense to pack up and travel again so soon. But what if there is something to it?"

"A curse?" Catherine asked. "A fairy great-great-grandmother? That's only for stories. If it had been so vital, someone would have told me," she added with resentment.

"Most stories have a seed of truth in them." Edgar's voice shook as she dried his back. "But you mustn't blame your brother if you were kept in ignorance. Your mother may not have felt it was appropriate for someone intended for a religious life."

"Ha!" Catherine snorted. "You should have heard the real histories of some of the nuns' families. I should have been told."

Edgar ran his hand through her curls and kissed her forehead.

"Perhaps," he soothed, "but it can't be changed now. Solomon has offered to go down on his own this week and see what he can find out. He was planning to go to Blois in any case."

"Another bridal prospect?" Catherine asked hopefully.

"Not likely." Edgar shook his damp hair like a dog. "He runs the other way every time a nice Jewish girl of marriageable age enters a room."

"He should take one of them," Catherine said sadly. "What is he waiting for? He likes women well enough. It's not right for him to refuse to marry. Who will he leave his share of your partnership to? Who will take care of Aunt Johanna and Uncle Eliazar when they're old?"

"I don't know, Catherine." Edgar finished dressing. "You would think that the sweet tranquillity of our home would fill him with the desire to have one just like it."

Catherine thought of the havoc that the children were probably causing at that very moment.

"Oh, well," she decided. "We can't force him to marry and we can't turn him out, so he might as well be useful. How long will it take him to return from Blois?"

Solomon was already trying to get information on what was happening at Boisvert. His old friend, Abraham the vintner, had family in the region. In order to learn the latest news, Solomon had resigned himself to passing an evening listening to a litany of the virtues of every unmarried Jewish woman in France, Normandy, Champagne, and Burgundy. At least so it seemed. Abraham's wife, Rachel, had made it her life's work to see him settled and procreating.

"She's not only beautiful, but even tempered, sweet as a dove," Rachel extolled her most recent find. "Her father will give you a house near Troyes. Think how convenient that will be."

"Very nice," Solomon said. Unbidden, his mind reminded him that Troyes was close to the Paraclete, where Edgar's sister,

Margaret, was staying with the nuns until her fate was decided. He pushed the thought away. Margaret's fate was not in his hands.

"Solomon, you can't enjoy this rootless life you lead." Abraham felt obliged to support his wife. "You've no home but a corner of a room in the home of Edomites!"

"Catherine is my cousin, for all she's a Christian," Solomon reminded them.

"And it's worth your life should the other Christians discover it," Rachel reminded him. "You survive on their goodwill."

"We all do, Rachel," Solomon answered. "And must continue to as long as we are forced to live among these idolaters. At least the Christians I depend on love me as I do them."

"But you need your own family," Rachel almost wailed. "You need a son to bring to the Torah."

"Rachel," Abraham said quietly. "You've done your best. We cannot continue to badger poor Solomon."

"Thank you." Solomon smiled ruefully. "Everything you say is true, Rachel, and I'm sure the women you suggest are all paragons of virtue and beauty. I don't know why I can't accept my obligation. But everything in me says that it's not time."

Rachel sniffed. "Well, from the gray I see in your hair, I'd say time is running out."

Solomon laughed at that. "Catherine tells me that there is a mixture that will cover the white hair. She swears she doesn't use it herself, but I have doubts. Now, what is the news from Blois? Is there a reason a man might send for all those of his blood to gather there? Even more, is there reason to stay away?"

Abraham tugged on his beard in thought.

"Henry, lord of Blois isn't yet returned from the Holy Land," he said. "That's both good and bad. When he's home, he and Geoffrey of Anjou are in a constant battle over border castles. But now that he isn't there to oversee matters, minor lords feel that they can chip away at their neighbors' lands with impunity."

"Do you think Lord Gargenaud's keep at Boisvert is in danger?" Solomon asked.

"It's probably the strongest fortress in the area," Abraham said. "Been there forever, as far as I know. Almost all the buildings are stone now. The ditches are deep and full of sharp stakes. The walls are thick. And the place has its own source of water within the keep itself, they say. I suspect that Paris would fall before Boisvert."

"Don't ever say such a thing, even in jest." Rachel signaled the serving girl to bring more wine.

"So you know of no reason why Edgar shouldn't take his family there?" Solomon wanted to be certain.

"The Holy One, blessed be He, has not given me knowledge of the future," Abraham said. "But it seems a safe enough place."

"Do you know any strange tales of the family of the lord?" Solomon asked. "That they have lives unnaturally long, for instance?"

Abraham shook his head. "Gargenaud is very old, I know. No one can remember when he was young. However, when they get past a certain point people tend to add to their age. I remember hearing about a woman in Rome who swore she was the daughter of Moses' sister. Some say old Gargenaud fought with Charlemagne or even his grandfather, Charles the Hammer. Nonsense, of course."

"Nothing else?"

Abraham laughed. "What do you want, demons flying around the towers by night? No, Solomon, nothing else."

Solomon thanked him for the information and the food. He didn't feel especially relieved that there was nothing sinister to tell Edgar. Even if there were no demons at work, something about this whole affair gave him the feeling that a storm was rolling toward them all.

Mandon huddled in the shadow of the church of Saint-Merry, shrinking closer to the wall whenever anyone approached her.

There are beings in the world who need masses of people about them in order to survive. But Mandon was one who diminished when forced to live long among throngs. Paris was agony to her. The streams here were tame for the most part, confined by stone embankments. This summer they had no force at all. They trickled their way to the Seine, too tired even to turn a mill. For one used to living always with the endless sound of water flowing, the muddy, clogged waterways were torture. She longed to return home but couldn't until her task was done.

What did it take to make these people heed the prophecy? Did they have no respect for tradition?

The next morning Catherine went down to the storage cellar next to the kitchen. The next moment, she was racing back up the stairs to wake Edgar.

"Rats!" she cried. "Everywhere! In the grain sacks and gnawing through the cheese rinds. The cellar is full of them!"

"How can that be?" he asked as he pulled on his leather *brais* and hunted for the thick boots that laced to his knees. "Damn! Do these up for me, Catherine, would you?"

Quickly she laced and tied the boots.

"I don't understand it," she said as she worked. "The traps were set as usual last night. But we've had no problem with rats in months. Where could they have all come from? It looks like one of the ten plagues down there."

Edgar was looking for a riding glove.

"Is Solomon up?" he asked. "Tell him to meet me in the kitchen. Have Samonie see if the neighbors have also been invaded. If it's as bad as you say, we may need to get dogs in."

Catherine found the glove and helped him get it on. "What should I do?" she asked.

"Go tell James that I need to borrow Dragon for a while," Edgar answered. "I know he'll want to come, too, but convince him that he should stay upstairs and guard you and the others."

"Edgar, I haven't let the dog sleep in the children's room for months." She followed him onto the landing. "Dragon is down in the hall, keeping watch. I'll go see that no one comes down until you and Solomon say it's safe."

Even on the third floor, they could hear the shouts, howls, crashes, and barks. Then there came a series of high-pitched squeals and skitterings on the stone floors. At last Catherine heard a cry of triumph, and soon Edgar and Solomon appeared at the bottom of the steps.

"They're gone," Edgar announced. "Dead or chased off. You can come down now."

"About half the stores have been contaminated," Solomon added. "The room will have to be emptied, scrubbed out, and resealed."

"Resealed?" Catherine asked.

Edgar started to remove his glove with his teeth, then thought better of it. He held his hand out so that Solomon could pull the glove off.

"There were holes in the two outside walls," Edgar told her. "As big as a fist."

"And a trail of greasy bread leading to each one," Solomon added.

"Someone *set* rats on us?" Catherine couldn't believe it.

"It seems so," Edgar said grimly. "Has Samonie returned?"

"Yes, she says no one else has noticed a flood of vermin."

"Then," Edgar said, "we have to assume that someone did this out of malice against us."

Catherine thought of asking in indignation who would want to do such a thing, but decided that would be naïve. The task would be winnowing down the list.

She sighed. "I suppose we'd better get to work then. We need to build a fire to burn the bodies and everything the rats destroyed. Then sweep out the cellar and lay new straw. Then see about replacing what we've lost before we leave for Boisvert."

She looked at Edgar, who looked at Solomon. All three nodded. If someone were trying to harass them, it was just as well that they were going to a well-defended place.

"This may be nothing more than the work of some trader who feels we cheated him," Solomon suggested.

"Can you name him?" Catherine asked.

"No," Solomon admitted. "No one has complained that I know of. But there are a hundred reasons besides your summons to Blois, especially since you were preparing to go there anyway."

"It may be that we're not moving quickly enough," Catherine said. "Edgar, can you send Martin to Vielleteneuse to ask my brother how soon they can be ready? I don't want to wait here until something worse happens."

"I don't understand," Edgar said. "I thought someone was trying to prevent us from learning of your grandfather's command."

"But someone else seems to be driving us there," Catherine answered. "At least it seems so. Saint Berthe's balancing rod! I can't stand all this ambiguity."

"It would be nice if people would just tell us what's going on," Edgar said. "But that never seems to happen. So, I'm deciding. Before our home is burnt down or we're all attacked by griffins, we're leaving for Blois. Solomon, can you leave at once and meet us in Chartres once you've investigated the area?"

"Of course," Solomon assured him. He gave a wry smile. "I feel as though we've all fallen into some winter's story and our only choice is to learn what part we must play. What am I?"

"The gadfly, of course." Catherine pushed him back toward the hall. "But it's the depths of summer and I'm certain I would know if we were in a *conte merveilleuse*. For one thing, we'd all be speaking in rhyme."

"Catherine." Edgar put his arm around her. "You're babbling. I think we should let Samonie and Martin start on the kitchen and storeroom while the rest of us go find some unpolluted food. You'll feel better when you've eaten."

"Samonie?" Catherine asked the maid. "What do you think?"

"Martin and I will work better without you all underfoot," she said. "We'll get some of his friends to come and help with the clearing out before he leaves with your message to Lord Guillaume."

"Just don't let them dump the rats in the stream out back," Edgar warned. "The water's too low to carry them down to the river."

Samonie nodded, then shooed them all out.

They soon found themselves settled around a rickety table between the bakeshop and a tavern along the edge of the Grève. The children sat on the ground underneath and played.

"Bread, cheese, and fresh berries," Catherine sighed. "Perfect."

"No beer?" Solomon said plaintively.

"I brought the pitcher." Edgar handed it to him. "Your turn to pay."

Solomon sighed and went in search of the beer cask.

While they waited for him to return, Catherine watched the activity in the square in front of them. The Grève was a major marketplace in Paris. It sloped down to the Seine, where barges unloaded goods from upriver. There were tables of cloth, pottery, and leather goods as well as foodstuffs, sausage, vegetables, and cheese. Many of the artisans came here to get the raw materials for their trades and make deals for future shipments.

The space was also dotted with carts from which people hawked fresh milk, sweets, and small ropes of bread, twisted into knots. Among them on this clear hot morning were jugglers, beggars, and cutpurses, all hoping to make their fortune from the citizens of the town.

Catherine loved each and every one of them. Paris in all its grubby glory was home to her, not some ancient pile of stones in the countryside. Why, then, was she being pulled to a place she could barely remember? It wasn't just the frightening incidents and enigmatic warnings of disaster should they ignore the summons. She could feel something inside herself answering a call to come back.

Peter crawled onto her lap, looking for breakfast. Catherine opened the slit in her clothing and he settled down. Solomon came back with the beer and then got cups of new milk for the older children. Edgar was laughing with his mouth full.

It was a perfect moment. A fleeting instant of mindless contentment.

Catherine had grown wiser over the years. She recognized it and treasured it as it passed.

Later that morning Solomon packed his saddlebag and sent for his horse to be brought round.

"You'll meet me a week from now, in Chartres," he reminded them. "Whether Guillaume and his family are ready or not."

They promised him they would be there.

"And don't become distracted by some new conquest," Catherine teased. "Unless she's one you mean to bring home."

Solomon grunted without amusement.

"As if I'd subject any poor woman to inspection by you and Marie, not to mention Rachel." He mounted the horse and gave them a quick smile. "Expect me alone in a week and don't make me wait! No, James, you can't come with me!"

It would have been nice to gallop away in a cloud of dust, but the road was so crowded he had to ease his way toward the city gate. That gave them time to make James let go of the stirrup and drag him back to the house.

"Catherine, why don't you take the little ones up for a nap," Edgar suggested as they came in. "You could use some more sleep, too."

James protested a nap loudly.

"I'm six! I don't want to stay with babies," he yelled.

Edana, at four, was more than happy to go up for a nap. Catherine sighed, not eager for a struggle with her stubborn son.

Edgar smiled. "Go on up," he told her. "James and I will see how the cleanup is going."

"Thank you, *carissime*," Catherine kissed his nose. "Just don't let him touch the rats."

"Of course not," Edgar sighed.

He let James climb up to his shoulders, warning him to duck as they went through the door to the kitchen. Edgar was Saxontall and most doors were designed for a shorter race. James always enjoyed the thrill of nearly being knocked unconscious by the approaching lintel.

They found Samonie, with a scarf over her mouth, bringing out baskets of torn grain sacks.

"I can pour some of this into new sacks," she told Edgar. "But a lot of it was eaten into and then peed on. Martin and his friends are outside. Did you check with the neighbors? We could get into trouble starting a bonfire on a day like this."

"They want to be rid of the bodies as much as we do," Edgar assured her. "I'll go out and see that it stays confined."

Martin had built a ring of logs and brushwood near the stream at the bottom of the garden. Two other young men were helping him pile the rats next to it, ready to toss on to the flames.

"There's going to be an awful stink," one said, wiping his nose.

"It can't be helped," Martin said. "It would be worse if we let them rot. That would just draw more of them."

For the thousandth time, Edgar wondered who Martin's father was. Samonie had been a serving girl at a castle in Troyes and her children were apparently the product of extra service to visiting lords. But she never spoke of it and he never dared to ask.

The boy was close to seventeen now, with a mop of thick, wavy brown hair, light brown eyes, and a nose that seemed made to look down. At his own request, he had apprenticed to Edgar and Solomon and was learning the difficulties of being a merchant firsthand. He had gone with them on the recent trip to Lombardy and acquitted himself well. He had the gift of saying less than he knew and noting when others said more than they intended. He had also shown himself to be completely loyal, something far more rare in Edgar's experience.

Samonie had given him a bucket of charcoal to increase the heat of the fire. Edgar set one of the boys to spreading it and sent the other to the bake house for a shovel of live coals. While they were occupied, he took Martin aside to discuss matters.

"Did you find out what made the holes in the wall?" he asked first.

Martin shook his head slowly. "I thought someone had simply hammered through the plaster, but the cuts were too clean. It's as if someone sliced triangles in the wall with a sword."

"I can't see that," Edgar said. "A sword would be too long. Even lying on your stomach, you couldn't do it. There'd be no way to put any force behind the thrust."

"I know, Master," Martin said. "But that is what it looks like. And there's more. Come see."

He led Edgar down to the stream.

"This is diabolical." Edgar could hardly miss the meaning behind the length of flattened plants. The trail went halfway up to the house.

"There are still bits of bread going from here to the storeroom." Martin knelt to show a few orts that the rats had missed.

James bent over Edgar's head to see what they were looking at. He overbalanced and tumbled off. Edgar reached out his left arm to catch him, but missed. He could almost feel his phantom fingers move through the child's body.

Martin twisted on the ground and broke James's fall.

"I'm not hurt," James told them.

"Thanks to Martin," Edgar said. "If you can't pay attention, you'll have to stay on the ground."

"I'll be careful, I promise." James grinned with confidence.

He began to climb his father again.

Once his son was established on his shoulders, Edgar returned to the broken plants and the bread crumbs. He found the conclusion too ridiculous to believe. He looked at Martin.

"Are you telling me that these were *imported* rats?" he asked. "There weren't enough in the parish?"

"It's the only explanation I have, Master," Martin said. "Of course, perhaps these are all false clues, left on purpose to deceive us."

"Now you sound like Catherine." Edgar sighed. "Let's deal with what we can see and touch and work from that. Very well. James! Stop yanking on my ears and help us. What can you see from my shoulders?"

"I can see the whole world, Papa," James answered calmly. "Over the wall and into the street. There's a man going by with honey sticks. Can I have one?"

"Not today," Edgar said, turning toward the stream. "Now what can you see?"

"Just the water, Papa." James sounded bored. "There are too many trees in the way. Oh! There's something at the top of the cherry tree! Do you see it? Like a gonfanon that soldiers carry."

Edgar tried to look up without sending James down again.

"Yes, there is something fluttering," he said. "Martin, can you climb up and get it?"

"I'm too heavy," Martin decided. "Rodric," he called to the boy shoveling rats. "Can you get that piece of cloth that's caught up in the cherry tree?"

Rodric was more than willing to change jobs. He went up the tree with ease and soon reached the cloth. There he stayed.

"What's wrong?" Edgar called.

"The *destrois* thing is tied to the branch," Rodric called back. "It's a complicated knot. It's going to take a while."

"I know him," Martin said. "Anything to avoid a nasty job."

While Rodric was struggling in the tree, the other boy had returned with the coals. Edgar and Martin had the fire hot enough to start adding corpses by the time Rodric descended.

"I got it!" he shouted. "It took forever, but I figured you didn't want me to cut anything this fine."

Beaming with pride, he handed the length to Edgar, who held it up to examine.

It was a long piece of very thin linen, he thought, almost like the strip a priest wears around his neck. But there were no crosses or fish or alphas and omegas on this. Nor was there a border of flowers. Instead, there were embroidered pictures of a mermaid smiling and beckoning from the water. A bit farther on, a man lay beneath a tree.

"It looks like writing at the top here." Rodric pointed. "Does it tell the story of the mermaid?"

"I don't know," Edgar said. "These words aren't in a language I've ever seen."

James looked down at it. "Let me see. I can read."

Edgar set him on the ground. "Yes, you can, James, but Mama reads better. I want you to take this in to her and ask her to take good care of it. Is that clear?"

James took the folded strip. "Yes, Papa."

Edgar watched him until he entered the house. Then he turned back to Rodric.

"Is there any chance that the cloth could have blown into the tree by accident?" he asked.

"No, my lord," Rodric said. "It was tied up there on purpose, I'd take an oath on it. That knot was like the ones the boatmen make, only worse. Who'd do such a crazy thing?"

Edgar didn't answer. He handed Rodric the shovel and set them back to work.

They were at it all afternoon. When the vermin had been de-

stroyed, Edgar gave the young men a *denier* each and treated them
to a visit to the bathhouse. It was nearly dusk when he returned
to the house.

Catherine was waiting impatiently.

"James told me that this flew into a tree and he found it," she
greeted him, waving the cloth in his face. "You might have given
me a little more information before going off to soak again."

Edgar caught at the cloth. "I'm sorry. I had rats on my mind,"
he said. "Martin's friend says this thing was tied to a branch so
tightly that a whirlwind couldn't bring it down. What is it?"

"I don't know," Catherine answered. "I thought you would
tell me. The handwork is incredible."

"But the writing," Edgar pushed. "What does it say?"

"I've been trying all afternoon," she said. "But I can't make
sense of it. The letters are like French or Latin, but I don't know
the words. I thought maybe it was closer to English."

Edgar examined it again. "There are no English letters here,
no-*eth* or *thorn*. Nothing I recognize."

Catherine sat on the steps as if too worn out to stand.

"What's going on?" she wailed. "Who left this and why? Is it
the same person who set the rats on us, or have an angel and a demon both been loosed on us, tearing from opposite sides?"

Edgar bent over and lifted her to her feet.

"The only answer I have is that everything seems to be leading us to Boisvert and it's time we left, before something worse
occurs. Tomorrow, if we can be ready."

Catherine nodded.

"The day after that, at the latest. We had almost everything
packed up before we were invaded this morning," she said. "Samonie and I need to get more supplies for the journey and finish
putting what we rescued back in the storeroom."

"Good." Edgar thought a moment. "And, Catherine, don't
forget to bring this embroidery strip to ask them about. It may be
part of your family legend."

"Definitely," Catherine said. "And if this is some sort of monstrous joke, I may use it to strangle whoever is behind it."

Despite their fear that they would be subjected to more threats and warnings, the family's journey to Chartres was calm. They were able to travel part of the way by river and then by roads that were well maintained and patrolled. This meant an inordinate number of tolls, but Edgar paid cheerfully.

They arrived at Chartres well before the week was up and found an inn to stay at while they waited for Solomon.

"You know," Edgar mentioned to Catherine once they were settled. "You might copy out the text from the cloth and take it to the cathedral school here. The best scholars left some time ago, but there may still be a master about who can decipher the language."

"I'll copy it," she agreed. "But you had better take it. I don't know anyone there. If I appear with some arcane words on a page, they might well think I want to use it for some dark potion."

Edgar laughed. "They might think the same of me. Do we have a plausible story as to where we found the writing?"

"Not at the moment," Catherine said. "Let me sleep on it. Don't!" she added. "I know you were going to say something lewd."

"No, you just hoped so," Edgar teased.

Catherine had to admit he was right.

By the next morning, she had decided that they should tell the clerics that the words were from an inscription they had found on a stone dug up on their land. It happened often enough that a plow turned up some old bits of wall with Roman writing. They didn't need to say that they already knew it wasn't written in Latin.

Edgar set off to the cathedral in search of a scholar. Catherine stayed behind to sit with Samonie and tend to her sewing, like a proper wife.

"It's been so calm the past few days," Samonie commented. "We must finally be doing whatever your sorceress wanted."

"Samonie," Catherine corrected her. "She wasn't *my* anything. I don't know what she was. And I never understood what she wanted."

"Still, it's nice to have a day or two without a disaster." Samonie wanted the last word.

"Yes," Catherine gave in. "I've enjoyed the peace, too."

It lasted until the cathedral bells rang None.

As the tolling faded, Catherine noticed a party approaching the inn. The elegance of the horses and the sedan chair made it clear that this was someone of distinction. She moved her stool back to give them more room to pass.

However, at a wave from inside, the sedan chair was set down directly in front of her. As Catherine gaped, the curtains were pushed aside.

"Sitting like a common alewife by the side of the road! You haven't changed at all," a woman's voice announced. "I can't believe we ever shared the same womb."

Catherine inhaled deeply. She wished Samonie hadn't tempted the fates.

"Agnes." She forced a smile as she held out her arms to her sister. "What a surprise! How wonderful to see you again."

Six

The town of Chartres, Sunday 5 kalends September (August 28) 1149. Feast of Saint Augustine of Hippo, bishop, theologian, and autobiographer, who really has a lot to answer for. 15 Elul 4909.

> . . . dont irai le messe oir
> Si com mes ancestre fist
> Et me grand guerre esbaudir
> Encontre mes anemis.
>
> . . . And then I will go hear the mass
> As my ancestors did
> And then I'll take up the war again
> Against all my enemies.
>
> —Aucassin and Nicolette, XXIX, II. 11–14

Apparently, the messenger from Grandfather had no trouble reaching Agnes in Trier," Catherine told Edgar sourly. "I'm rather sorry he did. She is, if anything, more annoying than I remember."

They were sitting in the room they had taken for the family

at the inn. Samonie and Martin had gone with the children to the market so, for the moment, Catherine and Edgar were alone.

Edgar grinned. "Are you going to take this opportunity to practice patience and charity and forgive your sister for marrying well, never spilling on her clothes, and always pointing out deficiencies in your character?"

"You forgot being blond and taking most of Mother's jewelry with her when she married," Catherine pouted. "That's a lot to forgive in one swallow."

"Then start with the jewelry and work up to the rest." Edgar reached inside her veil and pulled out a dark curl. "Personally, I prefer sable tresses. Scotland is awash in blondes."

Catherine tried not to smile. "You won't let me sulk, will you?"

"I haven't time to indulge you." He tucked the curl back in place. "Now, do you want to know what I found out at the cathedral?"

"Of course." Catherine was annoyed with herself for having forgotten. "What did the masters say?"

"That it isn't in a language any of them know," Edgar said. "I even asked if it could be Breton, but one of the monks speaks it and he's sure it isn't that, either."

"What about Saracen or Hebrew, but in Roman letters?" Catherine wondered. She held up the length of cloth again. "I don't know—it has a feel of being something almost familiar. In some parts I'd almost think it was French with terrible grammar, but it makes no sense. It must have something to do with the pictures. If the woman weren't a mermaid, I'd think it was the family story that Guillaume told us. He did say she had both her feet, didn't he?

"If someone is trying to send us a message, they're not doing very well," she muttered.

"You know, it might have been done by someone who

couldn't write," Edgar said, as he puzzled over the letters. "Perhaps the seamstress copied a few letters here and there and embroidered them just for amusement."

That idea bothered Catherine. "Sometimes people use chains of arcane letters if they want to cast a spell. Solomon told me that women ask him for magic words in Hebrew. If that's what this is, then it might well have been left as a curse upon us. We should get rid of it."

Edgar stopped her. "Catherine, don't start speculating on disaster. Why should the language be demonic? This could just as well have been left as a blessing. Perhaps one of the saints flew by the tree and put it there for us to find."

"A saint would have known to write in a language we could read." Catherine couldn't stop herself from arguing, even when the statement was absurd.

With a sigh she folded up the cloth and tucked it into a purse at her belt.

"Very well, now about your sister." Edgar guided her back to an immediate problem. "Have you told her yet that we are waiting for Solomon to meet us here before continuing to Boisvert?"

Catherine grimaced. "I was hoping you would do it. Or," she added wickedly, "we could wait for him to tell her, himself."

Agnes had learned of the family's Jewish connections a few years before. The very idea horrified her. She loathed the sight of Solomon and the easy way Catherine and Edgar included him in their lives.

"I couldn't do that to him," Edgar said.

"He might enjoy seeing her face when he walks in." Catherine felt a certain pleasure at the image.

Agnes was staying at a nearby convent guesthouse and had let it be known that she expected Catherine and Edgar to join her for the evening meal. In her perverse mood, Catherine considered bringing all the children and the dog but decided that would be too much. So she allowed Samonie to dress her stylishly and prepared for an unpleasant meal.

Agnes, of course, had brought servants, dishes, beds, tables, chairs, and pillows. Consequently, the room at the convent was as elegant as their home in Trier. Her husband, Hermann, rose to greet them as they entered.

"Good sister! Dear brother!" He hugged them warmly. "It has been too long since my Agnes and I have seen you. Have you looked on our fine son yet?"

"Catherine saw him this afternoon." Agnes joined her husband. She gave her sister a quick peck on the cheek and nodded coolly to Edgar.

As they were seated at the table, Edgar whispered in Catherine's ear, "It seems we're out of favor again."

"Saving her life wasn't enough, I guess," Catherine whispered back.

Not enough to erase Catherine's offenses of choosing Edgar over life in the convent, of accepting their infidel cousin, and, not least, for pushing their mother from being a woman who was merely deeply pious to one who was lost in religious mania.

Perhaps Agnes had a point.

They conversed politely through the meal, giving news of old friends and family.

"Your sister, Edgar," Agnes asked. "Margaret. Such a sweet child. Is she married, yet?"

Edgar froze, his spoon halfway to his mouth. "No," he said evenly. "She is continuing her studies at the Paraclete, as Catherine did."

"Ah, well, I'm sure that her grandfather will provide the convent a rich dowry should she decide to take the veil." Agnes smiled.

Catherine marveled at her sister's needle-sharp skill in knowing what would discomfit them most. Margaret was Edgar's half

sister, her mother an illegitimate child of the count of Champagne. Count Thibault had grown fond of his granddaughter and
had offered more than once to provide for her. Edgar resented the
count's interest all the more because there was nothing he could
do to discourage it.

"Margaret has not yet decided if she has a vocation for the
convent," Catherine jumped in. "As you know, Heloise will not
allow anyone younger than eighteen to take final vows. Margaret
has two more years."

"Of course." Hermann smiled at them. "My nephew, Peter,
still speaks of her. He sends greetings. You know, he is now a man
and I do not guard him anymore."

Agnes put her hand on his. "You aren't his guardian, of
course, but he still relies on you for counsel."

Hermann nodded affably. Edgar found himself liking the
man, despite his choice in a wife.

"Your French has improved amazingly since we last saw you,"
he commented. "I'm very impressed. It took me years to learn the
language."

Hermann smiled proudly. "My Agnes, she teaches me," he
said. "But it is not easy. Such slippery sounds, don't you think?"

"Oh, yes," Edgar agreed. "Very different from our tongues."

Hermann's good nature eased the tension of the dinner, as
did the clear wine he had brought from Trier. By time the sweetmeats were brought in, Catherine was feeling inclined to try to be
more charitable toward Agnes.

When the last server had left, Agnes sighed with relief.

"Now," she said firmly. "What are you two planning to do to
save us all from destruction?"

Catherine was stunned.

"Do you mean you knew about these stories, too?" Her lower
lip trembled. "I don't understand. If this is part of our legacy, then
why was I the only one not told?"

"Perhaps your head was so full of philosophy that you just didn't listen," Agnes countered. "Mother told me many tales of her childhood that you had no time for."

Catherine swallowed her tears. She resented Agnes's words deeply, even more because she feared her sister was in the right. Had she paid any attention to their mother's stories? She should have been more sympathetic, less concerned with herself. Catherine sighed. Sometimes sins of omission were harder to atone for than wrongs she had done.

The others were staring at her, Edgar and Hermann with worry. Agnes's expression was unreadable. Catherine tried to bring her attention back to the present dilemma.

"But you don't believe this myth, too, do you?" she asked. Agnes was always the sensible one. "Our lives aren't tied to a spring under Boisvert. That's nonsense!"

"Is it?" Agnes looked her up and down. "Then why are you here?"

"Because someone has taken great pains to send for us," Edgar answered for her. "And a man was murdered to keep us from learning of your grandfather's summons."

Agnes waved that away. "You are always being threatened. And for good reason. You never could leave well enough alone. If a man was murdered, I'm sure it was because of something unrelated to this. There is only one reason for either of us to have come on this journey."

She turned to her sister, her expression honest and pleading.

"You felt at once that you had to come, didn't you, Catherine?" Agnes leaned forward, her eyes fixed on Catherine's face. "Don't give me any complicated excuses. You know it, even if you won't admit it. You are going to Boisvert for the same reason I am. The curse is threatening Andonenn and she needs us. The mother of us all is calling us home."

Catherine couldn't avoid her eyes. Nor could she lie to them.

"Yes," she admitted. "I don't know who or what is doing it,

but I cannot deny the feeling that I'm being pulled to Boisvert whether I will it or not."

Catherine only managed to keep her temper in check until they had returned to their room.

"Wonderful!" She ripped her sleeves off with furious jerks. "Everyone in the family learned this damn story before they were weaned. Why did no one tell me? Am I not part of the family? Was I really that oblivious?"

Edgar picked up the shredded sleeves and put them in Samonie's sewing basket. From her cot in the corner, Samonie roused herself enough to caution them not to wake the children. Then she put the pillow over her head and went back to sleep.

Edgar and Catherine crawled into bed still in their shifts. The rings clattered as Edgar drew the curtains.

Catherine was still fuming. "If I'd known all along, I'd have understood the signs. I'd have known to ask the old woman more before she died."

"Sshhh." Edgar rolled over and drew her arm across his stomach. "We can't change that now. You musn't fret."

She drew breath to protest, but he turned swiftly and kissed her until he felt the anger drain away.

"No more tonight."

His body relaxed against hers and he was soon asleep.

But Catherine passed the darkness reliving the evening, thinking too late of what she should have said to Agnes and wondering how much her sister really believed of the family legend. It was nearly dawn before she slept.

Catherine had honestly forgotten about telling Agnes that Solomon was meeting them. So her conscience was clear when she and her sister returned from Mass at the convent the next morning and found him sitting with Edgar outside the inn.

Agnes stopped dead.

"This is too much," she hissed at Catherine. "What is that person doing here? You can't mean to bring him with us!"

Catherine smiled at her as she waved at Solomon.

"What took you so long, snail foot?" she called. "Did you have a nice visit in Blois?"

As they drew nearer, she could tell that Edgar had remembered to warn Solomon. He showed no surprise as he stood and bowed deeply to Agnes.

"My lady," he said. "You are looking well. Much better than the last time we met. Germany must suit you."

He looked at her and smiled.

Catherine knew for a fact that to most women, a smile from Solomon could win him anything from a free pitcher of beer to a week in a widow's bed. Agnes regarded him coldly.

"I prefer it to living at the house in Paris," she said. "Especially since my sister is not discerning in her choice of guests."

Solomon turned to Catherine. "So you told her about the rats." He smiled again at Agnes. "And have the good people of your village tried to murder any more Jews lately?"

"Solomon." Edgar felt it was time to intervene. "Agnes might be interested in hearing what you found out, if the two of you can be convinced to arrange a truce."

Agnes clenched her fists but nodded. Edgar looked at Solomon, who shrugged.

"Catherine?" Edgar motioned for her to sit. "Solomon thinks we should leave for Boisvert at once, rather than wait on your brother. There is some trouble between your grandfather and one of his neighbors."

Agnes joined them. "It isn't Foulques of Valleton, is it?" she asked. "He's had his eye on our land for years."

"No," Solomon said. "In Blois the word is that some castellan of Anjou is claiming that Boisvert is his through his mother's line. The bishop has offered to mediate, but the man won't consider it. He says Gargenaud must turn over the castle to him or face annihilation."

"No one in our family ever married into Anjou," Agnes said with certainty. "He's lying. What is this *avoutre*'s name?"

"Olivier of Château Boue," Solomon told them. "Mean anything to you?"

"Nothing," Agnes said. "He probably named himself. 'Olivier'! I suppose he has a brother named Roland. What nonsense."

"Hold up a moment," Catherine said. "Just how far back on his mother's side does this man base his claim?"

Solomon sighed. "You have it. Remember now, I'm only repeating what I was told. Lord Olivier says that he, too, comes from the line of your knightly forebear, Jurvale. Only his ancestor is from the man's first marriage, to a noblewoman, and not contaminated by Andonenn's unearthly blood. Therefore, he claims that his distant grandfather should be the true heir."

Catherine rubbed her forehead. The ache didn't go away.

"Is everyone here mad?" she asked quietly. "The bishop thought this claim valid enough to feel the need to negotiate?"

"It doesn't have to be true, Catherine," Agnes said. "Or even plausible. This Olivier only needs a battle cry."

"Do your sources say that Olivier is preparing an attack now?" Edgar asked.

"Not precisely." Solomon squirmed on the bench. "They say only that the land is unsettled. Everyone I spoke with had the feeling that something was amiss. The peasants are talking of bringing in the harvest still green, rather than lose it all. People swear they've seen strange fish in the rivers, with shimmering scales and golden eyes."

"How many people?" Catherine asked.

"It doesn't matter," Agnes said. "It's clear things are awry in the countryside all around Boisvert. We are the only ones who can put it right."

"You keep saying that, Agnes," Catherine said in exasperation. "But just how are we to do it?"

She didn't expect her sister to have an answer, but Agnes folded her hands and looked at them calmly.

"We must find out who is blocking the spring and stop them," she told them. "But first we must find the source and it will only reveal itself when all of the lady's children have returned to Boisvert."

They looked at her with deep skepticism. Agnes glared back.

"It's the truth! Ask Guillaume when he gets here," she said. "He'll tell you."

"But, Agnes, it's been centuries." Catherine spoke carefully, as to a child. "There must be thousands of descendants by now. Even if they could be found, they couldn't all possibly be brought together."

"That's as may be," Agnes said. "I only know the prophecy. The time has come and we must carry out our obligation." She stood. "If you've nothing else to discuss, I shall return to my rooms. I must let Hermann know what to expect when we arrive."

After she had gone, Catherine turned to Edgar.

"Do you think it's going to happen to me, too?" she asked. "Mother is mad; her brother was possessed and now Agnes thinks she can deliver Boisvert from an army."

The two men ignored her.

"How much do you credit these rumors?" Edgar asked.

Solomon thought a bit. "I had much of it from my friend Menachem. He does a lot of trading in Anjou. He said this tale of Lord Olivier's is being repeated as far as Tours. But even the Jewish scholars of Blois are uneasy. They talk of signs in the heavens or the numbers of our names all foretelling danger. Mostly I think everyone feels that there have been too many years of bad crops and too much uncertainty about who is lord of the land."

"Is all this likely to erupt soon?" Edgar pressed. "How great do you gauge the risk?"

"I saw no signs of a muster," Solomon said. "It's almost harvest. Not many men will leave the fields even if ordered to. It makes more sense to put off an attack until spring, when stores are low and you can keep your enemy from getting out to plant."

"That's the way they do it normally," Edgar agreed. "But there's nothing about this situation that's even close to normal."

"Edgar." Catherine had stopped musing on her own sanity. "We're only two days away from Boisvert. We've come this far. If I don't get some answers, you'll soon have to get a muzzle for when I start frothing at the mouth."

"You might as well continue," Solomon agreed. He stood and stretched. "I'm going to find a tavern where they actually have beer. No one's been out to serve us since I arrived."

"Aren't you coming with us to Boisvert?" Catherine asked in alarm.

"Not this time," Solomon told her. "For once, little Agnes is in the right. I don't belong in your adventure. Menachem needs me to help transport some wine to Saint Martin's. I'll keep my ears open and send word if I get wind of an army coming your way. At Boisvert, I would only be an intruder. However, I will escort you as far as the fork in the road. You go north to Boisvert and I'll return south to Blois."

Catherine wanted to argue, but she knew he was right.

She looked around. They had reached the hottest part of the day. It was odd that there was no one else in the road or the sheep pasture across from the tavern. Was everyone resting until the sun descended and the breeze blew up from the river? She had the sudden sensation that the three of them were the only ones left in the world.

"I have to go check on the children," she said abruptly, pushing herself to her feet.

When she had gone, Solomon and Edgar exchanged glances.

"The next market you go to," Edgar said. "See if you can find me a stout leather muzzle, just in case."

∞

Agnes was still seething by the time she reached the guesthouse. First she checked to see that the wet nurse was attending to her son. The woman, who spoke no French and could be trusted not to run off, was dozing by the cradle, one foot rocking automatically. Satisfied, Agnes went to pour out her grief to her husband.

"Catherine is just being stubborn," she complained. "She feels the force pulling us home as much as I do. Why won't she admit it?"

She was pacing around the room in agitation. Hermann took her arm and gently guided her to a chair. Then he gave her a cup of wine and waited until she had sipped enough for her breath to come more slowly.

"Now," he smiled. "You mustn't let her upset you so, *min trût*. Your sister was never one to accept anything as destined to be. At least not without a struggle. She is cursed with the ability only to see things exactly as they are. And if she doesn't understand what she sees, then she must find the truth behind it. You should be glad of that, *liebling*. Otherwise you might still be suspected of the murder of my brother."

"I know," Agnes sighed. "But sometimes I feel that she didn't come to Trier so much to save me then as to work out a particularly interesting conundrum."

Hermann laughed. "You know better than that! She could have solved any number of puzzles much closer to home. For all your differences, she cares about you. And you are fond of her, too."

"Perhaps," Agnes conceded. "But my fondness is hidden at the bottom of all the things she does to annoy me. The best I can do is pray for the safety of her soul. I long ago gave up on changing her in this life."

"That is my wise wife." Hermann kissed the top of her head. "And it's possible that we will be grateful soon for your sister's irritating traits."

Agnes looked up.

"Are you worried about this?' she asked.

"I find everything about it most unsettling," he admitted.

"But why didn't you forbid us to come, then?"

"Because I know you." Hermann smiled again. "My sensible Agnes does not insist on a long and difficult journey with little Gottfried, unless the necessity is urgent. A prophecy, a curse, or only the duty one owes to one's family, it doesn't matter why. You needed to come and so, I must bring you."

Agnes felt her eyes filling. Heaven had been so generous in giving her this man. It was too much to ask that God reform Catherine, too. She resolved to endure her older sister. After all, it would only be for a few weeks. They would be back in Trier by the feast of All Saints, leaving Catherine and her family in Paris to exasperate someone else.

Guillaume didn't relish facing Abbot Suger, his overlord and also currently regent of France. The abbot was a tiny man, acutely aware of his lack of stature. He had risen from a humble family to this exalted position through determination, perseverance, and unwavering loyalty to the kings of France. He was also a good master, demanding only what was his by right.

This was why Guillaume dreaded asking him for permission to leave Vielleteneuse, even if only for a few weeks.

"I've hired men to do the rebuilding of the keep," he told the abbot. "My bailiff will oversee the work. They hope to have it ready for us to move back in by Saint Nicholas's Day."

Suger listened sympathetically, now and then nibbling on the bowl of honeyed walnuts on the table beside his chair.

"A dreadful accident, this fire," he murmured. "We can only thank the saints that no one was killed and the village was spared."

"It was a miracle," Guillaume said sincerely. "Saint Denis was watching out for us. The people of the village will be sending a gift of thanks soon."

Suger beamed in delight. "We shall be delighted to receive it in his name."

Having thus oiled the wheels, Guillaume proceeded to his request.

He had expected Abbot Suger to refuse him and was surprised at the sinking in his gut when Suger agreed at once.

"I'll send some men to keep watch on the road," Suger said. "You can return from time to time to be sure the rebuilding is being done properly. Why should your household have to make do in temporary quarters?"

"Thank you." Guillaume's face showed his astonishment.

Suger offered him some nuts.

"You have been a good and loyal vassal," he told Guillaume. "I would think less of you if you refused a summons from the head of your family. Of course, I would have been disappointed if you had not sought my permission first."

"You are my liege lord," Guillaume said faintly. "My people and I are ever at your service."

"In the service of Saint Denis," Suger corrected. "How wise that the people of Vielleteneuse place all their faith in him."

Guillaume was nearly home before he realized the importance of the abbot's last words.

Marie came to greet him in the bailey. Guillaume slid down from his palfrey.

"The abbot knows about the rite," he told her. "You'd better have Conon tell the villagers that their donation of thanks to Saint Denis just doubled."

"Don't worry," Marie said. "Father Anselm has been burdened with confessions all week. Even though their homes were spared, the bolt of lightning was an unambiguous sign to most of them. Of course, there are some who say that the keep was hit because one of our guests tried to catch a glimpse of a woman's ritual."

"Who?" Guillaume was alert at once. "I'll have him whipped."

"I don't know," Marie said. "From what I've heard, the women terrified him sufficiently. Never mind. Are we still going to Boisvert?"

Guillaume nodded, his eyes surveying the ruin that had been his home and his responsibility.

"The abbot believes in duty to one's family."

Marie sniffed. "The way he's taken care of his own, I'd hope so!"

Guillaume ignored that. He was looking at the jagged burnt stalks of timber at the top of the tower.

"What's that thing?" he asked.

Marie tilted her head back to see where he was pointing. Between the blackened crenels of stone, something seemed to be caught on a piece of wood. It fluttered in the wind but stayed fixed.

"I don't know," she said. "I don't think it was there when you left."

"Have someone climb up and get it," Guillaume told her. "Hamelin!" he called to the soldier, who was coming up to take his horse. "Is it possible to get to the top of the tower?"

"It would be a tricky climb, but I think I could do it, my lord," Hamelin replied.

"Have a try," Guillaume ordered. "See if you can fetch that white thing waving around up there."

"But don't break your neck," Marie added.

Hamelin grinned and vanished into the keep.

Guillaume and Marie watched the top for him to emerge. Osbert, seeing that his lord's horse hadn't been seen to, came over. He looked up, as well. Soon the yard was cluttered with people all staring at the tower and wondering why.

"There he is!" Marie cried. "Be careful!"

Hamelin, covered in soot, was edging along the remains of

the floor. He leaned over to reach the object and gave it a tug. It held fast. He tried moving closer and teetered wildly on a loose board.

Everyone held their breath as he rocked far above their heads. After an eternity, he managed to get his arm around a merlon and find a solid spot to stand. From there, he used both hands to free the strip of white. Waving it over his head in triumph, he disappeared again, to cheers from all. A few moments later, amidst a deafening crash and a cloud of black dust, he fell out of the doorway, coughing violently.

Osbert ran up the steps to catch him. Leaning on his friend, Hamelin proudly handed the prize to Guillaume.

"What is it?" Everyone tried to see.

"Some kind of embroidery." Guillaume turned it over in his hands. "Is it yours?"

He gave it to Marie, who studied it a while. "Amazing!" she said. "You only got one tiny smudge on it. Excellent, Hamelin! Now go clean off and have some beer to clear your throat."

Several others decided to join him, seeing that after all it was nothing but a bit of cloth.

"Now." Marie sat on an empty keg and laid the cloth on her lap. "It wasn't done here, that I know. It doesn't look like church linen. These words aren't Latin. I know what that looks like. And it doesn't seem French, either."

Guillaume was more interested in the picture running across the top.

"It's a story, don't you think?" he suggested. "See, the knight chasing the deer. It must have got away, so he's gone to sleep under a tree. I wonder what it's about."

"The length seems to be complete." Marie examined the edges. "It's hemmed all around. That may be the whole tale."

"Well, that's boring." Guillaume was unimpressed. "I'm sorry Hamelin had to be put in danger just for a dull bit of needle-work."

"Perhaps," Marie said. "Don't you wonder how it got up there?"

"The wind, of course," Guillaume answered promptly.

"I don't think so, my dear." Marie folded up the cloth. "It seemed to me that Hamelin was untying it. And look, the only mark on it is from his fingers. It should be streaked with dirt."

She bundled the strip into her sleeve and knotted it.

"I think we should take this to Catherine," she decided. "She'll know what it says."

Guillaume sighed. "I suppose. All that schooling must eventually be of use."

He started walking around the keep, inspecting the repairs. Marie followed.

"I don't think you understand, my dear," she said. "This might be important. It was purposely left at the very top of the tower, in a place nearly impossible to reach."

"So?" Guillaume had more immediate concerns.

"So." Marie tried to match his stride. "This embroidery must be another sign."

Guillaume stopped. "Sign? Of what? And why? We're doing what the old woman wanted, if Catherine heard her aright."

Marie looked up at him. "I don't know," she said. "But having us and the children in a strong, fortified, unburnt castle is becoming more appealing each moment."

Guillaume's face was grim. "I don't need to hide," he said. "But I've told the abbot we are going to Boisvert, and so we shall go."

"Well, I've finished the packing, such as it is," Marie answered. "We can leave in the morning."

Despite her annoyance with Agnes, Catherine was forced to admit that traveling with her was not unpleasant. Agnes's animosity did not extend to her niece and nephews. Edana especially pleased her and the little girl spent most of the day riding in the chair with her aunt and baby Gottfried, emerging only when the motion became too much for her stomach.

It was a relief to Catherine to turn her daughter over to someone else, for her son needed the attention of at least three people to keep him from harm. James wouldn't stay anywhere for long. If he was riding with Edgar, he wanted Solomon. Then he had to get down and chase his dog, Dragon, along the path. The guards swore at them both as they ran in and out between the horses' legs.

"James!" Edgar shouted. "If you don't keep away from the horses, I'll put you and Dragon on a lead behind the mules!"

This threat restrained James only until the party stopped for a rest.

Catherine swore that James had been kneeling by the stream to splash water on his hot face. She had only looked away for an instant. The next thing she knew, there was a loud cry from the woods accompanied by Dragon's distinctive deep barking.

Her skirts caught on brambles as she ran toward the sound. She tripped on the undergrowth, landing in a tangle of thorns. Edgar passed her without stopping. He ripped the brush away with his good arm as he ran. Solomon followed right behind, his hunting knife drawn.

"James!" Catherine screamed as she tried to untangle herself from the grasping plants.

She heard Edgar's shout as he spied James, then louder barks and, finally, the voices of men raised in anger. With a final tug that ripped her *bliaut*, Catherine freed herself and followed the noise.

She plunged abruptly into a small clearing shaded by an enormous oak that blocked the sunlight, creating a space now filled with people and dogs.

Dragon was planted at the base of the tree, howling at something in the branches. At a discrete distance, a much smaller dog circled, whining worriedly.

"Where is James?" Catherine panted.

"Here," Edgar said.

He was holding the child tightly under his arm. Once Catherine caught her breath, Edgar handed him to her.

"He's not hurt," Edgar said sternly. "Don't fuss over him."

Once Catherine saw that James was in one piece and more excited than frightened, she had no intention of fussing. She was much more inclined to hunt for a good resilient birch branch to spank him with.

She set her son on the ground and held him firmly by the shoulders, kneeling to look into his unrepentant eyes.

"How many times have we told you to stay with us?" she scolded "You could have been lost in the woods and kidnapped by outlaws!"

"Dragon was hunting," James answered calmly. "I had to stay with him to see what he had caught. Look, Mama!"

Without loosening her grip, Catherine turned her attention to the man in the tree.

Edgar had finally managed to calm Dragon, but the other dog was still pawing at the trunk of the tree where his master was hanging.

"Drop your weapon and come down!" Solomon ordered him.

There was a pause, then a hunting bow clattered down, followed by a skinning knife in its sheath.

"That's all I have," the man called down. "I swear on the blood of the martyrs! Is that wolf tied up?"

"We have him," Edgar called back. "You're safe from attack."

There was the sound of muttering as if the man doubted him. But soon the tree started rustling and a pair of boots appeared from between the branches. One glance at the quality of the leatherwork convinced Catherine that this was either a very successful thief or a nobleman.

The man who dropped from the tree bore out her impression. He was wearing silver brooches on his tunic, which was also well made, with an embroidered collar.

"Now," he said as he dusted himself off. "Just what kind of

people are you to set a dog like that on a man hunting on his own land?"

Edgar gave James a stern stare and bowed to the man. "I apol‑ogize for the actions of my son and his pet. He shall be punished."

The enthusiasm drained from James's face, to be replaced by apprehension.

"Mama?" He tried to hide in her skirts. Edgar ignored him.

"What repayment can we give for your inconvenience?" he asked the man. "My name is Edgar of Paris. My partner, Solomon, and my wife, Catherine. The miscreant is my son James. He is, of course, abjectly sorry."

From the depths of Catherine's *bliaut* came a pitiful "Very sorry, my lord."

The man couldn't keep from smiling.

"A fine greeting to give your cousin, young man!" He gave James a tap on the head with his fingers. "I am Aymon, great‑grandson of Gargenaud, lord of Boisvert, as you are, James. I can‑not tell you how overjoyed we are that you have come. Are there others?"

"My sister, Agnes, and her family are with us," Catherine told him, too astonished at the coincidence to give more than a sim‑ple answer. "My brother and his wife and children should arrive soon."

Aymon closed his eyes and let out a long ragged sigh.

"Agnes came even from Germany!" He shook his head in wonder. "And Guillaume as well. I didn't believe it could happen. Oh, blessed Mother, we may yet be saved!"

He didn't give them time to question him.

"I have to fetch my horse, if your dog hasn't run him off," he told them. "I'll go through the woods and tell them of your ar‑rival. If you follow the road, you'll be at Boisvert before sundown. Hurry and welcome, welcome to you all!"

Seven

Somewhere in the forest in the county of Blois. Tuesday 3 kalends September (August 30) 1149. Feast of Saint Felix, martyr, whose breath could knock over stone idols.

Toutes les genz le conoissoient.
Tuit les conjoient et convoient
Aprés lui ot grant bruit de gent.

All the people knew him.
And all welcome him and
Follow after him noisily.

—Erec and Enide, II. 787–789

*T*he forest thinned as they came closer to Boisvert and the road widened enough for two horses to ride abreast. The party could now make better time. Overhead, the sunlight filtered through verdant branches that protected them from the heat, but the shade made Catherine uneasy. Too many things seemed to be coming out of trees lately, green women, new relatives. She glanced often at the overhanging foliage, half-expecting to see a pale face staring down at her.

Within a league or two, the woods grew even more sparse.

They passed by a hunter's tower and soon came upon a swine-herd, his few pigs out on a search for early acorns. When asked how much farther it was to the castle, he smiled vacantly and pointed in the direction they were already going.

"Do you think he's really stupid or just acting the way he thinks we expect him to?" Catherine asked Edgar.

"I think he didn't want to be bothered," Edgar said. "Or maybe he's deaf. Or he might have thought we were the vanguard of an invading army and has sent us in the wrong direction."

"You think it's a silly thing for me to wonder about," Catherine concluded.

Shortly thereafter the path rose gently in a long curve. When they reached the top, the woods ended, yielding to a stretch of fallow field, then long strips of grain, nearly ripe, interspersed with rows of grapes. These radiated out from a collection of houses built close to a high stone wall. Beyond the wall a village climbed the hill to a wooden palisade. And above that rose the castle of Boisvert.

Catherine had forgotten how massive it was. The fortress loomed above the village, blocking the afternoon sun. Its massive stones had been piled one upon another, not for beauty, but for protection.

Her ancestors had built the earliest keep in the days when the Northmen still ravaged the river valleys. Each generation had added to it until the castle spread across the top of the hill, three solid watchtowers joined by stone walls that enclosed an inner bailey. Below it was an outer bailey that was also ringed with stone. Outside that wall was a deep moat. The wooden wall that in Guillaume's keep was the only defense, had been erected here merely to keep livestock, children, and drunks from falling into the water.

Edgar gave a long whistle of astonishment.

"One could wait out Armageddon in a place like that."

Solomon rode up beside him. "Very impressive. I've no

doubt that when I return from Blois, you'll all have succumbed to the life of a noble and be dining on venison every night, quaffing huge vats of wine and wearing nothing but fur and silk."

Edgar laughed. "That's what they did at home in Scotland and I couldn't wait to leave. You'll be back by Michaelmas?"

"Before, if possible. We need to leave here soon after that if we want to be at Saint-Denis for the Lendit fair," Solomon answered. "And since what we sell there decides how well we survive the winter, I expect you to finish all this well before the end of September."

"Easily," Edgar promised him. "This summons was probably just an excuse for the old man to see how many of his descendants cared enough to come."

"Yes, I suppose," Solomon said with doubt. "That man in the tree didn't really say he was Gargenaud's *great*-grandson, did he?"

"It's possible; Catherine thinks her grandfather must be over eighty," Edgar replied.

Solomon shook himself. "This is all too strange for me, but be sure you make note of everything that happens. It will make a good story over the mulled ale this winter."

He bade them farewell and set off, seemingly unworried about traveling alone.

Aymon must have announced their arrival to everyone for, as the family drew closer to the castle, dozens of people came rushing out to greet them. Even before they were near enough to make out what was being shouted, they could tell the crowd was cheering. Several women were waving bright ribbons, tied to broomsticks or hoes.

"Saint Martha's miraculous stew!" Catherine exclaimed. "Why on earth are they so happy to see us? What do they think is going to happen?"

The gates opened wide for them and they entered the town.

As they started up the hill to the keep, the portcullis in the inner wall above them slowly lifted and a band of men emerged on horseback, fully armed. They crossed the drawbridge and stopped, motionless but for the flags carried by the squires that flapped back and forth in the wind.

The townspeople had cheered themselves hoarse and were now watching them hungrily as they passed through the village. All at once someone cried out.

"Look! Children! They have brought children!"

There was a collective intake of breath and then the cheering began again.

Catherine tightened her grip on Peter, slung sideways in front of her on the mule.

"What is this about?" she hissed at Edgar.

"How should I know," he answered. "It's your family. No, James! You may not get down. You're being punished, remember?"

As the villagers came closer, all reaching out to touch him, James decided that the back of his father's horse was a good place to be.

Hermann rode up along side them, easing his way through the people. He smiled in puzzlement.

"They are very friendly," he said. "I can't understand the words they say completely. They are happy to see children?"

"Apparently," Edgar said. "You understand as much as we do."

"Wait until Guillaume arrives with all his sons," Catherine added. "They'll be delirious with joy."

Hermann smiled again, not catching all of her comment. "Agnes fears they will tip the chair. She does not want the guards to hurt them, but too close the people come. Can you help?"

Edgar raised himself in the stirrups to shout at the crowd. As he did, Catherine saw the man at the head of the knights hold up his hand, palm out. The crowd quickly backed away in respectful silence.

"This is like a bishop's *adventus!*" she commented to Edgar. "All we need is trumpets."

"You had to say that." Edgar pointed at the squires, who now lifted their flagstaffs to their lips. The long horns gave one long blast that echoed across the plain below and set dogs to howling.

The knight who had given the command now rode toward them. The sunlight gleamed on his bald head. He had a closely trimmed white beard below a hawklike nose. Catherine opened her eyes wide in astonishment.

"Grandfather?" she said. She realized that she didn't remember what he looked like.

The man snorted. "Hardly, I'm Seguin, the son of Gargenaud's first son, Drogon. You must be my sister, Madeleine's, daughter. Is it Catherine or Agnes?"

"C . . . Catherine," she stammered. This old man was her first cousin? How many children did Gargenaud have? And when did he start having them?

"Agnes is in the sedan chair," she added.

"I bid you welcome in our grandfather's name," Seguin told them. "We are pleased that you understood the urgency of our need. We expect your brother in three days' time. He is the last."

"The last?" Catherine didn't like the sound of that.

"But you are weary from your journey." Seguin raised his arm and the other horsemen came forward to serve as escort as they entered the bailey.

"Welcome home to Boisvert!" Seguin roared loudly enough that those at the end of the procession heard him clearly. "Enter and welcome!"

As they passed through the gate, Catherine tried not to think of all the tales that began with the hero rashly entering a castle and finding himself in another world. And yet, coming through into the great outer bailey, she felt as if she had been transported into a bustling city totally apart from the village they had just passed through. There was activity all around her. Even in the heat, the ovens were blazing. A perspiring woman was removing fresh loaves and setting them on a long wooden table. In front of the stables, the farrier was examining the hooves of a brown palfrey. His assistant was having a hard time keeping the animal still.

And no wonder. Chickens fluttered everywhere, some chased by lean dogs, some by angry servants. Catherine could hear the calling of ducks and geese and the low snorts of pigs in their runs. Against the wall on one side ran a long row of wooden huts. Next to them stood barrels and baskets of food. The woodpile against a stone wall was higher than a man's head, even Edgar's.

"They seem to be well prepared for us," she said.

"It seems so," Edgar answered, looking around. "I don't think the king has this many servants."

"I wonder why the people of the village were so amazed that we brought the children," Catherine went on. "I was sure you told me that the message said they had to be here, too. Perhaps we didn't understand."

"If so, it will just be another thing to add to the list," Edgar grunted. "No, James, you can't help catch the chickens. You are going to meet your great-grandfather, so stop wiggling."

They halted by the stairs to the main keep. As soon as they dismounted, their horses were led away by stablehands. Other servants began unloading the boxes from the mules. Hermann helped Agnes, the nursemaid, and Edana out of the chair. Catherine expected her daughter to run to her at once, but the little girl stood quietly beside her aunt.

Catherine tried to ignore the pang.

Seguin dismounted, along with the other men. "Most of my knights are other cousins of yours to varying degrees." He waved in their direction. "You'll meet them properly this evening. My wife has prepared baths for all of you and assigned places to sleep and keep your goods. Follow me."

The stairs up to the inner bailey were wooden, warped with age except in a few places where boards had been replaced. Catherine ascended slowly, carrying Peter. The door at the top was designed not to greet guests but to give an armed man no room to enter. It was open. As Catherine approached, a woman came out and stood on the landing. Her *bliaut* was of crimson silk, heavily embroidered at the hem and neck with beads of glass. She wore a bright green head scarf, held in place by a delicate gold-link chain. Her face was slightly plump and little wrinkled. Only the lines around her eyes betrayed her age.

"I am Elissent," she said. "Seguin's wife. I bid you welcome in the name of Lord Gargenaud."

"Catherine, daughter of Madeleine." Catherine bowed. "This is my son, Peter, and my husband, Edgar of Wedderlie, in Scotland, with our eldest child, James. Our daughter is with my sister and her family."

She looked down. Agnes had stopped to give instructions to the porters about where the boxes should go. Edana clung to her hand and didn't even look up at them.

Elissent ushered them in. "My maids will take you to your room," she said. "Treat them as if they were your own."

Catherine stumbled on uneven stones as she entered the passageway. Despite lit torches, the narrow hall was dim. Another ploy to repel invaders. No wonder the castle had never been taken. There was no need for a protecting spirit with so much stone. The passage continued for several steps and then turned sharply to the right.

"*Os por le cuer be!*" Catherine exclaimed.

The dark tunnel ended abruptly at an enormous hall. Its high ceiling allowed the placement of several long, thin clerestory windows in the eastern and western walls that let light in from sunrise to dusk. Between them hung thick tapestries woven with images of animals and birds. They covered nearly all the stone. On either side of the room were staircases leading to wooden walkways, ending in doors that led to other parts of the castle. There was even a space above for musicians to play.

Long tables had already been set up and covered with light green linen cloths. A high armchair stood at the center behind the main table, its back to a cavernous fireplace built into the far wall. Empty in the summer heat, the hearth seemed to Catherine to be a dark open mouth inhaling the very air from the room. She tried to shake the thought from her mind, but she couldn't free herself from the sense that this ancient building was somehow alive and unwelcoming.

She stood uncertainly in the doorway until Edgar poked her in the back, moving her into the room. At once, a woman hurried up to them, her arms laden with soft cloths for washing.

"Welcome, my lord, my lady," she said. "My mistress was sure you would wish to wash off the dust of the road. Please follow me."

She led them toward a low door on the other side of the hall. As they followed her they heard the crackle of someone trying to run through the rushes on the floor.

"Edgar! Catherine!"

They spun around, not believing that it was a voice they knew.

A young girl ran toward them, her face alight with joy and her thick red braid swinging loosely.

"Margaret! How did you get here?" Catherine cried in delight. She held up the baby. "Peter, look! It's your aunt Margaret. It's a miracle!"

Edgar dropped James's hand and caught his little sister in a bear hug. She clung to him, shaking.

She seemed frail in his arms, this child of his father's second wife, the only mother Edgar had ever known. When Adalisa had died, Catherine and Edgar had taken Margaret into their home. But for two years past, she had been studying at the convent of the Paraclete, as Catherine had done.

"I'm so glad you're here," Margaret gulped, trying not to cry. "I was afraid you might not come."

"We had to," Edgar said. "But why are you here? You have no tie to these people. Why aren't you still at the Paraclete?"

She let him go and wiped her face with her sleeve before kissing Catherine and the baby.

"The abbess of Tart wrote to Mother Heloise and asked if I could be spared," Margaret explained. "She didn't want to send any of the professed nuns and she knew Catherine was my brother's wife. I think my grandfather may have been consulted, as well. So, I was put in charge of seeing that she arrived here safely."

It was a moment before Catherine understood the task Edgar's sister had been set. Her stomach contracted with dread and guilt.

"Oh, Margaret!" she cried. "You brought my mother here? How could they put the burden on you? I'm so sorry! Why couldn't they have let her stay where she was happy?"

Margaret smiled. "I was glad to come. I missed you all so much." Her eyes looked back to the entrance and the smile dimmed when she saw no one there.

"And really," she continued. "Apart from the fact that she never remembers who I am, I find your mother charming."

Catherine's stomach sank. She had known it was a possibility, but had tried to ignore it. She felt again the sharp fear that she deserved Agnes's reproaches. Madeleine had always been devout. Catherine's decision to enter the convent of the Paraclete had given her mother great joy. How could Catherine have known that her mother believed her to be Madeleine's expiation for the sin of marrying a converted Jew? When Catherine decided against the religious life, her mother felt betrayed. Eventually, this had led to her retreating into a pious madness.

Therefore, the news that her mother was only a few doorways

from her sent Catherine into a rare panic. At the moment, saving a legendary ancestress from a curse was so much more tolerable than coming face-to-face with the poor deluded woman who had borne her.

Her mind was still in turmoil as she busied herself organizing their assigned quarters.

"I'm so relieved that you finally got here." Margaret sat in the deep sill of the window in the room they had been given. "We've been here almost a week and I was becoming worried that I'd have to stay among strangers. Not that everyone hasn't been very nice to me," she added quickly.

"I'm just so sorry that you were made to be the guardian for my mother," Catherine said. "Where is she now?"

"Probably in the chapel with the priest. I think he's some sort of cousin of yours." Margaret fiddled with her long auburn braid. She had plaited it loosely over her cheek to hide the thin white scar that was all the visible evidence of an attack she had barely survived a few years before. The mark was not disfiguring, but she felt the curiosity and pity every time she had to meet someone new.

"The chapel. Of course. Where else would she be?" Catherine said as she laid out the clothes they would wear at the banquet that evening. "Even before her mind became fragile, she spent most of her days in prayer."

"As do all devout Christians." Margaret grinned at her.

Catherine laughed. "Yes, but they don't pray to a daughter whom they think has ascended bodily into heaven."

"Not usually," Margaret admitted. "But the nuns told me that she no longer believes you to be a saint. I think she's simply retreated farther back in time. She talks to me about the family as if you and your brothers and sister were still children."

"What do you think seeing us will do to her?" Catherine

dreaded the meeting. And yet, in her heart she longed to see her mother again.

Margaret shrugged. "I'm not a physician. Perhaps it will recall her to her senses."

Catherine was now shaking out a linen *chainse*. At Margaret's words, she gave it a hard snap that sent a cloud of dust and flower petals up from the floor, causing them both to cough violently.

With unsteady hands, Catherine set the *chainse* on the bed. She was appalled at her reaction. Of course she wanted her mother's mind restored. Or did she? How much of the events of the past few years would have to be explained? How much *could* she explain? Madeleine would be returning to a world that no longer held a place for her. Her husband was gone, her children married. Catherine was now mistress in her mother's home.

"Perhaps even then she would prefer to stay in the convent," Catherine concluded, pushing the fear away. "Will she be at dinner tonight?"

Margaret swung her legs off the windowsill and stretched, yawning.

"I don't know," she said. "Up until now, we've just had simple meals in the solar with the other women."

That reminded Catherine of another question. "Margaret, just how many of the family have come? Seguin said that Guillaume is the last. By my reckoning, this place should be stuffed with cousins."

Margaret took a pair of Edgar's stockings and unrolled them, looking for holes. She thought a moment.

"I haven't really asked, since I'm not one of you," she said. "It didn't seem polite. But I don't think there are more than two or three families. Elissent and Seguin are to all intents the lord and lady here. Aymon is their younger son. The older is called Raimbaut. I've only seen him once or twice. He's always out. Neither he nor his brother is married yet, which seems strange to me. There is the priest who seems to be related to you and a few others, mostly men."

"But I thought that all the people who are descended from this sorceress of the water were supposed to be here," Catherine protested. "There can't be only a handful of us!"

"Why not?" Margaret asked. "Think of how many people die without heirs. Perhaps some families became members of religious communities. That happens often enough. And then there are wars. What's really amazing is that Boisvert has passed from father to son for so many generations."

Catherine was unconvinced. "It still seems much too few. And what about bastards? You can't tell me all the men who ruled here were saints."

"Perhaps they only count legitimate children," Margaret said. "After all, my mother wasn't included in my grandfather's plans for inheritance."

"It's just all very peculiar," Catherine concluded lamely.

"I suppose." Margaret was being unusually thorough in her examination of the stockings. "Of course, Solomon is almost the last of his family, isn't he? I see he didn't come with you. Is he all right?"

"He's fine," Catherine said, avoiding the girl's eager face. "The same as ever. This didn't seem to be the best place to bring him, don't you agree?"

Margaret tried to hide her disappointment. "Of course. Your grandfather probably doesn't do much business with Jews. Solomon might feel uncomfortable."

"That's what we thought," Catherine said. "And, of course, he's not affected by this prophecy or curse or whatever, if it does exist. Nor should you be."

She stopped and looked at Margaret. She was nearly seventeen, much more beautiful than she knew, with her dark eyes and rich auburn hair. The scar she was so aware of was little more than a thread across her cheek. Even without the dowry promised by her grandfather, the count of Champagne, Margaret was a rich marriage prize. If only she could let go of her childhood attachment to Solomon! She wondered if those feelings would change if Margaret knew that one of Solomon's many conquests had presented him with a daughter.

Catherine turned away. She couldn't hurt Margaret more. The mute pain already in her eyes was more than Catherine could stand. Margaret knew well that she had only two choices in life, to marry a man the count approved of or stay at the Paraclete and take her final vows. The highest-born of the land were less free than the serfs in this. Catherine felt a pang of guilt that she had been allowed, with only a bit of opposition, to marry for love. She put her arms around her sister-in-law.

"I'm sorry you've been put to so much trouble," she said. "But it is wonderful to have you with us again. We've missed you so much!"

"Thank you." Margaret's voice was muffled in Catherine's robe. When she stepped back, her expression was once again cheerful. She put the stockings on the bed.

"We'll look like the poor cousins we are, I'm afraid," she commented, looking at the clothing. "All the women here seem to have an endless supply of silk and fur-trimmed gowns."

"In this weather? Then at least we'll be more comfortable," Catherine said. "Are they really that elegant? I wonder if Agnes brought Mother's jewel case. Maybe for the honor of the family she'd let me borrow a few pieces."

Edgar had left Peter for Samonie to watch while he and James explored the castle. He had intended to leave Edana, too, but she screamed so at being left with the baby that he had given in.

"Martin," he ordered the apprentice. "If you can keep a purse of garnets and tourmaline safe across Lombardy, Burgundy, and France, do you suppose you can see that a five-year-old girl doesn't go astray here?"

"Master, I know this ploy." Martin grinned. "I complete one task only to be set a much harder one. Very well." He went down on one knee. "My lady, I'm to be your knight and your steed. Do not abandon me, I beg you!"

Edana giggled and climbed onto his back. Edgar knew he wouldn't let her come to harm. Poor Martin had been pulling Edana out of trees and down from high shelves ever since she had started walking. The child was part monkey.

When they came down the steps to the bailey, the bustle suddenly receded and then stopped. Everyone was looking up at them.

Edgar smiled and waved politely as they descended. As they reached the bottom, a small crowd was waiting for them. No one said anything; they just stared hungrily at James and Edana. Edgar put his arm protectively across James's chest. For once, the boy showed no inclination to run away. There was a look on the faces staring up at him that daunted even James's unruly spirit. Edgar looked around for someone of authority. He saw no one.

"I thought we'd take the children to see the horses," he told the group at last. "If you'll let us through?"

He felt like Moses as the crowd parted before him.

"Master?" Martin whispered.

"Just keep walking," Edgar told him, not sure if the sea would remain at bay.

He could hear the murmurs as they passed but the words were unclear. They didn't sound threatening, more full of awe. This made Edgar even more wary. After they passed through, the crowd again closed behind them.

They reached the stables by following the sound of a hammer hitting an anvil. Their entourage stayed at their heels until they reached the huge forge, before which a brawny man was tempering a knife. Edgar turned to face the crowd.

"We thank you," he said, though for what, he had no idea. "I'm sure you want to return to your duties now."

"Gwan!" The blacksmith waved the heavy hammer at them.

"Them pigs is rooting under the fence again."

As last the crowd dispersed. Edgar thanked the smith.

"Why is everyone here so interested in my children," he asked. "Weren't we supposed to bring them?"

The man dipped the red hot knife into a pail of water and watched it sizzle.

"That you were," he said. "And we all savor the sight of 'em."

Edgar was not so blind a parent as to think his progeny were unnaturally remarkable. There had to be another reason.

"So where are all the other children?" he asked.

"Ain't none." The smith picked up his tongs and returned to the hearth.

"None? But I saw several running about when we arrived," Edgar said.

"Those are up from the village," the smith said. "There's none at the keep."

"What do you mean?" Edgar asked. "There must be."

"None I've seen." The man turned his back to them and refused to answer any more questions.

Edgar looked down at James who was hopping from one foot to the other in his impatience to see the knights' horses.

"Stay close to me, son," he commanded.

As they moved away, Martin voiced the thought Edgar was trying not to think.

"Are these people some sort of pagans?" he asked. "Who sacrifice babies to their idols?"

"Of course not," Edgar said. But, if not, he thought, what are they?

In the solar, Samonie was astonished at the number of women offering to help her wash, dress, and feed Peter. The word "hungry" kept occurring to her, too. One woman, very elegantly dressed, was more insistent than the others.

"My lady," Samonie told her politely. "You don't want to soil your fine clothes. We're trying to teach him but he's still not at all careful about where and when he squirts."

"Sounds like my husband," one of the other women commented.

The rest giggled. But the woman just rolled the sleeves of her *bliaut* up to her shoulders and pinned them there.

"Please," she said. "I have wanted a child for so long. Let me help."

Samonie sighed. There was nothing she could do. This was obviously a person of importance. She handed the woman the sponge.

"You have to wash him quickly," she warned. "He won't stay put for long."

She regarded the rest of the women.

"Do none of you have children of your own?" she asked.

They shook their heads.

"There are men here, aren't there?"

"Oh, yes, dozens of them," one woman said.

Samonie scratched her head. "Have they taken some sort of vow of celibacy?"

A roar of laughter answered that.

"It's the curse," the woman washing James whispered to her. "Once the well started failing, Andonenn couldn't protect us anymore. There hasn't been a baby born here in more than twenty years. Empress Judith's curse has doomed us all."

"Unless we can fulfill the prophecy and thwart the curse," another added. "And now that your mistress and her family are here, there's hope at last."

They all chorused agreement. Samonie took back the sponge and wrapped Peter in a drying cloth.

She had to find Catherine. A curse this powerful was more than she had counted on.

∞

Margaret showed Catherine the back steps down to the Great Hall.

"I feel so timid having to come down the main staircase with everyone watching me," she explained. "I knew there must be one that the servants used. I got lost a dozen times before I learned the way. It's amazing how huge this place is. It makes my father's keep seem like a hermit's hut."

"It probably started out as just a fortress tower," Catherine said. "As the years went by it must have been added to over and over."

"And in no particular pattern, either," Margaret said. "I think I'm going into an alcove and it turns out to be a whole other set of rooms. I was thinking of unrolling a ball of yarn as I go, to find my way back."

"I thought the story Guillaume told was preposterous," Catherine said. "Magic springs and hidden treasure. But this place does make me feel as if we had stepped into some ancient tale."

"I know." Margaret grinned. "They say there's a labyrinth underneath all this that comes out in the kingdom of the fairies."

"Has anyone been there recently?" Catherine teased.

Margaret laughed. "Not to admit it. Oh, Catherine! It is so good to be with you again."

As they descended the stairs, they were met by servants coming up, their arms full of boxes and bedding. They apologized to Catherine and Margaret as they passed, but their demeanor showed annoyance at finding two noblewomen in the working part of the keep.

"Agnes must plan to stay the winter," Catherine said, as a familiar coverlet passed them.

They came into the hall to find it being set up for the banquet that evening. In one corner some minstrels were trying to practice. The leader beat the meter on a small tambour, stopping every few moments to correct one of the players. Some of the men-at-arms had gathered at a table near the wall to play *trictrac* and throw lots. Their shouts almost drowned out the drone of the vielle. Around them all, people came and went, laying the places and setting up tables for water and towels.

In an alcove, Agnes was sitting with Elissent. When she saw Catherine and Margaret, she waved them over.

"Where have you been?" she asked. "Lady Elissent has been giving me some lovely cool cider and cakes. Thanks to her, I believe I have sorted out all the relations. It's sad how little we know of our cousins, especially when there are so few of us left."

"Really," Catherine said. "Agnes, you remember Margaret, don't you? Did Lady Elissent mention that she has come all the way here just to see that our mother arrived safely?"

"Why, thank . . ." Agnes stopped, a cake halfway to her mouth. "Mother? She's here? Why did no one tell me? I must go to her at once."

She started to rise, but Elissent put a hand on her knee.

"We understand her condition." She included Catherine in her explanation. "Your cousin, Father Ysore, has offered to attend to her spiritual needs and one of my women is seeing to her physical wants. She is greatly changed from when I last saw her, especially in mind. Perhaps you should prepare yourself before you go to her."

Agnes was confused.

"Mother thinks you're still six years old," Catherine explained. "And we're all living happily together in Paris."

Agnes set her jaw. "How happy she must be then! I would never rip that comfort from her. Nevertheless, I have a duty to my mother."

She stood to go, ignoring Catherine. At that moment Edgar, Martin, and Samonie arrived together, each clutching a child.

"Mistress, I must speak to you," Samonie began.

"Catherine, Margaret, come with me at once," Edgar said. "With your leave, my lady," he added to Elissent.

Catherine was fairly dragged across the hall.

"We're leaving," Edgar announced as they reached the main staircase. "There's something wrong here."

"A curse," Samonie inserted. "That's why there are no other children. All of these people are barren."

She hadn't meant the words to be overheard, but a sudden silence made them echo through the hall. They reached the old man who was just coming down the main staircase on the arm of a young woman. Everyone around them bowed.

"Nonsense!" the man roared. "The curse shall be broken. We will once again have children, a myriad of them, as soon as we restore Andonenn to her spring."

Catherine raised her face and beheld Gargenaud, lord of Boisvert. She knew him at once and wondered how she could have mistaken anyone else for this lion of a man. All the same, she gasped in astonishment.

After twenty years, her grandfather had not changed at all.

Eight

The town of Blois, Thursday, kalends September (September 1) 1149. Feast of Saint Anne, prophetess of Jerusalem. 19 Elul 4909.

Juxta quem vicam quaedam antiquissimae fossae visuntur . . . ex his fosse tempore messis, et occupatis circa frugum collectionem per agros messoribus, emerserunt due pueri, masculus et femina, toto corpore virides et coloris insoliti ex incognita materia veste operti.

Nearby this village one can see some ancient ditches . . . At the time of the harvest when all were working in the fields, there came from this ditch, two children a boy and a girl, with totally green bodies and in clothes of a strange shade and made of an unknown material.

—William of Newburgh
The History of English Affairs

$\mathcal{S}$olomon found his friend Menachem hiding from the heat in his storage cellar. The beaten earth walls were lined with casks that oozed a mixed aroma of wine and tar. Menachem was drilling a small spigot into one when Solomon arrived.

"Shall I help you test it?" Solomon asked hopefully. "You don't want to risk giving the monks of Saint Martin sour wine for their table."

Menachem grinned. "You have a talent for appearing just when there's drink flowing. Put a cup under this and tell me what you think, then."

Solomon caught the deep purple wine as Menachem turned the spigot. He took a long drink.

"Fantastic!" he said. "Too good for Edomites."

"Wait until you taste what I put by for us!" Menachem promised. "I'm glad you didn't delay in getting back. We need to go to Tours and return before the New Year."

"That's a bit over a week." Solomon put his cup out again. "It shouldn't take more than a day to take the wine downriver and another to get back. We could even walk it in time, if we needed to."

"I don't like doing things at the last minute," Menachem said. "And you forget a day to squeeze payment out of the cellarer at the monastery."

"Very well, do we leave Sunday?" Solomon asked, finishing the second cup.

"The next day, I think," Menachem said. "I decided to bring a couple of guards and they won't be ready until Monday."

"Guards? For a barge journey to Tours?" Solomon was suspicious. "I thought that route was well protected?"

"It is. It is!" Menachem answered. "I just don't like the rumors going around about Olivier de Boue gathering an army to attack Boisvert. His path would take him along the Loire at just the stretch we'll be traveling."

"Even this Olivier wouldn't be so stupid as to take wine meant for the monks," Solomon said. "And I thought you told me this threat of war was not substantial enough to worry about."

His friend seemed uncomfortable. "I don't think it is," he said. "But I'd rather have a few extra swords all the same. Now, we might have time for a game of darts before dinner. What do you say?"

Solomon agreed. Perhaps after a few bowls of wine Menachem would tell him just what had set him so on edge. Menachem recorked the cask and the two men headed up into the street.

Solomon looked around. The town was small, most of the buildings the homes of tradesmen or prosperous peasants. The houses of the Jewish families were interspersed among them. The inhabitants were all under the protection of Thibault, count of Champagne, and his son, Henry, count of Blois. Although Thibault was in Troyes and Henry on his way home from the Holy Land, their power was usually enough to discourage raids. That reputation and the fortress their ancestors had built on a spur of the river. Solomon had always liked Blois. There were enough Jews so that he could always count on a welcome from someone he enjoyed spending time with. The food was good and the wine superb. And it had been some time since anyone had tried to introduce him to a cousin of marriageable age.

He had intended to pass a tranquil few weeks here. Now his peace was broken by the worry that he had left Catherine and Edgar in a place of danger.

"So, what have you heard about this army of Olivier's?" he asked Menachem.

"Only that he's not only called in all the men who owe him service, but that he's also hiring soldiers," Menachem said. "A few locals have joined his army, but not many. We all grew up hearing tales about how the lords of Boisvert were wizards, descended from a powerful fairy."

"A good reason not to attack them," Solomon agreed.

"True, but Olivier is a vassal of Count Geoffrey of Anjou," Menachem explained. "And everyone knows that his family goes back to the Devil, himself."

"So I've heard." Solomon thought a while. "Do you think that Olivier can take the castle at Boisvert?"

Menachem shrugged. "Not without the Devil's aid, I'd say. The place looks as though it grew out of the rocks the day after the Flood. Even if only women and old men were left, it could still be defended."

Solomon relaxed. This was likely another one of the interminable feints the nobles made in their attempts to increase their holdings. He'd seen it before. Someone would sally out, burn a few fields, steal some pigs, and perhaps sit for a day or so in front of someone else's drawbridge. Eventually, the local abbot or bishop would be called in to negotiate peace. Annoying and disruptive, but that's how Solomon felt about most of the knightly class he had met. Even Edgar had moments of haughtiness that, while useful in trade, still irritated.

He let the worry slip away.

As they passed the town square, Solomon noticed an old woman crawling through the grass.

"Who's that?" he asked. "Does she need help?"

Menachem barely glanced at her. "Oh, that's only Berthe. She's probably looking for mushrooms or plants for her potions."

Solomon looked closer. The woman didn't seem as old as he had first thought.

"Is she a healer or a witch?"

Menachem laughed. "Who knows what she prays to, over her salves? But they work, I can vouch for it. When you're doubled over with a back that feels like it's being hit with hot irons, you don't question a remedy that lets you stand again."

"That's so." Solomon continued watching her until they entered the narrow street where Menachem and his family lived. There was something about the way she was moving across the green that seemed odd to him. It wasn't as if she was searching for mushrooms under leaves, but more as if she was carrying something on her back. He fancied that he could almost see the depression along the sides of her robes where a rider's legs would be.

Once he had lost sight of her, he shook himself. All these

tales of otherworldly beings, prophecies, and curses were addling his brain. What he had seen was the result of two cups of wine on an empty stomach.

"Is that a roast chicken I smell?" he asked Menachem as they neared the house.

"It should be two," Menachem said. "I left Hana plucking and singeing them this morning. And there's a sauce of black currants in wine to go with them."

The heavenly aroma drove out any curiosity Solomon might have had about the woman crawling across the green.

Berthe reached the public path. She stood easily, dusting bits of dry grass from the front of her *bliaut*.

"Well, that was strange," she muttered to herself. "But the instructions were very clear. I only wish it didn't take so long to find out if this works."

She made her way to her own house, not far from the river. Now and then she bent to pick up a pebble from the road. Most of them she let fall again after a quick look, but a few seemed to suit her and these were tucked into a rabbit skin bag hanging from her neck.

Berthe envied Lord Olivier. It was so much easier to attack a fortress with horses, men, and swords. Her way was tedious and exacting and required far too many nights without sleep.

But, if it worked, it would bring down Gargenaud in a way that no army ever could.

Catherine stared up at her grandfather. It had been so long since she had seen him that she had forgotten his face until this moment. Her memories were mostly of his booming voice, hurling orders at everyone in the household.

He was old. At least that wasn't in question. His eyes were filmy and his long hair and beard pure white. But his carriage was straight. He might have been helping the woman next to him, rather than using her arm for support. She appeared to be not more than twenty. For a moment Catherine wondered what it would be like to share her bed with someone four times her age.

His eyes must have been sharper than they appeared. Half-way down, he spotted Catherine gaping up at him. She blushed, fearing he could read her thoughts.

"Which one is this, Seguin?" he shouted at his grandson. "Or is she just some serving girl?"

Catherine stepped forward. "I'm Catherine, Madeleine's daughter. I'm pleased to see you again, Grandfather."

She bowed deeply, bending her knees until she nearly fell.

The couple reached the bottom. Gargenaud reached out and grasped Catherine's chin, tilting her face up. His fingers were hard as oak and strong.

He examined her features closely and finally released her.

"Yes," he said. "You're one of hers. I saw her this morning. Told me you were all babies. Thinks she's here for a wedding or some such. I never should have made her marry that man. Is he still alive?"

"I d . . . don't know," Catherine stuttered. "He left on pilgrimage some time ago."

Gargenaud snorted. "There's a coward for you. Hope he left his wealth behind."

Shocked, Catherine only stared at him. Her grandfather snorted again and moved on.

The question about her father had been unexpected. Hubert was now in the Occitan somewhere. To Catherine's pain and grief, he had recently left everyone he cared about to return to the faith of his ancestors. She didn't want to imagine what Gargenaud would say if he knew his son-in-law was again a Jew.

Edgar came to the spot where Catherine still stood, transfixed. He was trying not to laugh, but deep chuckles kept escaping.

"Sweet Virgin! I wish Solomon were here," he said. "He won't believe anyone could talk to you like that and not be shriveled by your tongue before he went two paces. So that's your grandfather?"

Catherine nodded dumbly.

"I begin to understand how this legend remains green." Edgar took her by the shoulder and guided her toward the table. "If the man can make my wife speechless, he must be more than mortal."

The rest of the company was far from silent. There were fifteen or so men, all of fighting age. A lanky priest was speaking with one of them. Catherine noted that the man was wearing more rings and pins than Father Anselm would have thought proper. He must also be from one of the landed families, for he seemed completely at ease among the knights.

The only women were Seguin's wife, Elissent, Agnes, her grandfather's companion, and Catherine, herself. There were no children to be seen, not even pages. Where was the rest of the family?

Agnes was an island of calm as she presented herself to Gargenaud and then introduced Hermann. Both of them seemed to meet with his approval.

This was confirmed as Agnes was seated next to Seguin, Hermann next to Elissent, with Margaret next to him. Catherine and Edgar were at the far end of the high table, well below the salt.

"I see that someone told Seguin that Margaret is his liege lord's granddaughter," Edgar said. He smiled at his sister, who gave him a pathetic wave from her place at the center of the table.

"Poor thing!" Catherine said. "I don't suppose we could rescue her?"

"Her only resort is to have a sudden faintness," Edgar said sadly.

"In this weather, it may not take long."

Servants came through first with bowls, ewers, and towels so that everyone could wash their hands before the first course was brought in. Then the food began to arrive.

"Saint Simon's spicy maggots!" Edgar exclaimed. "This is more than we eat in a year!"

They began with fresh greens in a walnut sauce and progressed to eels in jelly covered with a salt-and-fennel crust. This was followed by capons roasted on long skewers and served stuffed with eggs and spices along with a pheasant stewed with onions and then replumed. By the time the joints of ham were served, Catherine was near to fainting herself.

"More wine, my lady?" The server was at her elbow, ready to pour.

"Thank you, no," she gasped. "Edgar, I need to get out of here for a while. I think I'm going to throw up."

"You won't be the last tonight," he said.

He slid off his end of the bench to let her out. Catherine staggered in the direction of the privy, she hoped.

She went through the nearest doorway and soon found herself in a maze of narrow passages, some leading to storerooms, some to other hallways that twisted on each other and doubled back. Sometimes she could hear the voices from the hall. Then she would turn again and find only silence.

Her need for the privy outweighed all else. She didn't even wonder how she would find her way back. She would have been happy with an empty bucket or a discrete corner. Every way she turned was taking her farther into the depths of the castle. The wooden floor became flagstones and then uncut rock. Lanterns suspended from the walls gave way to torches.

"At last!" The sound of running water from behind a curtain told her she had reached her goal.

The cubicle was completely dark, so she left the curtain partially open. It didn't matter. Since she had left the feast, she hadn't seen a soul.

"I must be right over the moat," she guessed. "How far did I come?"

Once her most pressing need had been taken care of, Catherine realized that she was totally lost. From her childhood visit, she remembered being sternly warned never to wander alone through the castle. Children had vanished and nothing was ever found of them but little gnawed bones.

Catherine's nurse had known how to keep her in line.

There were no small skeletons in the dank corners, but the shadows seemed thicker now. Catherine tried to remember which way she had come. The best chance was to take any passage that angled upward. She kept hoping to run across one of the servants, sent down for more provisions. She wondered if Edgar was missing her, yet.

The summer heat hadn't penetrated this deep into the hill. The floor was damp and mossy and the wooden walls warped with age.

"How can there not be enough water when it's so wet down here?" she spoke her thoughts aloud.

"It will soon be as sere as autumn leaves," a hollow voice answered her from very close by. "You must not fail."

Catherine shrieked in terror and spun around.

There was nothing there but the shadow of a figure going down a passage to her left.

"Wait!" Catherine called after it. "I'm lost. Help me!"

It occurred to her that whoever it was didn't want to help her, but Catherine followed anyway. It seemed the only chance she had of reaching the hall. She hurried after the speaker.

There was no one in the passage when she reached it, but the torches were flickering as if someone had passed. Catherine made herself move more quickly. Her heart was pounding and she cursed the long skirts and sleeves that dragged on the floor and slowed her progress.

At the next junction, she spotted fresh muddy footprints on the stone. Ahead, she thought she heard someone moving.

"Please! Wait for me!" she called shakily. "I won't hurt you."

That was a stupid thing to say, she told herself.

Or was it? There had been fear in the voice, not menace.

The person was leading her upward. The floor became plank again and above her, Catherine could hear thumps that signaled entertainment had begun.

Where was everyone?

The next turn brought her to a spiral staircase. She lifted her skirts and climbed. A moment later she found herself at a doorway to the hall, on the opposite side from the one she had taken before. She could have sobbed with relief.

She paused a moment to adjust her clothing. As she did, there was a rustle from the next level of the steps. Catherine looked up and had a brief impression of a figure in the lantern light. A woman, very pale, in a shimmering robe that was years out of date. A woman Catherine had seen before, at Vielle-teneuse and in the forest. She looked back at Catherine.

"Don't forget her," she begged. "Your mother needs you."

Catherine leapt up the stairs. On the third one, her thin shoes skidded and she tumbled back onto the landing. Her head hit the edge of a chest, stunning her a moment.

"My lady!"

Catherine blinked. The priest was bending over her. "Are you hurt?"

"No, I don't think so." She felt her clothing for tears. "Did you see her?"

She knew before he answered that he hadn't.

Why was she the only one the woman from the woods ever spoke to?

Catherine sighed. "Would you mind escorting me back to my seat?" she asked. "I seem to have missed the jugglers."

Samonie waited until the children were tucked in and Agnes's nurse there to watch them. Then she set out to find someone who could tell her what was going on. There must be a servant here who knew the truth of the matter.

She started on the level where the guests were housed. It was
a sensitive task to casually wander through the rooms without appearing to be a thief. She had just decided that there was no one
working there, when a man came out of one of the cubicles.

"What do you think you're doing here?" he asked.

Samonie turned to run, but the man caught her, spinning her
around to face him. He squinted at her face in the dim light.

"Who are you?" he asked. He brought her face closer. "Wait, I
know you, don't I?"

Samonie gasped. He had known her well enough once. Six-
teen years before she had shared his bed for a season at the court
of Count Thibault. She hadn't given him her heart, but he had
been pleasant enough and treated her with kindness.

"I'm a servant to Lady Catherine, Lord Gargenaud's granddaughter from Paris," she told him.

He shook his head, trying to place her. She saw how the gold
hair was thinning and strung with silver.

"You're Samonie," he said at last and smiled. "Now I remember. I came back to the Christmas court at Troyes just to see you
but they said you'd gone."

"Yes, my lord Brehier." She bent her head humbly. No point
in telling him she had gone back to her mother's to have the baby.

"You look well," he said. "You live in Paris now? Is your mistress good to you?"

Samonie was taken aback. He seemed genuinely concerned
for her.

"I'm quite happy there," she answered. "And you?" she dared
to asked.

He shrugged. "Well enough. I've been here several years now.
Gargenaud is a hard man, but generous. He is a distant relation of
my mother."

Not enough, Samonie thought. It was clear that Brehier had
come down in the world. From a knight of Count Thibault to a
hired man-at-arms for one of his vassals was a long fall.

"That's good," she said. "Now I must find my mistress."

As she hurried back to the nursery, Samonie cursed herself. She should never have admitted who she was. It made no difference to him. She was only a casual affair from his youth. He was little more than that to her. And yet . . . no, she stopped that line of thought. Her duty now was to the present, to those she had sworn to care for.

There was no point at all in telling her son, Martin, that she had just seen his father.

Catherine waited until they were back in their quarters to tell Edgar of her adventure that evening.

"If you say I must have imagined all this," she said wearily, "I swear I'll send you up to sleep with the children."

"I'm sure you got lost," Edgar yawned. "I wouldn't be a bit surprised if some woman saw you wandering about and decided to have some fun taunting you. Everyone in this place is strange. Did you notice that no one bothered to introduce us to your grandfather's wife? I don't even know her name. Do I think your woman was a ghost or a river nymph? Perhaps. But I'm greasy and tired and I've had way too much to drink. Also, that music set my teeth on edge, with the horns and bells and badly tuned vielete. Can we sleep on it? Tomorrow I'll corner your cousin Seguin and make him tell me what's going on here."

"Yes, I suppose tomorrow will be time enough." Catherine sighed. "I'm sure Seguin will have a simple explanation for everything. But, just for tonight, carissime, would you mind if I slept between you and the wall?"

The next day started normally enough. The first thing Catherine heard was a male voice cursing loudly at an overenthusiastic rooster. There were groans from the passageway as people faced the morning with wine-induced headaches and overstuffed bellies.

Even the fresh herbs strewn among the straw on the floor couldn't disguise the reek of vomit.

Idly, Catherine wondered why no one in the *jongleurs'* tales ever had a hangover. All those heroes spent their nights at enormous feasts and the next morning woke up fresh to go jousting or dragon slaying. Of course, perhaps Roland had refused to blow his horn at the battle of Roncevaux not because he was too proud to summon help, but because the noise would have hurt his head more than a Saracen's blade.

She thought about sharing this interpretation with Edgar, but decided not to bother. Following her literary speculations, it occurred to her that none of the ladies of the *chansons de geste* had to step over the remains of someone's meal to get to the privy.

Catherine knew this was the fate that awaited her and it couldn't be put off much longer. She was reluctant to leave the bed. It was so comforting to lie with Edgar's back blocking the sight of the unfamiliar room. She didn't want to disturb the rhythm of his gentle whistle snore by climbing over him. Especially since he often misinterpreted the movement as the prelude to something she wasn't ready to get involved in.

There was nothing for it. Catherine felt around for her *bliaut* and pulled it over her head. As expected, the moment she started to slide across his body, Edgar reached for her.

"In a moment," she promised. "I'll be right back."

He grunted sleepily and let her go.

An instant later, she was back. He felt the pressure on the side of the bed and opened his eyes hopefully. Catherine was leaning over him. Her expression didn't hold the promise of any sex in the near future.

"Edgar, get up!" She tugged at the sheet. "Samonie found me in the passage. She's been up all night watching over the children. Someone tried to take Agnes's baby from his cradle. The nurse didn't wake, but Samonie was sitting by the bed and scared the intruder away. She thinks they would have taken Peter, too."

"What!" Edgar was up at once, throwing his tunic over his head and reaching for his belt.

They found a haggard Samonie still sitting between the children and the door. On the bed, James, Edana, and Peter were bright-eyed and bouncing to be let out.

Edgar laid his hand on Samonie's shoulder. He tried to find the words to thank her for her vigilance. She looked up at him and smiled.

"I didn't see who it was," she told him. "Someone in a woman's robes, but it was too dark to see the face. I called out and they ran away. I'd have followed, but I stopped to be sure little Gottfried was safe and Peter still in his cot."

"Thank you, Samonie. Now get some sleep," Edgar told her brusquely. "We'll take the day watch."

He and Catherine loaded themselves with their progeny and set out to find Seguin.

They ran him down in one of the storehouses, inspecting a delivery of cheese. He gave them a polite smile that changed to a frown as he saw their disheveled state.

"There was no need to bestir yourselves so early," he said. "Most of the household won't waken before None."

Edgar wasted no time with pleasantries.

"We came to Boisvert to help you," he said. "At great inconvenience. Now you repay us by trying to steal our children! Everyone in this place seems to be either bewitched or mad, and I'm taking my family out of it now!"

Seguin looked from him to Catherine to their rather grubby offspring in total bewilderment.

"Your children? Why should I steal them? What are you talking about?"

Edgar wasn't to be put off.

"When was the last child born here in Boisvert?"

Seguin grew still.

"Aymon was the last." He spoke quietly. "He's twenty now. It was some time before we realized anything was wrong. First Elissent and I thought it was something we had done. Then we realized that no woman living at Boisvert was conceiving. Finally we began to suspect that Andonenn's protection was failing.

"We were afraid the curse might reach to all her children. It gave us great joy to know that Madeleine's family has been spared. When I saw you, I felt the first hope I've had in months. That's all. I assure you that your children are precious to us. No one would harm them."

"Someone would." Edgar stepped closer to him, forcing the man to meet his eyes. "Our maid says there was an intruder in the nursery last night. She also said that yesterday one of the women made a fuss over Peter, refusing to give him back after his bath."

"Ah." Seguin thumped the cheese in embarrassment. "That would be Briand, Grandfather's new wife. She's become extremely melancholic lately. She longs for a child of her own."

"I see," Edgar said. "And, of course, the 'curse' prevents this, not her aged husband. So, why would that make her steal one of ours? What did she intend to do with him?"

Seguin's discomfort turned to anger.

"Nothing!" he shouted. "Do you think we're pagans who sacrifice infants to appease the gods?"

"Are you?" Edgar stared him down.

"Saint Andrew's flapping fish, man! Of course not!" Seguin stepped up onto the cheese cart to raise himself to the same height as Edgar. "The prophecy is quite clear. All the children of Andonenn must be present if the spring is to flow again. That includes yours."

"And just how are they to do that?" Edgar was far from mollified.

Seguin folded his arms. "That will only be revealed when the last ones arrive tomorrow."

Edgar backed away from him. Catherine and the children clustered around, making a tight family unit. Edgar held Edana closer.

"We won't be here tomorrow," he told Seguin. "Catherine, how soon can we be ready to depart?"

"Within the hour," she answered. "Instantly, if need be."

"No!" Seguin's expression changed to panic. "You can't go. Don't you understand? You'd be condemning us all!"

Edgar started herding the family back to the keep. "That's no concern of mine," he said over his shoulder. "Catherine, go find Margaret and let her know we're leaving. I won't have her trapped in this place, either."

"Of course," she said. "With any luck, we'll meet Guillaume on the road in time to tell him to turn around."

"No! Please!" Seguin followed them, wishing he could just call the guard and force them to stay. If it hadn't been for Margaret, he might have tried it. However, holding the granddaughter of one's lord captive was to guarantee swift and terrible retribution.

"Please!" he called again. "My lord Edgar, I beg you to stay. I swear on Andonenn's treasure that we intend no harm to your children. They are our future, too. If you only understood . . ."

Catherine paused and looked back. She touched Edgar's arm. Reluctantly, he turned to face Seguin.

"I have brought my family here against all logic and sense," he said. "I did this for love of my wife and respect for her people. You will need to give me much more in the way of explanation and reassurance before I'll even consider staying here another hour."

Seguin looked pleadingly at them. His bald head glistened with sweat that rolled down his face and into his eyes. He blinked, not noticing the sting.

"I can't tell you." The words were choked from him. "There are rules. Rules from before Grandfather's time, even. All I know is that we must all be together when the box is opened or we are doomed."

Edgar gave a snort of disbelief.

"What box?" Catherine asked.

"The one Andonenn gave to her eldest child." Seguin glanced about to be sure no one was in earshot. "It's so old that the silver lock has turned black as ebony. It is only to be opened in our most dire need."

Edgar rolled his eyes. "And this is it? What makes you think so? There's no sign of danger here, not from outside, at least. I see huge amounts of food stockpiled and no lack of water. Do you know the famine they're suffering in the north? That is dire."

Seguin shook his head. "You still don't understand. Follow me."

He led them to a low stone building. The walls had been piled up any which way from pieces of rock and old buildings. Catherine thought she spied the pale marble hand of an ancient statue stuck between two irregular pieces of granite. The mortar had fallen out and been replaced countless times over the centuries. Seguin opened the door.

The building had no windows. Seguin left the door wide, so that the sun fell on the circle of rocks that rimmed the well in the center of the room. They were bone-dry.

"You see?" he said. "A year ago, this was nearly overflowing, as it has been all my life. We never needed a windlass before to draw the water. Now every month we have to add a new length to the rope."

"Wells run dry," Edgar said. "Have you tried digging a new one?"

Seguin stared at him without comprehension.

"A new well won't save us," he said. "It's drying up at the source. And our family with it."

Catherine had been peering into the well. Beside her, James picked up a pebble and dropped it in. There was a long wait before they heard the plop. Catherine stepped back, dragging James with her.

"The legend says this comes from a spring under the castle, doesn't it?" she asked.

"Yes, deep beneath the hill, where Andonenn still lives," Seguin answered. "But she must have grown too weak to fight off the curse of Empress Judith any longer. You must see that it's our duty to save her as well as ourselves."

"No," Edgar answered. "I only see why I want to be far away from this place at once. It's all very well to have a fairy, or even a demon, on the family tree, but everyone else keeps them firmly in the distant past. They don't go trying to dig them up. If you people really believe some immortal water sprite lives beneath Boisvert then you're all mad."

A movement caught his eye. "Catherine! What are you doing? Are you trying to kill yourself?"

She had knelt down and was leaning over the edge of the well, her head tilted as if listening.

"Catherine," Edgar repeated. "This is not a good example for James and Edana."

Slowly, she stood. She faced Seguin, her face puzzled.

"I thought I heard a voice," she said, trying not to look at Edgar.

"I hear it, too," Seguin said. "She's calling us. Begging us to save her. How can you turn your back on her, cousin?"

"Catherine," Edgar said quietly. "It's only an echo of the voices from the keep. You know how water and pipes distort normal sounds. Don't let Seguin confuse you."

Catherine now looked at Edgar. "I don't know," she said miserably. "It may have been only a twisting of the sound of someone speaking in the keep, but it was so sad. It wrung my heart. Edgar, I must be sure. What if it's all true? I don't think that Seguin will let anyone harm the children. Perhaps we could at least wait until Guillaume arrives?"

Seguin's head fell to his chest. "Thank you, bless you, Catherine," he breathed. "My lord?"

Edgar's jaw tightened. "Catherine. Come with me."

Sequin waited, glancing nervously from one to the other.

Edgar's anger hit Catherine like a blow. She knew at once what she had done. But how could she repair it? She thought frantically. Of course! Once in a while those *jongleurs*' tales came in useful.

She came over to Edgar. He held out his hand to her, but to the astonishment of everyone, instead of taking it, she knelt before him, and placed her hand, palm up, below his as a vassal would to his lord.

"My husband," she said, head bowed. "I beg that you allow us to remain until my brother joins us, and my cousin Seguin is permitted to reveal the mystery. I ask this humbly for myself and in the name of my mother's family."

Edgar gaped at her in horror. Who was this woman and what had she done with his wife? Then Catherine looked up. He exhaled in relief. She wasn't insane or possessed. She was simply showing him a way to save face. If she felt that it was safe for them to stay, he would agree, at least for another day.

"Very well," he said in that haughty voice Catherine normally hated. "We shall remain here. But if I am not satisfied with Seguin's explanation, there will be no argument. We will leave at once."

"As you wish." Catherine smiled at him. He was startled and sickened to see fear, as well as apology, in her eyes.

What was this place doing to them?

Even as Seguin thanked him vociferously, Edgar had begun to regret his decision.

Nine

Boisvert; Saturday, 3 nones September (September 3) 1149.
Feast of Saint Ayou, native of Blois, abbot of Saint-Benoît
and master relic thief. 21 Elul 4909.

La vielle Matabrune ki en Jhesu ne croit
La dame se livre a duel et a destroit
L'un enfent aprés l'autre. . . .

The old woman, Matabrune, who had no faith in Jesus
Aided the woman in her pain of delivery And then destroyed
them, One child after the other. . . .

– *Beatrix*, II. 101–103

*C*atherine was shaking by the time they returned to the keep. She and Edgar had always kept their differences private, where they could fight as equals. After this public display she had no idea of what he was thinking or how he'd react when they were alone together. For the moment, he seemed involved with the children. She let him take them back up to the nursery while she slipped away.

She needed some time alone, to contemplate the consequences

of their decision to stay. The noise around her rasped her soul. She remembered that somewhere in the keep, there was a chapel.

When she finally found it, she was surprised to find Agnes standing at the door.

"You can't go in," she said. "Mother's in there. You shouldn't try to see her."

Catherine felt something inside her snap.

"I came to pray," she said angrily. "But what right have you to keep me from our mother? You've just seen her, haven't you?"

"Yes," Agnes said. "Elissent introduced me to her as a German countess."

"How impressive," Catherine said sourly. "And did that keep her from recognizing you?"

"Yes." Agnes looked away, blinking rapidly.

Catherine's anger ebbed.

"I'm sorry, Agnes, truly I am," she whispered. "But then what difference would it make if I saw her, too? You were closer to her than I. I'll be a stranger, as well. I just want to see her again. It's been so long!"

Agnes turned back to her sister. Catherine saw the tears glistening in the lamp light.

"You've changed less than I have," she answered. "And her feelings about you are stronger. You were the holy one, the gift to pay for her sins. We can't risk it. The nuns were right not to try to bring her to her senses."

She clasped her hands together in supplication.

"Please, Catherine," she begged. "I'm not doing this out of malice, I swear! Ask Margaret. Mother is happy now. Would you risk forcing her back into miserable reality?"

Catherine's lip trembled. She felt as if she were the child Madeleine believed her to be. All she wanted was to have her mother hold her and just for a moment, to be a child again. She gazed around Agnes to the chapel door. She couldn't stop herself. She took a step forward.

"Mama?" she called softly. "I'm so sorry."

Agnes threw out her arms to block the way, but Catherine didn't try to pass. Instead she turned around and stumbled back to her room. When Margaret found her sometime later, she had cried herself empty.

"Shall I come back?" she asked.

Catherine sat up, sniffing.

"No, of course not." She sighed. "When all this began, I thought that something here was calling to me. I wanted to see Boisvert again to be connected to the rest of the family. But it was a mistake. If our family isn't cursed, then the castle must be. I hate every stone."

"It's a strange place," Margaret agreed. "But not evil. I know what that feels like. There's a sadness here instead. Perhaps in your grief for your mother, you can't sense it. It's not in the people although they are affected by it. The soul of Boisvert itself is weeping."

"It's just the darkness of this room and all the hallways without windows that give you that impression," Catherine said as she wiped her face.

Margaret shook her head. "No, I don't think so."

Catherine never contradicted Margaret the way she did Agnes. If Edgar's sister said that a castle could be sad, then it was.

"Perhaps it's because it's been so long since there was a birth here," she suggested. "Do you believe it's true that our ancestress can no longer protect us from Judith's curse?"

"It seems as good an explanation as any," Margaret answered. "I only know that I wish I could help make everyone happy again."

Catherine smiled and hugged her.

"Then you don't think we were mad to come?"

Margaret laughed. "I didn't say that. But if you hadn't, I wouldn't have lasted long here by myself."

Catherine hugged her again. "Oh, Margaret, even though

awful things happened to us in England, it was worth it all to get you. I wish we could keep you with us forever."

"So do I." Margaret's laughter stopped. "Now, is there anything we can do besides wait for your brother to arrive so that Seguin may preside over the grand opening of this mysterious box?"

"Well, perhaps we could get a ball of yarn and see how much of this labyrinth we can explore," Catherine said.

"And if we find a door to another world?" Margaret was only half joking.

"Then we knit our way back home," Catherine grinned.

"My brother won't like us wandering off." Margaret hesitated.

"Margaret, we're not leaving the castle," Catherine reminded her. "And if we get lost, all we need to do is wind up the skein again to find our way back."

"Well." Margaret didn't need much encouragement. "It sounds harmless enough. And I'm very curious about what lies beneath the keep."

"Good!" Catherine said. "I'll go check on the children. You find a big ball of yarn and I'll meet you in the Great Hall."

They met a few moments later. Margaret was carrying a bag containing three balls of yarn, each as large as a baby's head.

"*Enodu!*" Catherine exclaimed. "We could find our way from here to Paris with that."

"The ladies all wanted to give me something," Margaret said. "They didn't even ask what it was for."

"That's what happens when you come from a powerful family," Catherine teased her. "If I had asked, they'd have given me the tailings from an old pair of stockings. Now, we need to tie one end firmly to something."

"What about the post at the foot of the stairs?" Margaret suggested.

"No, then it will go straight across the floor where someone will trip over it." Catherine looked around. "Here, the linen chest! It has big brass handles. That will work. Right against the wall and too heavy to budge."

The two women stared at the doorway Catherine had gone through the night before. Several people passed them, including Seguin, but no one commented.

"Perhaps all visitors explore in this way," Margaret said after another servant had gone by with no more than a glance at them.

"The way these passages twist, it may be that even the natives carry lengths of string," Catherine answered. "That could be why you had no trouble getting the yarn."

They deliberately chose any way that sloped downward. It wasn't long before they left the main keep far above. The walls became rougher and the floors more worn. The lower chambers and storerooms had been dug out of the hillside, cavelike. The ceilings were long boards propped up by wooden pillars. In some places, white roots reached out between the slats.

"We're so far below ground!" Margaret looked nervous. "How did they manage to create this honeycomb of rooms without bringing the castle down on their heads?"

Catherine had been trying not to consider how much stone and earth hung above them.

"Perhaps these tunnels started out as mines," she suggested. "Silver or copper. The keep might have been built over them."

"Who would do that?" Margaret was skeptical. "It's like building your house upon the sand. Actually, with all these holes in the earth I can't see why the castle hasn't collapsed."

"Margaret!" Catherine cried. "Please let's concentrate on the path. Everything has stayed here for centuries. I imagine it will last a few days more."

They continued in silence. Both of them were thinking of the curse and wondering if it had become strong enough to cause Boisvert to suddenly crumble around them.

"Catherine?" Margaret asked after a bit. "This section looks very old. How often do you think anyone comes down here?"

"I don't know. We haven't seen anyone for quite a while." Catherine paused, realizing what Margaret was saying. "There are torches every few paces, aren't there? They would have to be replaced almost every day. So this area must be used often. What for?"

Margaret looked around. They were in a long tunnel at the moment. The walls were thick blocks and there was no sign of a doorway or a branching passage.

"Perhaps Lord Gargenaud keeps wine down here?"

"We passed any number of storerooms full of wine casks three or four levels up," Catherine told her. "But, even if he did, why would anyone do anything so wasteful as to keep light going all the time?"

Before them, the passage bent to the right. A light glowed from around the turn.

"Aha! The answer may be just a few steps away." Catherine hurried forward.

"Catherine, stop!" Margaret called. "I've reached the end of the yarn."

Catherine went to the turn in the passage and looked back at Margaret.

"It slopes down and twists again," she said. "But there are no forks. We can't get lost."

Margaret stayed where she was. "No, Catherine, we can't take the risk of coming back and finding our Ariadne's thread gone."

"Who would take it?" Catherine pleaded.

"Who keeps the torches lit?" Margaret answered. "Catherine, you're responsible to your husband and children. You can't wander off into an adventure anymore."

"But," Catherine stood at the turn, "don't you want to see where this goes?"

"Not as much as I want to get back to the same world we came from." Margaret began to wind the yarn again. "Don't go any farther, Catherine. Which is more important, a mythical mother of your clan or the family waiting for us? Think of your children!"

Catherine wavered in the direction of the passage, one foot raised. At the end of this could be the answer to all her questions. She looked up at Margaret, already moving slowly back the way they had come. She seemed so fragile! Her thick red plaits had to weigh more than the rest of her. Yet she had survived seeing her mother slaughtered, being taken from her home to a strange land, and then a terrible attack by a mob. It wasn't cowardice that kept Margaret from continuing, but duty.

"Perhaps another day," Margaret promised. "When we have more yarn."

Reluctantly, Catherine joined her sister-in-law as they retraced their way back through the maze. But every few minutes, she paused and looked around, listening. She could swear she heard voices coming from the way not taken. No, she told her self. It's just my imagination.

They walked and walked.

"We should be getting close to the upper levels now," Catherine said at last. "It couldn't have taken us this long to go down."

"No." Margaret sounded worried. "I don't understand it. I'm following the thread. Here's where we tied the red one to the blue. But I don't remember this place. And, I think, no, I'm sure. We're going downward again. Catherine, how can this be?"

"We must have just forgotten," Catherine said, but there was doubt in her voice.

They continued past a few more turns. At last they came to a circular chamber with three passages radiating from it. The yarn stretched across the room and vanished into the darkness of the one opposite them.

"There's no light that way," Margaret said. "Catherine, you know we've never been here before! What should we do?"

She was near to panic now. She clutched the ball of yarn like a lifeline.

Catherine put an arm around her, as much for her own comfort as Margaret's.

"What choice do we have?" She tried to keep her voice steady. "Can you find the way back without a guide? Yes, it seems that someone has untied the yarn and sent us in a new direction. We don't know if their purpose is to hurt us or help."

"How could this help?" Margaret squeaked.

"I don't know," Catherine admitted. "But our only hope of getting back to the family tonight is to find someone to show us the way up and the best place to find someone is at the other end of this thread."

They were in the center of the chamber now. Margaret stared in terror at the black opening before her.

"I can't go in there," she stated.

"Not in the dark, *ma douz*." Catherine reached up and unhooked a torch from its sconce. "See, we'll not only have light, but a weapon of sorts."

Margaret gave in. She trusted Catherine more than she feared the void. "But I know we're doing this just as much because you have to know what's going on as to get out of here."

Catherine gave a shamefaced grin.

"Don't you want to know, too?"

Hesitantly, Margaret admitted to a slight bit of curiosity.

"But I'm tying the string to the sconce. I'm not getting lost a second time," she announced.

So, Catherine carried the torch and Margaret felt along the taut yarn. The two of them entered the tunnel.

It never occurred to Edgar that Catherine would go hunting for answers beneath the castle. Whatever the truth of the family legend, he was sure that everything that had happened was the result of living, breathing malice.

"Martin!" He stopped the young man on the way to the stables. "Is your mother tending to the children?"

"Yes, Master Edgar," Martin answered. "She's washing and dressing them for the arrival of Lord Guillaume's family."

"Really?" Edgar paused. "That seems a waste of time. They're always torn and filthy within an hour of joining their cousins. Oh, well, I suppose it's good to start out presentable."

He recollected his reason for hunting Martin down.

"I need to know more about the people here," he said. "There's little chance that any of the servants will tell me a thing, but they might talk to you. I want to know why, if there is no famine here, it appears as if Gargenaud is storing up for seven lean years. Is there truly a chance of our being attacked by this Angevin Lord Olivier? Also, do the folk of the village and the castle servants believe these legends? And if so, in what form? I've certainly seen no sign among them that they are expecting doom to fall."

"Perhaps they haven't been told that the well is failing," Martin suggested.

"Seguin has tried to keep it secret, I know," Edgar said. "But surely they must be curious about all this preparation."

They had reached the stables. It was occupied by several young men cleaning out stalls, a couple of men-at-arms mending harness, and one of the men who had been a guest at the banquet. Edgar had received the impression he was somehow part of the family, but they hadn't been introduced.

"See what you can find out," he said to Martin. "Without betraying anything that we have learned of this prophecy and curse."

"Then what information will I have to trade?" Martin objected.

"Give them my family," Edgar offered. "Say anything you like. You can even tell them how I lost my hand. I'm sure they're all wondering."

"Very well." Martin winced at the bitterness in Edgar's tone. "I'll do my best."

"Good. Start with the stablehands," Edgar said. "I'm going to see what I can get from him."

He nodded toward the man from the banquet, who was sitting by the doorway, holding a broken spur, apparently waiting for the blacksmith.

Martin had no trouble striking up a conversation with the stablemen. He started by taking care of the horses they had brought with them. While seeing to their needs, he asked about life at the castle. As Edgar guessed, they wanted him to give information about his life in return. When they learned that Martin had started life as a serving maid's bastard and managed to become apprentice to a trader, they were at first skeptical.

"Truly!" Martin insisted. "How could I lie with him standing over there able to deny it? My mother is now housekeeper at my lord's house in Paris. I grew up there. Last year I told him I wanted to learn the skill of trading. He and his partner took me on. We have only just returned from a profitable journey to Lombardy."

The young men gazed at Martin in hopeful respect. Each had dreams of rising above his station. This was the first time they had met a man who had actually done it. Then one of the lads, a tall blond who had yet to fill out to his recent growth, shook his head and went back to shoveling the stable floor.

"Maybe that sort of thing happens in Paris." He emptied the shovel with an energy that spattered the contents against the wall behind the wheelbarrow. "But this is Boisvert, where nothing ever changes."

"Why not?" Martin asked. "Your lord is old. When he dies, won't the new lord be looking for likely men to promote?"

The second young man laughed. "Do you know how many have grown old waiting for Gargenaud to die? Lord Seguin is his grandson and he's past sixty. They say Seguin's father gave up ever inheriting and so went and got himself killed in the Holy Land, trying to win a fief for himself."

Martin gave no sign that he'd heard this all before.

"How can a man of sixty still have a living grandfather?" he scoffed. "I've seen Lord Gargenaud. He's old, I'll grant you, but hale enough. He can't be as ancient as you think."

The blond looked around to see if anyone was listening. Then he leaned toward Martin.

"It's sorcery," he whispered. "Everyone knows it. One of the old man's ancestors made a pact with the guardian of the spring. There's some that say it was Gargenaud, himself and that he's immortal."

Martin sighed. He had hoped the servants would have a more matter-of-fact explanation for the strangeness of the place, but it seemed that the legend had saturated the minds of all who lived there. He hoped Edgar was finding out more.

Edgar was getting an earful, but not about Boisvert. He had approached the man in a casual manner, keeping his left hand hidden in the folds of his tunic to avoid the distraction of having to explain it.

"Good day!" he smiled. "That spur looks like it was smashed between two rocks. You must have taken quite a fall."

The man stared at him in glum resentment.

"I never fall," he said. "This is a cheap piece of shit some peddler stuck me with. Swore it was Cordoban steel. Hah! More likely Welsh tin. Crumpled the first time I dismounted."

"Too bad," Edgar said, wondering how any man could be so stupid as not to know the difference. "Think the blacksmith can fix it?"

"Not unless he can transmute the elements," the man growled.

Edgar blinked. This wasn't normal language to hear from a knight. It was time to find out more about him.

"I'm Edgar of Paris," he said. "From Wedderlie in Scotland by birth. My wife's mother is a daughter of Lord Gargenaud."

"I know who you are," the man interrupted. "And what. It was bad enough that Gargenaud sold his daughter to a merchant, but we needed hard coin then. But, you, born into the aristocracy, lowering yourself to take up the trade. You're no better than the Jew that sold me this spur!"

His voice had been steadily rising. At the end, he was standing, shaking the crumpled spur up into Edgar's face.

Edgar's gray eyes grew frosty.

"I do not sell to men like you, but kings and great lords of the church," he said. "And anyone who claimed this metal was steel must have assumed you'd know he was joking."

He grabbed it from the man's hand and tossed it over his shoulder.

"Saint Benoît's wrathful rod!" the man exclaimed. "If you weren't a cripple I'd flatten you!"

"Please don't let that stop you." Edgar's smile could have sliced through granite. "I'm sure you've had a great deal of practice on poor widows and beggar children."

"You arrogant . . ." The man drew back his arm to strike him.

Edgar's eyes didn't flicker, so when a hand caught the arm and yanked back, almost sending his assailant to the floor, the man was taken completely by surprise.

"Odilon! What do you think you're doing?" Seguin glared at him. "Lord Edgar is a guest here."

"Right," Odilon sneered, rubbing his arm. "He only came because he thinks there's a treasure to be found. What's honor to his kind? Well, you might as well go back where you came from, my lord peddler, because of all the stories about this place, that is the only one that's a total lie."

Edgar still hadn't moved. His total lack of reaction was making Odilon nervous. Seguin started once again to apologize. At last Edgar took his eyes off Odilon's face.

"My lord Seguin," he said calmly. "There is no need for you to make excuses for this man. I am presuming that he is another family member. He reminds me very much of Catherine's uncle Roger. He was subject to uncontrollable outbursts also."

Seguin winced. He remembered Roger all too well.

"Yes," he admitted. "Odilon is the great-great-grandson of Gargenaud's only brother. We are related in the third degree."

"I see," Edgar said. "Are there any others of his kin that I should be prepared for?"

"His brother, Ysore, is also here," Seguin told him. "The priest. You may have noticed him last night. You are safe from attack from him," he added dryly.

Edgar nodded, ignoring the slur. "So, this truly is a dwindling family?" he asked. "It's strange to me that anyone leaves Boisvert if, in doing so, they lose the protection of your magical forebear. I expected to find the castle crowded with Catherine's cousins."

"Those who stay are protected from early death," Seguin said. "At least they were. But only the lord lives beyond the natural span. There were never many children in each generation. Some entered the church. Others fought for the counts of Blois and died in battle. And now we have been cursed with barren wives. Only Madeleine's children have escaped this."

"Seguin." Only those who knew Edgar best would have seen how angry he was. "I have promised to stay here until Guillaume and his family arrive. I admit that I am curious enough to wait a day more for you to unveil all the secrets of this place, but the more I learn of you, the more I believe that you should all be left to molder in your myths."

He started to move away from them.

Seguin moved in front of him to keep Edgar from leaving.

Odilon crowded to the side, keeping him from turning around.

"You think this has nothing you to with you?" the young man shouted, rising onto his toes to look Edgar in the eyes.

At the other end of the room, the stablemen stopped even pretending to work. Martin wondered if he should grab a pitchfork and defend his master.

Seguin spoke more calmly but with the same passion. "Your children are of our blood, Edgar, no matter how diluted. If Boisvert falls, they will die, too. Only Andonenn's power has kept us strong all these centuries. Now it's fading and Empress Judith's curse will doom everyone. Only together can we defeat her. You must believe me."

He motioned to Odilon to move away from Edgar. The man didn't budge.

"Odilon!"

"Yes, cousin," the knight answered grudgingly.

"Apologize to Lord Edgar for your rash words," Seguin ordered. "You didn't mean to insult him so, did you?"

Odilon's jaw tightened. "No," he forced out. "I spoke without thought. I beg you to forgive me."

Edgar looked at him for a long moment. Then he laughed.

"How could I deny such a heartfelt and eloquent petition?" he said. "I wish no bad feelings between my wife's family and me."

"Thank you." Seguin relaxed, not noticing that Edgar had not accepted the apology. "My son, Aymon, says that he has spotted Lord Guillaume's party approaching. They should be here within the hour. Perhaps you'd like to tell your wife. I'm sure she'll want to be there to greet him."

Edgar took this as a dismissal. He bowed to both men and signaled Martin to accompany him.

"Did you find anything out?" he asked when they were clear of the stables.

"Only that this legend seems to have taken hold of everyone here," Martin answered. "The stablehands are worried that the line is failing and the castle will fall to the Angevins under Lord Olivier."

"Do they know about the well?" Edgar asked.

"They didn't mention it. They seemed more concerned that there were so few left of the family. They don't like being ruled by such an old man, even if he has otherworldly protection." Martin paused. "They know something's wrong. Everyone here feels it. It's like the hours before a storm."

They both looked up at an unrelentingly clear sky.

"Not yet, anyway," Edgar muttered. "Martin, go tell your mother that I want us to be ready to leave if I don't like what I learn at this revelation we're to receive tonight. I'm going to see if Catherine's found out anything useful. Do you know where she is?"

"I saw her and Lady Margaret this morning," Martin said. "I think they were planning on spending the day knitting."

"Knitting?" Edgar asked. "I don't think either one of them knows how."

Martin shrugged. "I must have been mistaken. Shall I help you look for them?"

"No," Edgar said. "I'm sure someone will know."

The walls of the tunnel were ragged stone that glinted with bits of mica and quartz. Narrow rivulets of water dripped through layers of moss that dangled from the ceiling. The torchlight shone only a few steps ahead. The floor was slippery and uneven so that Catherine and Margaret had to keep the light at their feet most of the time.

"This isn't a place where people come often," Margaret said, her voice hollow.

They were holding hands as they inched down the passage. With their free hands, Catherine clutched the torch and Margaret gripped the thin strand that stretched into the darkness ahead.

"No, this doesn't even look as though people made it," Catherine said. "But we don't seem to be going down anymore."

Margaret suppressed a moan of fear. "We don't seem to be going up, either."

Catherine squeezed her hand.

"I'm sorry, dear," she said. "Do you want to go back and take our chances in the lit sections?"

"No," Margaret answered. "We could wander forever. At least we know that someone has been this way recently."

Or something. They both thought it, but neither wanted to be the first to say it.

The torch began to flicker. At the same moment, Catherine felt a breeze on her face.

"We may be coming out," she said. "Once we get above ground, we can find our way back to the keep."

This cheered them both.

"I wish I'd brought a mantle," Margaret commented. "We've been down in the cold so long that I'm chilled through."

Catherine looked at her with concern. The girl's face was more than usually pale.

"It can't be much farther," she said. "Just around the next bend."

It wasn't the next bend, but the one after that that opened up into a small chamber. The sound of running water was loud and seemed to come from over their heads.

"Where are we?" Margaret's eyes searched the chamber for a passage out.

"In the cave of Andonenn," a voice said from the darkness.

Both of them screamed. Catherine dropped the torch.

It did not comfort them that they had found the person they had been following.

Edgar was becoming annoyed. Catherine and Margaret hadn't been seen all day. Samonie had given Peter gruel when the other children ate, but he still whined for his mother's milk.

"She didn't say where she was going," the housekeeper told Edgar. "But she must have meant to be back before None. Lady

Margaret was to attend prayers with Lady Elissent. One of the servants was looking for her a while ago."

"Catherine should know better than to leave without telling anyone," Edgar said. "Or at least Margaret should. Where could they have gone?"

He asked everyone he could find in the household. The guards at the gate swore they hadn't seen them leave. The women confirmed Martin's story of the yarn. But after that, they had simply vanished.

"It's the curse," Odilon said, giving Edgar a smug look. "You didn't take it seriously and now Judith has spirited your wife away."

Edgar glared at him and then at the circle of guards, servants, and relatives, all waiting to see what he would do.

"If that's so," he said at last. "Then I'm going to find out where and bring her back. If you're all too terrified to go with me, so be it. Martin!"

"Master." Martin was at his side. "Lord Guillaume has arrived."

"About time," Edgar said. He turned to Seguin. "You have until dawn tomorrow to show me a reason not to take my family and leave the rest of you to your madness."

Catherine chased the flaming torch as it rolled across the floor, scrabbling to get it before the flame was extinguished. As she reached for it, a hand came down and caught it. A feminine hand, with long white fingers. Catherine looked up.

"I know you," she accused. "You were old and you were dead. Then you were in the tree in the forest. Are you some kind of demon? What do you want and why have you led us into Purgatory?"

Ten

A cave beneath the castle, perhaps.

Li ver en sont rimé par grant maistrie
D'amor et d'armes et de chevalerie.

The verses are put in rhyme masterfully
Of love and of war and of chivalry.

—*Der Anseis de Cartage*, II. 6–7

I am no demon!" The woman gazed at them with scorn. "I am Mandon."

She waited for them to react. Margaret looked at Catherine. Catherine shrugged and shook her head.

"Mandon," the woman repeated. "The guardian. Has no one told you of me?"

Catherine looked at the woman with light, flowing hair sitting calmly in her clean flowing robes and then she looked at Margaret, shivering and dirty but determined. Something in her exploded.

"No!" she screamed. "No one mentioned you. Not one person told me to beware of an insane old crone who leaps under horses, then sheds forty years and runs off. No one said, 'Don't go into the tunnels beneath the keep because the same madwoman likes to turn people around until they can't find their way back.' Saint Thecla's barking seals! All I've heard are rumors and legends and garbled history. Now, will you take us back up or did you lure us here to slaughter and feed to your master?"

"What are you talking about? I have no wish to harm you." Mandon stood with a flowing movement, Catherine noted, and faced them.

She was tall, like the women of the north. The firelight caught a shimmer of gold thread on her *bliaut* and a sparkle of jewels on her fingers and about her neck. It was far from the worn gray robe she had worn in the outside world. Despite herself, Catherine felt a tinge of awe.

"So then." She stopped, unsure what to say next.

Margaret had caught only one thing.

"If you don't wish to harm us, then why did you trick us into coming to you?" she demanded, fighting not to cry like a sick child. "Why did you untie my yarn?"

Mandon studied her in puzzlement.

"You are not one of Andonenn's children," she said at last. "What are you doing here?"

"Freezing in the middle of summer," Margaret answered. "I don't care about your curse or your woes. I want to go back up to the sunshine."

Mandon reached out to touch the tear on Margaret's cheek. She seemed confused.

Catherine stepped between them.

"I don't know what you are," she said. "But you've played your mischief on me for the last time. You must have brought us here for a reason. If you aren't going to kill us, then tell us what it is and let us go."

Mandon moved away from them, back into the shadow.

"The stories are all true," she said softly. "The spring has been chained and the well that has kept us alive for centuries is drying. You must read the message and free Andonenn, or we are all doomed. Yes, even I shall die. She is my mother, too."

"What message?" Catherine asked. "The legend says nothing about a message."

"You have part of it," Mandon told her. "All the children do. She bade me see to it and I did, though at great cost. Join them; find the meaning. It will tell you what to do."

"Why don't you just tell me!" Catherine tried to shine the torch on the corner where Mandon was standing.

It was empty.

"Catherine!" Margaret's tears stopped. "She vanished. What do we do now?"

Gingerly, Catherine approached the corner. The wall was the same rough stone as the rest of the room. She had heard no creak of a door opening and closing. Mandon must be inhuman to . . .

"Wait."

The corner wasn't really a corner. As she came up against it, Catherine realized that there was a space where the walls should have joined. Instead they overlapped. In between there was room for a person to squeeze through.

"Look, Margaret." She laughed in relief. "There was no magic. She escaped through here."

She waved the torch behind the front wall. "And we can, too. This must be how she got up into the keep the other night. There's a staircase."

It seemed that they climbed forever. Catherine lost count of the steps after a hundred. But eventually they reached another dark opening. For a moment, both of them hung back, fearful of where they might come out. Then they heard the deep barking of a dog and the cries of children.

"Dragon!" Catherine called out joyfully. "James! Edana!"

She rushed through the doorway and was stopped by a soft barrier that threw her into Margaret's arms.

"Catherine?" Edgar's voice came from beyond the wall. "Where are you? We've been looking all over."

Catherine picked herself up. She realized now where they were.

"Margaret," she giggled in relief, then sneezed as dust filled her nose. "This is the Great Hall. We're behind the tapestry next to the hearth."

They emerged into a world of warmth and sunshine, filled with loud, normal people. Catherine ran to James and hugged him hard. The ghostly feeling of the tunnels had half-convinced her that, if she ever found them again, her children would have grown beyond her knowing. Edana was jumping up and down, her tunic torn, as usual. Catherine had never seen her look so beautiful.

"Yes, yes, Mama's home. Everything's fine." Edgar disentangled Catherine from her progeny and pulled her to her feet. "Now, where have you two been and what were you doing behind the tapestry?"

"Edgar, you won't believe it," Catherine began when Agnes bore down on them.

"Margaret, Catherine! Look at yourselves!" Agnes stepped back from them, her face an image of shock and distaste. "You're both filthy, your clothes crumpled and your hair! Saint Cunegund's red hot plowshares! You'll never be ready in time. Come with me at once!"

"But I must tell Edgar," Catherine protested.

"At once!"

Agnes was not to be gainsaid or interrupted. She shooed Margaret and Catherine like a pair of chickens toward the stairs.

"Agnes, I really think Edgar should know this," Margaret panted as she tried to climb one more set of steps.

"Is there a fire?" Agnes asked. "An army at the gates? If not, then it can wait. It will take more time than we have to make you two presentable by the time Guillaume arrives."

Edgar frowned as he watched them go. He was glad that no harm had come to his sister or his wife, but they should have known better than to wander off without telling anyone. It was the sort of thing he'd expect from James and Edana.

He went over to the wall hanging. It was old, done in the style of the Byzantines. He wondered if it had been brought back by one of the knights who answered Pope Urban's call to free the Holy Land. He felt the material. No, the moth holes were older than that. It hung flat against the wall, so how had Margaret and Catherine managed to hide behind it with no one noticing?

Edgar slid behind the hanging, feeling his way along the wall. He started when he saw a light that seemed to be coming from within it. Then his wrist felt empty space.

The light was coming from a torch lying on the staircase just where it turned, a few steps from the top. Edgar went down and picked it up. A cool breeze wafted up from the darkness, bringing with it the smell of mold. For a moment, Edgar was tempted to investigate, but he decided to wait until Catherine gave him her report.

Of course, there was no harm in asking one of the residents.

Edgar carefully snuffed the torch against the wall before returning to the hall. He looked around.

"Aymon!" He called the young man over.

"The passage behind this tapestry," he asked. "Where does it lead?"

Aymon gave him a look. "Nowhere, Edgar. It's a wall. They usually stay where they're put."

"No, I mean . . ." Edgar decided on another tack. "When was the last time these hangings were taken down?"

"How should I know?" Aymon answered. "Do I look like a laundress? Ask my mother."

"Thank you," Edgar said. "I will."

Aymon left, shaking his head. Edgar looked around for Elissent, but she wasn't in the hall. He watched Aymon directing servants as they set up the tables for yet another welcoming feast.
How likely was he to be lying? He'd spent his whole life in the
keep. He should know what lay under it, shouldn't he? But perhaps not. If one assumed there was a solid wall behind a hanging,
who would bother looking for a door?

Edgar had thought his family home in Scotland was strange,
but this was beyond anything he had experienced. Boisvert was
too big, too old. The people living here now skimmed along the
surface of the place like flies on a pond. It worried him that in the
depths there might be a gigantic pike, watching them all, waiting
to snap.

He wished Solomon were with them. These relatives of
Catherine's were all either mad or hiding something. Edgar felt a
strong need for someone to watch his back. There was no man at
Boisvert whom he could completely trust.

The bustle was increasing and the musicians had appeared.
They gave every sign of intending to practice. Edgar decided it
was time to take the children and find a quieter place to await the
arrival of Catherine's brother.

"James," he called. "Come with me. Bring your sister."

"What about Dragon?" the boy complained.

"He'll follow us," Edgar said sternly. "It's Edana you need to
watch out for."

"Master?"

Martin suddenly appeared at his side. Edgar gestured to where
James was resentfully tugging Edana toward them.

"I have to keep an eye on them and I need you to help me,"
he told Martin. "I don't like the way people come and go so
quickly here. Is there something you wanted to tell me?"

"Yes, Master." Martin also watched the children as if he were keeping them safe with his eyes alone. "My mother says that Peter is sleeping. She wants to know if Lady Catherine needs her."

"Probably not," Edgar said. "Agnes has maids enough for a cohort of women. As long as someone is watching over him."

The children had reached them. Edana held up her arms to her father.

"Not this time, deorling," Edgar said. "You're more than normally sticky and this is my best silk tunic."

"Come to me." Martin reached down to her. "I don't need to be fine for anyone."

Edana happily climbed into his arms.

Edgar watched Martin as he teased the little girl, all the while carefully mopping up the worst of the grime on her face with the tip of his sleeve. It dawned on him that he did have a man he could trust completely. He had been used to thinking of Martin as an odd-job boy, someone to run errands and hold the horses. Yet, on their recent trip to Lombardy, Martin had proved himself to be quick-thinking and utterly reliable.

"Martin," Edgar said. "I need your help."

Catherine and Margaret were rushed up to Agnes's room and divested of their outer clothing before they could do more than give a weak protest.

"Agnes, listen," Catherine tried as one of her sister's maids came at her with a comb and a determined expression. "We were lost down under the keep. Do you know how many tunnels there are down there? It's like a rabbit warren."

"Catherine, sit still so poor Mina can try to fix your hair," Agnes interrupted. "She may need goose grease to make it lie flat."

Catherine's thick, dark curls had been the despair of her blond mother. Just dividing it enough to braid took ages. It had been a relief when Catherine had been sent to the convent of the

Paraclete. When she took her vows, it would be cut manageably short.

But instead Catherine had come home and fallen in love with a British student. And her hair was as intractable as ever.

"Agnes," Margaret tried. "Don't you want to know what we discovered?"

"No," Agnes answered. "Why should I care about some musty antique you stumbled over? I'm not interested in secrets or treasure. I have everything I need. My only care is for the security of my family and also that they don't embarrass me by appearing at a banquet looking like women who've spent all day in a pigsty."

She opened a large trunk. In it were silk and linen robes so elegant that even Catherine was momentarily distracted. Agnes shook out a red one, embroidered with a pattern of spring flowers.

"If I lend you this, do you think you can keep from ruining it?" she asked Catherine.

"Probably not," Catherine answered. "I do have clothes of my own, you know. And, since you took all of Mother's, Edgar has been giving me lovely pieces of jewelry, too."

Margaret could see that this was about to disintegrate into a battle that had most likely started in the nursery.

"I'd like to wear the blue, if you don't mind," she interrupted. "I didn't bring much from the Paraclete and nothing fine enough for another banquet."

Agnes immediately turned her attention to Margaret, leaving Catherine to Mina's rough efforts to tug a comb through her hair. The pain brought her back to the issue at hand.

"There's a woman . . . down there," she told Agnes between jerks on her head. "I saw her . . . at Viellete . . . neuse and again in the . . . forest."

"What was that?" Agnes's face was buried in the trunk as she searched out a pair of hose to match the *bliaut* for Margaret.

"The woman we met today," Margaret said. "She said her name was Mandon."

"Mandon!" Agnes rose so quickly that she hit her head on the lid of the trunk. "You say you met her?"

"Yes," Margaret answered. "She led us astray and then showed us the way out."

"Mandon," Agnes repeated. "Are you certain that's what she said?"

"Of course we are! Ow!" Catherine said. The maid released her a moment to get another comb. "Have you heard of her?"

"Of course," Agnes answered. "I sometimes wonder if you slept through your childhood, Catherine. Mandon is Andonenn's messenger. She's supposed to appear to warn the family of danger."

"This woman was real, not a legend," Catherine said.

"Well, of course," Agnes said. "She's real and a legend. That proves we were right to come here. But why is she bothering with you?"

Catherine's temper was frayed. Her head hurt from the combing. Her feet hurt from all the walking and climbing. Patience was too much to ask.

"It may be that she came to me because I'm the only one whose mind isn't filled with stories about her," Catherine snapped. "This woman is flesh, just like us. I don't know what's going on, but I felt her hand and saw her breath in the air. She is human."

"That's as may be," Agnes said. "What do you think, Margaret? You saw her, too."

Margaret looked up from a tempting selection of earrings.

"Mandon seemed real to me," she said. "But very strange. She could be as addled as your poor mother. Perhaps everyone else who lives here knows all about her. After all, we haven't had time to meet everyone, yet. If so, I'm surprised that she's allowed to wander free. Catherine says she was at Vielleteneuse and Paris. Of course, she may have escaped from her keeper."

Catherine sighed. "I wonder if the true curse on the family is a tendency to madness."

"Speak for yourself," Agnes said. "Mother would be fine if it weren't for you. You were supposed to stay in the convent and pray for her sins."

Catherine made no retort. In part she felt that it was true.

"What about the message?" Margaret asked, once again leaping between the warring lionesses.

"Mandon gave you a message?" Agnes asked. "Why you and not me?"

"She said you already had it," Margaret told her. "Or part of it, at least. Do you?"

"We only had the one brought from Grandfather," Agnes said. "But that just said to come at once."

"No, it's more than that," Catherine said. "It's something she left for us, she said, something we have to interpret or solve. At least that's what I understood."

"So did I," Margaret said loyally.

Agnes found the hose and handed them to Margaret. She then dismissed the woman who had managed to force Catherine's hair into two long plaits.

"Now that you look presentable, I think you should find Seguin and tell him of your interesting adventure today. If there's a message from Andonenn, he'll be the one to decipher it. Now, I need to prepare myself for the banquet. I've taken far too much time attending to you."

Catherine was simmering as they left the room.

"Agnes always does this to me," she apologized to Margaret.

Margaret smiled. "I always wanted a sister," she said. "I hope you don't mind, but I rather like Agnes."

Catherine bent her head. When she looked up, Margaret was relieved to see that she was laughing.

"Don't tell anyone," she warned. "But I like her, too. Even though she maddens me with her arrogance."

Margaret made no comment.

When Martin had let his mother know that she was free for the afternoon, Samonie at first had no idea what to do with herself. In Paris there was never an empty hour. She thought about mending Edana's torn tunic, but decided that could wait. Then she happened to look out the window.

The children's room was high in one of the central towers of the keep and the view from it reached almost to Chartres. Samonie could see the fields reaching down to the forest. A few houses clustered in a tiny village near the forest and in a grove of fruit trees. As she watched, two tiny shapes dropped from one. It was a moment before she realized that the plums must be ripe enough to be worth stealing. The boys were running from a woman waving a switch.

"I came from a place like that," she murmured. "How long has it been since I walked barefoot through rows of barley or stole a plum from the tree?"

She made her way out of the keep and through the town gates, trying not to think of the climb she would have getting back. As soon as she was outside, she took off her leather shoes.

The barley field stretched before her. In the center was a hillock, too rocky or steep to plow. It was covered with grass and bushes and crowned by an ancient walnut tree. Samonie set off toward it. It seemed the perfect spot for a summer afternoon nap.

It didn't occur to her that someone at a tower window might be watching her.

∞

"Excuse me," Catherine asked. "Do you know where I can find Seguin?"

The man looked vaguely familiar. One of her other cousins?

"He's out at the portcullis, to greet your brother," the man answered. "Shouldn't you be there, too?"

"I don't think I could keep from laughing," Catherine said before she thought.

The man's eyebrows rose. "I see," he said. "You find our welcome ridiculous."

"Oh no, of course not," Catherine tried to repair her gaffe. "It's only in connection with Guillaume. And especially his children. I mean, I love them all but, well, you'll understand when you see them, cousin . . . ?"

"Raimbaut," he said. "I'm Seguin's elder son. You were presented to me before."

"Yes, of course," Catherine bobbed an apology. "There are so many new faces."

"Not really," he answered. "Perhaps if you had visited more, you would have less trouble identifying us."

Like most of the family, he was fair and of medium height. He appeared to be in his late twenties but Catherine knew that he had to be at least ten years older than she.

"Raimbaut," she asked. "Have I also been presented to Mandon?"

"Mandon!" he snorted in anger. "Now I know you're mocking us. Mandon doesn't exist. She's a tale for children. A being who travels wherever Andonenn's children live, who can appear young or old. Nonsense!"

"But then is Andonenn a myth, too?" Catherine asked.

"Of course not." Raimbaut stared at her as if she were a simpleton. "She is the mother of us all. We have it written in a book."

"Then it must be true," Catherine said.

Raimbaut did not notice the ironic tone.

"Right. It's all there, how she and Jurvale met and married and how she keeps watch over us," he told her.

"Could I see this book?" she asked.

"The monks keep it for us at Saint-Benoît," he said. "Ask them."

The blaring of trumpets interrupted them.

"That must be my brother," Catherine guessed. "Perhaps I should go greet him after all. Thank you."

She left Raimbaut looking after her with an expression of distaste.

Margaret had gone in search of Edgar. Catherine found both of them doing their best to keep James and Edana from being crushed by the crowd.

"I knew Guillaume's five children would impress them more than our paltry three," Edgar told her.

"Edgar, has Margaret told you about what we found today?" Catherine had to shout to be heard above the cheering.

He nodded. "We'll discuss it later."

Margaret tapped her arm to get her attention. Catherine leaned toward her. Margaret cupped her hands and spoke straight into Catherine's ear.

"He's mad because we might have been in danger," she said. "But he's certain that the woman we met was human. He wants to go hunting for her with Martin later."

Catherine answered close to Margaret's ear.

"Maybe now that Guillaume is here, Seguin will tell us everything."

"I hope so," Margaret yelled back. "There isn't much yarn left."

The sound of Guillaume's arrival reached Samonie only as a distant buzzing. She was lying beneath the giant walnut tree. The grass was cool and soft and the sunshine made gentle patterns through the leaves. She closed her eyes, reveling in the peace.

"You look as you did the day I first saw you."

Samonie's eyes flew open. Brehier stood above her.

She sat up quickly. "That was a long time ago."

He sat next to her. "It was a lifetime ago. I thought then that everything in the world was mine for the taking."

"Including me," Samonie said.

"Yes." He avoided her eyes. "Did I give you a choice or just come to your bed without leave? I don't remember."

"It doesn't matter," she answered. "I wouldn't have refused you."

"I'm glad," he said.

He took her hand. "Would you refuse me now?"

Samonie smiled on the face so like her son's.

"I don't see how I could." She lay down again, drawing him with her.

"Catherine, you'll never guess what we found tied to the timbers of the keep." Marie greeted her with a hug. "I have it in my purse. We could make no sense of it, but Guillaume thought you would know."

"What is it?" Catherine asked.

"Some sort of embroidery," she answered. "I'll show you as soon as we get settled."

"Embroidery?" Catherine echoed. "Is there writing on it?"

Marie nodded. "Mabile!" she chided her youngest. "If you hit your brother again, you'll get no dinner!"

"I think I know what it is," Catherine began, but Marie was too distracted.

"Good," she said. "I can't wait for you to tell us."

She was swept away in a jumble of children, servants, men-at-arms, and baggage.

"Margaret, did you hear that?" Catherine asked. "Remember the length I told you Edgar and I found in the woods?"

"Do you think it has something to do with Mandon's message?"

"I don't know," Catherine said. "I had the feeling that everyone was supposed to have a piece of it."

"Maybe they do," Margaret said. "Have you asked?"

Catherine sighed. "You have your brother's talent for making me feel an idiot," she said. "No, I haven't."

Margaret patted her shoulder. "We've been busy. You can't think of everything. If you did, why would you need the rest of us?"

The banquet that night was even more elaborate than the one welcoming Catherine and Edgar. They started with lettuce wrapped around pieces of trout and went on to rabbit pie with ginger and cloves, cold mutton, a soup of dried apples and figs, and then an array of cheeses and sweets. Catherine was glad that James and Beron weren't serving. The sugared violets alone would have been an irresistible temptation.

Beside her, Edgar only picked at the food.

"Are you still angry with me?" she asked. "If I had thought there was any danger, I wouldn't have gone."

"Yes, you would; I know you better than that." He put his arm around her. "I wasn't as angry as I was worried. Catherine, I can't lose you."

That shamed her more than a thousand reprimands.

"I'm sorry, Edgar," she said, suddenly wishing that they didn't have such a long, public evening ahead.

The musicians had been playing from the balcony all through dinner, but now they descended. As the trenchers were taken up and the hand washing bowls brought around, a group of players came in. They set up a small platform, with a wobbly painted tree stuck in it.

Edgar gave a low moan. "By the Magdalene's bangles! Not theater!"

The players finished their preparations and the leader signaled the trumpeter, who gave a sharp blast that caused the dogs to howl and all the diners to fall silent.

Senor, Dame, oyez cancon qui molt fait a loer
par itel convenent le vos puis je conter,
I tell you no lies, each word I do swear, sir
Is as true as the Gospel, the book we all treasure
The tale of a lost knight who did take his leisure
By a spring where a fairy did come for her pleasure . . .

"It's the story of Andonenn!" Catherine said in surprise.

"So it is," Edgar said. "Well, Guillaume told us there was one."

"It's not very good," Catherine commented. "The rhyming is very weak."

"No one else seems to have noticed," Edgar said.

It was true. All the others were listening raptly, except Agnes's husband, Hermann, who didn't understand the words. Some people were reciting along with the *jongleur*. Even Guillaume apparently knew bits of the poem.

"The story seems much as we were told," Edgar whispered after a while.

They had finished the meeting of the knight Jurvale and Andonenn and their happy marriage. Two of the players managed to portray all the characters in dumb show on signals from the singer. They had arrived at the point where Empress Judith tries to curse Andonenn's children. The actor playing Andonenn was wrapped in a blue mantle that they used for the Virgin in Nativity plays. This was not an accident.

Andonenn raised her hand in benediction over the assembly before her as the *jongleur* recited.

"La gentil dame Andonenn, qui fus moult preus et sage
courtoise et bele, brave and fair of face
Did bless her posterity to live in grace
That the evil empress should have disgrace
And Boisvert be safe in any case
As long as the spring flows within the place.

There was a collective sigh among the listeners. Catherine realized that every one of them believed in Andonenn, just as they did in Christ. Perhaps even more for she was their particular savior. Catherine suspected they would say it was no different than trusting in a patron saint, but the saints were merely intercessors with God. Andonenn's power was outside Christianity.

She noticed that the priest, Ysore, seemed just as content with the story as the others. Perhaps he believed Andonenn was somehow within the faith.

The tale came to an end with Andonenn's blessing. Gargenaud was helped to his feet as the players and musicians approached the table.

"Marvelous!" he told them. "Your best performance yet. We shall expect you here next year!" He took a silver chain from around his neck. "A small gift of thanks. My bailiff will see that you receive the usual rewards, as well."

They thanked him effusively and departed. Catherine was preparing to depart as well when Gargenaud made another announcement.

"At last all of Andonenn's children have come together to help her in our darkest hour," he said. "The time has come to open the casket that Richard, our father, left for such a time. It has been passed down unopened to the eldest child for three hundred years. Seguin, will you fetch it, please."

Seguin left the hall and returned with his cousin Odilon. Between them they carried a brass trunk. They set it on the platform the entertainers had used.

"Open it," Gargenaud commanded, handing Seguin a brass key.

"Jurvale's box is inside," Seguin explained.

He turned the key. It grated in the rusty lock. Everyone craned forward to see. At last the lid creaked open. Seguin reached in.

"My God!" he exclaimed. "How can this be? Who could have done this?"

"What is it?" a dozen voices called out.

Seguin took the box out of its container. It was small, only the height and depth of two hands outspread. The wood was black with age and the silver hinges tarnished almost the same color. But everyone saw the gash where the lock had been broken.

With trembling hands, Seguin opened the ancient box.

It was empty.

In the ensuing pandemonium, Catherine slipped out. Everyone else needed to touch the box, examine it for themselves. Some were weeping and others shouting. She had to get someplace quiet to reassemble the event in her mind. How had someone managed to open the brass trunk when Gargenaud kept the key around his neck? Most importantly, what would this do to the cult of Andonenn? With the treasure gone, how could she be saved?

Perhaps these thoughts directed her to search for divine counsel. Without noticing how, Catherine found herself at the chapel.

She paused at the door to take a candle from the basket on the floor and light it from the oil lamp. It was then that she heard the keening, a high wail that pierced the thick wood.

Someone else had sought refuge here. Catherine hesitated. A chill ran through her. What if it was a very old ancestor, bemoaning their impending doom?

Perhaps she shouldn't disturb them.

"Shame on you!" said a voice in her mind. "That poor soul needs comfort. Go in and pray with whoever it is."

Although it wasn't her original intention, praying didn't seem a bad idea. Catherine pushed the door open.

There, kneeling on the floor was a thin old woman. Her blond hair was shot through with silver and her skin lined. Her face was distorted by tears and blood.

Catherine stared in horror. In the woman's hand was a long

knife with a bone handle. The blade was still dripping blood. Before her lay a body. Catherine knew him instantly. It was the man who had chastised her this afternoon, her cousin Raimbaut, Seguin's firstborn.

She stepped toward the woman with some intention of getting the knife out of her hand. As she did, the woman looked up at her. Catherine gasped. It was impossible. How had she become so old? And how had she come to this?

"Oh, sweet baby Jesus, Mother," Catherine wept. "What have you done?"

Eleven

Boisvert, sometime after midnight. Sunday, pridie nones September (September 4) 1149. Trinity Sunday. Feast of Saint Moses, lawgiver and prophet, 1585 years before Jesus Christ. 22 Elul 4909. Not a feast of Moses in the Jewish calendar.

Onc n'est nus clers, tant soit enlatinés
Qui sache dire se puis fu retornés,
Ne se il est ou vu ou trespassés.
Dieu en ait l'ame! S'il est mort, c'est pités.

There are no clerks, who may have much Latin
Who know to say if he then went back,
Nor if he is seen or come across.
God has his soul! If he is dead, then it is a great shame.

—Chevalier Ogier

*W*hy was no one watching her?" Odilon demanded. "We all know she's mad."

He had somehow become the person in authority. Seguin and Elissent were too stunned by the murder of their son to take command. Aymon had taken one look at his brother's body and gagged. He had managed to get out of the chapel before throwing up into the rushes. No one had seen him since.

"There was no need to guard her every minute," Guillaume answered. "She's never been dangerous to anyone but herself."

"That's right," Agnes said. "The nuns say she's very gentle."

"I agree," Margaret added. "All the time I spent with her, she was completely docile. No one could have known she'd become violent."

"Of course not." Catherine couldn't believe what they were saying. "Because she didn't. How can you even think our mother would kill someone?"

Odilon rounded on her. "You found her, yourself, holding the knife. Raimbaut's body was still warm. What else should we think?"

"Any number of things!" Catherine shot back.

The problem was that she couldn't come up with any. All her mind could hold was the image of her mother kneeling in all that blood.

They had all convened in a solar room and sent the servants away. Gargenaud had been put to bed protesting that he wanted to know what was going on; he was the lord here, after all. His silent wife, Briaud, followed after him uttering soothing promises.

Odilon sat in the high-backed chair. His brother, Father Ysore, stood next to him, nervously fumbling at the silver cross hanging from his neck. Guillaume, Marie, Agnes, Hermann, Catherine, Edgar, and Margaret had fitted themselves in as best they could on stools or leaning against the wall.

Catherine couldn't stop the tears. They just appeared in her eyes and slid down her face. Her nose was running, too. Of course she had no handkerchief and she didn't dare use the sleeve of Agnes's silk *bliaut* as one.

"Here, use mine." Edgar waved his left sleeve in front of her face. She quickly wiped her face and nose.

"Now, let's work this through." Odilon drummed his fingers angrily on the arm of the chair.

"This horrible murder proves that the curse is gaining power," he announced. "No one has ever died within these walls. Not for hundreds of years. We can't blame poor, deluded Madeleine for her crime. She is obviously under the influence of some evil force."

Edgar had had enough.

"You can't blame her, because she didn't kill the man," he said firmly.

"What are you talking about?" Odilon sneered. "She was found by your own wife."

"Catherine saw her mother next to Raimbaut's body," Edgar said. "Holding a knife. That doesn't mean Madeleine killed him."

His calm common sense washed over Catherine like a salve. She gave one last sniff into Edgar's sleeve and stood.

"He's right," she said. "Mother is half the size of Raimbaut. He was attacked from the front. The knife pierced his heart. How could she have had the strength to do that?"

"Satan can pour his power into the weakest of vessels," Ysore objected. "And he can make them seem greater than they are. Raimbaut may have thought a wild beast or a monster was upon him."

"Then why did he make no effort to fight back?" Catherine asked. "I saw him. His hands were uncut. His clothing unmarked except by his blood."

"Perhaps it was a more enticing form then," Odilon suggested. "That would speak to all your objections."

Agnes had been sitting numbly, holding Hermann's hand like a lifeline. Now she came to life.

"Wait," she said. "Are you saying that Mother became a seductress and lured Raimbaut into the chapel to slaughter him? That's preposterous. And do you then believe that she also opened that box of yours and stole whatever was inside it? How could she have even found it, or taken the key? Maybe you think that two demons infiltrated the castle? Perhaps an army of them, all shape-shifters."

"Good for you, Agnes," Catherine said. "Even under the influence of the Devil, I don't see how Mother could have opened the boxes without being seen. And, if you say that it was sorcery, then there's no reason that any of us couldn't have been influenced as well. You could have done it yourself, Odilon, and not even know it."

"Nonsense!" he roared. "It's well known that Satan chooses the weakest among us, those who can't resist his wiles. Of course it was Madeleine."

There was something wrong with that logic. Catherine tried to reason out the flaw.

Edgar had been puzzling over something else. "Where did she get the knife? And where is it now?"

"I have it," Guillaume said. "I wrapped it in my cloak and brought it with me. I didn't want the children to find it."

He looked around for a place to set it. Catherine stood and pushed the stool she had been sitting on to the center of the room. Guillaume laid the dark cloak on it and uncovered the knife.

It had a long blade, thin from many sharpenings. The bloodstains had mostly rubbed off onto the material and the metal shone as if newly polished. The handle was of horn, knobbly and scratched.

"Does anyone know who this belongs to?" Guillaume asked.

They all shook their heads.

"It looks like a skinning knife," Odilon said. "But the blade is finer than any I've seen. No one here has one like it."

"What are those odd marks?" Agnes asked. "They look almost like letters."

"Let me see." Catherine squatted next to the stool and peered at the knife handle.

"K . . . A . . . R," she made out. "Then maybe *mirg abun*. It doesn't make any sense to me."

She turned it to the other side, but the blood was caked so thickly that she didn't have the stomach to clean it enough to read.

"Some devil's tongue, no doubt," Ysore surmised. "Perhaps Hebrew."

"No," Margaret spoke up at once. "I've been studying Hebrew for some time and the letters aren't right, nor are the words."

Ysore shrugged. "Saracen then."

"It's odd," Guillaume said, looking over Catherine's shoulder. "The handle looks ancient and yet the blade must be newly made. It shows no rust at all. Who would put a fine knife like that onto a scarred old hilt?"

"Well, unless you'd rather believe that this was forged in hell and only appeared here tonight," Edgar said. "I think our first duty is to find out who owns it and where they were when Raimbaut was killed."

"That sounds very well," Odilon said. "But who will admit to being the owner? And as for where, all of us at least were in the hall together. Everything you propose still leads back to poor Madeleine."

"Shouldn't we be trying to find out what was in the box?" Catherine asked. "Or do you already know? Wasn't it supposed to be something that will break this curse?"

"Yes," Odilon said. "That's the story Seguin told me. No one has ever opened it, to my knowledge, and there's nothing in the legend that even hints at what the contents were."

"Is there a reason why anyone would want to steal it?" Edgar asked. "Wasn't there a treasure somewhere in the story?"

"Yes, but Andonenn guards that." Odilon dismissed the idea. "Richard's legacy was to save us, not find a horde of gold."

Edgar scanned the faces of the others. All of them showed agreement with Odilon's statements.

"Then what should we do?" he asked them all.

No one answered. They all looked at each other, waiting for someone to take the lead. Even Odilon had no more to say. Finally, Agnes got up, pushing at a crick in her back.

"I intend to go to the nursery and check on my son," she announced. "If he is safe and well, then I'm going to see what comfort I can give my frightened and confused mother. After that, I shall be in the chapel, praying for the soul of my cousin Raimbaut."

She beckoned for Hermann to come with her. He rose at once, his normally cheerful face grave as Agnes explained in German the gist of the outcome of the meeting.

"Perhaps I should go with her," Margaret said. "I'm really the only one Madeleine is familiar with. If you will permit me?"

She addressed this to Odilon, but her eyes flickered to Edgar and he gave a slight nod.

When she had gone, Marie gave a sigh that became a yawn. "I'll leave it to the rest of you to uncover the hows and whys. Someone must see that your cousin's body is prepared for burial. Father Ysore, can you do a funeral Mass? I have the impression that you haven't had many opportunities."

"I have a missal," Ysore said. "I need to have the priest from the village to assist me. We should be able to arrange to say Mass in the church there just after Tierce."

"Why not our own chapel?" Odilon asked.

"Because we have to clean and purify it after the spilling of blood." Ysore spoke to his brother as to an ignorant child. "Everyone knows that."

"I don't think it's good to go outside the castle," Odilon said. "The knowledge that there has been a death here will unnerve the villagers and a murder even more so."

"You can't avoid that, cousin," Guillaume spoke up. He, too, was fighting sleep. A late night, a heavy meal, and undiluted wine could not be overcome even by the shock of violent death.

"True," Catherine agreed. "They'll all know what happened as soon as the first cock crows. And we should not let our fear keep us from honoring Raimbaut with public worship. If so, then Satan does indeed have a hold upon us."

Grudgingly, Odilon agreed.

Catherine and Edgar also stopped by the nursery on the way to bed. Catherine's candle revealed Edana and James tucked snugly between Samonie and the wall, with Peter's small cot next to them. Samonie stirred and lifted her head.

"There was a lot of noise a while ago," she whispered. "Everything all right?"

"Nothing to fret about tonight," Catherine said.

Samonie nodded, checked Peter's covers, and fell back to sleep.

Catherine put her arm around Edgar's waist as they found the passage back to their own bed.

"Thank you for defending Mother," she whispered. "You do think she's innocent, don't you?"

"I think it's far too convenient to be able to blame her," Edgar answered. "In my experience, the Devil doesn't need to be so obvious as to work through a frail woman."

"Of course." Catherine stopped. "That's what was wrong with Odilon's theory. Mother's body is weak and yes, her mind isn't very hardy either, but that isn't what one needs to fight Satan. It's faith. Mother is the most devout person I've ever known. Even when I was a child, we had family prayers twice a day. We never passed a church or a shrine without making an offering. I can think of no way she could be tempted or tricked into aiding Lucifer."

Edgar started her walking again while he examined her conclusion.

"I think you're right," he said at last. "Also, making us think that the murderer is someone too weak to defend herself is just the sort of clever nastiness that evil delights in."

"So we'll do what we can to catch the real villain, won't we?" Catherine leaned against him, her startling blue eyes pleading.

"Not if it puts the rest of us in danger," he answered, looking away to avoid temptation. "That means you and Margaret as well as the children."

Catherine bit her lip. "I don't think we are in physical danger, despite all warnings," she said. "Not if Raimbaut was killed by a living person rather than a dead woman's anathema. Raimbaut was the heir after Seguin. We are strangers here, and no threat. We have no claim on Boisvert."

"But it doesn't appear that Gargenaud is about to die anytime soon," Edgar pointed out. "I'd have made sure of his death before risking such a blatant murder. And after him, Seguin still lives and may last as long as his grandfather has. You don't think Aymon or Odilon killed Raimbaut to place themselves closer to inheriting?"

"I suppose not," Catherine said. "You're right. It would make more sense to get rid of Seguin or Grandfather himself. So why is Raimbaut dead?"

"That is what I intend to find out." Edgar kissed her on the nose. "But not until I've slept. Agreed?"

"Willingly," Catherine said. "Just help me out of these outlandish clothes and into my bed."

"Willingly."

The town of Blois had the usual array of churches and monasteries. Solomon was used to the sound of bells at all hours and had no trouble sleeping through it. So he was more than annoyed to be awakened early Sunday morning by something ringing directly under his window.

He wrapped the sheet around his waist and stumbled over to stick his head out.

"Stop that racket!" he shouted.

The ringing ceased at once. He started to go back to bed when his name was called.

"Solomon of Paris! You up there!" It was a woman's voice, cracked with age.

Solomon went back and squinted at the bell ringer.

It was Berthe. She grinned up at him with blackened teeth.

"I need your help!" she called. "Pull on your *brais* and let me in. This isn't news for the gossips to hear."

Blearily, Solomon came downstairs, wondering where Menachem and his wife had got to. He opened the door and Berthe rushed in, carrying a large cowbell. She glanced at him in disappointment.

"I didn't say, put on your tunic, too," she lamented. "I like to see a nice solid, hairy chest on a man."

"Sorry," Solomon told her. "What is it you want from me?"

"What? Am I not a guest? Have you no drink to offer?" She sat on a bench next to the cold hearth and waited.

Grumbling under his breath, Solomon went to the cask and drew cups of beer for both of them. He handed Berthe hers and watched while she drained it and held the cup out for more.

"Not until I know why you're here," he said. "How do you even know my name?"

"Mandon from the castle told me," Berthe said. "She was here last night. Things are going bad up there. You need to get back to succor your kin."

"I have no kin at a castle." Solomon's eyes narrowed.

"Of course you do." Berthe waved the cup under his nose. "But that's nothing to me. It's them at Boisvert I care for. We've got to leave at once. You have a horse?"

"Yes, but . . ."

"Good. My bag is ready." She set the bowl down on the bench with a reproachful sigh. "You get the beast and meet me just outside the gate on the road to Chartres."

"Look, I'm not going to Boisvert." Solomon tried to keep her from leaving. "I have business here and I'm not welcome there."

Berthe pushed him and his protests aside.

"They don't want me there, either," she said. "And I've got herbs to tend to and chickens to feed. But that's no matter. This is duty. Now, go get your things. I'll be waiting."

With that she was gone.

Solomon stared at the empty cup and his own, half full. He drank the beer and started back upstairs. The woman must be cracked. And yet, she knew his name and that he had family at Boisvert. Who had told her? Had Catherine or Edgar sent a message through one of the servants there? It didn't seem likely. Blast it! He had been having such a nice dream.

He had finished dressing when Menachem and his wife returned.

"Where did you go so early?" Solomon asked them. "What's wrong?"

"It's that Lord Olivier, may he be cursed to damnation," Menachem answered. "He's on his way to lay siege to Boisvert. He's learned that Count Henry is on his way home from the Holy Land and he wants to take the castle before the count can raise an army to stop him."

"But you told me that Boisvert can't be taken by siege." Solomon couldn't understand why his friend was so upset.

"It can't," Menachem said. "Everyone knows that. It's the safest place to be. But Olivier will come through Blois to get there. You know what that means."

Solomon did. The first thing any would-be conqueror did was to scour the land around to find provisions for his men and horses and then to destroy anything that might be of use to his enemy.

"I told you the omens were bad, didn't I?" Menachem said. "I'm taking my family to Pucellina's mother in Troyes until this is over. You can come with us if you like."

"Thank you, no," Solomon said. "I have to leave anyway."

"If you're going back to Paris, would you take Abraham his share of the profits from the wine sales?" Menachem asked.

"No, I'm not going back right away. It might be better to find someone else."

Solomon filled his saddlebags, adding a round of Pucellina's cheese and some of her dried fish. For all he knew, the people at Boisvert would have nothing but pork to eat.

Catherine woke Sunday with a fierce headache and the fervent wish that the day before had been a nightmare. She rolled over. Edgar was gone. Instead, Samonie was bending over her.

"Hurry, Mistress," she said. "You need to get dressed for Mass."

"Oh, Lord, Samonie," Catherine moaned. "I can't even lift my head. I must have drunk a vat last night."

"Then it's time for penance," Samonie said, not without sympathy. "I'll get a cool compress for you to hold to your face. You can pretend you're weeping."

"What's the news?" Catherine asked as she gingerly climbed from the bed. "How is my mother?"

"Doing better than any, I'd say," Samonie said. "She seems to think she had a vision of some martyr, Saint Maur, perhaps. She asked Lady Margaret if he had left any blood as a relic."

"Poor Mother!" Catherine said. "Poor Margaret. And Raimbaut's family, how are they?"

"That I don't know." Samonie helped Catherine with her shift. "From what the kitchen folk say, they're more horrified by any death in the place than they are at losing their son."

"Grief takes people in different ways," Catherine said. "Will they be well enough to come to the Mass, do you think?"

"Lady Elissent won't," Samonie was certain. "She's in her bed sobbing like a proper mother. They gave her a sleeping draught, but it's done nothing. Seguin might pull himself together to come down. I don't know if anyone's bothered to inform the old man.

And no one's seen Aymon since last night. That's suspicious. Think there might have been a bit of Cain and Abel there?"

Catherine had put on a dull-colored *bliaut* suitable for a sad occasion. She handed Samonie the comb to do her hair. Samonie hummed as she worked.

"You seem extremely cheerful considering there's been a murder here," Catherine commented. "Does he have a name?"

The humming stopped. "Mistress," Samonie said. "I'm so sorry! How disrespectful to the poor dead man! I don't know what I could have been thinking of!"

"Samonie," Catherine said. "I've known you a long time. You have served us faithfully, giving up the chance for a better life. I don't begrudge you a bit of pleasure, as long as it's not with a murderer."

Samonie crossed herself, dropping the comb. It stuck in Catherine's hair.

"Never fear, this is no stranger, but a friend from long ago," Samonie told her. "Long before I met you."

She sighed.

"What is it?" Catherine asked.

Samonie resumed combing. "It's silly, I suppose. It's only that he's getting old. That must mean that I am, too. Odd how I can ignore the years until I see someone I knew as a girl and realize how they've aged."

"Nonsense!" Catherine said. "You're not much older than I am and I refuse to think of myself as decrepit. We're only affected by Raimbaut's death and the ancient walls around us. Everything will be fine once we're back in Paris."

"Yes, I'm sure you're right," Samonie said wistfully. "It's strange, though. I think I like him better now that time has marked him."

After that they were silent, each considering her own mortality and the random way death had intruded again into their lives.

The small parish church in the village was crammed. No one could remember a death at the castle; it was rare enough among the villagers and peasants. They all believed that Andonenn's blessing fell on them, too. Seguin's men-at-arms did their best to keep people back so that the family could enter, but the villagers knew their rights. This was their church, not the lord's and they demanded to be allowed in.

Catherine and Edgar made their way through the crowd slowly, keeping Margaret between them. Ahead, Guillaume strode with the arrogance that knows people will make way. For once, Catherine was grateful.

Raimbaut's relatives were clustered at the right side of the altar. The church was too small to have railings or a rood screen, so someone had brought a folding screen from the castle to shield them from inquisitive eyes.

Seguin was there, looking pale as a corpse himself. Odilon stood next to him. The rest of the family was represented by Madeleine's children and their spouses. If anyone thought it was strange that the mother of the mourners was thought to be the killer, no one mentioned it. Catherine adjusted her veil to keep her face hidden. She saw Ysore, assisted by the parish priest, getting ready for the Mass. There was a row of knights and soldiers across the front and a number of castle servants along with more important villagers just behind them.

But where was Aymon?

Catherine searched the faces of those in the church, wondering if he had come in but been unable to join them. Under cover of the general chatter, she asked Margaret.

"He hasn't been seen," she told Catherine. "Seguin is half-furious that he's run off and half-afraid that someone has attacked him, too."

"I hadn't thought of that," Catherine said. She told Margaret about Samonie's theory that Aymon had killed his brother. "Do you remember if he was at the table all through dinner and the entertainment?"

"No," Margaret said. "People came and went all the time. It was a long evening."

"I think he needs to be found before we start accusing him," Edgar said. "He may have been attacked, as well."

Catherine gave a start. "I never thought of that! How awful! He may be lying someplace hurt or . . ."

"Hush!" Margaret warned her as people turned to stare. "First, we should pray."

Catherine subsided until the end of the Mass, but her mind was not on the soul of the departed.

Samonie and Martin were waiting for them outside the chapel.

"We couldn't get in," Martin told them. "But we gave the responses as best we could from here."

"My mother always said that God hears us wherever we stand," Catherine said. *And sees us no matter in what dark place we sin,* she added to herself. Madeleine's faith had been all-encompassing.

"Gargenaud's wife is with Raimbaut's mother," Samonie said. "One of the women told me that Elissent keeps calling for Aymon. Was he at Mass?"

They all shook their heads.

"If he's gone into that tangle of corridors underneath the keep." Guillaume had overheard them as he passed; "there'll be no finding him this side of the Last Judgment."

"How do you know about the tunnels?" Catherine asked.

"I was fostered here, remember?" he answered. "Raimbaut, Odilon, Brehier, and I played hide-and-find down there all winter. And had our hides tanned many a time for going too far and having to be fetched out."

"What about Aymon?" Edgar asked.

"He was too little when I was here," Guillaume said. "But no doubt he took his turn later."

The rest of them began to organize a search of the underground tunnels. Samonie fell behind. No one would ask her opinion. She had heard nothing after Brehier's name, in any case. Could Guillaume have meant her Brehier? Was that why he was at Boisvert now, because he'd been raised here?

Well, what of it? This was a logical place for a knight of Count Thibault to train. The lords of Boisvert were his vassals. Brehier had never told her where he came from. They hadn't talked much at all in their early meetings. She had never thought to ask, since she hadn't expected to ever see him again.

She'd been fooled once before, by a man who'd wormed his way into her bed in order to bring ruin to Catherine and Edgar. She would never forgive herself for that. Brehier might want nothing more than her company, but she would now be on guard for any sign of mischief on his part.

Of course James wanted to go with the party when he saw them gather to search the tunnels. Edgar explained to him that, of his cousins, only Gervase, the oldest, was allowed to accompany the men. James was not appeased. He set his jaw in a remarkable imitation of his father's stubborn face and retired to the nursery to pout.

"Keep an eye on him," Edgar warned Catherine. "He's as willful as you are."

Catherine laughed. "Worse. He's as determined as you. Be careful down there. I wish I were going, too. At least it's cool."

The day was the hottest of the summer, without a cloud to conceal the earth from the eye of the sun. Catherine and Margaret took the children up to the women's solar, where they could remove the heavy *bliauts* and wear only their loose shifts.

After a while Agnes joined them, carrying her infant son and followed by the wet nurse, carrying a blanket and bag of provisions.

"Hermann has gone with the other men," she announced. "Edgar remembers enough German to tell him what's happening. I've been to see Mother. She's sleeping for now."

The two women laid out the blanket and unwrapped the baby from his swaddling, then proceeded to oil him all over before setting him down to air.

"Now, you children watch where you're playing," Agnes warned the cousins. "Stay away from this corner. Anyone bothers my precious Gottfried and you'll be eating standing up for a week."

None of the children seemed particularly terrified by this, particularly since Agnes followed the threat by giving each of them a honey stick from her bag.

For a few moments they all simply sat listening to the gurgle of the baby and the slurping as the children sucked on the sweets. The heat pulled out all energy, even that needed to think.

Some part of Catherine's mind was still working, however, and was trying hard to get her attention.

What had happened the night before?

They had all been crowded into the hall, everyone hot, greasy, and too full of wine. The brass chest had been opened with Gargenaud's key and the box inside found with the lock broken and nothing inside. Then someone had screamed and they had all rushed off. Was that the order?

"Agnes," she asked, "what happened to the box?"

"What box?" Agnes yawned.

"Richard's," Catherine said. "The one that held the secret of our redemption. The one that we had to wait to open until the whole family was present. The one that someone else had smashed open anyway. Where did it go?"

"I don't know," Agnes said. "Marie?"

"It must have been cleared up with all the tables and such last night," Marie answered.

Catherine sat up straight. "You mean this sacred family relic was just carted off to a storeroom by the servants?"

Marie shrugged. "Why not? The treasure was gone."

"Don't you want to know where?" Catherine was waking up. "Who took it? What was it? What will happen to us all if it's not found?"

"What do you mean?" Agnes looked up from where she was playing with the baby.

"Well, the whole point of the thing was that Richard left it to be opened in our greatest need," Catherine explained. "The well is drying up and death has entered the keep. Even I can see things are dire. So, is no one interested in finding this thing that is supposed to save us?"

Marie was quiet for a moment.

"I suppose the murder drove it from our thoughts," she said. "Mine, at least. Perhaps Seguin thinks that when Aymon is found, he will have it."

"If Aymon still lives," Agnes added.

They all nodded solemnly.

"Well, I don't see that there's anything we can do," Marie said.

Catherine was trying to form a plan when, suddenly, Margaret spoke up.

"I think we should have a look at that knife."

They all stared at her. Then Catherine got up. She went to the wall where her *bliaut* hung from a hook and reluctantly pulled it over her head.

"Margaret is quite right," she said. "Will you keep guard over my children while she and I go and do so?"

"Do you even know where it is?" Agnes asked.

"Guillaume has it," Catherine said. "I want a good look at it. It's time we stopped letting a legend control our lives."

Twelve

That same afternoon; the road from Blois to Boisvert.

Beau sire Dieus, dist Charles, donne-moi du jour tant
Que me puisse vengier du domaige pesant!

Great lord God, said Charles, give me just one day
That I may avenge this heavy crime!

—*Roman de Galien*

"*W*ould you mind moving your arms a bit higher?"
Solomon asked Berthe.

She was riding pillion behind him, gripping him around the
waist for dear life. Solomon found the way she kept twiddling her
fingers very unnerving.

She chuckled. "You wouldn't begrudge an old woman a bit of
fun, would you?"

He reached down and moved her hands. "Yes, I would."

"Just close your eyes and pretend I'm young and beautiful,"
she suggested.

"I don't have to," he answered. "You're in back of me. I
thought you wanted to be at Boisvert as soon as possible."

He felt her shrug. "I do. I was just passing the time. This is a tedious ride."

"If you must pass the time," Solomon said, "you can tell me what your interest is in the people at Boisvert. Do you have family in the village?"

"Don't you really want to hear what I know about the family you have there?" Her hands tightened again, digging into his stomach.

"I told you, the only connection I have there is my partner and his family," he said. "The only reason I agreed to go with you was to warn them of the army coming to attack."

"That's right," Berthe said. "You're a good friend to them. You and Edgar are renowned among the traders. A Christian and a Jew, English and French, fair as an angel and dark as Satan. Everyone knows you."

"How flattering." Solomon's voice was sour.

"So it is," she answered. "Some wonder about it, but I know this Edgar married your cousin, the daughter of Hubert of Rouen. I remember when Hubert first came to Boisvert. Old Gargenaud knew what he was, but he smelled the money and a way to get his youngest daughter away from the castle. He knew even then that the curse was getting stronger. I remember your father, too."

Solomon stiffened. Berthe laughed.

"He came with Hubert once. Nice-looking man, but acted as if he was about to be crucified. Haven't seen him for years. I heard he turned monk."

Solomon didn't answer.

"Ah, must be true then, or you'd be quick enough to deny it," she concluded. "Is he still in the monastery?"

"My father is dead," Solomon said in a tone that threatened violence if she mentioned him again. "Now, you haven't told me why you want to go to Boisvert."

"I didn't, did I?" she said. "Ah, well, I've a niece in service there. I'm a bit worried about her. She's been poorly lately."

"Of course." Solomon didn't believe her. "You have a reputation of your own . . . for cures."

"And other things," she cackled. "Can't you make this horse
move any faster?"

"Not if you want to keep your seat," he answered.

She loosed one hand to give him a slap on the back.

"Don't you worry about me," she said. "Let's just get there."

He urged the horse to a quick trot. Against his back, he felt
Berthe joggling up and down, but the old woman made no com-
plaint.

Solomon hoped that he could be rid of her before anyone he
knew saw him.

The small chapel was empty except for the stone altar and fresh
straw on the floor with flowers strewn over it to eliminate the
smell of death. The attempt hadn't worked.

Catherine and Margaret knelt and crossed themselves, murmuring a quick Ave Maria. Then Catherine took the candle from
next to the door and used it to light three more along the wall.

"Now," she told Margaret. "Let's have a look."

Margaret unrolled Guillaume's cloak to reveal the stained
knife.

"Catherine," she asked. "Why did we take it here to examine?"

"If we went out in the sunshine, everyone would want to see,
too," Catherine answered. "And also, if there is something evil in
it, then we have more chance of fighting it in here."

"That makes sense," Margaret admitted. "But it didn't protect Raimbaut, did it?"

"Trust you to find the flaw in my logic," Catherine sighed.
"Now, the letters engraved on the shaft made no sense, but I
thought there were also some on the hilt. Can you make anything of it?"

Margaret wrapped her sleeve around the blade and held the
handle up to the candlelight.

"I see a K . . . A . . . something worn . . . then OLUS," She squinted, tilting the knife. "This has been well used. The next letter is an M, maybe. See what you can make out."

Catherine took the knife gingerly. "You're right," she said. "This isn't a ceremonial knife. No jewels or silver inlay. It looks like the sort you'd find in a kitchen."

"Wonderful," Margaret said. "That means anyone in the household could have taken it."

"Yes, probably." Catherine was still studying the carving. "I can't make out the letters after the M, the next part is DEDIT."

"It's in Latin?" Margaret asked in surprise. "'Dedit' means 'Gave.' So it reads KA something, OLUS M, something DEDIT."

She and Catherine looked at each other and spoke at the same time.

"Karolus mei dedit!"

"Charles gave me!"

"That's not grammatical," Catherine commented. "But maybe there wasn't any more room on the handle."

"Charles is not that common a name anymore," Margaret said carefully. "Of course, this does look very old. You don't think it was a gift from the Emperor Charles, do you?"

"I don't know." Catherine turned it over. "You'd think there would be an IMP after Karolus. And it is very plain. It could be that the maker just learned the letters and did the carving to pass the time."

"I don't suppose there's a Charles living here at Boisvert," Margaret said.

"I don't think so," Catherine said. "But, if it belonged to one of the people living here, you'd think someone would have recognized the knife."

"Yes," Margaret nodded. "And the same if it belonged to the kitchens. It seems odd that no one has recognized it."

"Perhaps it was brought in," Catherine said. "Brought especially to kill Raimbaut with."

Margaret didn't like that line of inquiry. "You mean by one of us? Or your mother?"

"Of course not!" Catherine was shocked. "But anyone living here could have bought it from a peddler or at a stand in Chartres or Blois."

She held the handle and examined the blade.

"It's newly sharpened," she said, wincing as a line of blood appeared on her thumb.

Margaret shrank back from the glistening metal.

"To make it sharp enough to kill?" she asked, her voice shaking.

Catherine sighed. "Probably."

She studied the blade further, now at the hilt, where the iron had been inserted into the wood.

"You know," she said slowly, "I don't think all of this stain is blood." She scraped a bit with her finger. "This seems like rust."

She thought a moment. "Margaret," she said. "I have a suspicion. We need to find what happened to that treasure chest. I want to check something."

The hall was in chaos. Edgar found his brother-in-law in the middle of a shouting match among five or six of the men-at-arms, Seguin, and, oddly, the priest, Ysore.

"If Aymon's gone to ground, we'll never find him!" Guillaume growled. "No one knows where all the tunnels lead."

"But he may be hurt!" Seguin's face was taut with shock and grief.

"Or he may be hiding." Ysore's words cut into the noise.

Seguin whipped around to challenge him. "My son had nothing to do with his brother's death! He loved Raimbaut."

Guillaume stepped between the two men before Seguin lost his temper enough to strike a member of the clergy.

"If he's hiding, it may not be from justice, but from the murderer," he suggested.

Seguin liked that idea even less.

"Are you saying my son is a coward?" He whirled about to face Guillaume.

Edgar moved into the circle. "Guillaume is only saying that we don't know," he told Seguin. "But we won't unless we find Aymon. Could he have left the keep without anyone noticing?"

Seguin shook his head. "His horse is still here and his dog. He wouldn't go without them."

"Then we'll have to try the tunnels," Edgar concluded. "I have never seen them, but I'll help in the search if you need me. I like Aymon. I don't want to think of him lying in the dark, hurt and unable to reach us."

"Very well then," Seguin said. "Who will come with us?"

"Who knows the tunnels?" Ysore asked.

Seguin scanned the faces around him. "Guillaume, you spent enough time down there. Ysore, don't tell me you didn't. Anyone else?"

One or two of the men raised their hands.

"Where's Brehier?" Ysore asked. "He and Raimbaut were always leading me down there and then running off until I got lost and cried for help. He should be one of the guides."

Seguin pointed at two of the younger men.

"Go. Find him and bring him back with you now."

Edgar took advantage of the lull to draw Guillaume aside.

"How do you feel about this?" he asked quietly. "Especially with your wife and children here."

"I've been meaning to bring Gervase here for a long time," Guillaume answered. "He should know that my family isn't only lowborn traders. It wouldn't hurt the others to learn about the place, as well."

"But there's a murderer loose," Edgar reminded him.

"That should be nothing new for you," Guillaume retorted. "I've put a guard on Marie and the children. Yours, too. I'm not a fool."

"Of course not," Edgar said quickly. "Far from it. But all this about fairies and river nymphs, I don't know how to take it."

"Andonenn is the guardian of the spring," Guillaume said. "And of our family. I don't worry about what else to call her."

"No," Edgar thought. "I suppose you don't. It must make life much easier for you."

The men soon came back with Brehier, who was fastening his belt as he followed them down the stairs. Guillaume snorted.

"You haven't changed," he said.

Brehier glared at him. "I was in the privy," he explained. "So you think that Aymon is below the castle?"

"Yes, can you think of any place he'd make for?" Seguin asked.

Brehier twisted his mouth in an effort to think. "There are a couple of corners that he always chose when we were playing hide-and-find. And didn't he have some sort of cave where he kept his secret treasures so his parents wouldn't find them?"

"Yes," Guillaume said. "I'd forgotten that. I don't know if I could find it again, could you?"

"I think so," Brehier answered. "At least I remember the general direction. Do you want me to go now?"

"Yes," Seguin said. "Take Edgar here and someone else to run back if you get into trouble. Guillaume, you take a couple of men and search in another section. Aymon may have found a new place to hide since you were children."

He stopped and scratched at his beard. "I always wondered how he disappeared so thoroughly when there was work to be done."

Seguin continued giving orders, some of them twice. Edgar recognized the signs of a man who was doing anything to avoid having to think about what was happening. He went over and introduced himself to Brehier.

"I imagine Seguin doesn't think I'm of much use." He held up his arm. "But my apprentice, Martin, has proved himself both agile and intelligent. Martin!"

He waved the boy over.

Martin came at once, his face alight with excitement.

"Lord Brehier and I have been asked to seek out Aymon in the passages below the castle," Edgar explained. "I need you to come with us and mark the way. If we have any trouble you'll need to come back for help."

"Yes, Master," Martin bobbed his head. "Should I bring a cudgel? Will there be monsters?"

Edgar laughed. "You sound like James. I hope we'll not come across any monsters, but a strong cudgel isn't a bad idea. Run get one. We'll start out as soon as you get back."

Brehier watched him go. "A well-set-up lad," he commented. "Where did you find him?"

"He grew up in my household," Edgar explained. "He's the son of our housekeeper."

Brehier gave a start.

"What's his age, do you know?" he asked casually.

"Seventeen or so, I think," Edgar said.

Martin returned a moment later bearing a stout stick.

"That should frighten the monsters," Edgar assured him.

Martin grinned. "It might even bring James into line," he suggested.

Edgar sighed. "Not for long, I'm afraid."

"Are we ready?" Brehier asked, staring at Martin. "The doorway next to the hearth is the closest."

When the hall had finally cleared, Margaret and Catherine ran quickly down the stairs from the upper floor.

"Why are we sneaking, Catherine?" Margaret asked. "We aren't doing anything wrong, are we?"

"Of course not," Catherine answered. "Did you want to explain to all those men that we want to examine the family relic? Now, where did you say it was?"

"Against the wall over by the linen chests." Margaret led the way. "I'd forgotten. I saw the servants push it there last night."

She went along the row, lifting saltcellars and throw rugs to see each wooden box. Catherine followed.

"Here!" Margaret said in triumph. "Now let's see if they left the little box inside."

The brass chest had been covered with a stained tablecloth. Catherine pushed it aside and lifted the lid.

Inside lay the pieces of the box that Jurvale's grandson, Richard, had left to protect his descendants. Catherine assembled them carefully.

"I don't think that the person who stole the treasure did more than rip this apart to get at it," she said. "At least I hope there was no more damage."

Margaret brought over a lamp to shine on the dark wood.

"Oh, thank you," Catherine said. "Yes, I thought there was a padding of some sort. I wonder what the material is? Ancient silk, maybe?"

Margaret looked at the brown crumbling material. "I have no idea. Is there still an impression in it?"

"I think so." Catherine held the box carefully, trying not to unsettle the contents.

Margaret took the knife from her sleeve and held it lightly over the faint hollow.

"You were right," she said in amazement. "It fits exactly. This was the treasure? A kitchen knife is supposed to save you?"

"It seems so," Catherine said. "But I don't understand it. Why would an old, plain knife be so important?"

"Maybe it's magic," Margaret suggested.

"If so, then we haven't found the secret of using it." Catherine dismissed the idea.

Margaret laid the knife carefully back in the box, just to be safe.

"Edgar is going to hate this, you know," she said.

Catherine nodded. "Richard's heir killed with Richard's knife. It's almost mythic. I wish I could get rid of the feeling that we've wandered into some epic poem."

"It is chilling." Margaret shivered to prove it. "I don't feel up to behaving like a heroine."

Catherine set down the box and hugged her tightly.

"You've already been a heroine," she said. "You never have to do it again."

Margaret shook herself out of the hold and laughed. "My sister-in-law, the prophetess?"

Catherine feigned insult. "In this family, a spot of prophecy shouldn't surprise anyone."

She sat down, serious again.

"I could use the Sight to work this out," she said. "Did someone in the household know that this knife was in the box? How could they, if it hadn't been opened since the time of Louis the Pious?"

Margaret plopped herself on the floor. She brushed the straw aside and began writing in the dust.

"We need to lay this out like a problem in logic," she told Catherine. "First, what do we know for certain?"

"There's a box. There's a knife. There's a body," Catherine answered.

Margaret drew a square, a long line, and a stick figure.

"Lovely," Catherine said. "Soon Mother Heloise will be asking you to draw the capitals in manuscripts."

Margaret made a face at her. Catherine grinned back, glad that Margaret had shed her fear.

"First the box," Margaret said. "We know someone opened it before the ceremony last night."

"Yes," Catherine said. "But we don't know who or why or if they knew they would find a knife. And if they knew, did they intend to use it to murder Raimbaut?"

"Catherine, you were taught better than that," Margaret chided. "No speculating. Now the knife."

"We know it appears old," Catherine considered. It had been some time since she'd had to think in logical steps. It was a useless skill when dealing with the minds of children.

"We also know that it was recently sharpened," Margaret added. "That would mean it was taken at least a few days ago, but maybe months or even years."

"Very good!" Catherine said. "I hadn't got that far."

"And there is carving on it, in what we are fairly certain is Latin," Margaret continued. "Along with letters in a language we can't read. Anything else?"

"When it was found, Mother was holding it and it was covered in blood." Catherine spoke evenly. "We only assume that it was used to kill Raimbaut."

"Good," Margaret said. "Not proven, but I would say it's a valid assumption." ·

"And the body?" Catherine asked.

Margaret absently rubbed the figure until it was no more than a smudge on the floor.

"That's the real puzzle," she said. "Although perhaps if we knew more about the other two, everything would be clear. All we can say is that he was the elder son of Seguin and that he's dead, stabbed through the heart with a knife."

"From the front," Catherine added. "It doesn't make sense. Why was he in the chapel instead of the hall with the rest of us? Why didn't he try to defend himself?"

"The last point is what worries me," Margaret said. "People are saying that he wouldn't have feared your mother, so she could get close to him without his sensing danger."

"But if she came at him with a knife, he could have disarmed her easily," Catherine said. "Whatever people say, I don't believe she did it. Logically."

"I agree," Margaret said. "Logically."

They both sighed.

"Now what?" Catherine asked.

"I don't know," Margaret said. Her glance strayed to the corner where the *jongleurs* had left the chest with their instruments. She gazed at it for so long that Catherine waved a hand in front of her face.

"Margaret?" she asked. "Are you having a vision?"

"No." Margaret stood up suddenly. "But I may have just had a revelation. Where do the players keep themselves in the daytime?"

Martin was enthralled by the dank tunnels.

"I was only jesting about the monsters," he told Edgar, "but now I'm not so sure."

"Want to turn back?" Edgar teased.

"Of course not." Martin jangled the leather bag around his neck. "With all the charms and bits of martyrs' bones my mother gave me, the Devil himself would turn and run."

Brehier was in the lead, but turned around every few moments to watch the other two.

"Your mother," he started. "Is she the woman I've seen with Lady Catherine?"

"More likely the one you've seen chasing my children," Edgar answered. "They lead Samonie a hard life."

Martin smiled. "You know she loves it. Especially since my sister died. She told me they soothe the hurt in her heart."

"Really?" Edger was genuinely surprised. "Irritating and disobedient as they are, I feel the same. It's good to know they don't torment her too much."

They walked in silence for a few moments; then Edgar and Martin began discussing the recent journey and making plans for what they should offer for sale at the Lendit fair that fall. Brehier listened with interest.

"It's a bit further yet," he interrupted them. "Aymon loved the remote caves. You were just in Italy?"

"Lombardy," Edgar answered. "We met some Genoans there and traded for African spices and stones, among other things."

"And Martin is learning this trade?" Brehier asked. "Not just tending animals and running your errands?"

"Well," Edgar laughed. "That is a large part of apprenticeship, but he's been present at the negotiations. I hope he's kept his ears open."

"Of course, Master," Martin assured him. "Watching you and Master Solomon at work is as good as a troop of jugglers, acrobats, and dancing bears!"

Edgar cuffed him lightly. "Show more respect, young man, or we'll send you in to explain to Abbot Suger why his incense is twice the cost of last year's."

Brehier listened to them in wistful amazement, all the while keeping his back to them as he led the way through the underground passages.

"Not far now," he told the other two. "It appears that you're doing well, Martin. Your father must be proud of you."

"I don't think so," Martin said. "I doubt he knows my name. I certainly don't know his."

"Oh, I beg your pardon," Brehier said.

"Thank you, my lord," Martin said. "But you needn't worry. It used to bother me, when the children in Troyes would mock me for it. But now it doesn't matter. I've made my own life."

"Yes," Brehier whispered. "So you have."

They had finally reached the part of the labyrinth where Brehier thought they might find Aymon.

"It was somewhere down this way." He indicated a moss-lined passage. "There are only a few other branches to this tunnel. I know that at the end of one of them there's a cave. It even had a sort of basin where water collected. Aymon loved it. He brought down skins to sleep on and baskets of sausage and cheese."

"And a friend from time to time?" Edgar suggested.

"Probably," Brehier said. "For such a big place, there's remarkably little privacy in the keep."

"That's always the case," Edgar agreed, wondering why the subject seemed to embarrass the man.

"I think one of us should stay in the main passage and the other two explore the side paths," Brehier suggested. "Perhaps Martin and I can go. If we find anything, Martin can come back for you. If we don't return in the time of ten *Nostre Pères*, then you should go back for help. Is that agreeable to you?"

Edgar nodded. He hated being the one left back, but had to admit that Martin and his cudgel would be of more use if there were something at the end of the tunnel waiting to attack.

Brehier went first. As he was about to follow, Edgar drew Martin aside.

"Watch yourself," he warned. "Brehier seems an honest man, but with all that's happened here, it's better to be on guard."

"Don't worry, Master," Martin said. "I've learned a number of tricks from Master Solomon. He always expects trouble."

As he waited and recited Virgil in his head to count the time, Edgar reflected that Martin would be fine.

They weren't gone long.

"Nothing," Brehier said. "A short passage ending in a rock wall. There's another just a few steps up."

They went through the same procedure at the next opening. Edgar was reaching the end of his memory of Aeneas' journey when he heard a call echoing from the darkness.

"Coming!" he called back and hurried down the tunnel.

He found Brehier and Martin standing in the cave Brehier had described. A lantern stood on a rock and next to it was a pile of wolf skins and a linen bed cloth. On the floor was a basket. Edgar peered into it. There were bits of cheese stuck to the bottom.

"Someone's been here recently," he said. "Do you think he heard us coming and ran?"

"No," Brehier said. "There's only one way out."

"So he must have come here right after we found Raimbaut's body," Edgar said. "Ate and slept perhaps and then left, but where to?"

"He may be planning to return," Brehier suggested. "Maybe he went to find more food."

"Maybe," Edgar said. "Brehier, there are any number of ways down here from inside the keep. Is there also a way out?"

"You mean into the village?" Brehier asked. "Not that I know of, and Guillaume and I hunted long enough. A way past the guards after Compline would have been all the treasure we could have asked for back then."

"But could there be?" Edgar persisted.

"I suppose," Brehier admitted. "We never found the end of some of these tunnels. But, as far as I know, no one's ever found one."

"Master?" Martin said quietly.

"Yes?" Edgar turned to him.

"When we first met Lord Aymon, he was out hunting near here," Martin began. "We took the road, and he said he would go back through the woods."

"I remember," Edgar said.

"Well," Martin went on slowly. "I thought that he would ride on some forest path."

"Of course," Brehier said. "And so he did. I saw him in the hall shortly before you arrived."

"Forgive me, my lord." Martin hunched as he spoke to diminish his effrontery. "Did you see him ride in? Because I noted his horse and, when I went to the stables, it wasn't there."

"What?" Brehier said. "Are you certain?"

"Is there another place he might have left it?" Edgar asked. "In the village?"

"No." Brehier shook his head. "And no reason for him to."

"That's very interesting, Martin." Edgar looked at him with

approval. "I wonder where the tunnel comes out. It must be close to the forest."

Brehier was trying to comprehend this. When he realized what they were saying, his reaction was strong.

"That bastard found it!" he exclaimed. "The road to freedom! And didn't share it with anyone! Guillaume will be furious."

"But now that we know it exists, we can, too," Edgar said. "Instead of traipsing around in the dark, we should go to the place where we first met Aymon. All we need to find is where he keeps the horse. The entrance to the tunnel must be near it."

Solomon was overjoyed to see the towers of Boisvert in the distance. His passenger was testing the limits of his patience.

"Do you want me to take you to the castle to find your niece?" he asked.

"And have everyone in the town see me come in with you?" She poked his ribs. "A woman alone has to consider her reputation. No, leave me outside the town. I'll make my own way in."

"Whatever you wish," Solomon said gratefully.

There were only two places to look for entertainers in the daytime. They weren't in their beds, and so Catherine and Margaret went down to the village. They found them sitting on a bench outside the tavern, well into their second pitcher of beer.

"*Dex vos saut,* beautiful ladies!" The leader tried to rise and bow but was hampered by the bowl of porridge on his lap. "How may we serve you?"

"We'd like to know more about the *chanson* of Boisvert," Catherine said. "Margaret, would you get these fine men another pitcher?"

"With pleasure." Margaret vanished into the tavern.

Now the leader managed to stand. "Please, my lady." He gestured dramatically toward the bench. "Join us and we shall give you a private recitation."

Catherine took the offered seat, even though it was unidentifiably sticky.

"You needn't trouble yourselves to that extent," she told them. "I understand it takes several nights to tell the whole tale. I only want to ask you about part of it."

"Give us beer and a little bread, my lady, and we are yours for as long as you like," the leader told her. The other two men nodded agreement. "I am Alceste, and my comrades are Evander and Julus."

"You all must have had very educated mothers," Catherine commented.

"Indeed." Alceste gave an ironic smile.

Margaret returned with the pitcher and filled their bowls.

"We are at your service, my ladies," Alceste prompted.

Catherine looked to Margaret. This had been her idea.

"We don't know the legend of Boisvert," she began. "We'd like to know what it says about the treasure that Andonenn is guarding."

Alceste leaned back and closed his eyes. He stayed that way so long that Margaret thought he had gone to sleep. Evander noticed her confusion.

"He has to go through the *laisses* in his head," the *jongleur* explained. "You can't just jump into the middle."

All at once, Alceste came to life.

Louis the king was pious and brave
His people he wished for Christ to save
Nevermore that they be pagan lore's slave
But Richard had vowed by the old king's grave
To honor the final command he gave
And so by night he crept to the nave
Of Charles' chapel, with only a stave
The treasure to rescue and hide in a cave
Though Queen Judith in anger might rave
There to guard it beneath the wave.

As he spoke, Evander automatically mimed the action of Richard creeping into the deserted chapel and taking something from a shelf. Then Julus became the angry queen, shaking her fist as Richard retreated with his prize.

"Does that help, my lady?" Alceste opened his eyes.

"There's nothing more that says what the treasure was?" Margaret asked without much hope.

"No, only that it was something Louis thought smacked of pagan superstition," Alceste answered. "And it can't have been very big. The next *laisse* says that he put it in a bag and carried it on his horse."

"Is it the same as the box that was opened last night?" Catherine asked.

"Oh, no." Alceste leaned forward, looking into his beer as if it could read the future. "That's very clear. The box contains the key to the treasure."

"Like a map?" Margaret wondered if the writing on the knife might be a code of some sort.

Alceste closed his eyes again. They all waited.

Open the lock in your darkest hour
Children of Andonenn needn't cower
To save her you shall have the power
Follow the guide left in the tower
It will lead you to Andonenn's bower
Fear neither storm nor shower
Insert the key into the flower
Find the treasure and win the dower.

Alceste opened his eyes and smiled at them. "Does that help?"

"I don't remember that part," Julus said.

"I don't either," Evander agreed. "The lines are too short to act properly."

"It's at the very end," Alceste told them. "We hardly ever get that far."

Catherine wished she had a writing tablet. These were the clearest instructions she'd ever heard in a poem. Of course, now they had to find a guide in a tower. And it did seem to ruin her theory about the knife having been in the box. There must be a real key somewhere. Did the person who stole it already have the guide?

It was looking worse for Aymon. She hoped he was found soon.

"Thank you," she told the *jongleurs*. "That does help. We are grateful for your help."

"How grateful, Lady Catherine?" Alceste asked with a smile.

Margaret fumbled in a bag at her waist and found three silver *deniers*. She handed them to the men. Alceste looked at it with approval.

"Coins of Troyes are always welcome." He got up. "Come, brothers! We can now drink wine like the nobles."

As they started down the path, they were forced to move aside for a man on horseback coming up. The sun was behind him, making his features hard to make out. When he saw Catherine, he stopped and dismounted. She squinted and then started in surprise.

Then he saw Margaret, already running toward him. His face lit with joy as she leapt into his arms.

"Solomon!" Margaret cried. "I'm so glad! I've missed you so very much."

"And I you, precious." He hugged her.

Looking over her shoulder, Solomon saw Catherine's expression and all the happiness drained from his heart.

Thirteen

Sunday afternoon. The village of Boisvert.

*Surge, vade, et dic populo Deo ne timeat, sed firmiter toto corde
credat in unum verum Deum; eruntque ubique victuri.*

Rise up, go and tell the people of God not to be afraid but
with all their hearts believe firmly in the one true God; and
they shall be victorious everywhere.

—*Gesta Francorum*, Part 25

*S*olomon quickly released Margaret.

"I'm sorry, sweet," he said. "For a moment, I forgot you were
no longer ten years old."

Her arms were shaking. "Yes, of course. How could I be so un-
mindful of my age?" she stammered.

"Catherine!" Solomon called. "I have serious news. I need to
speak with your grandfather."

Catherine's face changed at once. "Come with me," she said.

They hurried up to the keep, Solomon leading his horse and
walking with Catherine. Margaret followed slowly behind.

"Why is she here?" Solomon asked. "No one told me."

Catherine explained about her mother, giving a rapid recitation of all that had happened since they arrived.

"Now, what is it that's brought you here?" she asked.

"I should tell your grandfather first," Solomon hedged. "He's the lord here."

"Seguin seems to be the one giving orders," Catherine said. "But with one son dead and the other missing, he may not be too receptive."

"Catherine." Solomon stopped in the road to gape at her. "Don't you ever go anywhere peaceful?"

"Apparently not," she answered, linking her arm in his. "Solomon, we really need to have a talk."

He pulled away. "No, we don't. Please take me to whoever is commanding the defense of this place. I have no time for any other discussion."

"Of course."

Catherine led him into the bailey and waited while he saw to his horse. Margaret joined her a moment later, flushed and ill at ease.

"How silly of me to be so bold," she said. "I might as well have been Edana's age. Don't tell my brother, will you?"

Catherine looked at her sad, pleading expression and her heart ached for both of them. Why couldn't Margaret have an easier life?

"I won't say a word," she assured the girl. "As long as you don't forget yourself again."

"I won't." Margaret sounded defeated. "I'll go in and see if Seguin has returned from hunting for Aymon."

"A good idea. Thank you," Catherine said.

Solomon returned soon. He didn't ask where Margaret had gone.

"You know I wouldn't be here if it wasn't important," he told Catherine.

"I do." She understood the unspoken apology. "Are we in danger? Should we return to Paris?"

"I don't think there's time," he said.

They entered the hall and found only Gargenaud and his wife, Briaud, waiting for them.

"I was told that a stranger had ridden into the village and was coming this way," he greeted them. "I sent the girl to find Seguin, but if you have a message to deliver, then give it to me. I'm still lord here."

Solomon bowed to him.

"I bring news from Anjou," he said. "Olivier de Boue has raised an army and is proceeding toward Boisvert with great speed. I have this from people who have seen them and fled their homes before his advance. You have no more than a day or two in which to send for aid and gather your people into the keep."

He bowed again.

Gargenaud sat motionless. Catherine wondered if he understood what Solomon had said. Then he raised his arm.

"Briaud," he told his wife. "Have the bells rung. Send my bailiff to me at once."

She nodded and withdrew.

"Thank you, young man." Gargenaud waved him away. "Go down to the kitchens and tell them I said to feed you."

"Grandfather," Catherine interrupted. "This is my husband's partner, not a paid messenger."

"He's not hungry?" Gargenaud asked.

Solomon touched Catherine's arm. "As a matter of fact, I am," he said. "Thank you, my lord."

"Seguin!" Gargenaud shouted. "I told you that bastard was going to attack. Seguin!"

He noticed Catherine. "What's wrong with you, girl? Go fetch my grandson at once!"

"Yes, Grandfather," Catherine bobbed quickly and ran from the room.

Edgar knew they were nearing the surface again when he heard the bells.

"How long were we down there?" he asked Brehier. "It can't be Vespers, yet."

"We only ring the church bells on Sunday morning and holy days," Brehier told him. "That's the alarm. We need to get back at once."

At an underground junction farther on they ran into Guillaume and his group.

"Is it fire?" Guillaume asked, his memory of disaster still fresh.

"Don't know," Edgar panted. "How much farther to the hall?"

"Not far now." Guillaume was running, too. "I don't hear any screams."

"Is that good or bad?" Martin asked Edgar.

"Neither. It just means the children aren't there."

The men exploded into the hall, swords and cudgels ready to attack.

The huge room was empty.

At the first clang of the bells, people had poured from every cranny of the castle. Samonie and Marie arrived, herding children before them, the youngest on their hips. Soon after, Agnes, her husband, and her household followed. In between came servants and the few ladies of the court, supporting Elissent. Last came an angry Seguin.

"Who ordered those bells to be rung?" he shouted.

"I did," Gargenaud answered. He strode into the hall, back straight as if he had just dropped twenty years. "We have to prepare for a siege. Everyone! Out to the bailey!"

Catherine stepped out onto the staircase down to the bailey, pushed by the others. She looked down and felt as if she were about to descend into a flood. People were pouring through the gates and across the drawbridge. It appeared that the entire village was trying to fit into the space. Some were pulling goats and pigs, or carrying cages of chickens or rabbits.

Samonie nudged her from behind. Catherine took a deep breath and plunged into the crowd.

Halfway down, she spotted Margaret's red braids. Pushing with her elbows, she managed to clear a path to her.

"What's happening?" Margaret asked.

It was Marie who answered. She leaned against the castle wall to catch her breath.

"Everyone knows that when the bells sound, the entire village should head for the protection of the keep," she told them. "We have the same custom at Vielleteneuse."

Catherine surveyed the chaos around her. "Wouldn't it be better just for a few select villagers to see what was wrong first?"

Marie shook her head. "There might not be time. It could be flood, fire, or invasion. Better to have everyone safe."

Now it did seem to Catherine that people were collecting, as she had done, in family groups, counting noses, staking out a space. Some even had the presence of mind to bring bedding.

She wished Edgar would return. There was no sign of Solomon, either. Where had he vanished to?

"Mama!" James tugged on her sleeve. "Is there going to be a battle? Can I fight, too?"

"No, and of course not!" Catherine told him sharply.

James glared up at her, then sat on the ground, arms crossed, with a face of stubborn anger. Catherine sighed. Samonie handed Peter to her. Of course he was hungry again. She held him up and looked at him sternly.

"Don't you become like your brother," she warned. "I couldn't manage two of you."

She sat on the ground beside her sulking son.

As she waited for Peter to finish nursing, Catherine looked around the bailey. Things were becoming more organized. People had found places for themselves and all were now waiting tensely for someone to tell them why they had been summoned. When Gargenaud appeared on the landing above them, in mail and helm, a spontaneous cheer went up.

"People of Boisvert!" he cried.

There was instant silence, except for the bleating of a goat.

"My people!" Gargenaud held up his sword. "The walls of this keep have protected you all your lives. They always shall. I have just learned that a foul usurper, Olivier de Boue, is on his way with his paltry army. He believes that he can force us to turn over Boisvert. But this is Andonenn's home and she will allow none but those of her blood to hold it."

Murmurs began from the mass of people below. Gargenaud held up his hand.

"We have withstood worse than Olivier can give," he stated proudly. "But we must prepare to fight him off from within these walls either until our men defeat him or Count Thibault sends us aid. You have nothing to fear!" His voice rose. "We are well sup plied, thanks to your good efforts. There is food and water enough to last out a dozen Oliviers. But we must see that there is nothing left in field or village that will sustain these barbarians. My grandson, Seguin, will tell you what must be done. In Ando nenn's name and by the mercy of Our Lord, we will prevail!"

He raised the sword so that it caught the sunlight. The flash gave the impression that the fire of the sun had leapt into the blade and into the man holding it.

The roar was deafening. Gargenaud bowed his head in thanks. Then he backed through the doorway to the keep. Seguin replaced him at once. He descended the stairs, calling out orders as he came.

"Gather what you can from the fields. Burn the rest. Bring

everything from your homes, then burn all those outside the walls."

Someone gave a roar of anguish. Seguin stopped, searching for the source of the cry.

"Landris, stop whining," he ordered. "Houses can be built again. Or do you want to stay and defend it with a mattock and scythe?"

"He'd cut off his own foot," another man shouted.

The laughter broke the spell. The crowd dissolved into collections of frightened but resolute people, each concerned with protecting his own.

Catherine saw Solomon at last.

"Where's Edgar?" he asked when he was close enough to be heard.

"I don't know," Catherine said. "He went hunting for Aymon."

"Oh, yes," Solomon said as he reached them. "The prodigal son. Look, Catherine, I need to leave. Your grandfather wants me to get to Troyes as soon as I can to tell the count what's happening and have him send men to lift the siege."

"But that's so dangerous!" Margaret had been listening.

Solomon smiled at her. "Not a bit. Who would bother a simple trader? Anyway, I'll be well ahead of Olivier's army."

Catherine wished she could send Margaret with him. She had no reason to be caught up in this. But seeing the way Margaret was gazing up at Solomon, she couldn't risk it. She loathed herself for not trusting them. Still, she didn't and that was all there was to it. Perhaps Edgar would see the matter differently.

"When do you go?" she asked.

"Within the hour," he answered. "There's still enough daylight for me to be well on the road, perhaps as far as Chartres today."

Catherine looked down at Peter, now asleep against her

breast, a trickle of milk running from the corner of his mouth. She wanted him out of it. She wanted all of them out of it, home and safe in Paris. Gargenaud hadn't told these people that the well was drying up; that there had been murder here only last night. She had tried to deny the curse but this threat was too great.

"Solomon . . . ," she began, but was cut off by Marie as she saw Guillaume come out of the keep.

"Over here!" She waved her scarf until he spotted her.

Edgar was right behind him with Martin and another man. Samonie gasped.

"Are you all right?" Catherine asked her.

Samonie nodded, staring in amazement at her son and his father standing together like old friends. Catherine followed her gaze but saw nothing to remark upon.

"It doesn't appear that they found Aymon," she said.

Edgar and Martin headed toward them. The other man wandered off toward the stables. Edgar's mouth fell open when he saw Solomon.

"What are you doing here?" he asked. "Don't you know we're about to be attacked?"

"I'd heard something about that," Solomon said. "Don't worry, I'll be away from here shortly. Think you can hold out until I return with the count's army?"

Catherine started to laugh. "I can't see you leading the charge," she told him. "But you don't need to kill your horse racing for help. You can see that Boisvert is impregnable."

"Yes," Edgar said. "Solomon, as long as you're here, Martin and I need to discuss something with you."

The three of them moved to a spot under a tree where no one had yet set up a tent.

"That's odd," Catherine said. "Why do they look so worried?"

"We're about to have an invading army at our gates," Marie suggested.

"But the only way Boisvert could fall is if we were betrayed," Catherine said.

They looked at each other, then down at their children.

"Aymon?" Marie asked in a whisper.

"Oh, Saint Genevieve!" Catherine breathed. "I hope not."

"What are you whispering about?" Margaret asked.

"Nothing, *ma douz*," Catherine smiled. However, she began to reconsider her decision to keep Margaret at Boisvert rather than chance her being seduced by Solomon. In her core, she knew that Solomon would never hurt Margaret. He would die to protect her, even from himself.

Solomon listened to Edgar's tale of their underground expedition.

"I remember where we met Aymon in the woods," he said. "It makes sense that he should stable the horse not far from there. Between that stretch of forest and the castle there's nothing but open field."

"Do we have time to hunt for it before Olivier is upon us?" Edgar asked.

"Can you afford not to?" Solomon returned. "If Aymon has turned on his family, then he could lead Olivier's men through the tunnels and up into the heart of the keep."

"I know. And even if he hasn't, he could be captured and forced to tell the way in." Edgar bit his lip. "Martin, could you ride to Troyes for us?"

"Of course." Martin lifted his chin proudly.

"No, Edgar," Solomon said. "They killed the last messenger, remember? Martin has too much the look of a man on a dangerous mission. Who would suspect a grizzled old Jew of racing off to save a Christian lord?"

"I'm not afraid," Martin protested.

"An even better reason for me to go," Solomon told him. "Fear keeps one watchful and alive."

Edgar gave in. "Yes, you're right, Solomon. Martin is too

valuable here. Anyway, his mother would kill us if anything happened to him."

Solomon grinned. "I'm off, then, as soon as I fill a skin of wine."

"Good." Edgar put his arm around Solomon's shoulder. He spoke softly but with sincerity. "Watch yourself, man. My wife and my sister would kill me if anything happened to you."

Solomon nodded, his throat too tight to speak.

"Well, I suppose we should prepare ourselves for an extended stay," Marie said. "I wish we'd brought more of our men than just Hamelin and Osbert. There aren't enough swords here even for a good sortie."

"I wish I'd brought more clothes for Edana," Catherine complained. "Samonie and I spend half our time mending as it is."

"Let's get them all back inside and take stock of what we do have," Samonie suggested.

They went back to the hall, now busy with every sort of activity. Old rushes were being swept out, tables moved, boxes brought in and stacked against the walls. Guillaume called to Marie as she started up the stairs. She turned back.

"I'll meet you in the solar," she told Catherine.

Guillaume was pulling on his beard in irritation. Marie gently drew his hand away from his face.

"Someone has to take charge," he told her. "Elissent is still prostrate with grief and that wife of Grandfather's is useless."

"It's not my place," Marie pointed out, a cold dread rising in her heart. "Briaud is the one to make decisions."

"Have you seen her?" Guillaume snorted. "She barely speaks. I don't know if she knows how. As far as I can determine, she does nothing but attend to my grandfather and comb her hair. If there is any suspicion of witchcraft, we need look no farther than her. For now, we need someone to apportion the food and see that the weakest of the villagers have a place in the keep rather than the bailey."

Marie sighed. "If Seguin asks me, I'll do it, but I won't put myself in a place I have no right to."

Guillaume kissed her. "I knew I could count on you."

Marie patted his cheek. "You know, my dear, there are times when I wish that you couldn't."

"Catherine, Martin and I are going to see Solomon on his way." Edgar found her surrounded by linen, trying to keep Edana and Peter from tangling themselves in the lengths.

"You won't be long, will you?" she asked. "There's so much to do."

"No, we'll be back before sunset," he said. "But if you need someone, Brehier here has offered to help. He grew up at Boisvert and knows its ways. He'll be of more use than I."

"Not for everything." Catherine fluttered her lashes.

Edgar shook his head. "No one would ever believe you'd been schooled in a convent, woman; you're shameless."

"I know," she said contentedly. "So hurry back."

Solomon was waiting at the gate.

"The place looks strong enough," he commented. "If you can plug the hole, there's no reason why you can't hold off Olivier's army."

"Don't dawdle, though," Edgar said. "I have no desire to spend the winter keeping James from falling off the parapets."

Solomon promised. At the edge of the forest, he took his leave of them and headed north. Martin and Edgar entered the wood near the place where they had first encountered Aymon.

"It can't be too deep in the forest," Edgar thought aloud. "He'd have to protect the horse from wolves and the weather."

"A cave, perhaps?" Martin said.

"The land seems flat apart from the tor that Boisvert is built on," Edgar answered. "But it's something to watch for."

They found the clearing where Dragon had treed Aymon. Nothing more had been disturbed. On the far side Martin discovered a narrow path, no more than beaten grass, not much traveled.

"Excellent!" Edgar said. "Let's see where it leads."

As they left the clearing, Edgar stopped and looked back.

"I was just thinking," he said. "Remember that little noisy dog trying to climb the tree to reach his master?"

"Aymon's dog?" Martin said. "Of course. I wondered what he could be using it to hunt for. Squirrels?"

"Annoying little thing," Edgar said. "But, have you noticed it around since Raimbaut was killed?"

Martin thought. "I can't say I have. Does it mean anything?"

"I don't know, but it's something to keep in mind."

The trail wound among the trees with no obvious direction. Sometimes it doubled back on itself. Edgar was beginning to suspect that they were following a deer track that would soon vanish, leaving them to find their way back by starlight.

Martin was riding in the lead. Edgar had fallen into meditation on their situation and whether or not they would be able to leave the castle in time for the fair at Saint-Denis in October. How long did sieges last? He'd only been in the one at Durham and that had been over in a matter of days. But he'd heard tales of towns that had run out of food and started eating horses, rats, and even each other. If they could only find this secret entrance, perhaps they could all flee through it and be away before anyone noticed.

He didn't notice that Martin had pulled ahead of him and was now out of sight. A crash and a cry brought him back.

"Martin!" he shouted. "Are you hurt?"

There were more sounds of thrashing about. Edgar hurried to the place where he found Martin stuck in a thornbush, his horse gazing at him indignantly.

"Did she throw you?" he asked, as he dismounted and set about rescuing the boy.

"No, I ducked to avoid a low tree limb and slid off," Martin said. "I was careless. Ow! These spines are worse than a hedgehog!"

"The undergrowth is unusually prickly around here," Edgar said as he pulled Martin out. "All about, except for there."

He pointed to a stand of plants, some flowering red and yellow.

"Elfwort, althaea, some kind of spurge," he said. "All of them grow where the soil is damp and marshy."

"I wish I'd known," Martin grumbled, pulling briars from his *brais*. "I'd have waited to land somewhere soft."

"Mmm hm." Edgar had noticed another deer track along the side of the patch of herbs. "Can you walk?" he asked Martin. "This trail is too faint to see from horseback."

This time he led the way. The trees grew more thickly here, almost as if they'd been deliberately planted to block the way.

"If it gets any more dense, the horses won't be able to turn around," Martin warned.

"Yes, I guess we should go back," Edgar conceded. "I was so sure this was the way."

There wasn't much space to circle in. Edgar's horse brushed into a chestnut tree draped in vine and started, dancing sideways farther into the foliage.

"*Avoi!* There now!" Edgar tried to calm him. "It's all right, just relax and . . . Martin?"

"Yes, Master."

Edgar's voice came from within the tangle.

"Come here. I think we've found Aymon's stable."

Martin pushed the vines aside and stepped into a natural chamber. The foliage hid the place from view, just as a willow tree might, but the high chestnut limbs allowed enough space to keep a horse tethered. A log had been hollowed out and filled with water and a pile of hay left in a withy box. One more thing made it certain.

"His horse is still here!" Martin exclaimed.

"Very observant," Edgar said. "But that must mean Aymon is still somewhere at Boisvert."

"Should we take it back with us?"

"Yes, we don't want Aymon able to flee."

"Um, Master."

"What, Martin?"

"I don't think he's going to flee."

Martin pointed to a boot sticking out from the underbrush. Edgar knelt and touched it. The foot was still inside.

Quickly he uncovered the body.

"Come help me, Martin!" he said. "Hurry! We have to get him back to the castle. He's still alive!"

It was hard in the midst of all the bustle, but Brehier finally managed to find Samonie alone.

"I met your son," he told her. "He's a fine young man."

"Thank you." Samonie tried to brush past him, protecting herself with the layers of cloth draped over her arms. "I need to take these rags to Lady Marie. She wants to be ready in case we need bandages."

"We have time yet." Brehier took her hands. "I won't ask why you didn't tell me. You might have left word with someone in case I returned, though."

"Really." She retrieved her hands. "What should I have said? You have a bastard by a scullery maid, come claim him, and by the way, she has a daughter already by another man. Then what? You take us all home to your mother? Don't be absurd."

"You admit he's mine?" Brehier asked.

Samonie gave a short laugh. "Isn't it usually the man who wants to deny it? You saw it for yourself. His color is darker but the face is yours." Her voice softened. "Just as you looked when I first saw you."

She made another attempt to get by him.

"What?" she asked. "I've told you that Martin is of your making. He's a boy to be proud of. You can sleep well knowing that, if you like. I'm not going to shame you by noising it about. That should help your sleep, as well. Now may I get on with my work?"

Brehier lowered his arms.

"Is that what you wish?"

She stared at l..m in consternation. "Yes, I'm happy in Paris. Mistress Catherine is good to me, as is Lord Edgar. I don't want to lose my place because you kept me from my duties. Anyway, what else is there for us?"

His shoulders drooped. "That's true. I should have said something eighteen years ago. What have I to offer you now?"

Samonie took a step toward him. No. She made herself stop and tried to think with an organ above her waist. This was a man she had barely known a lifetime ago and now didn't know at all. What did he want from her?

"I have everything I need," she told him. "But, if you want to pass the time, I noticed a nice window nook not far from the garderobe on the second level. I might be willing to meet you there after Compline tonight, if I'm not needed elsewhere."

Catherine managed to reorganize the family's possessions, noting the things they would soon run short of. Agnes's tendency to bring everything from her silver goblets to winter cloaks didn't seem so foolish now.

"Don't fret," she told herself. "It will all be over soon. They'll negotiate a truce, or Count Thibault will send an army to drive Olivier away. We'll be home before Michaelmas."

It was only when the last article had been put away that she thought of something.

"Margaret?"

From a partition farther down the passageway a head stuck out.

"Do you need me, Catherine?"

Catherine went down to where Margaret had created a narrow space for herself, the same size as she had at the convent.

"I can't believe I've been so unnatural," Catherine said. "All of this going on and I never once wondered what happened to Mother. Do you know where she is?"

"Don't worry," Margaret assured her. "They don't have her in chains. She's in a room next to the solar. Agnes asked one of her maids to attend her. I looked in on them a while ago. Madeleine doesn't remember anything about finding the body. At least, I don't think so. She asked if her stained robe could be brushed clean. I told her I wasn't sure and she said, 'Wash it at once. Blood comes out of wool if you get it soon enough.' Then she returned to her stitching."

Catherine shivered. "I'm a coward, Margaret. I thought I wanted to see her again, but really, I'm afraid of meeting a stranger. I want my mother again."

The moment she said them, she wanted to call the words back. Margaret's lip trembled.

"*Deorling!*" Catherine held her. "I'm sorry. At least my mother is still with us in the flesh, if not in mind. I didn't mean to remind you. Oh, how I'd love to put a lock on my tongue!"

"Never mind," Margaret told her. "At least I have a family that loves me. So many people don't."

"Speaking of which, where is our Vandal horde?" Catherine asked.

"Helping," Margaret said. "Even James and Bertie. Agnes has them sorting and carrying for her. She seems to have a talent for making people want to be useful."

"I know," Catherine agreed. "It always made me furious."

Marie had arranged a simple evening meal for the household. She wasn't sure what they would do when everyone from the village was camped in the bailey and every corner of the hall. *Sufficient unto the day is the evil thereof*, she reminded herself. At last everything seemed to be running smoothly. If she only could sit down for a moment.

"Marie!"

Of course not. She sighed. "Yes, husband? What do you need?"

"Some of that salve of yours." He rolled down his hose to show her a scrape that went all across the side of his calf. Marie noted that the stocking would need mending, too. She didn't bother asking what he had done.

"I'll send Evaine to fetch it," she told him. "I had thought we wouldn't need the medicines so soon."

"Ha!" Guillaume said. "When you have time, I spotted a boil on one of the villagers' necks that needs lancing, an eye that's gone red and runny, and some idiot trying to walk on an ankle as big around as a rutabaga. These people think that Andonenn will cure them, so they don't treat anything."

"I'll have a look at them in the morning," Marie promised. Her back and legs ached and she was so tired her eyes wouldn't focus.

She didn't even turn her head to see what the commotion at the gate was. Someone would tell her soon enough.

She sank into an armchair piled with soft cushions and let her head fall back.

A moment later she was brought up to complete wakefulness by Edgar's voice.

"We found him in the forest," he was saying. "We thought he was dead at first, but then he groaned. We got him home as quickly as we could, but I don't know. He's badly wounded."

She opened her eyes to see a procession entering the hall. First came Edgar, explaining to Guillaume why they had been in the forest. He was followed by a stretcher borne by two men. At the side of it walked Seguin. He looked like a man on the edge of the abyss. Lastly, Edgar's apprentice, Martin entered, carrying what looked like a hunting bow.

The men set the stretcher on the long table where she had planned to serve dinner. Seguin held out his hand to her.

"Please, Lady Marie, your husband says you have some skill," he pleaded. "We know nothing of illness or wounds. I beg of you, by all the saints, don't let Aymon die."

Fourteen

Monday, nones September (September 5) 1146. Feast of Saint Gennebaud, first bishop of Laon, who committed the sin of having children with his own wife. He finally locked himself in a cell to avoid temptation and achieve sainthood. 23 Elul 4909.

Mais cho est bien voirs que l'on dist.
Li buen, li biel el siecle muerent,
Li lait li malvais i demeurent.

But it is very true what people say.
The good, the beautiful soon leave the world,
The ugly and the evil live on.

—*Silence*, II. 2136–2138

Elissent roused from her bed of grief to rush to the side of her surviving son.

"I knew he couldn't have hurt his brother," she sniffed. "Look what that murderer did to him. But he'll get better. You can make him better, can't you, Marie?"

Marie examined Aymon's wounds. "Possibly," she said. "He

must have lain outside for several hours. He's very weak and some of these cuts are deep. He'll need constant care."

"He shall have it." Seguin stood behind his wife, his hands on her shoulders.

"I don't understand it," Elissent said. "None of this should have happened. We were supposed to be safe here."

Seguin patted her soothingly. "I know. Something is terribly wrong. We did everything we were told to. The curse ought to be broken. Instead . . ."

He closed his eyes. One son laid out for burying, the other perhaps dying. Outside, an army was gathering to lay siege to his home. He had sent riders out to his vassals to come to the aid of Boisvert, but no one had yet returned. Seguin felt that even God had cast them off.

But he couldn't let anyone know his despair. There were nearly four hundred people looking to him for protection. The few trained soldiers he had, needed his leadership. If only he knew what to do.

He gazed on the face of his son. Aymon was flushed with fever. Marie had warned him that suppuration might set in. She had potions and powders. One of the servants had been sent out to get fresh dung from a white dog. He didn't want to imagine what that was for. The requisition reminded him that Edgar had said something about Aymon's dog being missing. How could anyone know in this chaos?

Seguin gazed down on his son. He knew that there was nothing more he could do here. Aymon's life was in the hands of Marie. He prayed that she had more influence with God than he did.

Edgar and Martin were waiting when Seguin came down from the sickroom.

"I don't know how to thank you," he told them. "Aymon would never have been found if you hadn't gone looking. But how did you know where?"

"Didn't Brehier tell you about the passage out?" Edgar asked.

"I haven't seen him since yesterday morning," Seguin said. "What passage?"

They explained. "But we haven't found the entrance, yet," Edgar ended. "We found Aymon first. It was more important to get him back here. With your permission, Martin and I will return to the forest and resume searching."

"There was a rumor when I was a boy about an underground path into the forest," Seguin said. "But I always thought it was just the wishful dreams of the fosterlings. Aymon discovered it, did he? And never told a soul."

He sighed, shaking his head. "He was no captive. Why did he need a secret way out?"

"A woman, perhaps," Edgar suggested. "Someone married or unsuitable."

Seguin rubbed at the knot in his neck. "What does it matter now?"

"Why he kept it secret is of no importance, I agree," Edgar said. "But I believe we need to find this passage before Olivier's men do."

"Yes, of course." Seguin was alert again. "However, there's much more to be done here, if we're to survive until relief comes. The walls are strong; we have food. The water may hold out. But we have no serious defense weapons. We haven't needed them in generations."

"First let us find the passage so that it can be blocked," Edgar said. "Then Martin and I will aid you in building a defense."

Seguin looked at Edgar's arm. "You? What can you do?"

Martin stepped between him and Edgar.

"My lord," he said quickly. "You would be astonished."

Catherine felt completely useless. When Marie had been called to care for Aymon, Agnes had taken over as chatelaine. She was superb at it. From a mass of frightened people and piles of be-

longings, she was creating order. There were even moments of
calm. Margaret had been pressed into service as nursemaid for
Madeleine again. Edgar and Martin had gone off somewhere
without even telling her. When Catherine had asked what she
could do to help, Agnes had suggested condescendingly that she
stay out of the way.

So that's what Catherine was doing. She sat on a chest in the
corner of the hall watching the activity. She wondered why there
was so much preparation going on if the dispute with Olivier was
going to be resolved quickly. After a few hours of observation, she
concluded that people weren't so much fearful as excited. It made
a change from their daily life and brought neighbors together.
Catherine was skeptical about how long that would last.

She also wondered which of the bustling individuals was really trying to destroy Boisvert. Had someone been hired to murder the heirs, thus reducing Gargenaud to despair? Was one of
these seemingly honest villagers planning to open the gate to the
enemy?

And where was Mandon while all this was going on? The
mysterious woman had gone to immense lengths to get them all
here and left them wandering without direction. Did she simply
intend to hide under the castle and wait to see what would happen? If Olivier conquered them, would she become the guardian
for him, instead? Or would she fade away as Judith's curse ate
down to her lair?

No answers came. Her speculations were as useless as she was,
Catherine thought gloomily.

Slowly she became aware that, across the hall, there was one
other person who wasn't bustling. There was something familiar
about her. Catherine concentrated, squinting at the figure to see
her better.

"Saint Perpetua's oily athlete!" She slid off the chest in surprise.

The old woman was huddling in a corner. She seemed feeble,

limbs shaking with age. But, when Catherine looked at her steadily, she saw someone not much older than she, hair grayed with ash, lines on her face accentuated with brief strokes of kohl.

She had seen this trick before.

Catherine went bounding across the hall, dodging boxes, bales, and babies as she ran. The woman saw her coming and tried to get away, but Catherine was too quick.

"Mandon!" she cried, grabbing the woman's wrist. "Why are you just sitting here? What are you going to do about this?"

The woman shrank back in fear. Catherine peered more closely at the face and blinked. It wasn't Mandon.

"Who are you?" she demanded.

"Berthe, good lady," the woman croaked. "My name is Berthe. What is it you wish me to do?"

Catherine didn't let go. "Tell me the truth."

"My lady," Berthe pleaded. "I don't know what you mean? The truth about what?"

The image of the bewildered old woman was so good that Catherine doubted for a moment. If she hadn't seen Mandon transform, she would have believed herself mistaken. She brushed her fingers over Berthe's cheek.

"It doesn't even come off," she marveled. "But I can tell. You're too much like her. You must know Mandon, too. I saw it in your eyes when I spoke her name."

Berthe tried to break loose. Her strength convinced Catherine that she was right. She needed both hands to keep hold of the woman. In the struggle, Berthe's scarf slipped off, exposing dark roots.

"There," Catherine said. "What kind of woman dyes her brown hair gray?"

"Hush!" Berthe told her. "People are watching."

She stopped fighting Catherine.

"If I tell you what you want to know, will you pretend we never met?"

"I can't promise that!" Catherine declared. "Not without knowing what you intend."

"Then take me to Gargenaud and have him judge me." Berthe rubbed at her wrists.

"Judge you for what?" Catherine asked tightening her grip. "Pretending to be lamb dressed as mutton? I don't think that's a crime. What crime do you think you should pay for?"

"I'm only here like everyone else, for protection," Berthe insisted. "I've done nothing wrong."

"Maybe not," Catherine said. "But you know things I need to understand. Tell me about Mandon and what your connection is with her."

"You wouldn't believe me." Berthe laughed.

"I'll believe the truth," Catherine said quietly. "It would be nice to hear it for a change."

Berthe studied her for a long minute.

"The truth is," she said in a low voice, "that I'm here to help my sister. Do you believe me?"

Catherine released her grip on Berthe's wrists. Her fingers slid down the woman's arm until she was clasping both her hands.

"Yes," she said. "Oddly enough, I do. Come with me."

In a remote chamber of the castle, just above the chapel, Margaret was forlornly trying to get Madeleine to eat something.

"I assure you, my lady," she said. "This isn't a fast day. The cook has sent up lovely fresh berries and cream and a loaf still warm from the oven. That must tempt you."

"Oh, it does, Sister Margaret," Madeleine said. "But I will resist the temptation. I have vowed to fast in penance for my sins."

"What sins, my lady?" Margaret asked. "Did the priest set you this penance?"

Madeleine shook her head. "Of course not. I promised my husband that I'd tell no one, especially not a priest. Do you know my husband? He's a merchant, very rich. He's gone now, to Spain,

I think, or perhaps Poland. I haven't seen him for a long time. The children miss him."

"Then you must keep up your strength for their sake," Margaret said patiently.

"I hadn't thought of that." Madeleine looked so contrite that Margaret felt dreadful for deceiving her.

While Madeleine was occupying herself with the berries, Margaret wandered over to the long, thin window. Through the thick glass she could see movement. Shouts of command echoed across the bailey, cries of sudden anger, even laughter.

Life was going on down there and she was trapped in a quiet cell tending to a madwoman. And, when all this was over, she would return to the convent. A wonderful convent, to be sure, but still not exactly at the center of things. Of course, she could marry. Her grandfather was eager to arrange a good match.

She only wished there was another choice.

"It's a terrible thing to marry a Jew."

Margaret spun around. Had Madeleine been reading her thoughts?

"What did you say?"

"He said he'd been baptized, you know," Madeleine continued conversationally. "And he's never tried to convert the children. But he never takes Communion. Sometimes I think he hates me for keeping him from turning infidel again. I pray and pray that he will receive the grace of a true believer, but I must be doing something wrong."

She looked down at the almost empty berry bowl.

"My faith must not be strong enough."

"Of course it is!" Margaret knelt beside her. "You are the most pious woman I've even known. But should you be talking of this?"

Madeleine was puzzled. "I can't tell the priest or my friends but, Andonenn, I thought you would understand."

"Andonenn!"

Madeleine's eyes focused on her. "Oh, how silly of me! You're Margaret, the girl from the Paraclete. I hope someday my Catherine will become a nun. She'd be happy in a place like that."

"Yes, I'm sure she would." Margaret was trying not to upset Madeleine. "But what about Andonenn? Have you seen her?"

Madeleine nodded. She put down the berry bowl and looked around for her sewing. Margaret handed it to her.

"Andonenn?" she prompted.

"I used to spend hours with her, when I was a child," Madeleine said as she stitched a border on a child's tunic. "I was the baby, you see, and a girl. No one really had much time for me, so I would go down to the spring and talk with Andonenn. I think she enjoyed it as much as I did."

Margaret had to swallow a few times to steady her voice before asking the next question.

"You know where Andonenn's spring is? Do you think you could find it again?"

Madeleine put down her needle and thought a while. Then she resumed her sewing. Margaret thought she wasn't going to answer. Finally, Madeleine turned and smiled at her.

"I'm sure I could," she said. "If we ever go to visit Boisvert, I'll take you to her. I know she'd enjoy meeting you."

Margaret fell back on her heels in surprise. She had no idea what to do next. One thing she was sure of, Catherine must know about this at once.

She looked at Madeleine. There was no way she could leave her alone now. Not with Catherine's mother babbling about her husband being a Jew. Margaret chewed her tongue in frustration. She went to the doorway and looked out. With all the activity in the castle this must be the only corridor completely unoccupied.

Margaret made a decision. Who knew when someone would come to relieve her?

"Lady Madeleine," she said. "Do you feel like taking a walk?"

∞

Edgar and Martin made their way back to the chestnut tree where they had found Aymon. This time they brought along sickles for cutting the brush and vines.

"It can't be far from here," Edgar said, whacking through the overgrown herbs.

"I don't see any rocks that could be a cave," Martin replied. "Do you think there's a door in a tree? I've heard of those."

"No idea," Edgar grunted. "You'd think there'd be some sort of path, if Aymon came this way often."

"These woods are so crisscrossed with tracks that we'll never find the right one," Martin complained. "Damn! I just backed into a patch of nettles!"

"We'll have to get you leather *brais*," Edgar commented. "You shouldn't be out here bare-legged."

"Nice to mention it now," Martin muttered.

They continued swinging, clearing the undergrowth in patches, but finding nothing.

"Maybe we were wrong," Edgar said at last. "There must be another explanation. Or the entrance is a lot farther than we thought."

Martin wiped his face with his sleeve. "Where else can we look?" he asked.

Edgar shook his head. As he did, he caught a flash of color between the vines hanging from the chestnut, not a dozen paces from them.

"Martin, get down!" he hissed, throwing himself to the ground. Had they been overheard?

Martin obeyed without understanding. He lay on his stomach with his nettle-stung leg against something thorny. He clenched his teeth and tried not to move.

Edgar tried to count the number of men at the tree. He only saw two, but there had been that brief glimpse of red. Both the men he could see at the moment were in dark green under clinking chain mail.

"Are you sure he said it was here?" one man called to some-one beyond Edgar's sight.

"Fifteen paces from the chestnut," a voice answered almost above Edgar's head. "In the direction of the keep."

Edgar dared take a breath. They had been looking in the wrong quarter. He waited until the sounds of the men grew dim-mer, then risked nudging Martin with his foot.

"We have to follow them," he mouthed.

Martin nodded. "But we have no weapons but these," he whispered, clutching the scythe.

"Then we'll have to be very careful not to be caught," Edgar answered.

They crept after the three men, who were not making any at-tempt at stealth. Edgar wondered why. This was enemy territory. Had they been told that there was no danger of being spotted? Had Aymon betrayed his family and then been betrayed in turn or was there another spy within the castle?

The undergrowth was so dense that only the sound of the sol-dier's voices kept them on the trail. They peered through it to see where the men had stopped at last. When he saw the spot, Edgar realized that he could easily have passed it without a glance. It was only a pile of weathered stone, half the height of a man. The entrance was a triangular hole made where two flat pieces had been propped. It was so narrow that Edgar doubted a fully armed man could squeeze through.

The soldiers had brought a pot of coals wrapped in canvas. One of the men took a staff wrapped at one end with rags soaked in pitch. He put it against the coals and blew on them until the pitch burst into flame. Then he lit another from it. Finally he and the man in red carefully pushed their way between the rocks, each holding a torch before them.

The last man was left sitting on the outcrop, loosely holding a crossbow.

"We have to get in there," Edgar whispered in Martin's ear. "Can you get behind the guard?"

"Yes, Master," Martin answered.

Edgar put his hand over Martin's mouth.

"Do it," he breathed. "I'll get his attention."

Martin slid into the brush, trying to sound like a passing badger rather than a man. Edgar waited a moment and then stood and stepped in front of the guard.

The man sprang up, his crossbow ready to shoot. He relaxed slightly when he saw Edgar's handless arm.

"Who're you?" he demanded.

"Name's Edgar, who are you?" Edgar responded. "You come from the castle yonder?"

"Maybe," the man answered. "What business is it of yours?"

"I like to know who's aiming at me." Edgar smiled. "I'm not armed, you know, just with this."

He held up the sickle. "Promised a lady I'd bring her fresh herbs for her bower. They like that, you know."

The guard did not appear convinced. Edgar was glad to see Martin rise onto the stones at that point and fall heavily upon the man. The crossbow flew into the air.

"Catch it!" Edgar yelled as he threw himself on the man, sitting hard on his back.

Martin picked up the crossbow and held it on the guard.

"Press it to his neck," Edgar ordered. "Let me get hold of it while you tie him up."

Martin took Edgar's place while Edgar took the crossbow. He pulled off the guard's hose and tied his hands and feet together, so that the man was trussed like a piece of game.

"Now," Edgar asked. "Whom do you serve?"

"No one," the man barked.

Edgar tapped him with the crossbow.

"Not Olivier de Boue?" he asked.

"Never heard of him," the man answered.

Edgar tried another angle.

"Who told you how to find this?"

"Godfrey," the man answered. "The man in the red cloak."

"And whom does he serve?" Edgar asked, pushing the point of the bolt deeper into the man's neck.

"No one!" the man shouted. "We are all lordless men. That's why we're trying to find the treasure!"

Edgar looked at Martin.

"What treasure?"

"Everyone knows about the treasure under Boisvert." The man was as contemptuous as anyone can be while bound hand and foot and bent back like a bow.

"I don't," Edgar said.

"Look." The man tried to sound ingratiating. He wasn't good at it. "There are only the three of us and a lot of gold and jewels and suchlike. We could use another pair of . . ."

He looked up at Edgar's arm, the crossbow balanced in the crook of his elbow. "Strong arms are always welcome," he finished. "There'll be enough treasure for all."

Edgar put down the crossbow. The man gave a long exhalation.

"Martin, I think we should hang him from a tree so that he stays fresh while we're gone," Edgar decided. "Run back to the horses for some rope."

"Yes, Master. Where are we going?" Martin asked.

"Down that rabbit hole," Edgar said, pointing. "Are those coals still hot?"

Martin uncovered the pot. "Glowing, Master."

"Good, while you're getting the rope, see if you can find anything for us to use for light."

Catherine wasn't sure where she could take Berthe to ensure that the woman wouldn't run away. She finally settled on the nursery, now occupied only by the German nurse with Agnes's baby, Gottfried. She smiled at the woman, and in her halting German, told her she might have a break.

Catherine bent over the baby's cradle. Gottfried was sound asleep, his mass of golden curls making him look positively angelic.

Berthe leaned over the baby, too.

"A blessing on you, child of Andonenn," she said.

Catherine quickly drew her away, to a bench against the wall. "Now tell me," she demanded. "How can you help us?"

Berthe smoothed her skirts as she sat and adjusted her scarf. Age was slipping from her like melting ice.

"I'm a healer." She smiled at Catherine.

"Then shouldn't you be down helping Marie tend to Aymon?" Catherine said.

"She'll do well enough," Berthe said. "There is worse sickness in this place. The soul of Boisvert is ill unto death."

She was so determined to sound portentous that Catherine felt herself becoming more annoyed.

"We have priests for that," she said stiffly.

"Oh?" Berthe raised an eyebrow. "Do you mean the one in the village who can't read his own name and learned the Mass by rote or the one in the castle who spends all his time hunting with his friends?"

Catherine squirmed on the bench. "You have a point," she admitted. "And what is the nature of this spiritual sickness?"

"You know already," Berthe said. "You've seen it. Those who stay here do nothing but rot. That's why no woman can conceive. That's why death has entered the gates. That's why, unless we can treat this illness, unless we can remedy it, Boisvert will fall."

Catherine waited for the trumpet blast. There was something about Berthe that made her feel she was listening to *jongleurs*.

"Why does this matter to you?" Catherine demanded. "Who are you? Who is Mandon?"

Berthe gave her a sly glance.

"We are two sides of the coin." She grinned. "I'm the one that always loses the toss."

"That tells me nothing," Catherine said.

"The task before us is more important than old history," Berthe insisted.

"It's not old to me." Catherine sighed, but it was clear she would get no further answer. "Very well, then. How do you intend to cut this 'rot' out?"

"That depends on how deep it runs." Berthe stood and rummaged in the large cloth bag she had slung over her shoulder. She took out a knife in a wooden sheath. With a dramatic flourish, she drew it out. Catherine gasped.

It was the mate of the one that had killed Raimbaut.

"Where did you get that?" she cried. "Stay away from the baby!"

"Shame on you, Catherine," Berthe said. "As if I'd so much as snip one of his curls! This was given me by my mother, who had it from hers, who had it from hers, and so on back to the time that Boisvert was really made of wood."

"Is there writing on it?" Catherine's interest overcame her fear.

"Once was." Berthe held the knife out. "Can't hardly see it anymore . . ."

She held out the knife to Catherine, who took it and held the handle up to the light. She could make out a *K* but the letters at the end, what she could see of them, were different. It wasn't a language she knew but there was something familiar about it.

"What did it say?" she asked

"Don't know. A warning, a blessing, maybe the name of the first owner," Berthe answered. "I heard you were the smart one."

"Not always." Catherine sighed. "So what do you intend to do with that? And what about Mandon?"

"In time," Berthe said. "You've met her, have you? A meddle-some woman."

Catherine agreed. "You must be related. Sisters?"

Berthe smiled. "Of sorts. Don't fret about it. First, we have to find the rot and, if it hasn't run too deep, cut it out."

"Is that what happened to Raimbaut?" Catherine's brittle trust in this woman evaporated. "Was he rotten?"

"Perhaps," Berthe said. "But it wasn't my knife that cut him."

She headed for the doorway.

"Where are you going?" Catherine cried. "We can't leave the baby."

"Bring him then." Berthe didn't pause.

"Agnes will kill me," Catherine said as she scooped Gottfried into her arms. "She's so fussy about how he's cared for."

The thought gave her some pleasure.

"Do you know where you're going?" Catherine asked as she trotted after Berthe.

"Oh, yes, I was a child here," she answered.

Catherine had already suspected that.

They went into a section of the keep that Catherine hadn't seen before. Berthe crossed the gallery and into a wing on the other side of a great hall. The floor dipped a bit where the new room had been joined on. Berthe hurried on.

They finally reached a large wooden door. Every inch of it was carved with a frieze of twining plants. In the center was a tree whose branches wove into the vines along the edges. Beneath the tree the carving became that of a knight and a woman. They sat demurely on either side of the trunk, perhaps discussing the weather. Catherine smiled in delight.

"Look, Gottfried!" she exclaimed. "It's Jurvale and Ando-nenn."

Berthe strode up to the door and knocked loudly.

There was no sound from within.

"The room may be empty," Catherine said.

"He's in there." Berthe knocked harder.

As they waited, Catherine studied the carving of her ancestors. It was very well done. She must remember to show it to Edgar.
Each finger was delicately shaped, even to the nails, and the
feet. . . . Catherine looked again. Peeking out from beneath Andonenn's skirt was something that looked very much like a fishtail.

"Berthe, do you see this?" she asked.

Before Berthe could answer, the door opened. Catherine had
wondered where her grandfather and his wife vanished after the
evening meal and where they spent their days. Now she knew.
She was rather sorry she had learned the answer.

Briaud stood before them wrapped in a long length of silk.

"I thought you'd find a way in," she said, staring at Berthe
with loathing.

"Um, perhaps this isn't a good time for a visit." Catherine
was staring at the curves barely hidden by the cloth.

"Don't worry, we're done for now," Briaud told her, hitching
the silk up on her shoulder. "He won't want it again for hours."

"Grandfather?" Catherine said.

"Bring them in and shut the door," Gargenaud shouted.
"There's a draft in here."

Berthe charged in past Briaud. Catherine followed more hesitantly, praying that her grandfather was wearing more than his
wife. She held baby Gottfried up to her face. He was still sleeping. How could he do that? Her children had wakened if someone
sneezed. If only he would start crying so she could have an excuse
to leave.

Gargenaud was lying in an enormous bed. He had pulled up
the sheet, at least, but the sight of his bare chest, white hair
gleaming with sweat, caused Catherine's stomach to contract and
her head to fill with unwanted images.

Berthe was not intimidated. She marched to the bed. Putting
her hands on her hips, she addressed the lord of Boisvert.

"I've come to save you, you old fool," she said. "How long did you think you could hide the truth behind silly stories and ceremonies? There's a real army not a day away. Do you intend to frighten them into surrender with legends?"

Gargenaud drew himself up in anger. The sheet slipped alarmingly.

"How can you, of all people, doubt the legend?" he roared. "Look what happened when you tried to escape it."

"At least I didn't die of boredom as this one will." She jerked a thumb at Briaud, who had moved nearer to Catherine, her eyes fixed on the baby.

"We don't need your help," Gargenaud told her. "No army can breach these walls."

"And who will lift the stone that's blocking Andonenn's spring?" Berthe asked. "You don't even know where it is. How long can you last without water?"

"There's enough to last until we find the key," Gargenaud said. "Briaud, stop drooling over that child and come here. I've a kink in my back.

"Leave her be," Berthe said. "She knows she'll get none of her own until you're dead. Not unless you leave here. But you may have no choice, old man. You've abused Andonenn's gift and forces are coming together to take it back from you."

"You're as addled as poor Madeleine," Gargenaud jeered. But his voice held a flicker of doubt.

Berthe sat down on the bed. "You know better than that, Father. I'm more sane than you. But you're not so far gone that you don't know how much you need me now."

The old man glared at her.

"I need no help from you," he said. "You are an unnatural child and have no place here. Andonenn's true children will save her without you."

He finally noticed Catherine and the baby.

"Which one are you?" he asked querulously. "Get about your

business. Do I have to get up and show you the door? Briaud! My back!"

Catherine and Berthe made a hasty retreat.

"If it weren't for my promise to Mandon," Berthe muttered, "I'd let that old man burn."

At the moment, Catherine would have been happy to do the same.

Fifteen

Somewhere underground. That afternoon.

"This torch isn't going to last very long." Martin looked
worriedly at the wad of feebly burning cloth he had wrapped
around a chestnut branch.

"Then let's hope we find these men soon," Edgar said. "At
least we know we haven't missed them. There haven't been any
forks in the tunnel yet."

"What do we do when we find them?" asked Martin, acutely
aware that they were poorly armed.

Edgar had been wondering the same thing. He knew the men
had left their swords and bows with the guard. What else might
they have?

"I'll think of something," he said.

He sounded so confident that Martin ceased worrying.

Edgar cursed his own rashness. Even before he had lost his hand, being around fighting men had made him resentful. He was the youngest, destined for the church and of no value in a society of warriors. Whatever lip service they might give to religion, they all really believed that God was on the side of the strong. They sneered at the monks and made jokes about beardless men in skirts. It always made Edgar want to attack them like a rabid dog. The men at Boisvert had the same effect on him.

Yet, in this case, what else could he have done? There wasn't time to go to the castle for reinforcements. He couldn't chance the men getting back to Olivier with news of a back entrance to the unassailable castle. The only thing was to attempt to capture them.

He only wished that he wasn't risking Martin's life along with his own.

There was a sound up ahead and the glow of light reflected around a bend. Edgar put a finger to his lips and then gestured for Martin to put his torch down. They would need all three hands to deal with the thieves.

Slowly they crept toward the light. It flickered but didn't move forward. Edgar felt a shiver run up his spine. Were they creeping into a trap?

Edgar waved Martin to stay behind and eased cautiously into the light.

He almost trod on the remains of the torch, guttering out on the damp ground. Just beyond it lay the body of the man in green, his arm outstretched as if he'd thrown the torch as he fell. In his back was a short metal arrow, not fletched. Its copper color was bright against the dull shade of the man's tunic.

"What happened?" Martin asked from behind him. "A thieves' row?"

"I don't know." Edgar knelt next to the body. "He's dead, but only a few moments. It looks like he was running away from something."

They both stared into the tunnel. Martin picked up the torch. Edgar nodded. Without speaking, they ventured again into the darkness.

They found the body of the second man lying faceup a few yards farther down the passage, another copper arrow through his throat. His red tunic was stained a deeper crimson that pooled in a hollow in the floor. Martin felt a squelch as he stepped in it.

"He must have been shot first," Edgar said. "And his partner was hit trying to escape."

"But from what?" Martin's voice shook.

"Someone who was already down here," Edgar said. "This passage seems to already be well guarded. Martin, we don't need to worry about these men giving away the secret entrance. Let's go back, fetch their friend, and take him back to the castle for questioning."

"What about them?" Martin asked, indicating the bodies.

"We'll send men back to collect them," Edgar decided. "Seguin will want to put a guard here, I'm sure, until the passage can be blocked from inside."

"You don't think he set the guard." Martin stated this as a fact.

"I wish I did," Edgar said. "But I believed him when he said he didn't know this tunnel existed."

"I wonder where it comes out," Martin said.

"So do I," said Edgar. "But not enough to face whatever killed these men. Let's go."

"Catherine, where have you been?" Agnes snatched the baby from her as she entered the nursery. "I came up to see how my sweet Gottfried was and I found an empty cot. Do you know how I felt? Oh, my precious child." She covered his face with kisses.

"I had to leave, Agnes, and couldn't let him stay here alone," Catherine explained.

"Then you should have told the nurse," Agnes answered. "You have that much German. Don't I have enough to do without having to fear that my son has been abducted?"

"I only took him to Grandfather's room," Catherine told her. "He was asleep most of the time."

"Just don't do it again," Agnes said. "And what possessed you to go there?"

Catherine sighed. "It's a long story. Do you really want to hear it now?"

Agnes put a hand to her forehead. "No, I don't care as long as he's safe. I just wish we were all home in Trier."

"Yes, that would be nice," Catherine said. "I'm going to follow your suggestion and find out what my own three are up to."

She found Berthe waiting a little way down the passage.

"You might have come in to help me explain," she grumbled.

"I've talked enough today," Berthe answered. "Now I have to find Mandon. I shall meet you this evening. Do you still have the other knife?"

"I gave it to Seguin," Catherine said. "Are you sure you'll be able to locate Mandon. I don't think she can be found unless she wants to be."

"I know her tricks," Berthe answered. "Now, go tend to your family. It's them I'm doing this for. If it weren't for the children, I'd let this place fall."

Their crowded chamber was a refuge in an alien world. Samonie was mending a tunic for Edana when Catherine entered. James, with his cousins Hubert and Beron, was down in the Great Hall busily running errands for Agnes, but nine-year-old Evaine had stayed to help amuse Edana and Peter. Her face lit when she saw Catherine.

"Aunt Catherine!" she said. "I'm teaching Edana her letters. She's very quick."

"Or you may be a good teacher," Catherine told her. She took the stylus and board, wrote an 'E' in the wax and held it up. "Do you know that one, precious?"

"That's for Edana," the child answered proudly.

"Very good." Catherine gave her a hug. When she tried to let go, Edana held her more tightly.

"Mama," she asked sadly. "When can we go home?"

"Don't you like it here?" Catherine asked.

Edana shook her head. "It's too big and the green lady scares me."

Catherine looked at Samonie, who seemed as surprised at she was.

"What green lady?" Catherine was afraid that she already knew the answer. Evaine answered for her cousin. "The one who comes up at night, when you are at dinner. She's pretty, but her hands are so cold. She wants us to come to her rooms to play, but we always tell her no."

"That's very smart of you, Evaine," Catherine said. "I can see you're a good guardian for the little ones."

Evaine sighed. She knew that all too well.

"Samonie, I thought there was always someone here." Catherine tried not to sound accusing.

"Either I or one of your sister's maids are with the children every minute," Samonie insisted. "And someone stays in the anteroom after they are put down to sleep. I don't see how anyone could get in."

"If it's Mandon, there may be no way to keep her out," Catherine said. "She knows all the hidden doorways. Evaine, if she comes again, I want you to call Samonie at once. She'll send for me."

"Will the lady hurt us?" Evaine's eyes were round with fear.

"Absolutely not," Catherine answered. "But you are still not to go with her, no matter what she says."

Evaine crossed her hands over her heart. "I promise, Aunt."

Edana still clung to her mother. Catherine tickled her until she loosened her grip.

"*Ma douz*, will you stay here with Evaine for a while longer," she asked. "I'm going to find Papa. Then we'll both come up and play with you."

Reluctantly, Edana agreed.

"I'm not sure how long I'll be," Catherine added to Samonie. "Edgar and Martin went off somewhere after they brought Aymon in. I'm hoping they're back by now."

"Are we really going to be besieged?" Samonie asked.

"It seems so," Catherine said. "But I'm sure it won't be for long. Solomon has gone for help and Olivier may give up even before it comes. Once he sees the fortifications here, he'll realize that it's impossible to take the castle."

Samonie pretended that she believed this.

In the short time Catherine had been with Berthe it seemed that the atmosphere of Boisvert had undergone a definite change. It was odd, Catherine thought, that before, when only rumors menaced them, the place had felt full of lethargy and despair. Now, when there was a real threat and a murderer at large, people seemed almost cheerful. Everyone she passed was intent on their task, not rushing but purposeful. She marveled at this as she made her way to the hall. Finally, she decided that most people must prefer to have a real enemy to fight rather than rely on the whim of legend to decide one's fate.

Catherine wasn't sure she wanted either option. This visit had made it clear to her that, unlike Agnes and Marie, she wasn't meant to be an aristocrat. Their rather modest home in Paris felt like heaven to her. And, at this moment, it seemed almost as far away.

Martin was in the hall, washing his hands and face at a basin. Catherine was relieved to see him.

"Where did you go?" she asked. "Where's Edgar?"

She stopped, staring at the stains on his washing cloth. "Is that blood?"

"Don't worry, Mistress," Martin said. "It's not ours. We found Aymon's bolt hole. Some others had got there first."

"But you're unharmed?" Catherine asked. "Edgar as well?"

"Yes. He's gone to ask Seguin what we should do with the prisoner."

"Prisoner!"

"We left him with Brehier," Martin told her. "I think he's a spy for Olivier, but Master Edgar isn't so sure."

"Just where *were* you?"

Martin was saved from answering by the arrival of Edgar, bursting to tell her what they had done.

"Edgar!" Catherine was horrified when she heard. "If someone hadn't got to those men first, you and Martin might have been killed! Copper arrows, you say? That's bizarre. I wish we knew who your savior was."

"I'm not sure I want to," Edgar said. "I have an image of a Grendel-like creature lurking in the dank caverns."

"What's a Grendel?" Catherine asked.

"Just an English story. It's a monster from the marshes."

"Wonderful," Catherine said. "Thank you, Edgar. As if my imagination hadn't already conjured enough otherworldly beings to populate the world under the keep."

"Now that I've seen it, I'm more inclined to believe your family's tales," he admitted. "But at least we no longer need to fear Olivier's men attacking us from below."

"So really, all we need to do is stay here, keep our heads down, and wait until help comes." Catherine was satisfied to do that.

She didn't see Edgar's face as he said, "Yes, of course."

"At least we don't have to endure any more of those banquets," Catherine prattled happily. "Agnes is putting us all on something close to Lenten rations."

"Good, I was getting bilious from all that meat sauce," Edgar said.

"I don't think you understand," Catherine teased. "That means stopping up the wine barrels, too."

"Smart woman," Edgar said sadly. "It will be needed. Don't worry, I can live quite well on beer, even the way you French flavor it."

"How shall we amuse ourselves, stuck in here for a week or more?" Catherine asked with lascivious intent.

Edgar wasn't really listening to her. "I promised Seguin I'd see about the defense engines. The don't even have a *brigola* in this place. I need to find Hermann. I know there were at least two at the castle in Trier. He can check my design. I'll see you this evening, *carissima*." He dropped a lopsided kiss on her forehead and went off in search of Agnes's husband, Martin at his heels.

Catherine was left in the middle of the hall, purposeless again. She was about to return to the nursery, where at least she could be sure of a welcome, when Margaret beckoned to her frantically from the stairs. Catherine hurried up, glad to be wanted.

"Catherine," Margaret said, when they met. "Please, please forgive me. Something awful has happened. I seem to have mislaid your mother."

Out in the bailey, Edgar had found carpenters and the blacksmith. They all knew in principle what he wanted, but none of them had ever constructed a *brigola* before.

"Will it fit on the parapets?" one man asked. "The walkway isn't that wide and you need to make the arm long enough to send the rock or whatever far enough."

"How will we get it up there?" another worried. "The stairs twist too much for wood of any length."

"We'll bring it up the outside," Edgar said.

"With arrows flying at our backs? Not likely."

This came from a voice at the back. Several others murmured agreement.

"We'll do as much as we can before Olivier arrives," Edgar told them. "And the rest by night, if we have to. This is the best hope we have for protecting the houses between the village walls and the castle. Your homes, I believe."

They showed more willingness after that. Edgar was soon assured that all the materials were available. He set the men to working immediately.

When they had scattered to their tasks, Edgar noticed that Hermann still appeared concerned.

"I know," Edgar said to him in German. "It won't be much if Olivier has a strong force. Do you think he's wealthy enough to have serious siege engines?"

Hermann chewed his lip. "Even if he were, the hill is too steep for a belfry. They might try ladders, but we should be able to stop that. I'm worried about two things: fire and battering rams."

"There's still water enough to douse flaming missles," Edgar argued. "And, as for the latter, the gates are strong and iron bound, even below, and the bailey has a moat around it."

"Have you seen how the water level has gone down?" Hermann pointed out. "A man could wade it. It wouldn't be hard to throw down some planks and push a battering ram across on wheels."

"So, we get boiling oil to pour from the portcullis," Edgar said.

"That would be a start." Hermann did not sound convinced.

"Well, what would you have me do, man?" Edgar demanded. "Wait for the saints to save us, or for this Andonenn to emerge from her cave and drive the invaders out?"

Hermann smiled. "Of course not, good brother. We must do everything we can to defend ourselves. I only wish there were more we could do. I pray to the saints and the Virgin as much as any man, but in the end, who knows if he will be deemed worthy of divine aid?"

Sadly, Edgar agreed. He thought of all he loved in the world, now inside the keep. It seemed that God wouldn't be so cruel as to let them come to harm. But he had lived long enough to know that God's intentions and his didn't always agree. It wasn't enough to be good. After all, look what happened to Job.

So he set to work, doing the only thing he could to try to keep them safe.

Catherine was sure she had misheard.

"You mislaid her?" she asked Margaret. "But how? You two were left in a very small room."

Margaret looked down at her shoes, embarrassed to meet Catherine's face.

"Madeleine told me that when she was a girl, she had seen Andonenn. She said that she remembered the way to her home."

"And you believed her?" Catherine asked. "You know she's mad. She doesn't even know her own children."

"Yes." Margaret looked at her. "But she's much less confused when she talks about the past. She seemed so certain. So I took her to look for the way down. We didn't go the way you and I did, but outside. Only once we got out there she became confused. Things were different and she couldn't understand. I turned away for only a moment and she vanished!"

"Out in the bailey?" Catherine was incredulous. "How can that be? Someone must have seen where she went?"

"I asked everyone," Margaret insisted. "They all said that they'd seen us come out, but no one noticed her after that."

Catherine fought for calm. "Margaret, she can't have vanished into the air."

"I know." Margaret was well into a state of panic. "But I looked everywhere. Catherine, I even got a stick and poked it into piles of hay."

"Perhaps she slipped back into the keep," Catherine suggested. "Have you checked the chapel or her room?"

"Yes, both of them," Margaret said. "I just came from there. Oh, Catherine, what can we do? Your family is going to be so angry with me!"

"No, no," Catherine said automatically. "We should be grateful to you for taking care of her so selflessly. If Agnes says one word, I'll . . . Well I don't know, but she'll regret it."

Margaret couldn't help but smile at Catherine's nursery behavior. It was only a flicker, though. The gravity of the situation quickly weighed her down again.

"What should we do?"

Catherine couldn't be angry with her. She was so pathetically conscious of her failing. As if anyone could guess how a deranged woman would act. Margaret never should have been given such a responsibility. For one moment, Catherine was tempted to wait and see if anyone even missed Madeleine. She pushed the thought away in horror, but it lingered at the back of her mind, taunting her.

"We'll have to tell the others," she concluded. "Agnes and Guillaume should know and perhaps Seguin or Brehier or one of the others, who was a child here, might remember a hiding place she loved."

Margaret's shoulders sagged, but she nodded agreement.

"Where is everyone?" she asked.

"The men are in the village setting up traps in case Olivier's army breaks through the lower walls," Catherine said. "Agnes could be anywhere; she flits about so."

"Is there anyone else who might have been here when Madeleine was a girl?" Margaret asked. "I can't tell how old most of these people are, but there must be a servant who knew her then, don't you think?"

"A servant? I don't know." Catherine thought. "But someone, yes. I met her a little while ago. Only I'm afraid she's disappeared, too."

Margaret sighed.

"People do seem to vanish here and then reappear when least expected," she said. "I suspect that Boisvert is full of doorways into the world of fairies."

"From what I've seen, there could be portals to Purgatory, or even an underground route to Rome." Catherine was becoming as disgusted as Edgar with the enigma of the place. "No wonder people are pleased to have an army to fight."

"No matter where she's gone," Margaret said, "we must find her."

"I know." Catherine squared her shoulders. "I'll have to go down and tell Seguin. He may not want to spare people to search, but they were willing to do it for Aymon, so they'll have to for Mother."

"Aymon, I almost forgot him," Margaret said. "How is he?"

"Samonie says he still lives but hasn't wakened yet," Catherine told her. "Marie thinks he might eventually. I hope he can tell us who attacked him. There's a guard by him constantly. Seguin won't take the chance that the murderer might want to finish the job."

"If he wakes, he can tell us who killed his brother," Margaret said. "Perhaps there should be two guards."

"There were guards on Mandon at Vielleteneuse when she pretended to be dead," Catherine mused. "She vanished from there and we know there are no tunnels under that keep. It's practically marshland. I wonder if it's a talent the women of Boisvert learn."

"Or perhaps there's a charm they recite to become invisible," Margaret suggested.

"If so, it wasn't passed down to me."

Catherine went down to the village to find Seguin. Margaret insisted on accompanying her to take the blame if need be.

The houses had been stripped, even the shutters taken up to the castle. Unripe vegetables still grew in the gardens, but any bean that showed a hint of plumpness had been picked. Cows wandered the common pasture but pigs, goats, and fowl were all gone from their pens. A few dogs scavenged in the feeding troughs or growled at the many cats, which no one had tried to collect.

They found Seguin overseeing the digging of holes in the earthen road. Men had put stakes and sharp rocks at the bottom, covered the hole with mats, and then scattered dirt over the mats, hoping to hide them. On the narrow paths between the houses people were stringing trip wires and others were strewing caltrops amidst the refuse and straw. These would stick like a nail in the foot of both men and mounts.

Margaret and Catherine stepped more carefully after seeing this.

When they found Seguin and explained that Madeleine was missing, he immediately stopped what he was doing.

"Pagan," he ordered. "Carry on with this. I'll return as soon as I can."

"Where were you when she vanished?" he asked Margaret as they climbed back up to the bailey.

"Between the storage sheds and the well house," Margaret told him. "She said there was a way to reach Andonenn, but she wasn't sure where it was."

"Did you look in the well house?" Seguin asked, starting to run.

"Of course." Margaret sprinted after him.

"Did you look *in* the well?"

Margaret stopped so abruptly that Catherine ran into her.

"She couldn't have! There wasn't time!" Margaret protested.

"I hope not." Seguin ran over the drawbridge to the stone building that covered the well. The door was open.

"Did you leave it like this?" he asked Margaret.

"No, I'm sure it was closed," she answered. "A woman yelled at me not to let the chickens in."

"Dear Lord," Seguin breathed. "Just as I feared."

"No." Catherine grabbed his shoulder. "What are you saying? Mother would never drown herself."

"Not intentionally," Seguin said. "But she was hunting for Andonenn. Don't you see? This is the way to the source."

Catherine felt cold all over. "This is nonsense. There are a hundred other places she could have gone."

Seguin didn't answer but began turning the windlass to bring up the water bucket. He seemed to be having trouble getting it to move.

"Catherine," he spoke quietly. "Perhaps you should go find your brother and sister."

"I have to stay here," Catherine said. She didn't think her legs could move.

Margaret felt as if she were being slowly strangled. This was all her fault.

"I'll get them," she managed to say.

Catherine didn't notice her leaving. Her eyes were on the rope slowly winding. All she could hear was the creak of the windlass as it fought against the weight of whatever was coming up. She tried to think logically. A body was too big to fall into a bucket. The wall around the well was too high to fall over accidentally. Her mother wasn't so careless of her own safety.

Or was she?

Catherine realized with a stab of guilt that she didn't really know. For the past ten years, Madeleine had been safely tucked away in the convent of Tart. Apart from occasional messages saying that she was well, they had heard little. Catherine's father had given the nuns enough to support her for another twenty years, if necessary. Catherine always included Madeleine in her prayers. The nuns had told her that seeing her eldest daughter would only confuse the poor woman. That had been an excuse not to visit. And Catherine had gone on with her life, married, had children, lost one to illness, had another stillborn. She had traveled to England, Spain, and Germany.

Madeleine didn't even know that Catherine had children.

And all the while the creaking continued as the bucket made its way up from the depths.

Seguin grunted and pulled harder on the crank. At last something showed at the rim of the well.

Something dark was caught on the chain holding the bucket. It hung down over the side, tipping it. Seguin reached out and swung it closer until he could grab the sodden material. He pulled at it until the last bit appeared, dripping profusely.

It was a woman's veil.

Catherine felt her knees give way as she fell, sobbing, onto the stone floor.

And then Margaret was there, her arms around Catherine, weeping, too. From somewhere, Guillaume's voice was raised in disbelief and horror. Agnes's shrill demands for an explanation pierced the air through all the other cries. Catherine buried her face in Margaret's *bliaut* and willed them all to go away.

A moment later she felt herself transferred into Edgar's arms. He spoke to her softly with a calm detachment that soothed her enough to catch her breath.

"It looks bad, I know," he said. "But your mother may not be down there. She could have leaned over the wall and the veil come loose and fallen. We'll go on searching."

Catherine clung to this hope. Seguin had unhooked the bucket and was attaching the lantern used to check the level of the water. They all waited breathlessly as he lowered it.

"My God!" He exclaimed.

Catherine's stomach lurched again.

"I had no idea the water was down this far!" Seguin finished. "But I see nothing floating in it. There's no body."

Guillaume came to look.

"Nothing," he said. "Of course her clothes could be weighing her down."

"Guillaume!" Agnes protested.

"I don't want to have false hope," he stated. "After all, if she didn't drown, then where has she gone?"

Seguin stared into the well. "I have to agree. All signs say that Madeleine is down there. Her body may be caught on something or it may have sunk. If so, it should reappear in a few days. Until we know for certain, we need to find another source for drinking water."

Catherine was appalled by his callousness, but the others accepted it as necessary.

"There's not much in the cisterns." Agnes spoke as if from a distance, but her voice was steady. "I checked this morning."

"There's beer enough for a week or two," Guillaume said. "We'll know before then. Poor Mother! But perhaps it's better than living in twilight. She's at peace now."

Margaret was still in tears. "I should have watched her with more care!" she sniffed. "This is all my fault."

Catherine came out of her own shock enough to defend Margaret, but she needn't have worried. No one could feel resentment in the face of such contrition.

"You couldn't have foreseen this," Guillaume said. "I forgive you any small lapse in attention. Any one of us might have been with her."

Agnes didn't speak at first. Then she bowed her head.

"It's true," she said. "She's always been so docile. I wouldn't have expected her to do something like this."

She stared at the well. "I still can't believe it."

Edgar repeated that there would still be a thorough search. "I'll question everyone," he promised. "If she still lives, she'll be found."

His words gave them some comfort but they had no real hope.

Death had come to Boisvert again.

Marie hadn't left Aymon's side since Edgar and Martin brought him in, although she had done everything possible in the first hour. His wounds baffled her. They didn't look as though they'd been made by a blade, at least not the one that had dispatched Raimbaut.

She also couldn't understand why he hadn't wakened. The cuts were deep but not in the most vulnerable areas. She had been able to staunch the blood and it had stopped flowing not long after. His color was pale, but not deathly, and his pulse was strong. His breathing was deep and even. The fever had ebbed. In her experience, people with this type of injury regained consciousness quickly.

Perhaps there was some enchantment involved. Marie did not have any training in how to counter that, except through prayer and holy relics. They didn't have any relics to speak of, and Elissent had been praying hard for her son all day. She was now sleeping fitfully, sitting on the floor by the cot, holding Aymon's hand.

Marie rubbed her eyes and yawned. She'd been up since first light, had chewed on a dry piece of bread softened with bacon grease a few hours before, and eaten nothing since. A while ago there had been some commotion in the hall, but no one had come to tell her about it. She wondered if they were already under attack.

There was silence all around, the velvet silence of a summer afternoon when everyone with any sense is sleeping until the evening brings a cool breeze. From the rafters she could hear the cooing of the doves that had escaped from their cote yesterday.

Marie's head drooped.

"Mother?"

Her eyes flew open. "Yes, Gervase. What is it?"

Her eldest son seemed frightened. Marie came fully awake. "What has happened?" she demanded.

"I don't know." Gervase took her arm, trying to get her to stand. "Father told me to come get you. But it must be something terrible. Mama, he was crying!"

Sixteen

The castle keep, that evening.

Occidit hic pietas, regnet et impietas
Vita perit; mors seva fuit, bachatur et ensis
Nullus ibi parcit, Mars ubi sceptera regit.

Here piety is killed and impiety reigns
Life is lost; cruel death is rampant and the sword has free rein
No one is spared, where Mars holds the scepter.

—Bishop Guy of Amiens
Carmen de Hastingae Proelio, II. 497–501

"Why is Mama crying?" James tried to climb onto the bed where Catherine was curled. "Did a bad man hurt her? I'll kill him for you."

"James!" Edgar dragged his son away. "There'll be no talk of killing. Mama is sad. Put that sword down before you hurt your little brother."

Peter was standing next to the bed, unable to climb it. Catherine's convulsive sobbing was frightening him, too. Not having a wooden sword to express his feelings with, he resorted to a high shriek.

The noise roused Catherine. One look at the panic in her baby's face was more potent than a slap. She swallowed her tears and lifted him up next to her.

"There, there." She rocked him in her arms. "It's all right. Mama is here." Her voice faltered. She hugged him closer. "Mama won't go away."

He tugged at the front of her *bliaut* and she rearranged herself so that he could reach her breast. He sucked eagerly. In a few moments, both of them were asleep.

Edgar took James outside.

"Don't worry, son," he promised. "Mama will be fine. You can come with me. I have to help the men make throwing machines."

That interested James. He went willingly, but his curious mind was still trying to figure out who had made his mother so unhappy.

Edgar found the village craftsmen assembled, as Seguin had commanded, but none of them looked very happy about taking orders from a one-handed Englishman. Edgar decided the only thing was to dive in. He only hoped the men would have the decency not to mock him in front of James.

"Now," he told them. "What I'd like you to make is rather like a mangonel or petrary, only the arm is positioned farther out on the base and there's a sling at the end instead of a basket."

He drew his design in the dirt with a stick. The carpenters, wheelwright, and blacksmith crowded around.

"What're all the ropes for?" the blacksmith asked.

"We need a man at the end of each one to counterbalance the weight at the throwing end," Edgar explained. "You fit the sling along this channel."

He dragged the stick along a line at the bottom of the diagram. "Then fill it with stones or bits of metal and secure it.

When that's done, the men grab hold of the ropes and pull down hard, all together. At the other end, someone releases the sling and it throws the stones well over the wall and into the army camped below."

The men studied the diagram with interest. Finally, one of the carpenters spoke up.

"We can turn out two or three of these in a matter of days," he said. "The problem is finding enough men strong enough to put some force into the pulling."

Edgar scratched his head. "What about putting baskets at the end of a couple of the ropes? They could be loaded with more rocks and balanced up high, maybe on ladders or a platform. When we're ready to fire, we can pull out the support. The baskets would drop with much the same force as if a large man yanked the rope."

He sketched a crude pair of laundry baskets tied to the end of the ropes.

"They might tip before we were ready," the carpenter ventured. "We ought to secure the tops with lids tied on some way."

"That would be safer," Edgar admitted. "Are we agreed to try? If the baskets don't work, it wouldn't take much to free them."

The men seemed gratified that their suggestions were attended to and approved the plan heartily. They divided the labor and dispersed at once to begin work.

Edgar took James and went to tell Seguin of his progress.

"Good work!" Seguin said. "You may think it odd we have no such things prepared, but I never thought we'd need them. It's been centuries since there has been a serious threat to Boisvert."

Edgar was mindful of the little boy listening to every word.

"The walls here are strong," he said. "We can certainly wait until winter drives Olivier home to his own castle."

Seguin had not been around children for a long time. He didn't mince his words.

"We'd be fine if my aunt Madeleine hadn't been so inconsiderate as to drown herself in the well, which was already running low," he answered sourly. "Without fresh water, we won't last a week."

"Papa?" James voice was less certain than usual. "Is Mama crying because the army will kill us?"

"Absolutely not." Edgar squatted next to him. "We are all safe here and we'll be going home soon."

He glared up at Seguin, who had the grace to be embarassed.

"That's right," he told James. "We have the high ground here and brave people to defend the keep. Olivier de Boue is no more to us than a fly to a bull. Their mangonels and *ballista* will never crack our walls or reach up to the keep. I promise you, young man."

"Is that an oath?" James suspected he was being teased.

Seguin nodded. There was no laughter in his eyes.

James was satisfied.

Edgar was more uneasy.

"We should have a trebuchet ready in a couple of days," he said. "I had an idea for something that would make it possible for even women to load and release it, but I'd like to do a trial first. Is there time?"

For reply, Seguin pointed out across the field to the woods from which smoke was rising.

"They'll be here before nightfall," he said. "By dawn they'll have set up camp just out of range of our arrows. Then we'll know the size of the force marshaled against us."

Edgar was astonished that his first reaction to the news was relief. He had doubted Catherine's theory about the pleasure of having a solid foe to battle. Now he was forced to agree. It helped him to concentrate on an enemy at the gate rather than a phantom within the walls.

"Lord Seguin! My lord!"

They both looked in the direction of the shrill voice. Seguin smiled at the sight of Evaine racing up the stairs to them, her braids flopping against her shoulders.

"What is it, child?" he asked gently as she stopped to catch her breath.

"Mother sent me to find you," she panted, flushed with importance. "She says I should tell you that your son has finally awakened. He's asking for you."

Seguin didn't answer but closed his eyes and crossed himself, murmuring a prayer of thanksgiving.

"Take me to him at once," he told her, taking her hand.

Aymon was sitting up on his cot, supported by his mother and a thick pile of cushions. He was pale but alert.

For once, Seguin could not hide his emotions.

"My dear boy!" he exclaimed. "I feared I had lost you, too."

"You nearly did, Father," Aymon told him. "If Brehier hadn't found me in my hiding place in the woods, it might have become my tomb. I was very foolish."

"But what happened?" Seguin asked. "Why did you run from your home and who attacked you?"

"I don't know who," Aymon said. "As to why, I'm ashamed to say that when I saw Raimbaut lying there dead I was so distraught that all I could think of was to get away and hide until the worst of my grief was spent."

"No one would have scolded you for immoderate grief." Elissent stroked her son's forehead.

"You have no idea who attacked you?" Seguin prodded. "You must remember something."

Aymon's face creased as though thought was painful.

"I remember getting my horse," he said. "And riding into the woods. I left him under the chestnut tree as usual. As I was taking off his saddle, I heard a noise. Then I felt a rush as of someone running toward me. After that, all is empty until I woke to my mother's face."

He gave her a tender smile.

"So," Seguin said. "Marie, when may he leave his bed? We'll have need of him in the coming days."

"He's still very weak," Marie said. "I'd not like him to do more than walk a few steps until the end of the week."

"Nonsense!" Aymon cried. "There's an invader approaching. This is no time to lie abed. I'll be at your side tomorrow, Father."

Elissent shook her finger at him.

"You'll do as you're told, my dear," she admonished. "You are now the heir to Boisvert. You have a responsibility to stay strong and healthy so that when the curse is broken and Andonenn restored, there will still be one of her children to govern it."

"Mother." Aymon brushed her hand away. "I am not a child, nor an invalid. As soon as my legs will support me, I will be out on the walls, defending my home. That is my duty."

"You are a worthy heir," Seguin beamed. "I'm proud of you, son."

Marie and Elissent exchanged a glance. If they could manage it, Aymon would find himself unable to stand for at least five more days.

Once her body had wrung out her tears, Catherine found that all feeling seemed to have left her. She couldn't make herself understand that her mother was dead. Instead of pain, she had nothing inside but a great hollowness where sorrow should be. How could she be so callous? What kind of unnatural child was she?

Instead, Margaret was the one she grieved over. The poor girl kept herself away from the family as much as she could. She spent the night in the chapel, praying for forgiveness. She refused to eat. No number of assurances that no one blamed her could reduce her guilt.

Catherine was horrified to realize that, in some part, she was angry with Madeleine for dragging Margaret into the tragedy of her death.

She was more than angry with Berthe. All the woman's mys-

terious allusions and promises of help were as much a fable as Andonenn. She was either mad or evil, or both. No wonder she
hadn't returned.

Gargenaud had been told of his daughter's drowning. He sent
word that he would remain in his room that night. Seguin had de-
livered the news and remarked to his wife that the old man was
prostrate, but not with grief.

Catherine heard of this, of course. She, Agnes, and Guillaume were the only ones who mourned Madeleine. To everyone
else her death was an inconvenience, a sign of coming disaster or
a very thoughtless act of water pollution.

"Edgar," Catherine said, when he came up to the room to get
his straw hat. "I am ashamed to be related to these people. I
hereby vow that I shall never say a word against your family
again."

"Why not?" Edgar asked. "My family is dreadful, with one or
two exceptions, like Margaret. And these people do have their
good points. I rather like your cousin Seguin. Odilon and his
priest brother, I could survive without. Neither has done a thing
to help us prepare to defend the keep. I hear that Odilon has been
sharpening his sword and checking his mail for broken links, all
the while bragging about what he intends to do. But he hasn't offered to lead a sortie. And that Ysore hasn't even said a Mass for
the soul of your mother."

He found the hat and put it on. Catherine noticed that his
nose and the back of his neck were already reddening. She gave
him a towel to tuck under the crown and hang down. But nothing
would really protect Edgar's fair skin from the summer sun.

"There's smoke rising from the forest," he said quietly as he
left. "By tomorrow we'll know just how strong the walls of
Boisvert are."

Catherine was so drained that it was hours before she realized
what he meant. She had forgotten all about the army coming to
besiege them.

∞

On his way out, Edgar stopped by Aymon's bed.

"It's good to see you in the land of the living," he said.

"Thanks to you and Brehier." Aymon smiled. "I don't know what I was thinking of, to wander off like that with a murderer on the loose."

"You were overwhelmed by grief and not in your right reason," Edgar consoled him. "Aymon, we know about your secret tunnel. Brehier and I found the entrance in the forest not far from where we found you. But we weren't able to trace it back to the keep. How does one reach it from the inside?"

Aymon's face was blank.

"Secret tunnel?" he said. "I don't know what you mean."

"Aymon." Edgar tried to keep his patience. "It's not ten paces from the tree where you tie your horse. This is not the time to guard a childish need for secrecy. The safety of all here depends on blocking any way in. If Olivier's men find the entrance, they can creep in and kill us all in our beds."

"That would be horrible," Aymon agreed. "But I can't help. I know of no such tunnel. I know of no such passage from the keep. Are you sure you didn't just find some old pagan cave? There are a few around here. I sheltered in one once when caught out by nightfall. I'll never do that again. I heard moans and cries all night from the damned souls who worshipped there."

"No." Edgar was losing patience. "It was a passage just like the ones under the castle. I'd go back and search it again if there weren't an army in the way."

"I've no idea what it was." Aymon yawned. "Sorry. Those women worried so much that I wouldn't wake up and now they keep giving me sleeping draughts."

He closed his eyes.

After a moment, Edgar gave up.

It made no sense. Aymon must have known about the tunnel. If not, then who had told the thieves that it was the trail to a treasure? The prisoner was talking readily enough, but no amount of persuasion had convinced him to name the one who had sent them to Boisvert. Edgar was inclined to believe that he didn't know.

As if aware that cheerful sunlight was inappropriate, dark clouds began to blow from the west. Seguin's only comment was to ask Edgar if rain would affect the tension of the ropes of his trebuchet.

It seemed to everyone else that Heaven was commenting on the battle to come. If only they knew what side it disapproved of.

Not even the children slept well that night. Peter fretted so that Catherine took him out onto the castle wall where a line of people stood silently as a cool breeze stung their eyes.

The fields below were dotted with flickering campfires stretching almost to the forest. The wind brought snatches of sound: the shouts of men and the neighing of horses, hammer blows as tents were set up, clanking metal.

Catherine found Edgar and Margaret.

"How many are out there?" she asked them.

"Hundreds, I'd say." Edgar was trying to count the points of light. "I had no idea this minor lord could raise such a force. He must have hired mercenaries, as well as his own men."

Catherine moved closer to him, staring into the night.

"There will be some sort of parley first, won't there?" she asked.

"Seguin has asked for volunteers to take a message to Olivier, asking his intentions, that sort of thing," Edgar said. "I don't think this will be solved with words."

"Our father and brothers would have gone out to fight before the army got this close," Margaret said. "Why are we waiting?"

"We don't have the men our father did," Edgar told her. "Our keep wasn't as strong as this and, our father cared little about what happened to the people inside."

"Ah, yes," Margaret remembered.

By mutual consent they returned to their chamber. Catherine laid the sleeping Peter on the bed with his brother and sister.

"Samonie?" Catherine saw that the woman was leaving the room, a pillow and blanket under her arm. "Aren't you staying with us tonight?"

Samonie shook her head. "I love you all dearly," she said. "But eight people in a room this size can be too close. I think I've earned one night of uninterrupted sleep."

Catherine was not as obtuse as Samonie hoped. She merely smiled and wished her housekeeper a pleasant evening.

It took Samonie some time to find Brehier without appearing to be looking for him. She finally found him sitting on a sawhorse next to the ovens.

"Hello!" He stood to greet her. "I've been hunting everywhere for you."

"Really?" she asked. "Whatever for?"

He bent down and whispered a suggestion in her ear. She laughed.

"Aren't you on duty tonight?"

"No, Guillaume and I spent all day down below, trying to discover the other end of the tunnel we found. It must link into the maze somewhere. We went as far as we dared, farther than either of us had ever explored. Finally we had to turn back or risk losing the way back. It must be found. We can't defend all the ways up."

"What about the man you captured?" Samonie asked. "Has he told you anything?

"Not even his name." Brehier made a face. "He keeps repeating that he's nothing but a common thief, hired in Chartres to help dig out a treasure."

"Could he be telling the truth?"

"I have no idea," Brehier told her. He took the blanket and pillow from her. "That's for Seguin and Odilon and Guillaume to decide. I'm only a poor relation."

"You are!" Samonie was taken aback. "You never said so."

"Why else do you think I came back here?" he asked. "At Boisvert, none of Andonenn's children would ever be turned away, no matter how distant the tie."

Samonie took a moment to digest this fact. Brehier tried to see her face in the torchlight.

"Does this mean you won't sleep with me tonight?"

"What?" She recalled why she was there in the first place. "Of course I will."

She was just wondering what Catherine would think if she knew that her son, Martin, was of her kin. Then she thought of the curse. It couldn't reach that far, could it?

She had lost her daughter. She had no intention of letting her son die, too.

If only she felt certain that she could trust his father.

The next morning brought a thick mist that seeped under doors and flowed around the buildings and mounds of belongings and into the covers of those sleeping out of doors.

Edgar observed it from the window, trying to catch sight of anything moving up the hill toward them.

"It will burn off soon," he predicted sourly.

Catherine sighed. She was growing to hate the sun. How could she ever have complained about the dank Paris winters?

They waited all morning for some sign from the enemy camp.

"He should have sent out a challenge by now," Seguin worried. "He can't expect us to simply surrender."

"We should show him we won't," Odilon stated. "I have a dozen men ready to make a sortie."

"Why?" Edgar asked. "We're safe in here."

Odilon got up and moved away from him. "So that he knows we're not cowards," he sneered.

"Of course," Edgar answered. "And be sure that we're fools."

"Enough!" Seguin shouted. "The enemy is not in this room."

"Are we so sure of that?" Odilon asked under his breath.

Edgar heard him and presumed that Seguin had, too. But the lord made no comment.

"Edgar," he asked. "Those *ballista* of yours, will they be ready?"

"Yes, my lord," Edgar answered. "Your workmen are most skillful. It would be good to have a pile of stones to throw and smaller ones to fill the baskets."

"I'll set people to gathering them." Seguin nodded approval.

Odilon was growing restless.

"I still think some of us should ride out," Odilon grumbled. "Let them know there are men here who will fight."

Seguin was silent for a while.

"Odilon, Guillaume."

The two men straightened at the steel in his voice.

"You want to do a deed of courage? Very well, Odilon, you may make a sortie."

Odilon gave a broad smile. "Thank you, my lord! I'll have my men prepare."

"And mine," Guillaume said. "I've only Hamelin and Osbert, but they're both strong and brave, worth ten any day."

"Good," Seguin said. "You're to go out with a maximum of fanfare, horns, drums, and swords. Make sure all eyes are on you."

"What are you planning, cousin?" Guillaume asked.

"That entrance in the forest is still our Achilles' heel," Seguin told them. "I propose sending two men to find and enter it while Olivier's men are occupied."

"You want me to be a damned hunter's blind!" Odilon was outraged.

"Exactly," Seguin said. "I don't want to be another verse in the family epic. My only goal is to protect my people until either help arrives or winter sends Olivier home. Shout threats and flourish your weapons, but I hope that will be all. I have already asked Thierry and Lucius from the village if they will undertake to find the tunnel. They know the forest paths better than any."

"What are we to do?" Odilon complained. "Turn tail if they want to fight?"

"We retreat." Guillaume was firm. "You may stay and die in glory, but I have a wife, five children, and two hundred villagers depending on me to stay alive."

Before Odilon could protest further, Seguin gave a roar of approval.

"Very good, cousin!" he said. "We don't have enough good warriors to throw any away. Now, everyone. There's no time to lose."

Edgar had to admit as he watched them go, gonfanons fluttering in the breeze and armor shining, that they did look impressive. Seguin rode in front, with Odilon on his right and Guillaume on his left. The metal on their harnesses gleamed and their shields caught the sun, sending blinding rays onto the tents of the enemy. Edgar told himself they were fools, but he knew that part of his anger was that there was no chance of him joining them.

They rode straight across the fields and up to Olivier's camp. No one noticed the two men in peasant garb slithering among the ruins of the houses outside the wall. They blended in with the dry fields and vanished in the direction of the forest.

A few moments later, there was a bustle from among the tents and a similar party emerged. The two groups of horsemen met in the middle of the field and stopped.

By the gestures it was obvious that Seguin and Olivier were discussing the situation. Seguin pointed out the thickness of the walls of Boisvert and Olivier countered with the size of his army. As this continued the movements grew more threatening, although no one yet had drawn a weapon.

Finally they seemed to come to some agreement. Both parties wheeled about and galloped back to their own sides.

∞

Seguin dismounted and took off his gloves.

"That idiot hasn't a drop of Andonenn's blood in him," he said. "It will please me greatly to send him whimpering back to Anjou."

Guillaume went to where Marie, Catherine, and Edgar were waiting.

"It was all I could do to keep Odilon from offering a personal challenge," he grunted. "He seems to think this is no more than a tourney. Have Thierry and Lucius returned?"

"No," Edgar said. "But we don't know how long and twisted the passage is. Or how far they had to circle to get to the opening."

"Mmm." Guillaume looked worried. "I hope this parade gave them enough time. Wearing mail in this weather is as close to hell as I ever hope to be."

They waited all afternoon, each moment expecting the men to appear through one of the entrances to the Great Hall.

The sun was low in the sky, and Catherine and Edgar were standing on the wall looking out toward the invaders.

"I wish we knew what they planned," Catherine sighed.

"Olivier doesn't have enough men to throw them against the walls," Edger considered. "With all the traps we set in the village it would be almost impossible to get siege engines very close. He must know he can't starve us out."

"What if he is waiting for the gate to be opened by someone already inside?" As soon as she said it, Catherine was sorry that she had given her fears form.

Edgar started to answer when the clammy evening was shattered by a horrific scream from Olivier's camp. It was so loud and high that dogs began to bark and the doves were startled from their nests.

A horseman rode out from the camp, carrying something slung on the horse in front. While he was still out of arrow range, he reined in and unceremoniously dumped his burden onto the dusty road.

"What . . . what . . . is . . . it?" Catherine's mind refused to admit to what her eyes saw.

"It's Thierry." Edgar's voice was flat. "They've cut off his hands and feet."

"No, it can't be. Please, dear God, it can't be." But she knew it was.

Catherine could now make out the figure, crawling up the road on knees and elbows. The cuts had been cauterized but he was still trailing blood from fresh raw wounds.

"Papa, what's going on?" James tugged at Edgar's tunic.

"James, go in at once!" Catherine said sharply.

"No!" Edgar rarely spoke in that tone, but when he did, Catherine obeyed.

Edgar picked his son up and held him so that he could see the man moving with agonizing slowness toward the castle.

"Do you see what they've done to him?" he asked James.

The little boy nodded, horrified.

"Edgar, he's only six!" Catherine pleaded.

"Yes." Edgar didn't look at her. "Old enough to remember."

"Papa," James whispered. "Why . . . why did they hurt him?"

"This is what Christians do when they go to war," Edgar answered, his words clear and cutting. "You must swear two things to me, son, if you decide to be a warrior. Never treat anyone with such evil."

"No, Papa, never." James's cheeks were red and his eyes round with fear.

"And," Edgar went on, "become strong enough that no one will be able to ever do such a thing to you."

James's glance went to the leather-covered stump where his father's left hand should be.

"I swear," he said. "On my soul, Father."

Catherine reached out for the boy.

"Let me take him in now," she said. "Edgar?"

Something in him seemed to burn out. He handed her their son.

James clung to her tightly with arms and legs. Catherine looked into Edgar's eyes, afraid of what might look back. Their sea-gray shade had darkened to cold iron. She blinked and saw the sea wash back, salt tears glittering on his pale lashes.

Seventeen

Three weeks later. 4 kalends October (September 27) 1149, Michaelmas Eve. 16 Tishri 4910, the second day of Succos.

Li quens Rollant ad la buche sanglente
De sun cheval rumput en est li temples.
L'olifant sunet a dulor e a peine
Karles l'oit e ses Franseis l'entendent.

Count Roland's mouth was bloody
From his cracked skull and brain.
He sounded the oliphant in grief and pain
Charlemagne heard it and his Franks took heed.

—*La Chanson de Roland*, II. 1785–1788

*B*efore he died, Thierry swore to them that he had not divulged the existence of the tunnel. He had told his captors that he had been hunting and knew nothing of Boisvert. Olivier had insisted that he and his companion were spies and punished them accordingly. The other man had died after his feet had been cut off. He had said nothing about another entrance, either.

Gargenaud ordered that Thierry be buried with honor in the family vault.

The next day Olivier attacked with a charge that cost him many men, thanks in no small measure to the trebuchet Edgar had designed and that the workmen had improved upon. Even the lower walls remained unbreached.

Olivier was undaunted. Even though they had no weapon that could reach the defenders, the assault continued every morning for ten days, as if Olivier felt he had no need to conserve his forces nor any interest in how little damage they were doing.

At this point everyone at Boisvert had been pressed into service, carrying stone, filling the baskets, making new arrows for the archers. There was not enough time for anyone to sleep or prepare food nor, with the state of the well uncertain, was there a chance to wash. The inhabitants became increasingly grimy, their faces lined with gritty sweat.

Now and then Olivier would let loose a shot from a mangonel and there would be a thump and shake as the boulder hit the walls.

"Why does he bother?" Marie cried in vexation as the stool she was sitting on rocked with the vibration.

"To rub out nerves raw," Agnes answered. "In my case, it's successful."

Eventually, the daily assaults ended, and Olivier contented himself with an occasional charge against the gates when they least expected it. These were easily repulsed by the archers on the walls.

"I don't understand it," Seguin said. "He hasn't tried a battering ram on the lower gate. Not even flaming arrows. Why not?"

"Do you think he knows that we can't use the well?" Odilon asked, with an apologetic glance at Guillaume.

"How could he?" Seguin asked.

The unspoken answer lay between them. There was a traitor.

"Perhaps he wants to keep Boisvert in good repair for when it belongs to him," Odilon suggested.

"There's no way that will happen," Seguin said. "Especially if he continues his siege in this halfhearted fashion."

"We should be grateful," Guillaume added. "It gives us more time to try to find the passage that leads out to the forest."

"Does Aymon still insist he never knew about it?" Odilon asked.

"Yes," Seguin said. "He says he found the stable and made use of it. That was all."

"I wish we could get out to explore from that end." Guillaume tugged his beard in frustration.

"Better stay far away lest Olivier find it," Seguin reminded him.

"Well, Count Thibault will surely arrive soon with enough men to drive Olivier back to Anjou," Guillaume concluded.

"Huh!" Odilon said. "If Thibault ever got the message. What will you wager that the count knows nothing of our trouble? Do you really think this Solomon cares what happens to us?"

"I don't like Solomon," Guillaume told them. "But it's because he's arrogant and an infidel. Other than that, he's trustworthy. It may be that Thibault wasn't in Paris or Troyes and Solomon had to track him down elsewhere. But he won't abandon his mission."

Odilon shook his head. "You've been contaminated by your sister. She and her husband are obviously far too friendly with the man. No one is coming to save us."

"That's not true!" Guillaume felt odd defending Solomon.

Seguin interrupted. "I don't know which of you is right. It doesn't matter. What we must do is find a way to defeat Olivier on our own."

"And what has happened to Andonenn?" Odilon wanted to know. "We did everything we were supposed to. Instead of being our salvation, that magic gift from Charlemagne turned out to be a knife that killed the best warrior we had. We have a foe without and a curse within. How are we supposed to fight both at once?"

"I own the knife makes no sense." Seguin sighed. "But Andonenn has protected us this long. We must have faith in her yet a while."

The men were sitting beside the empty hearth in the Great Hall. It was late in the evening and their faces were lit by only a small oil lamp hanging from an iron sconce. Varying emotions were reflected in them, but the predominant one was irritation. There was no need yet for fear or despair, but each man felt that the days of calm punctuated by sudden shrieks of men or the *whoosh* of objects hurled at the wall were only a stalling ploy. Guillaume finally said what they all were thinking.

"He's waiting for something, or someone."

"So are we," Seguin said. "But even if he brings in a thousand more men, we can still keep them from breaking through. The slope is way too steep for battering rams or belfries."

"There's something we're missing." Odilon tapped his teeth with his meat knife.

From outside there was a crash as a boulder flattened an empty chicken coop.

Seguin paid it no mind. "Yes," he agreed. "But what? What have we failed to see?"

"Mama." Edana climbed on Catherine's lap. "I want to go home."

"So do I, *deorling*." Catherine tried to smooth her daughter's tangled hair. "But we still have work to do here."

Edana nodded wisely. "That's what the lady says."

"What? What lady?" Catherine feared she already knew.

"She asks me and Evaine why you aren't helping," Edana told her. "I always say I think you're trying. Is that right?"

"Yes, it is," Catherine said. "I didn't know you still saw her. I thought Evaine promised to call if she came again."

"She told us not to," Edana confessed.

"Edana, I am your mother," Catherine said sharply. "Your first duty is to me. Now, you must call if you ever see her again. I need to speak with her. Do you understand?"

Edana seemed worried but she promised. She hugged Catherine and ran out to play with her cousins.

Catherine sat for some time, pondering the message that Mandon had given Edana. Not doing enough to help? What more could they do? Berthe had vanished. No one else had admitted to seeing her and Catherine was half-convinced she and her matching knife had been a dream. Mandon only spoke to children, apparently. They had prepared the best they could to hold out against Olivier de Boue. They had followed the commands of the legend. What else was there?

Through the window she could see clouds gathering again. Hopefully, there would be rain soon. After a few days, when Madeleine's body had not floated to the surface, Seguin had decided that the water might be used for washing and, after boiling, for cooking. But there was the fear shared by them all, that Madeleine was still in there, caught on something or weighted down by her clothes. No one wanted to drink from a grave. Rain would be a blessing.

The fact that her mother's body was still missing gave Catherine a shred of hope. Perhaps Madeleine was still alive. But, if so, where was she and why hadn't she been found?

Catherine pressed her forehead against the stone edging the window.

"We're missing something," she muttered.

Brehier also felt there was something that had been overlooked. Olivier's sorties were too desultory. His men must be getting hungry by now. There wasn't that much left in the fields. They did nothing beyond making sporadic raids on the countryside and occasionally hurling stones over the walls. Olivier had to be waiting for something, but what?

Someone should go and find out.

Brehier thought of what had happened to the men caught spying. Death didn't frighten him particularly, but how much torture could he endure?

He honestly didn't know.

After debating the subject with himself, he decided to go to Edgar.

"This isn't a decision I can make," Edgar told him with alarm. "You should talk to Seguin."

"I can't," Brehier insisted. "He's my lord and kin. It's the same with the others. They knew me as a child and as a man returning home with his tail between his legs. Seguin half believes that I am the one who betrayed us."

"And, if you are, what better way to get out than to offer to go among the enemy again? It would give you the chance to tell Olivier what the situation is in here?" Edgar pointed out.

"Yes, I thought of that," Brehier said. "I'm wondering if Olivier is stalling because his spy hasn't been able to get out to report. But it isn't me."

Edgar remained unconvinced.

"There's another possibility," Brehier continued. "I thought of you as soon as it occurred to me. Can you teach me to recognize different kinds of siege engines?"

"Why?" Edgar asked. "What do you think he could be constructing?"

"Something we won't notice until it's too late," Brehier answered.

Comprehension dawned in Edgar's eyes.

"You can't go alone," he said. "It would take too long for you to find it. They'd catch you for certain. You need someone to go with you. Martin and I can take the west side, go over the wall by the middens, and slip into the forest by night. We'll be able from there to see what they are up to. There's not enough going on

where we can see. I think most of the army is building some en-
gine in the forest."

"No," Brehier said quickly. "Not Martin."

Seeing Edgar's puzzlement, he added, "He's too inexperi-
enced. And not you, either. If I let you fall into their hands, I
would be just as sure to die as if Olivier captured me. And I doubt
your wife would be as gentle as his torturers."

"Then it will be to both our advantage for me to accompany
you." Edgar smiled. "I'll leave Martin here, if you like. I don't like
risking the boy, either. But, if you want me to keep this from Gargenaud and the rest of the family, the only way is by taking me
with you. And, if you are the traitor, you had better pray that you
never fall into Catherine's hands."

"I swear you can count on me." Brehier offered Edgar his
hand.

Edgar clasped the hand. "I am depending on it."

"Shall we meet by the gate tonight after Compline?" Brehier
asked.

"No, the guards will be alert and we'll spend the time stum-
bling in the dark," Edgar said. "Better in the twilight just before
dawn. This time of year we might be lucky and get a ground fog
that will conceal us better than night."

"Tell no one," Brehier cautioned. "There is still a deceiver
living among us."

"Yes, I know," Edgar answered, wondering if he was talking
to him.

Margaret was sorting through the clothes she had brought with
her. There hadn't been much to begin with. Agnes seemed to
have an inexhaustible number of clean *chainses* and five or six
fine *bliauts* to wear over them. Margaret had brushed and spot-
cleaned the stains on her things as best she could and aired the
clothing that touched her skin, but she was beginning to feel as

shabby as some poor serf who had but one change of clothing for the year.

There must be a bit of ribbon or a length of brocade to brighten the dull colors and cover the grease spots. She dug down to the bottom of the bag.

The thing she came up with surprised her. She'd never seen it before. It was a piece of embroidery about as long as her arm and as wide as her hand. The design was crude, a knight standing with one foot on the chest of his enemy, then the same man receiving a box of sorts from his lord, no, his king. The rough figure wore a crown. The next part showed the same knight riding toward a tower on a hill where a female figure waited. There was writing, too, but Margaret couldn't read it.

She couldn't understand how this had gotten into the bottom of her clothes bag, but she did have a good idea where it had come from.

She rolled the embroidery up and tucked it into her sleeve. Now, where would Catherine most likely be?

Agnes was not as well prepared as it seemed. She realized that most of her strips of old linen had been set aside for bandages. Now she realized she would need a few of them back.

"Marie," she asked, grateful to have found her brother's wife alone. "Do you think you could spare some rags. All of mine are soaking in a pail of cold water."

"Yes, of course." Marie went at once to her cache. "I have plenty and I'm not due to need them for another week or two. Now, what's this doing here? How odd."

She held up the cloth that had been discovered at the top of their burnt-out tower.

"Saint Gertrude's slipping sandals!" Agnes exclaimed. "Do you know what that is?"

"No," Marie answered. "Do you?"

"Not at all," Agnes said. "But I have another piece of it, I think. It was hanging outside my window the morning we left Trier. I asked Hermann if the writing at the top were German and he said it rather looked like it, but he couldn't make it out. Now, where did I put it?"

"If you can find yours, I'd like to compare them," Marie said. "Guillaume thought someone was trying to tell Andonenn's story in tapestry. But why it would then be hung from the tower, I can't imagine."

Agnes took the wad of rags and went back to her room. She was certain that she had packed that embroidery piece. A search of her clothes boxes turned up nothing. She asked her maids, but no one remembered seeing it.

The nursemaid overheard them as she entered, bringing Gott-fried to his mother. She made a guilty noise.

"Oooooh, my lady," she said. "Forgive me. I thought it was for the baby."

"Why ever would you think that?" Agnes asked. "And what did you do with it?"

"It has a picture of saints and magic writing," the woman explained. "I want little Gottfried to have all the protection I can give him."

"That's very commendable," Agnes told her. "But I don't think the cloth has any power to do that."

She ended on a note of doubt. For all she knew, it might have. She held out her hand for the embroidery piece. The nursemaid laid the baby on a cot and took off his long *chainse*. She turned it inside out and there it was, loosely stitched around the hem of the garment.

"I'm afraid he's soiled it a bit," she told Agnes. "Shall I rinse it out for you?"

Agnes nodded. "I'll be in the solar with Lady Marie."

At the same time, Margaret was showing her discovery to Catherine.

"I think it belonged to your mother," Margaret said. "But I

don't know how it got in with my things unless she put it there."

"It looks like another piece of the one from the tree in our garden," Catherine said, studying the design. "But, look, this one seems much older. The colors of the thread have faded."

"Perhaps it's a family pattern?" Margaret suggested.

"I suppose," Catherine said. "But I've never seen it. I wonder where she kept it."

"Your sister might know," Margaret said.

Catherine sighed. "Yes. Mother talked with Agnes much more than with me. We'd better take this to her. I don't know what it means, but at the moment we have no other hope."

Seguin was on his way to consult with his father when he decided to check on Aymon's condition. Despite initial improvement, his son was still too weak to leave his bed. Marie had said nothing, but Seguin feared that there had been permanent damage. Aymon's legs were unnaturally still beneath the sheet.

He found Elissent sitting with him. She was reading from a book of psalms in French and Aymon was trying to appear interested. He greeted his father with enthusiasm.

"At last," he said. "Someone who can rescue me from my overprotective nurses! Father, look at me. I'm doing much better. I can hear that you need me."

"When you can get out of bed on your own," Elissent responded, "I won't try to keep you in it."

Aymon grimaced. "It's true my legs are still a bit weak, but put me on a horse and I'll be fine."

Over his head, Seguin's eyes met Elissent's. She gave a small, sad shake of the head.

"One more horseman will make little difference," Seguin told Aymon. "There's no point in riding out to attack Olivier when all we need to do is wait him out. You stay where you are until your mother and Marie say you're completely recovered."

"But I feel so useless here!" Aymon thumped the bed in frustration.

"We all do, to some extent," Seguin tried to assure him. "Waiting is not natural to men trained to fight. We can't even get out to hunt. You're not the only one on edge from lack of occupation."

"Have you spent more time searching the tunnels?" Aymon asked.

"No, I don't want to risk losing anyone else," Seguin said. "Whoever attacked you and killed your brother may still be hiding down there. The doorways down there are guarded now, but it would take an army to go through every one of the old passages safely."

Aymon leaned back on his pillows, not entirely mollified.

"I wish I had seen the face of the one who struck me," he sighed.

"Perhaps you'll soon remember more about him," Seguin said, patting his shoulder. "A sound or a smell that might help us identify him."

Aymon shook his head. "There's nothing. I was so agitated by the sight of my brother's body that I would not have noticed a lion ready to pounce."

"Of course," Seguin said. "And we're grateful that you, at least, survived. Marie says it's a miracle that none of the blows penetrated your liver or heart. It's strange that the thrust that killed your brother was so precise and your wounds so clumsily made."

"Are you sorry it was not the other way around?" Aymon asked sharply.

"Of course not," Elissent answered for them both. "Your father was only making a comment. You and Raimbaut were equally precious to us. Isn't that so, husband?"

Seguin blinked. He had been following his thoughts.

"Yes, yes, of course," he said just a fraction late. "Couldn't bear to lose the both of you. Stay put until you're entirely well. I'll come by later."

He left abruptly. Aymon looked after him with a wistful expression. Elissent didn't notice; she had resumed reading the
psalms.

"They all match," Catherine said, looking at the row of embroidery pieces. "But it still seems that there should be one more."

She pointed at a space where the floral borders didn't match.

"If we could read the language we'd know for sure," Marie
said. "I can't believe that not even the monks of Chartres knew
what it was."

"It could be some incantation," Catherine suggested. "The
words that will open the way to Andonenn's spring."

"It might be the language of the fairy people," Margaret
said. She frowned. "But then how would they expect us to pro-
nounce it?"

Marie had been studying the pieces.

"Could the words be a ruse?" she asked the rest of the women.
"Perhaps we should make more note of the pictures."

"But that's just the story we all know," Agnes objected. "The
text must be a message for us. Why else leave these strips all
over?"

"Why indeed?" Catherine wanted to know. "None of us
found this until we had already decided to come here. Why go
to so much trouble putting them in places where we might not
find them? Why not just wait until we had arrived and give
them to us?"

The other three were silent.

They all looked at each other. Finally Margaret said in a
small voice, "Isn't that the way legends work? Everything must be
done in its own time, according to the rules."

Catherine didn't know whether to laugh or shriek. Mindful
that there were various children around, she managed not to do
either.

"Does this look like a legend?" she asked them. "Do the heroines of *chansons* ever go weeks without being able to wash their hair? Or run out of blood rags? Or have to wipe a child's runny nose? We're real women. This Mandon has been trying to shove us into guises we have no right to take. Why are we trying to follow her rules?"

"Because it seems the only way to survive and return to our true lives," Marie answered.

Agnes shook herself as if waking. She gave Catherine a bemused smile.

"Why would we believe anything so stupid?" she said. "Catherine's right. We've let Boisvert ensorcel our minds. What we should do is track down Mandon and sit on her until she tells us what's going on and what we have to do to make things right again. Never mind these pieces of cloth."

"Agnes, this isn't our home," Marie reminded her. "We can't take such liberties."

"Why not?" Even timid Margaret was fed up. "No one else is going to do it. Elissent is too occupied with Aymon and Briaud . . ."

She trailed off. The other three silently filled in their opinions of Briaud.

"We have to find Mandon first," Marie said bitterly. "She seems to be able to get into the nursery no matter how many of us are stationed at the door."

"Of course!" Catherine hit her forehead with her palm. "*Quam stulta sum!* There must be a secret opening there like the one she slipped through in the tunnel. We know the room so well we never thought of looking for a hidden door."

As one, the women gathered up their children and headed for the nursery.

Brehier was quite certain that he was going to come back from his mission with Edgar, but just in case, there was one thing he had to do.

Martin was playing *merel* in the bailey with the stablemen. The small pile of coins indicated that the game was more to kill time than serious gambling.

"Martin!"

The boy's head came up. He smiled.

"Yes, my lord Brehier. What may I do for you?"

"If you could come with me, please," Brehier answered. "I need to have a talk with you and your mother."

"Nothing here . . . ah . . . ah . . . choo!" Agnes sneezed from behind a wall hanging.

They were dismantling the nursery trying to find Mandon's entryway.

"Where does she come from when you see her?" Marie asked Evaine.

"I don't know, Mama," the girl answered. "I wake up and she's just there. I know I said I'd call you but she told me that if I did, there would be no hope of ever freeing Andonenn. Did she lie to me?"

"I don't know, *ma douz*," Marie answered. "But it was wrong of her to try to convince you to disobey me."

"I've been all over these walls," Catherine said, pulling a long cobweb from her braid. "If there's an opening, I can't find it."

Edana had been sitting on the floor with Marie's youngest, Mabile, both watching the search with interest.

"Are you looking for the lady?" she asked.

"Yes," Catherine answered. "But we can't find the door to her house."

"We know, don't we, Mabile?" Edana said.

Mabile pulled her thumb out of her mouth long enough to confirm this.

"You do?" Catherine knelt next to them. "Where?"

"Right under us!" Edana laughed, as if she'd just performed a complicated trick.

Instantly the girls were picked up and deposited on top of the clothes chests. The spot where they had been sitting was covered by a moth-eaten deerskin.

"I remember that," Agnes said. "It was here when we were children."

Catherine tried to pick it up, but the skin was stuck to the floor.

"Margaret, would you run down and see what's below this?" she asked. "I can't find a hook or anything to open it so it must be on the other side."

Margaret was back in a moment.

"It's just a room full of boxes," she told them. "The ceiling is painted with branches and leaves as if you were lying under a tree. The paint is cracked and peeling."

Agnes gave a quick intake of breath. "That was Mother's room," she said sadly. "She used to tell us about it when we were little."

"I wonder if that was where she went to find the way to Andonenn," Catherine said.

Marie was more interested in immediate dangers.

"Could there be some sort of trapdoor, Margaret?"

"I couldn't see one, but with all the foliage, it would be easy to miss," Margaret answered. "And I don't think that was Madeleine's way out. We went outside the keep when she was looking for it again."

"James?" Catherine said.

The boy knew that tone. He looked guilty even though he didn't know what he was about to be accused of.

"Where is your wooden sword?" she asked.

"Right here, Mama," he answered, both relieved and puzzled.

"I need to borrow it for a moment," she told him.

He handed it to her. "Are you going to fight off the soldiers? Dragon and I will help you."

"No," Catherine said. "I'm going back down with Margaret.

I'll tap on the ceiling until you hear me under the skin. When you do, stomp on it to let me know."

The room was small, with only one narrow window. It seemed to have been created as an afterthought from a corner. Two of the walls were stone and two made of wood. Catherine tried to figure out where the skin was above them. She climbed onto an oaken chest and began to tap on the ceiling with the sword.

After a few tries, there was an answering stomp.

Catherine got down long enough to put another box on top of the chest.

"Steady this for me, would you?" she asked Margaret.

Carefully, she felt around the area beneath the deerskin.

"There's something here," she grunted. "Oh, no, I think it's just a knothole."

She pulled her finger out of it and, to her surprise, the ceiling came with it. There was a squeal from above and then the opening was ringed with faces.

"Well," Catherine announced. "Now we know how Mandon gets into the nursery. The next thing is to figure out how she gets in here."

Samonie was out by the kitchens, trying to beat the dust out of a *bliaut* of Catherine's. When she saw Brehier and Martin heading toward her, she dropped the beater and crossed her arms.

"Samonie," Brehier began without preamble. "I have to leave Boisvert for a time. Before I go, I want us to explain things to Martin."

"What things?" Samonie asked in suspicion.

"All of them," Brehier answered. "Including some you don't know."

Samonie sat on an upturned washtub.

"Then I'd better start," she said. "Martin, I met Brehier in Troyes, when I worked at the castle of the count. It was a long time ago. He had more hair then."

"Saint Peter's crowing cock, woman!" Brehier interrupted. He doesn't need to know all that. Martin, I'm your father."

Martin stared at the both of them for a while; then he nodded slowly.

"You always said he was a knight, Mother," he said. "I apologize for not believing you. Thank you, my lord, for telling me."

Samonie stood up and brushed off her skirts.

"If that's all," she said. "I have work to do."

"No, that's not all!" Brehier took her by the shoulders and set her back down. Then he turned back to Martin

"I didn't know you existed," he explained. "I wish I had. I haven't done much in my life to be proud of and it would have given me comfort to have been able to remind myself that I, at least, had produced such a fine son."

Martin tried to suppress the smile, but it would appear.

"I shall try to be worthy of your esteem, my lord," he said.

From her washtub, Samonie broke in. "Go on, Martin, say it. You know he's dying to hear it, don't you?"

"Father!" Martin said.

"If you'll have me," Brehier answered.

"Now are we finished?" Samonie tried to get up again.

"Not quite," Brehier said. "If I should die in battle, I want you to be able to claim what little I have. It isn't much but it, and my name, are yours, my son. I have written as much on a paper I left with Ysore. And I also want to give you this."

He took out a small parcel wrapped in cloth. As he opened it, Martin realized that the parcel was the cloth.

"I had it from my mother," Brehier said. "Who had it from hers and so forth. It was my great-grandmother who was of Boisvert."

As soon as she saw what it was, Samonie snatched it from him.

"You've had this all along and told no one?" she asked. "I vow that each member of your family needs a keeper!"

"Would you consider taking on the job?" he asked.

For once, Samonie was speechless.

"Say yes, Mother." Martin took the embroidery. "Don't worry. I'll see that cousin Catherine gets this immediately."

"Don't be saying that to her now!" Samonie warned. "I'd slap you, myself, for such disrespect."

After Martin had left, Brehier smiled at Samonie.

"I was asking you to marry me," he said.

"A fine thing," she answered. "Both of us well past our prime and you likely to be killed tomorrow."

"True," he answered. "What do you say?"

"I say, come back alive and with all the important bits still attached, and I'll consider it."

Samonie tried to turn away, but he caught her and kissed her hard. After a moment she gave up trying to be sensible.

Eighteen

The fields outside Boisvert, just before dawn. Thursday
3 kalends October (September 28) 1149. Michaelmas, the
feast of Saint Michael the Archangel. 18 Tishri 4910,
the fourth day of Succos.

Trebuchet

*E*dgar was glad of the fog, even though his skin was dripping and clammy and his feet were freezing. Olivier's guards would not only have a hard time seeing him, but would also be confused as to the direction of sounds. He didn't know why, but he had often noticed that it was harder to locate the source of a noise in fog than in total darkness.

He and Brehier had met at the wall behind the middens and slipped over it, dropping onto the rocks below. At that point there was room enough for only one man at a time to pass between the wall and the hill. Gargenaud had felt that this, plus the noisome garbage pit on the castle side, would discourage invasion. And a spy who came in this way would be instantly smelled out.

Edgar moved carefully along the line of brush where the fields met the forest. On his left, he could make out the tents of Olivier's army. All was silent.

He had counted on the fog to hide his movements, but it also made it difficult to locate where Olivier's guards were stationed. He hoped they were all fairly close in.

He stepped on a loose pile of damp leaves, lost his balance, and fell with a squashy thump. His left arm flailed toward an exposed root and he cursed mightily to himself, knowing he had nothing to catch himself with. He lay at the bottom of a natural trench, dew soaking into his cloak, expecting any moment to find a sword tip at his throat.

Once he had caught his breath, Edgar pulled himself to a crouch and peered through the brush. He saw no one heading toward his position.

It bothered him that there was so little movement from the camp. Even at this hour sentries should be pacing and cooking fires started. The circle of tents seemed almost empty. Could Olivier have given up the siege and crept away by night?

Or could he be laying a trap?

Edgar wondered where Brehier was. Catherine would call him a fool for having trusted the man. He fervently hoped he'd be back within the keep before she woke. He hoped he'd get back at all. Catherine shouldn't have to find herself a widow so soon after her mother's death.

With a sigh he continued closing in on the camp. He was armed only with a long hunting knife and he had no intention of getting close enough to anyone to use it.

The closer he got, the more deserted the camp looked. His heart beating loudly in his ears, Edgar reached the first tent. It was empty.

So was the next and the next.

Edgar began to relax. Perhaps Olivier had received word of a relief army approaching and decided to retreat. He allowed himself to stretch to his full height.

"Get down!"

Edgar hit the ground. A few feet away, Brehier signaled from behind a tent flap. Edgar crawled toward him.

"Are you mad?" Brehier greeted him.

"There's no one here," Edgar answered.

"This reconnaissance was your idea," Brehier said. "Don't you realize that you were right?"

"Gudesblod!" Edgar swore. "Did you see where they went in?"

"Not far from Aymon's stable," Brehier answered. "They don't seem to be using the tunnel, though. Maybe our prisoner is what he says, a common thief."

"Or maybe we captured him before he could report its location," Edgar said. "Now what? Do you know where they are?"

"Too close," Brehier told him. "They've left this camp up as a blind and have made clusters of huts in the woods much closer to the walls. I nearly walked right into one of their 'villages.'"

Edgar quaked at the thought of how he might have done the same. When he fell, he could have slid right to Olivier's feet.

That brought another thought.

"Brehier," he said quietly. "If you had devised a phantom camp to fool the enemy, would you keep an eye on it to be sure the enemy didn't find out?"

"Oh, yes," Brehier answered.

They both thought this over.

"We're going to have a hell of a time getting out of this alive, aren't we?" Edgar said.

"Unless we can turn hedgehog and burrow home," Brehier answered.

"It seems," Edgar sighed, "that we're the only ones who can't."

Edgar was so preoccupied the evening before that Catherine hadn't been able to tell him about the embroidery pieces or the hunt for Mandon. She had planned to the first thing in the morning but, when she opened her eyes, he was gone.

"Samonie?" she called through the curtains. "Do you know where Edgar went?"

There was no answer. She poked her head out. Samonie wasn't there.

Catherine threw on her clothes. How late had she slept? The sun didn't seem to be very high. Was there an early Mass for Saint Michael that she hadn't been told about?

She hurried into the passage and up to the nursery. The children were all sound asleep, the nurses dozing by the doorway. The heavy iron brazier they had placed over the trapdoor was still in place. At least Catherine needn't worry that Mandon had made an appearance that night.

In the hall she found guards just coming off their watch and servants sweeping the rushes into piles to carry out to the middens. No one else was up.

Where could Edgar and Samonie have gone?

Catherine was becoming alarmed. She went back to her room to fetch her outside shoes. To her amazement, Samonie was lying on her cot as though she'd been there all night.

"Where have you been," Catherine demanded, shaking her. "Where's Edgar?"

"Master Edgar? I don't know," Samonie yawned. "I'm sorry. I was with Brehier most of the night, but we didn't sleep. I must have a bit before I start my duties today."

"Samonie, that's not my business," Catherine said. "You haven't seen Edgar, then?"

"No, but Brehier left while it was still dark out," Samonie said. "He told me he had to meet a man about a mine. Mistress, I need to tell you something."

"A mine," Catherine repeated, not hearing any more. "Of course. Edgar was suspicious that the siege has been too easy. He thinks that Olivier has brought in engineers to tunnel beneath the walls."

"He wouldn't be so careless of his life as to go out there to find out," Samonie told her.

"Yes, he would," Catherine said, torn between fury and terror.

"But the walls here are too thick to be brought down by tunnels," Samonie said. "If they were, the place would have fallen centuries ago."

"If someone had told Olivier about the underground passages." Catherine deliberated the possibility and decided it was all too likely. "Then the engineers would only need to create a new one that would connect with the others. From there they could gather the soldiers into groups and overwhelm us before we knew what had happened."

"So Master Edgar decided to find out," Samonie said dully. "And Brehier went with him."

"Samonie, we have to do something," Catherine said. "The answer has to be in those tapestry pieces. If we have to solve that idiotic puzzle to save ourselves, then we shall. Come with me."

Samonie dragged after her, trying to tell her body that, even if she hadn't slept, she had at least spent most of the night on her back.

"Elissent?" Catherine was at the door to the sickroom. "Could you spare a few moments? Samonie will stay with Aymon."

"Mother, I don't need a nurse, or a guard," Aymon complained from his bed. "I'm nearly well now. Once this weakness leaves my legs, I'll be as good as new. You can leave me alone for a space. I'd rather like some time to myself."

Elissent seemed doubtful. "What if that murderer comes after you again?"

"I have a knife," Aymon said, grinning. "I'd love a chance to give a bit of what I got. But it's not going to happen. He probably escaped into the forest right after I was attacked. No one else has been hurt, have they?"

"No." Elissent was still uncertain. "But what if you need something?"

"I'll shout for a maid," Aymon told her. "Go on. You need some rest. Catherine, after she does whatever you need, would you see that she gets a few hours' sleep?"

"Of course, Aymon," Catherine said. "You really are looking much better. I'm sure you're in no more danger than anyone else at Boisvert."

She finally managed to drag Elissent away on the condition that Samonie was left on a bench outside the door, to rush to Aymon's assistance at a moment's notice.

"Now what is it?" Elissent was annoyed at being dragged from her son's side.

"We need you to look at some embroidery," Catherine explained.

"Oh, really! At a time like this, we need to be doing something more productive than stitching altar cloths," Elissent sniffed.

Catherine took her up to the solar where they had laid out the pieces.

"I thought you might have the missing one," she told her. "But then last night we found what I think is the final piece. We still aren't sure what it means, though. We were hoping you could help."

Elissent's annoyance evaporated when she looked at the long panel of embroidery. Her expression was replaced by something that seemed like fear.

"I've seen this before," she said. "But not for years. Just after Seguin and I were married, Gargenaud took it off the wall and cut it into pieces, one for his daughter, Madeleine, and the rest for his sons. Seguin's father, Fulk, took his to the Holy Land. I imagine it is still there. It looked similar to this."

She touched the piece that Agnes had received.

"What about this one?" Catherine showed her the one Margaret had found.

Elissent fingered it. "This looks like the original. All the others are new. They are much like the old ones, but not quite. Perhaps it's just the colors, but they don't seem right."

"And this?" Catherine directed her attention to Brehier's piece.

Elissent stared at it. It was a scene beyond the end of the story. The first part showed the knight and his lady at home in the castle with children around them. Then an image of a great storm cloud darkening their home. The last two showed the lady kissing her lord good-bye and, finally, the lady, holding the treasure box, standing in front of a gate of three stones, one foot raised to enter.

Elissent shook her head. "I've never seen this before. There was a story, but I . . ." She felt the material. "This isn't from Gargenaud's tapestry. It's much older. Where did you get this?"

"Brehier had it from his great-grandmother," Catherine said.

"Did he now?" Elissent said. "I heard that long ago there was another tapestry. But it was lost at the time of the raids from the Northmen. Gargenaud's was a copy of it. There was no panel showing Andonenn's departure. Everyone knows that."

"None of us do," Marie told her. "Yet we and all our children are in jeopardy because of the secrets you here at Boisvert are so determined to keep."

"This makes no sense!" Elissent insisted. "The original pieces were scattered before any of you were born. Who made these copies?"

"Mandon?" Catherine suggested. "Or perhaps her sister, Berthe of Blois?"

"You keep talking of Mandon," Elissent said. "But no one has seen her for years. She's just a poor madwoman who hides under the castle. She must be dead by now. All that generation had weak minds. Madeleine isn't the first, you know. Living here would send most women into madness. And she has no sister that I ever heard of, certainly not in Blois."

"Very well." Marie tried to make peace. "All we need to know now is if there is anything in the total picture in this tapestry that can help us defeat Olivier."

"No," Elissent said firmly. "It's nothing but a story. It means nothing now."

"But what about . . . ?" Agnes began.

Marie shushed her. "Thank you, Elissent," she said. "We are sorry to have disturbed you for no good reason."

"I understand your worry," Elissent told her. "But Boisvert can't fall even if the water fails. You need not fear."

When she had left, Marie looked at the others.

"Was that of any use at all?" she asked.

"Well, we know that Brehier's section of the tapestry was new to her," Agnes said. "And that someone copied all but Mother's so that we would get them. And Elissent suggested that the last piece is the part of the story where Andonenn goes back to the spring."

"I'm sure of it," Catherine said. "I wonder if the writing would tell us where she went."

"Since we can't read it, we have to hope it doesn't," Marie noted.

They all glumly agreed.

"This is the end of the story, right?" Catherine said.

"Yes, that's been established," Agnes told her.

"I was just remembering the *jongleur*," Catherine said. "The end of the saga of Jurvale and Andonenn. What was it?"

Open the lock in your darkest hour
Children of Andonenn needn't cower
To save her you shall have the power
Follow the guide left in the tower
It will lead you to Andonenn's bower
Fear neither storm nor shower
Insert the key into the flower
Find the treasure and win the dower.

They all turned to stare at Margaret. She blushed.

"It was easy to memorize," she said. "Tumpty-tumpty and tumpty-tump. It just stuck with me."

"How can you put a key into a flower?" Agnes asked.

"'Fear neither storm nor shower,'" Catherine said. "And Mother went outside to find the way to Andonenn. Don't you see? It's not one of the doors within the keep. It's somewhere beyond the walls."

"Or by the well," Margaret said. "Maybe she didn't jump in. Maybe there's a secret doorway in the well house, too."

"Even if we find the door, we don't have the key," Agnes objected, but there was hope in her voice.

Catherine had been staring at the last panel.

"Edgar told me that the opening to the tunnel in the forest looked like some of the pagan stones you see in the countryside. You know, three slabs piled up like a doorway to nothing. Only these marked the entrance. Don't you think this picture of Andonenn going home looks the same?"

The others crowded around.

"It could be," Agnes said. "But the only way to find out is to go see it and, in case you've forgotten, there's an army between us and the forest."

"There has to be a way," Catherine said. "We must do more than simply wait to be conquered or rescued."

At that moment, their frazzled nerves were further assaulted by a sudden explosion of angry screams mixed with shrieks of pain. As one, the women ran toward the sound.

Elissent was in the hall outside Aymon's room. She was holding Samonie by the arm with one hand and, with the other, was beating her fiercely with a stick.

"You disobedient, lazy, traitorous woman!" she yelled as she struck. "What did they pay you? Where did they take him?"

"Stop!" Catherine cried, as she tried to grab the stick from Elissent.

Margaret threw herself over Samonie. "Don't hurt her, please!" she begged.

Agnes and Marie helped Catherine restrain Elissent.

"Let me go!" She struggled in their arms. "That woman is a traitor! She let Olivier's men in to kidnap my son!"

"What?" Marie asked.

"It's not true!" Samonie shouted through a swollen lip.

"It is!" Elissent insisted. "I never should have left him so helpless. I came back and his bed was empty and this slut sound asleep when she should have been watching!"

"I was tired," Samonie protested. "And I did drop off, but I'd have heard if anyone had carried Aymon away. He would have called for help."

"That's right," Elissent said. "My poor boy! And no one but a serpent in our home to hear him!"

"Elissent." Catherine was firm. "Samonie would never betray us. If Aymon has been abducted, she had nothing to do with it. Considering how many secret doorways there are in this place, he could have been taken out through a revolving seat in the privy!"

"How can you mock at such a time!" Elissent sobbed.

"I beg your forgiveness." Catherine sighed. "But you have also overstepped yourself. Samonie is my servant. It is not your right to strike her."

She knelt next to the maid, who was holding the side of her

face. There was a red mark across her hand. Catherine moved it to examine her bruised cheek.

"Marie, would you make a poultice for this?" she asked. "Margaret, take Samonie to her bed, please."

They both nodded and, their arms wrapped protectively around her, took Samonie away to be cared for.

Agnes remained. She could see how angry Catherine was. Someone had to stay to assure that there wouldn't be another murder.

"Elissent," Catherine spoke from between clenched teeth. "I am sorry for your loss. It grieves me that death has come to Boisvert. It grieves me even more that my family and I have been brought into this. We came here out of respect for my grandfather and our heritage.

"We have been insulted and put in mortal danger. You have lied to us repeatedly. If it weren't for the threat to my children I would say now that Boisvert deserves to be conquered."

"I say the same," Agnes stated, to her sister's amazement. "Catherine and I are going to uncover the truth if we have to do it with spades and buckets. I'm sick to death of you and your ineffectual husband. And I think you have terrible taste in clothes!"

Elissent stared at them a moment and then covered her face with her veil and stumbled, weeping, in search of someone more sympathetic.

Agnes brushed her hands together.

"So, what do I have to do to set a trap to catch this Mandon person?" she asked.

Edgar and Brehier were making their way back through the woods up to the village walls. The fog had lifted and been replaced by brilliant sunlight. It was a going to be a lovely day. They crept as quietly as possible, praying that all of Olivier's watchmen were busy guarding the mining operations.

"A few more yards," Brehier whispered. "Then we'll have to sprint for the wall and hope that our own men don't shoot at us."

"There isn't one inside who doesn't know me on sight," Edgar said. "I'll go first. Ready?"

There was no answer. Edgar turned and came face to face with the point of a crossbow bolt.

The day wasn't going as he had planned.

"This yarn is stiff with dirt," Agnes commented, holding it up with distaste.

"It's been wound through a lot of floors," Catherine said.

They were in Mandon's tunnel. Agnes and Catherine had found the passage from the storeroom simply by pounding and clawing at every possible area.

"If we start at the place where she was last seen," Catherine had explained. "We have a chance of following her back to her lair. It's not a great chance, but it's all we have."

Agnes had not argued. While Catherine went to get the yarn and change her clothes, she had made her own preparations for confronting Mandon.

They had told Marie and Margaret where they were going and overridden their mild objections. When they met at the passage door, Agnes was wearing a short *chainse* with a cord belt and a cloak that came just past her knees. She had twisted her blond braids into a knot and hidden them under a flopping cowl.

Despite her anxiety, Catherine smiled.

"You make a very attractive young man," she said.

"So do you," Agnes said. "Although it unnerves me how much you look like Solomon. All you need is a beard."

"There wasn't time to grow one," Catherine said. "Shall we go?"

This time the yarn was tied to the handle of the trapdoor. No one could untie it without being seen by those in the nursery.

They descended a spiral of stone steps that passed through the landings above ground and continued into the depths.

"This is not at all what I expected," Agnes said, gazing with distaste at the slimy walls. "From the tales, I thought it would be draped with glittering gossamer and jewels."

"I swear, I'm going to have strong words with the next poet I meet," Catherine muttered.

They came to a fork.

"Which way?" Agnes asked.

"The one on the right," Catherine answered.

"How do you know?"

"I just do," she answered with older-sister logic.

Agnes followed, willing to trust her for the moment but ready to blame her if it all went wrong.

"I am Edgar, lord of Wedderlie," Edgar announced quickly. "And this is Brehier of Boisvert. We demand to be brought to Lord Olivier."

"Right," the man at the other end of the crossbow said. "You look to me like an outlaw come out of the woods to see what he can grab."

Edgar stood up carefully. The bow moved upward with him but shook a bit. Edgar was a head taller and he held himself like a man used to being obeyed. A sliver of indecision entered the man's mind. He uncinched his belt and tied it around Brehier's wrists. Then he looked at Edgar's one hand and tried to think how he could be equally restrained. He made a decision.

"All right then," he told them. "You! Lord Whatever! You go ahead. And remember, you try to run for it and your friend gets a hole through him."

He kept the point of the crossbow against Edgar's back as they walked.

"What's your ransom value?" Edgar asked Brehier as they came closer to Olivier's camp.

"My horse has more than I do," Brehier answered. "But let's hope it doesn't come to finding out."

Edgar had planned to make a move when the guard stumbled on the rough ground. But the bastard was part goat and soon he had brought his prize into the camp and up to a large tent with a pennant flying from its ridgepole.

He handed them to the guard at the tent flap.

A few moments later they were manhandled inside. Edgar opened his mouth to explain who he was. But what he saw robbed him of speech.

A dark young man in a crisp linen tunic, a gold brooch at his neck, must be Olivier. But Edgar and Brehier were transfixed by the man sitting next to him.

Aymon smiled at them with wicked glee.

"Catherine, if I find out that there's a dry, clean pathway to Mandon, I will never let you hear the end of it."

Agnes was glad that they had decided to dress like men for this. Her shoes and hose were spattered with muck. She shuddered to think what a long skirt would look like.

"Are we almost there?" she asked.

"I'm not sure," Catherine admitted. "This doesn't look like any place I've been before. We're going up again; did you notice?"

"Is that good or bad?"

They went a little farther. Catherine stopped and pointed.

"I think it's good," she said.

At the end of the tunnel they could see sunlight sneaking in between piled-up rocks. If they were taken away, there would be a hole about knee height.

Automatically, Agnes dropped her voice.

"It must be the entrance to Andonenn's tunnel," she said. "We could all escape through here."

"Unless there are guards on the other side," Catherine said as the light flickered, as if someone had passed in front of the entrance.

"But it's our best chance," Agnes replied. "Let's leave the end of the yarn here and go back to tell the others. Hermann will be so happy. He wants to go home where people understand what he says."

"Not yet," Catherine said. "We need to follow the way Andonenn took."

"We have, only in reverse," Agnes told her.

"No, when we entered this part, there was another on the left," Catherine said. "The answers are down there."

"You don't know that," Agnes said. "We should be getting back. Perhaps Edgar has returned."

"You're right, Agnes," Catherine said absently. "You go back. Tell them what we've found. I'm going to get to the bottom of this, even if it leads straight to Hell."

Agnes sighed. "Well, when you put it that way, I suppose I'll have to come, too."

Brehier stared at Aymon in disbelief.

"You murdered your own brother!" he shouted. "How could you?"

Edgar hadn't thought of that question. In his family, fratricide was almost a tradition.

"It was clever of you to wound yourself so you wouldn't be suspected," he complimented Aymon. "How did you do it?"

"What do you mean?" Aymon asked. "Your blasted guards shot me. I would have been halfway to Rouen by nightfall if I hadn't been hurt. You can't imagine how awful it was to come to and hear my mother's voice grating away at the psalms!"

Edgar turned his attention to Olivier.

"Lord Brehier and I request that our ransom be set, and a messenger sent to Paris so that I may raise it, my lord," he bowed politely.

Olivier popped a ripe plum in his mouth, chewed a while, and then spat out the seed.

"Seems to me," he said at last, "that ransom is for knights captured in battle, not spies."

"I beg to differ," Edgar smiled. "It is not what the man was doing when captured, but how much he can pay."

Olivier ate another plum.

"Yes," he agreed. "That sounds right. Unless we find this fabulous treasure Aymon insists is hidden under Boisvert, it may be all I get from this campaign."

Brehier gave a snort.

"Treasure! You didn't come all this way for that, did you?" he laughed. "If you believe in that, I have some excellent relics to sell. Our Lord's sandal strap. John the Baptist's leftover locust leaves. The miter of Saint Peter from when he was bishop of Rome. What will you offer?"

Aymon rose and punched him hard enough to knock him over.

"I hate poor relations," he said. "You were always annoying, you and Guillaume and Raimbaut. You all said I could play hide-and-find with you, and then you never looked for me!"

Brehier struggled to stand.

"And this is what happened when I did." Blood dripped from the corner of his mouth. "You'd be dead now if Edgar and I hadn't found you."

"Did you also try to stop the messengers?" Edgar asked. "You only got one and he had already reached me."

"That was the first plan," Aymon said. "When you all came anyway, I had to think of something else."

"And what about the bit of cloth with the strange writing on it?" Edgar asked.

"I don't know what you mean," Aymon answered. "Any more than that story about the outside tunnel. You've been listening to too many stories with a full wine flagon in your hand."

"And Mandon?" Brehier said cautiously.

"Oh, she's real enough," Aymon said. "Some bastard child of Gargenaud's, I think. She's totally mad, but harmless. He won't let us drive her out. She steals food from the kitchens at night, you know."

"You *mesel!*" Brehier cried. "You made them think it was me!"

Olivier was getting bored with the bickering.

"I don't care about your myths, or who Aymon has done away with, as long as the treasure is real," he said. "Take these two out and tie them up well until I decide what to do with them."

As they were dragged out, Edgar overheard Aymon say to Olivier, "It's there, I promise. You are no more than another shovelful from breaking into the chamber. There are more riches there than in the whole town of Genoa."

The alternate way down was much drier than the one they had taken under the keep. Bits of shiny stone sparkled in the light of the lamp Agnes carried.

In less time than they expected, Catherine and Agnes found themselves in a large cavern. On the wall hung a large version of the embroidery pieces. In the center was a table covered with a white cloth. On it was a tall silver pitcher and four silver cups.

Agnes reached out and took Catherine's hand.

"Welcome, children," a rich female voice greeted them. "I knew you would find the way."

The professional prisoner trussers had had no difficulty with Edgar's missing hand. They had simply pinioned his elbows painfully behind his back.

"This wasn't exactly what I had intended us to do," he told Brehier.

"It's better than I feared," Brehier answered. "I thought the rope would be around our necks."

They were silent for a while, each gauging the possibility of rescue or escape.

"By the way," Brehier said after a while. "I've asked Samonie to marry me."

"Really?" Edgar said. "What did she say?"

"She doesn't mind, if you don't object," Brehier said. "She thinks I asked her just because of finding out I'm Martin's father, but that's not it. She's a fine woman. One to grow old with."

"I'll not argue that," Edgar said. "She cooks well . . . You're what?"

At that moment a roar of triumph came from Olivier's army.

"What is it?" Edgar was positioned in the wrong direction.

"It sounds like they've broken through into the passage." Brehier sagged. "Now there's nothing to stop them from overrunning the keep."

"Damn it!" Edgar struggled impotently at his bonds. "We've got to get out of here! Someone has to warn them!"

Nineteen

Andonenn's cave. The same time.

Chi voel a fin mon contie truire
Beneois soit qui le vos conte
Beneois soit qui fist le conte
A cials, a celes qui oirent
Otroit Jhesus cho qu'il desirent.

Now I wish to finish my tale
A blessing on the one who tells this
A blessing on the one who made the tale
To those, men and women who listen
May Jesus give them all they desire.

—*Silence*, II. 6702–6706

"*M*andon," Catherine said flatly. "It's time to stop playing games. No one is coming to save you."

"But here you are," Mandon said.

"Didn't I tell you she would find a way?"

Another woman walked out of the shadows. She had combed out the hair dye and washed the lines from her face.

"Where have you been, Berthe?" Catherine wasn't thrilled to see her. "Did it amuse you to lead me about and then abandon me? Do you know what happened to our poor mother?"

"Yes," Berthe said. "I'm so sorry. Did you bring the other knife?"

"What? No?" said Catherine.

"Yes." Agnes brought it out from the bag at her waist.

"At last!" Both women reached for it.

"Agnes, what are you doing?" Catherine tried to go for the knife, as well.

"Catherine, it's all right." Agnes pulled away from her. "Evaine told me that Mandon had asked for it."

Mandon took the knife gently and set it on the table. Berthe brought out her knife and set it next to the one that had killed Raimbaut.

"Now we have the key," Mandon said.

"You might have just asked for it at the beginning," Catherine said sourly.

"Not until we knew which of Andonenn's children was trying to destroy us," Berthe explained.

"And now you do." It wasn't a question.

"Yes," Mandon said. "It will be hard on Seguin. He never should have married that woman. Good fruit comes from good stock. Elissent was of the family of Empress Judith. She was bound to breed traitors."

"Oh, yes, Judith, the one with the curse," Catherine remembered.

"Elissent?" Agnes asked.

"No, it was Aymon," Catherine told her. "Marie couldn't understand what had made his wounds nor why he wasn't able to walk when nothing vital had been pierced. But I didn't suspect him until he ran away. I knew Samonie would have wakened if anyone had tried to take him. And now I think I know what wounded him."

She pointed to a quiver of short copper arrows.

"You two did it, didn't you?"

"We couldn't let him leave," Berthe said. "We needed him to direct Olivier's engineers."

At last Catherine understood why there had been so little activity in the enemy camp. Edgar must have suspected this. Her heart froze. Someone had told her he had been seen this morning in the bailey with Brehier. They couldn't be so foolish as to have left the safety of the walls to find out.

"Olivier can't breach the walls, so he's digging under them," she said.

Berthe nodded. "If one knows where, it isn't hard to penetrate one of the tunnels.

Agnes was becoming more bewildered. "You wanted Olivier to undermine Boisvert?"

"Not exactly." Mandon smiled. "You'll understand soon. But first, we must assemble the key. The time is come to retrieve the treasure."

The only treasure Catherine could imagine at this moment was to have her family around her and all of them safe at home. Still, after all they'd been through, she could spare a moment to see what Andonenn had been protecting all these years.

Mandon and Berthe picked up the knives again. Both Catherine and Agnes stiffened. Then the women carefully twisted the blades. There was a click and the metal slid from the hilts. The pieces hidden within the handle were oddly serrated. Catherine watched in growing comprehension as the women turned the blades around and inserted them back into the wood so that the serrated pieces were now sticking out. They looked very much like keys.

Berthe and Mandon moved toward a dark opening in the cave.

"Come with us," they beckoned.

Catherine and Agnes followed. Mandon set a lantern on a long table and then walked around it. On the other side was a huge empty basin carved from the stone.

"This was Andonenn's pool," Berthe told them. "The one where she brought Jurvale. Until Seguin married Elissent, it was always full of clear water. But Judith's curse grew stronger with her kin under our roof. It made the earth slide and stopped the flow of the spring. We knew that, even if he knew what had happened, the curse would keep Gargenaud from digging it out."

"Wait." This was too much for Catherine. "You arranged all this? People have died! The castle is about to be taken over. Those poor guards were tortured to death by Olivier's man!"

"We know," Mandon said. "It grieves us, as it did to kill those clumsy thieves. We shall have to answer to God for our deeds someday. But we at least know that we have saved Andonenn and given the treasure back to the world."

Agnes leaned over and whispered to Catherine. "I'm sorry I blamed you for Mother's madness. It's obvious that this place addled her mind before we were ever born."

"You realize these women are our aunts," Catherine whispered back.

"*Himmel!*" Agnes exclaimed. "Is this what will happen to us!"

The women appeared not to have heard them. They stepped into the dry pool and went to the center, where a square pillar stood. They inserted the knives into slots on either side of it and turned.

For a moment, nothing happened. Then the block began to move with a creak that made Catherine's back teeth shriek in agony.

Mandon lifted the top off. Berthe reached in and took out a parcel wrapped in ancient sheepskin. She cradled it in her arms as she brought it over to Catherine.

"Of all Andonenn's children, we feel you are the one who

can use this most wisely," she said as she handed her the treasure.

Catherine took the object. It was heavy. She started to unwrap it, but Berthe stopped her.

"Not here," she said. "There isn't time. Please, share a cup of wine with us. It is the last from Andonenn's dowry. To honor her. Then you must take the treasure and leave."

"A cup of wine?" Catherine was disgusted. "Is this some weird pagan ritual or do you intend to poison us?"

Agnes touched her arm. "I don't think they mean us harm," she said. "Although I'm not completely sure. Let's drink. What difference does it make? Olivier's army will soon overrun the keep. I want to get back to Gottfried and Hermann. If we are going to die, I want to be with them."

Mandon smiled with childish joy at their acquiesence. Carefully she poured an equal amount from the pitcher into each of the silver cups. She gave one to Agnes and, after she had shifted the treasure to balance against her chest with her left arm, one to Catherine. She and Berthe lifted theirs.

"To Andonenn's children and saviors," Berthe said. "May you continue to be blessed."

Catherine tasted the wine. Then tasted it again. The first sip made her think it had spoiled. There was a fizz to it. But it didn't have the rotten smell of bad wine. It was more like tasting stars. She drank the rest eagerly. If it was poison, it was the best she had ever tasted.

"Now hurry!" Mandon pushed the two of them out of the cavern and toward the tunnel. "Follow the string. Quickly now. Don't worry. Everything is going according to plan."

"But why all this mystery?" Catherine called back over her shoulder.

"It was the only way to do it," Berthe called back. "We needed to make a miracle. Now run!"

∞

Edgar's arms and legs had gone completely numb.

"What's happening now?" He strained painfully to twist enough to see.

"I'm not sure." Brehier craned his neck to get a better view. "The engineers broke through a while ago into one of the tunnels. Olivier immediately sent his soldiers down. They must be on their way up to the keep by now."

"We've got to get free," Edgar said desperately. "Before the guards come back."

"Keep struggling," Brehier suggested. "Maybe a rope will snap."

Preposterous though it seemed, Edgar had no better idea.

"Damn," he said. "I've pulled a muscle in my leg."

"Edgar, something strange is going on," Brehier said a while later. "The soldiers are coming back. It looks like they're wet."

"Wet? There are no baths at Boisvert," Edgar said. "The well is drying up. What could they have landed in?"

"I don't know, but more are coming," Brehier reported. "They appear soaked as if they'd been caught in a sudden rain. Edgar, I think Aymon directed them to dig into the underground spring!"

"How?" Edgar said. "No one knows where it is."

"They do now." Brehier was getting more and more excited. "They aren't climbing out now, but bodies are gushing out on the water. Some of them aren't moving."

Edgar felt tears sliding from the corners of his eyes.

"The siege is over, Brehier," he said. "Olivier can't get into Boisvert. They're safe. Catherine and my children are safe."

Catherine and Agnes were up to the lower storerooms when they heard the roar behind them. They looked back. The stairs they had just climbed were now rapidly being covered with water.

"Catherine," Agnes said. "Mandon and Berthe are down there. They'll drown."

"I know," Catherine said. "They did, too. Agnes, there's nothing we can do. They wanted us to be saved. And the treasure."

"Whatever is in that box had better be worth it," Agnes said. "But I don't believe it will be."

"I don't, either," Catherine agreed. "There is nothing worth the price that's been paid for it."

They entered the hall to find it full of people. Everyone from the castle and village seemed to be gathered there. Wine and beer were being passed and liberally quaffed.

"Mama!" James raced up to her. "Mama, we won!"

"We did?" Catherine bent to receive his hug. "Where's your father?"

"He didn't come back yet," James said.

"What? But he's been gone for hours!"

James caught her panic. "Mama, they won't cut off Papa's other hand, will they?"

His shrill voice rose over the joyous chatter of the others.

"Of course not," Catherine said.

She realized that everyone was looking at her. The box containing the treasure slid to the ground.

"What has happened to my husband?"

No one wanted to answer. From the corner of her eye, Catherine saw Samonie, sitting by the hearth. She wasn't rejoicing.

Catherine went cold all over. The room was too full, the faces leering. Everything was spinning. Her head fell back and she collapsed into her sister's arms.

In the woods, Edgar was considering the situation.

"The one problem with Olivier being washed out of Boisvert is that he has no reason now to keep us alive," he told Brehier.

"Aren't we still worth a ransom?" Brehier wanted to know. His efforts at breaking the ropes around his ankles had only made his feet go numb.

"Maybe, but it's more likely he'll be so angry at wasting all these that he'll slaughter us in spite."

"You seem calm for a man convinced he's about to be killed," Brehier complained.

"My family is no longer in danger," Edgar said. "Solomon will see that they are cared for. I'd like to do it myself, but this is a fair trade."

"I would have liked to get to know my son," Brehier sighed. "But at least I know that I shall leave something behind me when I die. Do you think they'll let us have a priest?"

They both were silent, thinking of the sins they would not have time to do penance for. From the mouth of Olivier's tunnel, there were wails of anger and grief.

All at once, the cries changed to ones of fear. Brehier looked up.

"Horses," he said. "I hear horses. You don't think that Thibault has come to save us at last?"

"Catherine? Catherine? Please wake up." Margaret was rubbing her temples with some acrid oil. "Solomon came back! He brought men to lift the siege. Everything is all right. They found Edgar. He's fine."

The words penetrated slowly into Catherine's unconscious.

"Here, *deorling*," a deep voice interrupted. "Let me have her."

It was the sound of his heartbeat against her ear that brought Catherine to herself again. It was so constant and reassuring.

Margaret had expected that Catherine would fly into hysterics when she realized Edgar was alive, but she only turned in his arms so that she could hold him more tightly. He looked down into her face. The expression was so intimate that Margaret had to turn away. They would have only a moment before being overwhelmed by the affections of their children.

Margaret was happy that the ordeal was over. She never wanted to go below ground again, not even into a root cellar. It would be good to return to the Paraclete, where life had order and sense and legends were safely in the distant past. These people were not hers. She didn't belong in their world.

There was an empty alcove on the far side of the hall, half hidden by curtains. Margaret made her way there, planning to hide until the celebration ebbed.

Someone else had already had the same idea.

"Solomon!" Margaret stepped toward him

He stood. "How are you?" he asked. "I'm sorry it took so long for me to return. Your grandfather is not an easy man to track down."

"I'm fine," she said. "I . . . that is, we were worried about you."

Solomon wished he knew how he felt about her. He knew he loved her; he had since she was a child. But he was terribly afraid that it was more than an avuncular fondness. When he was traveling, her face and voice, the auburn braids, seemed to be in his thoughts all the time. When he was with another woman, he felt her sadness. And now, the sight of her, so much in pain, broke his heart.

"Margaret," he said. "You know there is nothing I wouldn't do for you."

"Except convert." She smiled to take away the sting of the words.

"I can't any more than you could." He turned toward the window, unable to look into her eyes. "But even if I did, it would still be impossible. You know that. Your grandfather has other plans for you. And your brother would never let me cross his threshold again. You know it as well as I do."

"Yes." There was an ocean of grief in that word.

"You only feel like this because I bring you presents," Solomon tried to tease her. "Wait until young lords come courting you. You'll see what a poor catch I'd be."

Margaret came and stood beside him. They both stared out the window into the village and the fields beyond.

"Solomon," she said at last. "Do you love me or do you just feel pity for my hopelessness?"

Now was the time to do the noble thing. He should cut himself off from her forever. She deserved a rich, happy life, free of regret.

He opened his mouth to lie. She turned her face up to his, her large light brown eyes shining with tears. The words escaped him before he could react.

"Oh, my life and my soul," he said. "I shall love you until I die."

He held her close until her tears were spent. They both knew he must never see her again.

Edgar had the unpleasant task of telling Seguin that Aymon's body had been washed out of the tunnel with those of Olivier's soldiers.

"He was no traitor," Seguin stated firmly. "He planned it all so that Andonenn could be freed and Boisvert protected again. It was Mandon who killed Raimbaut. She was wickedly insane. I should have had her locked up years ago."

Edgar didn't argue. For all he knew, the man was right.

It wasn't until things had settled down and the villagers returned to what was left of their homes that Gargenaud made his appearance.

"We shall have to get that poet to add more *laisses* to the story," he announced. "Raimbaut and Aymon died heroically to save us. They have guaranteed that Boisvert shall stand forever. Andonenn's treasure is still protected."

"Aren't we at least entitled to see it?" Odilon asked. "If I'm to be the next lord of Boisvert, I should know what I'm guarding."

Before Catherine had recovered from the joy of Edgar's return, the box had been taken away by one of Gargenaud's men. She hadn't seen it since.

Now it was brought out, a plain wooden casket with a latch

but no lock. Gargenaud had it placed on a table. He signaled Seguin to open it.

Catherine was in the front of those pushing forward to get the first glimpse.

Seguin slowly opened the lid. His expression changed to consternation.

"What is this?" he asked. "It's just an old book!"

"I told you there was a book!" Guillaume said from the back of the room.

Seguin held it up. It was a thick codex, the vellum pages rippling with age. The covers were leather-covered wood boards, studded with precious stones.

"Is it a book of magic?" Odilon asked.

"Perhaps some lost letters of the apostles," Ysore suggested.

Seguin opened it. He studied the first page, written in clear Carolingian uncial. He went to the next page, and the next.

"It must be written in some secret language," he said at last. "I can't make out a word of it."

Catherine was finally able to get a look.

"This is the same language as on the tapestry," she said. "Hermann, didn't you say it seemed a bit like German?"

"Yes, but not," he said. "A few words the same, but there is no sense to the phrases."

"I remember reading somewhere that Charlemagne had a book made of all the pagan legends of the Frankish people." Catherine tried to read the lines again.

"Yes," Edgar added. "But his son, Louis, and Louis's wife, Judith, had the book destroyed so that it wouldn't influence good Christians."

"You think this is it?" Seguin asked. "This is what Jurvale stole? We've spent three hundred years guarding this? My sons died for nothing but an old pagan book?"

"It would seem so," Catherine said. "And, oddly, Judith has won, after all. I doubt there's a person alive who can read it."

∞

Catherine and Marie were gathering up their possessions and packing them any which way, so happy to be going home that they didn't care what got wrinkled or broken.

"If we hurry, Solomon and Edgar may still reach Saint-Denis in time for the Lendit fair," Catherine said.

"Guillaume has rented a house in Paris from Abbot Suger for us to stay in until the keep is rebuilt," Marie almost sang. "A winter in the city! We can see each other all the time!"

"And Brehier says he doesn't mind living with us at all." Catherine couldn't believe her luck. "Edgar wants to build a room for him and Samonie at the back of the house. I was so afraid I'd lose her."

"Even though it was awful," Marie considered. "Things have ended just like in the stories, after all."

Not quite. Catherine knew there had been no magic, no miracles. Just two women determined to control events to get their way. The legends were no more than smoke to conceal the reality.

They had brought all the bundles down to the hall for servants to take down and load onto the donkeys. Catherine was saying good-bye to Odilon and Seguin when Agnes came down.

"Catherine, where are the earrings I loaned you?" she said. "The ones of Mother's. I need to put them in my jewelry casket before I lock it."

"You said I could keep them," Catherine answered. "I already put them in the boxes."

"I didn't," Agnes answered. "I distinctly said you could borrow them while we were here because you hadn't brought anything decent."

"No, you didn't." Catherine's voice rose. "I have lots of nice jewelry. I wanted them because you made off with all Mother's things and I have nothing to remember her by."

"I deserved every piece," Agnes shouted back. "You ran off to the convent and then to get married. I was the one who stayed home and took care of her. You were always so selfish!"

"Selfish! What do you call a person who won't let her sister have a small pair of earrings?"

"Catherine, stop bullying your sister. Agnes, let Catherine have the earrings. You have plenty."

"Oh, Mama!" they answered together.

Realization hit. They both froze and turned slowly.

Madeleine was standing before them, very much alive. More alive, Catherine saw with a shock, than she had been in years.

"You two are much too old to squabble like children," their mother told them firmly. "I understand from Andonenn that while I was ill, you both went and got married. She says you both have children of your own. And high time, too. Please, take me to meet my grandchildren."

"I take back every doubt I had," Catherine said through tears. "There was magic after all."

And now, the *chanson* is complete.

a way that didn't require him to show up because there was literally nothing for him to contest. I wondered, when he opened that final envelope that said I was legally free of him, if he felt powerless for the very first time in his life. I gave him something he couldn't fight or bully his way out of. The golden boy, who had been raised to feel entitled to anything he wanted, couldn't have me.

As quickly as I became an officer—in the blink of an eye and after the work of moment after interminable moment—I had my life and my future back. I walked from the courthouse to the Social Security office and left with a new card with a new name. *My* name. Taking a deep breath, I realized I had left with something else too, another kind of union—the army, for better or for worse, would consume my next three years. I stuck the Velcro name tag with MESTYANEK embroidered in bold black standard-army print on the right side of my chest above my shiny gold lieutenant rank, directly across from the US ARMY tape nestled over my heart. I drove east, toward Fort Campbell, Kentucky, and the famed 101st Airborne Division. I was assigned to the 159th, a Combat Aviation Brigade, scheduled to deploy to Afghanistan in less than three months.

against a military officer is a crime under the military justice system also, and I held the proof of his plan. I was an officer too, even if I was entry level.

I filed for divorce.

And Jeff did as he promised he would: He tried to destroy me.

He submitted phone records to my schoolhouse commander, attempting to prove my conversations with a friend showed I was guilty of a military crime. When I fought back and shared the recording, the commander dropped all charges. He rightly assessed the incident as a messy marital situation.

"Don't forget, Lieutenant Poole," the commander chided, using the name that had begun to make me shudder. "As a woman in the army, everyone will be watching you, all the time, in everything you do. You'll need to run faster, jump higher, work harder, and keep your nose much, much cleaner than any of your male colleagues."

He warned me that if something like this happened in the "real army"—meaning when I got to my unit—it *would* be the career-ender Jeff threatened. As I stood at attention to close out the brief investigation, the commander added, "You'll need to be better than your husband, too. Don't forget that. Dismissed."

As far as I know, nothing ever happened to the male Lieutenant Poole for lying, or for his honor violation, but I didn't pursue it. After he'd threatened me, and after I'd seen the opportunity to use the distance to take my life back, I never took his calls again. When I had him served with divorce papers, he used the Soldiers' and Sailors' Civil Relief Act to avoid a summons, which can shut a divorce down for as long as a service member is on active duty. He seemed intent on fighting me at every turn. Conveniently, he'd left me nothing to fight over. All the debt from our ill-advised wedding, the fancy "officer car" he'd insisted we buy, the vet bills for the dog he wanted, and anything else we'd spent "jointly" were in my name only. He had the dog, the furniture, and all the money in the bank account.

But I didn't care. I'd been left alone with nothing before, and I was better equipped to handle it than I had ever been. I wanted out. So I took all the debt and let him keep the rest. I refiled for the divorce in